MYRACLES IN THE VOID

WES DYSON

WONDERLOVE

WONDERLOVE

For author contact and more visit WesDyson.com

Cover artwork by Franziska Stern

Paperback ISBN: 978-1-7379105-0-3

Copyright © 2022 WONDERLOVE, LLC

per la famiglia,
related and not.

CONTENTS

ACKNOWLEDGMENTS

This book came to be what it is through the efforts of many wonderful human beings. I am so grateful to everyone who lended their time, energy and support to the vision of this story. This remains the easiest page to write.

I want to specifically thank my developmental editor, Cate Hogan, for her unwaveringly kind and thoughtful guidance. Listening to the excitement in her voice was absolutely instrumental in getting through the early drafts. I still cannot believe anyone understood what I wanted this be book to be. She was really the first to believe in it.

Thank you to my proofreader, Monti Shalosky, for her incredible eye and her patience with Hop's wild dialect. It couldn't have been easy, a'kay? Her commitment to giving this book the best presentation possible meant a great deal to me.

My thanks to Smith Publicity for believing in this project, but a special thanks to Andrea Kiliany Thatcher, who not only acted as this book's brave publicist, but also provided me with the insights and encouragement needed to feel secure in the absolutely terrifying process of publishing.

I would also like to thank a group of special beta readers — Kaylee Haynes, Meghalee Mitra, and Eric Wyman — whose interest in this story, even in its early, difficult stages, helped me feel like it was something worth pursuing. Your thoughts and impressions really helped shape this story.

Nothing is ever self-made. I thank you all so, so much.

MYRACLES IN THE VOID

CHAPTER I
UNFORGIVING HOP

THE RED TIDE is COMING!
Water Level Low.
SPRYT Sightings Highly Expected.
Un-luck + Disaster To All Who Encounter.
BLOCK EVERY OPENING.
— *Mayor Tanning*

What a delightful sign to have hanging in front of one's home — a mix of "watch out" with "you're on your own." But that's living in Hop for *ya, a'kay?*

As a floating port in the middle of the sea, there weren't any roads to or from Hop. On their own, indeed. But it wasn't always so lonely. Fifty years ago, Hop was a bustling pitstop for the hundreds of trade ships sailing across the Domus Gulf every year. A place to "hop" from one side of the gulf to the other. Being a travel hub made it bursting with exotic goods and fresh ideas. But the wild waters of the gulf were hard to predict, and they only seemed to grow more dangerous over time. One shipwreck was enough to send thoughts and prayers, but after ten and twenty ships washed back blown to bits, it started to nip at the profits. Soon traders found alternate land routes that may have taken longer, but at least weren't so death-y.

Practically overnight, Hop and its people were forgotten like a used hanky in a puddle. Trapped on a floating port amid the unforgiving sea, a stagnant idea stuck to them — anything made would just be *un*made. What was to stop anything they worked hard to build from falling to pieces like Hop did? *Nothin' lasts but salt in yer ass* became the most graffitied words on the splintering streets, a series of long planks called "Boards." Was there any point in shining your shoes, doing your hair, brushing your teeth? They would all end up dirty, tasseled, and yellow. *Un*done, eventually. Was there any point in building relationships, then? Nothing lasts but the salt in their asses, indeed.

Just behind that friendly "red tide" warning sign on Boulie Board, a skinny wreck of a home rose from the battered planks. Its number, 76, was drawn large and wide on the front and side in "Hopper White," a local specialty paint whose main ingredient was seagull poop. Nothing could be wasted in Hop, not even waste. The pieces that made up the home had a kind of *widely used* look about them, like maybe that wall had once been the barnacled belly of a rowboat, and before that, it was a sign that said HOP: POPULATION 600. Its door was a full fourteen shades of a should-I-touch-that sort of green and was cracked at the bottom up to the knob. Its two sea-weathered windows were small and narrow like suspicious eyes squinting at the neighbors. By Hopper standards, the Izz family actually had quite a fine little nest.

The only reason the Izz house somewhat outshined its raggedy neighbors was because of the family's firstborn, Gaiel Izz. Gai liked to fix things when they broke. Something about broken objects made him queasy, compulsive even; a roar in the belly yapping at him to make it better. As for the things he couldn't fix, he'd at least insist on putting a sheet of soggy newspaper over it or something. In fact, he patched so many holes in his clothes with newspaper that it became the dominant fabric. It crinkled as he walked.

One special night, this industrious fifteen-year-old was lying motionless on the floor in one of the home's damp upstairs bedrooms. His right ear was practically suctioned to the floorboards as he listened carefully for any signs of movement downstairs. He'd been listening so long his ear had become a bright, throbbing mushroom. This night, he'd embark on his most ambitious fixing project yet — his twelve-year-old sister, Lynd.

While Gai may have been on the floor, he wasn't *out of bed*. The floor was both of the Izz children's bed. Many, many things floated by Hop in the strong currents, like sunken ship junk or garbage from far off Electri City on the mainland. But few were "cozy" materials for them to scoop out and use to make bedding. Since nothing came in or out of Hop, if a Hopper wanted something new, they'd best grab a scoop and pray to Zeea that whatever they needed happened to be floating by that day. Gai once scooped an armful of braided anchor rope and wove it into a nice blanket. He looked over at Lynd sleeping on it, snoring like a ship headed out to sea — *Twaahhh!* Peaceful as she seemed, her little hands kept pulling at the fraying edges of the rope-blanket, almost like tearing it apart soothed her as a babe suckling their thumb would. She was definitely not a fixer like her brother. Truly, she was quite the opposite.

Gai hadn't heard a peep or a creak downstairs for quite some time and began to imagine their mother, Mape, had fallen asleep in her favorite rocking chair again. He then carefully studied his sister's breathing. Slow and steady. *Lynd's asleep, too*, he thought. *It's now or never.*

The boy crept over to their narrow window. As usual, Mamma Mape heeded the mayor's spryt warning outside and boarded up their windows nice and twice, like a good Hopper. He dared not risk yanking them open and letting the briny night mist blow in and wake up his sister. All he wanted near the window was a single piece of wood he'd hid above the pane — a reach too high for either Ma or Lynd to find. Pulling it down, he remarked just how *new* this forearm-sized chuck of wood was. It didn't have nail wounds from its time as a post or curly grooves where worms had eaten it. It didn't smell like rot. It was the least Hop-like piece of wood he'd ever seen. It was even delicately curved — perfect for his plan to fix Lynd. But it was only part of his plan.

Gai stuck the wood into the waist of his pants and quietly scurried to the only other opening in the Izz household — the toilet. Or, in Hopper terms, the "dumper." The floorboards creaked as he entered the small room with a generous hole cut in the floor for elimination of all kinds. Gai could hear the whooshing water directly beneath. Sometimes it splashed up at him if the chop was particularly rough. He peered down into the wet darkness, and his stomach churned like the sea. Did he absolutely have to fix Lynd tonight? After all, he could easily just curl back onto his floor-bed and no one would know a thing. Should he use the bathroom first? His sister snored so loudly and abruptly in the next room — *Twahh-twahhh!* — that he nearly wet himself right there out of fear. He exhaled, hoping his fears would sort of just blow out of him. "I have to. For Lynd."

Getting through the dumper hole was the easy part. Finding his footing in the nasty, molding jungle of posts that held up Hop below was indeed a trick. It was sticky and slippery in all the wrong places. This area was called the "Under Board," and it was nowhere anyone ought to be. It was closer to the dangerous water, smelly as a dead cod, and who knows who could be sneaking around in the dark with him? And let's not even mention the chances of getting a splinter. But Gai believed his plan was worth the risks. His sister needed help. He went carefully and only breathed in with quick mouth-gulps. In about twenty gulps, he found his way under the house and back up onto Boulie Board proper, gasping for what counted as fresh air in Hop.

He'd made it out of the house. He'd actually done it. He was outside in the middle of the Hop night for the first time ever. And he was alone. It was time to find the *ingredients* he needed for his plan to work. Leaning near the front door of 76 were two long nets — scoops, as they were cleverly called — about three times his height. He snatched one and tippy-toed to the Board edge, listening for anything that wasn't the sound of rushing water. There were plenty of characters to encounter in Hop's darker hours — nosey neighbors, thieves, rival scooper gangs, *spryts* even. Anything was possible. "Definitely should've used the bathroom first."

Gai lowered his scoop into the strong currents below. "A'way, Zeea. Gimme some luck." His handle bent three times with fresh catches before he pulled it out. "Balls at ya," he huffed, pawing through the dripping net. "All watermoss." The boy plucked out a small crab from the tangled watermoss. "Well, there's a nice crabby for Emilie in here, at least. More than we scooped earlier—"

"Ya snuck out to get pet food?" someone spoke behind him.

Ahh! Gai dropped everything but the crab and spun around with it in his hand like its tiny claws were a weapon. *Pinch, pinch.* In the dim light, his not-at-all-sleeping, absolutely-faking-it sister stood chest-high to him. Her wavy hair was dark as the night around her, so she was all cheeks and eye-whites. "Lynd." His shoulders relaxed. "I thought ya were asleep? Get back inside."

"I know." She sighed. "Finally had to fake snore to get ya to leave . . . Did ya just wee yer pants?"

"No! What? Never! What?"

"But durin' that thunderstorm—"

"I told ya that was the *rain* leakin' through the roof!" He came close to whisper. "How'd ya even know I was gonna sneak out?"

"I didn't." Lynd reached for his newspaper-patched shirt and crinkled it. "But ya sound like a rat chewin' on garbage when ya move."

"Ya think yer so smart," he huffed.

Gai then noticed a thin sliver of wood gripped tightly in his sister's hand. It was about the length of her foot and as thick as a finger. She was mindlessly playing with the splintering edge the same way she did with her blanket.

"At least ya listened to Ma," he said. "Always bring somethin' to snap when ya leave the house. Just in case."

She ignored him and looked at the crab, "Gaiel Izz, the good boy, snuck out for the first time. To get Em pet food?"

"Yeah," he lied, stone-faced.

Lynd bent the tip of that piece of wood in her hand off with her bare thumb. *Snap!*

The boy flinched, "A'kay. A'kay. Don't get mad. *Please at ya.*"

"Waitin'," she sung, rocking on her heels.

"Keep yer voice down," he whispered. "I'm just lookin' for somethin', a'kay?"

"I *knew* it," she said, pointing to Mayor Tanning's red tide warning sign. "Ma said the sign's about spryts comin'. Yer out to find one without me, ain't ya?"

"Spryts?" he scoffed. "No. I'd like to *live.*"

"What's so important, then?" Lynd whined.

"Get. Back. In. Side," he said with all the older-brother-authority he could fake. "Wait, how did ya get out?"

"All I had to do was break those boards over the window," she said proudly. "I pulled apart that rope blanket ya made me and climbed down."

"Ya don't say." Gai wiped off a layer of Under-Board muck from his arm. "Anyway, get back in. I won't tell ya again."

Snap! She broke off another piece of the wood in her hand.

"Fine." Gai tossed the crab back into the water. "I'm not out here for food. I'm not out here for spryts. What's tomorrow?"

Lynd smiled wide. "My birthday . . ."

"A big one." He fanned out both his hands. "Yer gonna be thirteen fingers old."

She grabbed one of his hands and closed it. "Ya still talk to me like I'm only five fingers."

"Still got the claws out?" He turned his back to her and sat down, dangling his feet over the edge of the Board. "All's a'kay. I didn't scoop what I need to make yer present anyway."

"Ya risked sneakin' out . . . to make me a *present?*" Lynd sat next to him and wrapped her arm all the way around to his other shoulder. "Thanks at ya! I love it — *will* love it. Whatever it is. *What is it?*"

"Will ya keep yer voice down? I don't wanna think what'll happen if someone finds us out here." He pointed down, "Someone could crawl right up from the Under Board and grab us."

"A'kay. . ."

"And yer stabbin' me with yer broken wood."

"Oh, sorry at ya." Lynd shriveled a bit in embarrassment.

He sighed. "No, lucky ya brought that thing. Or Boulie could've gotten a new crack in it instead. Or *I* could've."

"I-I don't—"

"I know ya don't mean to break things," Gai interrupted, peering down Boulie Board to the center of Hop.

All the Boards started in a central point and radiated out like spokes on a wheel. At night, the center glowed faintly yellow with a few bright electri lamps. Most Hoppers could never afford fancy Electrian toys like flameless lamps, so having one was sort of a status beacon. Note, having high status in Hop still meant one's toilet was a hole in the floor.

He whispered, "Remember the time we scooped a lamp?"

"Mhm. Was the happiest I saw Ma since Pa left," Lynd said. "We should've kept it."

"She was right to sell." Gai pointed to each yellow light. "Light makes ya easy to spot. I'd rather not have any extra targets on our back."

"Ya think Pa could be back for my birthday, Gai?"

The boy turned away. "I thought ya got tired of askin' me that?"

Lynd stood up. "A'way."

"Finally," he yawned. "I'm ready for bed."

"Bed? There's no bed when ya got a present to make." She offered her hand. "Let's head to the center. Everything that floats by collects there, so maybe we'll scoop what ya need?"

Gai shot to his feet. "Have ya lost yer brains? Every spot down there is claimed by one scooper gang or another. Ever heard of the Wicked Wikets? They'll net us up like clams!"

Lynd had already started walking down Boulie while he was babbling. When he finally finished, she whispered, "I wish ya weren't such a sogg sometimes."

"What'd ya call me?" The word struck Gai right in the beating heart. Sogg. *Bump. Bump.* Was that what he was? *Bump. Bump.* Sogg was Hopper slang for a useless person, like when someone would scoop something they thought was nice at first, but turned out to be all soggy and unusable. What an unforgiving term. How could he fix being a sogg? The boy picked up his scoop and banged it like a gavel. "Back home, now!"

Lynd stopped. But she wouldn't turn around. Her little shoulders rose and fell with a sigh. "We only go outside to work." She began sniffling. "Everything's too dangerous. Can't even remember the last time Ma stepped out onto the Boards. We can't make any friends because—" *Snap!* She broke the wood in her fist again. *Snap!* Then another piece. *Snap!*

"All's a'kay," Gai said softly, gesturing with his palms open like Lynd was a wild, bucking horse. Breaking things was some kind of release for her. When she got upset, she *had* to break something. If she didn't break something with her hands, then something would just break around her — hands-free. It was frightening to the boy and terrifying to their mother, who tried her very best to ignore it. That nice crack in their front door was Lynd's doing, as were four more just like it inside the Izz home.

Boulie Board's planks began to rumble under their feet as if the waves were pounding the Under Board. The posts rattled. Gai's cheeks rippled. But the boy knew this was no seaquake. It was Lynd's bizarre destructive power boiling up to the surface again. The boy hobbled to his sister, softly singing a song their Pa used to play, "We've been here before . . ."

Lynd's fist loosened.

"With yer hand in mine," he continued.

The planks eased their quaking. Lynd's shoulders settled down away from her jaw.

Gai sang, "In my heart, there's a window. And it sees through time . . ."

Lynd turned to him and smiled as if nothing super crazy just happened.

"See," said Gai. "All's a—"

Waaahhhhhhhh! A loud horn blared from a few houses down, followed by heavy, clanking footsteps coming at them fast. Gai took Lynd's free hand and led her to the edge of the Board, where they both climbed down to hide in the Under Board.

The noisy boots banged right above them, pounding back and forth like they were searching around. Then, sniffing them out like a dog, they stepped right to the edge from where the Izz kids had just climbed down. Gai and Lynd huddled tightly just beneath and held their breath. They dared not make a sound. Finally, after a few long beats, the boots clanked back to where they came. The boy and girl exhaled together with relief.

"Mrs. Shakk," Gai said. "Our favorite neighbor."

"Why does she have to use that yellin' horn?" Lynd plugged her ears. "Makes my head wanna explode."

"Satisfied?" Gai waved her to the edge. "Let's get home quick before someone else comes. Or you get upset—ugh—before someone else comes."

Lynd stayed leaning in the crux of two beams.

"A'way, Lynd. Ya gotta admit this is way more excitement than anyone promised ya when ya went to bed."

She grasped the wood tightly in her hand. But did not break it this time. "A'kay."

"Wow." Gai gently put his hand on her shoulder. "Pa's old fiddle song really calms ya up, yeah?"

Lynd only offered a tiny smirk.

As the boy began his climb back up to the Boulie, two more stomping feet rushed toward them again. Who knew the Boards were so busy at night? Gai ducked back under and waited for whomever it was to pass.

Clink. The person dropped something just as they were walking above Gai and Lynd. "This rotten old sachet," a woman said, picking it back up. "Everythin' else in this world's got a hole in it, 'course this does too, she says." The woman then walked down toward the center of Hop, muttering, "Zeea, I pray this is worth it."

"Gai," Lynd whimpered. "That was *Ma!*"

"What?" He tried to peak through the spaces between Boulie's planks. "What did she mean 'worth it'? What's she doin'?"

"She *never* goes out!" Lynd smacked his shoulder. "We have to follow her!"

"No, Lynd. We're goin' home."

She scoffed and paused, glaring at him. "Yer *such* a sogg. What if somethin' happens to her?"

Bump. Bump. The sogg remark. That made two times. A fist-sized lump formed in his throat. Where did she get an idea like that? *Bump. Bump.* He looked at the wood still clutched in his sister's hand. All that destruction nonsense started the night Pa left. Was that why he was a sogg? Because he couldn't fix her? He was trying. He did his best to fix everything that broke in the house due to her strange power. He was even sneaking out to make the perfect present, one that actually might calm Lynd when she needed it. Maybe then the destruction would stop. He could patch up a few cracks, but what else was he supposed to do to fix Lynd? *Bump. Bump.* Put a piece of newspaper over her?

Lynd turned and said, "What if somethin' happens to her like P—"

"Stop!" Gai accidentally shouted. He went to cover his mouth but then puffed out his chest instead. "Ya won't keep up with Ma, jumpin' on the dinky ones." He leaped from beam to beam as a monkey moves through tree limbs.

She giggled. "Lead the way, wetleg."

CHAPTER 2
THE RED TIDE

The Under Board was a thick forest of support beams, crisscrossed in haphazard ways. The Izz children were forced to wind their way under the homes of their neighbors, where globs of who-knows-what dripped on their heads. It didn't smell like just a tea spill, that's for sure.

Lynd noticed something was sticking out of Gai's waistband as he crawled. "Is that part of my present?" she asked.

He simply wiggled it back down into his pants and kept moving.

Lynd followed her brother's every move through the beams. She reached and jumped, grabbed and shimmied, all with that thin piece of wood she needed in case the urge to break something arose. No telling what could happen if she didn't have that close at hand. As she went to grip the next beam, that all-important sliver of wood slipped and fell all the way to the rushing water below. *Oops.*

She didn't tell Gai.

The boy kept a sharp ear up at the planks above, listening for their mother's next steps. Where in Esa was she going at this late hour, anyway? Especially when she never went outside during the day. As far as the children knew, she hadn't been out of 76 since their father disappeared five years ago.

Lynd couldn't bear the silence any longer. "'Ey, Gai."

"What?" he replied sharply.

It was so dark that Lynd only knew where to go by following her brother's silhouette in the dim glow of Hop's center ahead. "Ya think Ma could be out lookin' for spryts?"

"What's with ya? No one *wants* to find a spryt, Lynd. Ma says they're dangerous as a deathfish."

"What do ya think they are, then?"

"I heard they look like spooky red doom dots," Gai said. "Some say they're *ghosts*. All the souls lost in the gulf come back to haunt us."

"Ghosts?" Lynd stopped in her tracks. "Do ya think . . . one of them could be Pa?"

Gai almost slipped off a beam. "Pa is not *dead!*" His voice cut through the air like a razor. "He just . . . left and hasn't come back yet."

"I-I don't think he is either." She touched the back of his shoulder, but Gai snapped it away and continued his march.

After a few quiet moments, he softly said, "Ya really don't remember the night he left?"

"No, I wish." She mimicked his moves from post to post.

Her brother kept quiet, leaping through the knitted beams even faster.

Finally, Lynd said, "Wanna know what I think spryts are?"

"No," he mumbled over the roaring sea below. "Y'already made me lose Ma."

"Oh, just thought ya'd like to know," Lynd said. "Since one was in our room last night."

"In our—?" A wave crashed on the posts and splashed Gai's whole left side. He turned his entire body around in one jump, shaking the wooden lattice. "Where was I? Why didn't ya say anythin'? Did it touch me?"

"No." She laughed.

Gai stood motionless. "What *was* it?"

"Kinda like the light electri lamps make, just not yellow. A bright red dot, like ya heard. And it zipped around like a bug tryin' to get out."

"So, it was a ghost?"

"No," she said. "I mean, it didn't *say* anythin'."

"Did ya stomp on it?" Gai was both glued to the post and her story. "How'd it even get in?"

"I was asleep, having another dream about Pa comin' home. He was with Uncle Baald on the ship. Anyway, when I woke up, there it was!"

"But Ma boarded the windows?"

"It was just a tiny thing." Lynd's voice started to break up. She cleared her throat. "But then it left, right out a crack. I dunno, Gai, I felt like if I could've caught it, somethin' wild would happen . . . Do you think spryts could be dreams?"

"Doubt it," Gai said. "What about that scooper who said one blew a hole in his scoop? Or Mayor Tanning, who swore he saw two hit each other and they exploded all crazy?"

"Bad dreams," said Lynd. "But what if I caught mine and my dream of Pa comin' home came true?"

"I miss Pa, too," Gai said softly. "But we're not touchin' any spryts, ya got me? A'way. We gotta find the other parent, now."

They continued stretching and reaching for the beams, sometimes having to bend their bodies in slithering ways. Most Hoppers were asleep, silent and unlit above their heads. But soon, yellowish electri lights were peaking through the cracks. Then the Under Board boards started to jitter a bit with footsteps above. Garbled voices, small and booming, rained down. "We're right under Tanning's Vice House," Gai whispered. "Cover yer ears. I don't want ya to hear the way these people talk."

"I'm not a baby!" Lynd half-yelled over the sounds of clinking cans, roaring voices, and falling dice above. *What're ya lookin' at, ya quirk?*

Gai smirked, looking back. "I just don't want ya to pick up any new names for me."

Lynd glanced up at the golden lights of Tanning's Vice shining through the floorboards. No children were allowed in, so who could blame her for peeking? She tried to make out who was in there by the shapes of their shoes. Mrs. Shakk had ones made out of metal buckets that she hammered around each foot; and hers were the least interesting ones. Lynd then heard a familiar voice up there — *Just lemme play, she says!*

Lynd pressed her eyes up closer to the floorboard. "I think that's Ma!"

She tilted her ear to the voices just above. First was a man's voice
— *Yer gonna bet that necklace on one game of Elix or Ruin?*
That's right, she says. I'll bet on Elix this time!
"Yup. Ma's up there," Lynd whispered.
Gai's brow twisted in disbelief. "In the Vice House? She *gambles?*"
The two children were glued under those planks of wood, like
boogers. The boy grabbed a nearby beam to leverage himself higher
and felt that it was wrapped around many times with fishing wire. He
couldn't believe his luck. It was precisely what he needed for Lynd's
present — a wire he could pull tight over the nice piece of wood he
found. He wanted to make a fiddle like Pa had. But what if this
fishing wire were wrapped around that beam to hold it in place? He
was afraid to take it and have the whole place come down on them.

"It's my girl's thirteenth tomorrow," Mape continued in the room
above them. "I'd like to get her somethin' good for once."

"All the times ya been in here, Mape," the man muttered, "Ya
promised ya'd never bet that necklace."

"Promises are the easiest things to unmake," Mape said softly.
"I'd rather my girl have shoes than me have a necklace, she says."

Lynd felt her cold toes curl around a splitting Under Board pole.

The man in the room chuckled. "Alright, Izz. Deal her in! Look's
like yer up against Mrs. Shakk for the win."

"A'way, Lynd." Gai stepped on the next beam beside her. "I don't
wanna hear how this ends."

Lynd stood still, staring up at the cracks. If she wanted to, she
could yell to her mother. She could tell to stop, to not bet her only
real possession on a gift for her. Her heart became so heavy. Her eyes
welled up.

"Lynd . . ."

"I miss Pa, Gai. That's all I want for my birthday." She started to
fully bawl. "Ma shouldn't have to do that!" She kept squeezing her
fist. But that trusty piece of snapping wood had fallen into the
water. *Krak!* A beam right beside her splintered instead.

Gai whispered. "It's a'kay, Lynd. Just snap the wood in yer hand
—" He then saw it was gone.

Krakk! Snnap! More posts and boards started breaking around her,
seemingly in sync with her sobs.

Gai reached out to her, "Where's yer—*whoa!*" Chunks of the

splintering wood were flying through the air like a storm was ripping bark off a tree. The Under Board began shaking, and so too did the Tanning's Vice House above. The patrons yelled, "Currents are pickin' up!" and "Another storm's rollin' in! Nothin' lasts!" The floorboards banged with footsteps as they vacated.

The beam with the fishing wire wrapped around it snapped in Lynd's destructive chaos. Gai quickly grabbed it and began to wrap it lengthwise around that lovely curved un-Hop-like piece of wood he brought. Once it was tight, he plucked the wire with his fingernail as if it were an instrument. *Ping!* "We've been here before," he sang. *Ping!* "With yer hand in mine."

The rumbling stopped. "Pa?" Lynd opened her eyes and wiped a tear.

"What do ya think?" he said, "Sounds like Pa's fiddle a little, yeah?"

"Ya made that for me?"

"It's what I came out to make, yeah." *Ping.* "I thought if I could learn to play it, maybe . . . happy birthday." Of course, the boy was thinking his sister's destructive nature was only becoming more and more dangerous. He worried what would happen, exactly, when he finally couldn't calm her? What if Pa never came home?

Lynd sniffled a few more times and took the instrument from him. She smiled. "Ya remember when Pa first brought that fiddle home?"

"How could I forget?" Gai said. "Ms. Shakk heard him playin' and told the whole Board. Then they came and painted 'QUIRKS' in front of our door."

"It took us forever to wash that off." Lynd started to laugh through her crying.

Gai smiled. "Hopper White really sticks."

"He was playin' it in my dream, Gai. I keep hearin' that song. Mrs. Shakk is there, too . . ."

"A'way. I think ya scared everyone up there back to their homes. We can climb up here and walk back. Just be careful."

"A'kay."

The children used the outer scaffolding and climbed directly up to the Boulie's ledge unnoticed. Lynd had a new present, and they even managed to sneak out for the first time without getting caught.

As a bonus, the Vice House didn't crumble on top of them. But the children walked with a heavy, defeated shuffle all the way home. That's Hop for ya. There just aren't enough little wins to take away the big lose of living there. Their mother was gambling for presents. Their father was thought to be dead. And they were trapped forever in a dangerous place surrounded by unforgiving waters. Whose light would dare shine there?

"What's *that?*" said Lynd. "Did ya see that?"

"Let's just get home, Lynd. A'kay?"

"Never mind." Lynd sighed hard. She held up her fiddle and plucked it. *Ping.*

Gai stopped and turned to her abruptly. "Don't play it here!"

She stopped walking. "But, I wanted to hear—"

"Neighbors can hear, too! I don't want any repeats of that night. We'll find a safe spot tomorrow to play, a'kay?" He turned and marched to 76.

Ping.

Gai finally turned, enraged. "Lynd, I said—" But his jaw fell. Terror washed over his eyes. He pointed behind his sister.

Lynd turned around. Her mouth hung oval, stunned. Hundreds of bright red specks were tossing about in the air above the center of Hop like fireflies.

The yellow electri lights all started shutting off one by one as the neighborhood realized — just as Tanning's fair warning signs warned — the spryt lights were out tonight. Swarms of dazzling rubies danced over the port and surrounding water. The Izz children couldn't run, they couldn't speak, they couldn't look away. The curious lights seemed to avoid boarded-up windows, walls, posts and twine as if they were *thinking.* They dipped near the water by sleeping scoopers, who still had their scoops tied to poles in the curling currents. The tiny dots didn't seem to be aiming to go anywhere in particular, just dashing and drifting delightfully.

Gai whispered, "These are?"

"Spryts!" Lynd finished, her eyes ticked about like she was trying to follow every one.

Most of the lights were still far down Boulie, back over the center, making them feel less imminently terrifying. But then a few drifted up from sides of Boulie Board near their feet. The danger literally came close to home.

"Lynd," whispered Gai. "We should get back inside."

"Y-yeah," she said, turning. "Sure."

The two slowly walked the short distance left to their home, careful not to touch any of the lights as they gently floated past. Gai reached for the rope Lynd used to sneak out and pulled himself all the way up to their room. But Lynd paused on the Board. She plucked that note one more time. *Ping.*

Right in front of the Izz house door, that one with thirteen shades of oh-Zeea-I-am-not-touching-that green, another shimmering spryt rose from the churning sea.

Gai waved down at her frantically, afraid to actually yell. What if a neighbor heard?

Lynd played the first two notes of the song their father used to play from memory. *Ping. Bung.*

The spryt flickered its red light and seemed to dance with the notes.

"I knew it," Lynd breathed, stepping closer to it.

"Lynd!"

The spryt began to bounce casually from their door to the tip of Boulie, a pier toward the open water. Lynd followed it with the fiddle in hand, grinning.

Gai rounded the sill and headed back down. "Per course, ya gotta do this to me!" He jumped down and hit Boulie so hard he thought his bones were screaming at him.

"I knew they were dreams!" Lynd said, dancing about like she was mimicking the floating spryt. They went further and further to the railless end of the Board. "Gai, help me catch it!"

Gai chased after her. "Lynd!" Stormy waves began mashing up against the posts, shaking the whole Board. He couldn't even see her anymore, only the red dot she was chasing. He was about twenty plank boards from the tip of Boulie. "Get back inside!"

"I'm not gonna let Pa get away again!" she yelled.

He limped after her. Only thirteen planks away. He could barely make out where she was against a forming thunderstorm rolling in from the gulf.

Nine planks away. "We've been here before." His sister was at the very edge of Boulie, facing the violent water, pinky-plucking her instrument for the red light. "With yer hand in mine." The spryt hovered above her. "In my heart, there's a window . . ."

She reached up and grabbed it. An impossibly brilliant crimson light engulfed her entire body.

Krack! A glowing red gash formed in front of Lynd in the open air, jagged and quick as lightning, as if the sky itself had just ripped open like a firecracker.

"Look out!" he cried. Then everything in his view ahead — the open water waves, the pier, and his sister — shattered like it was painted on fallen glass. The planks of Boulie Board's tip tore apart like an invisible ship just crashed into it, two, then five, then ten planks in, right under Gai's feet. He collapsed with it all to tattered Under Board below.

"Lynd!" He gripped a post, avoiding the deadly descent into the rushing currents. Fractured pier pieces flew through the air, a few striking the boy as he dangled for his life. Finally, he pulled himself to an unbroken part of the Board, rolling onto Boulie. He got to his knees and begged to see any sign of her. He cried out against the thunder over Hop. "Lynd!"

There was nothing. No spryt. No dream. And worst of all — no Lynd.

CHAPTER 3
LIKE A SHIP CRASHED INTO ME

The only time Hoppers spoke to one another was when there was a good rumor to spread. Safety was their excuse — to warn everyone about what's-their-name doing you-know-what. Rumors traveled even faster when there was danger or mystery involved. Ones about families who were already poorly thought of spread even quicker. The Izz girl's disappearance, for instance, was already the talk of the town before breakfast was ready the next day.

Mamma Mape and Gai didn't sleep at all. A few scoopers got together for a search party, but they scooped no signs of Lynd. Mayor Tanning spent the day interrogating the only witness, and the boy brought all his truth to bear, sneaking out to make a present, the Under Board, and, of course, the spryts.

"Ya think I was born last week, boy?" The mayor bashed his fist on the three old oar paddles he used for a desk. "I was yer age when they built these Boards, and now the whole edge of Boulie's gone! Spryts been around — causin' trouble, yeah. Maybe shockin' a few scoopers outta their seats. But ya expect me to believe some little red light caused all that?"

"What else could it be?" said Gai. The color was drained from his face due to lack of sleep. "Lynd touched the spryt. And then everything ripped to pieces!"

"Ripped to pieces, ya say?" The mayor twisted his sticky-looking beard to a point and said, "Not the first Izz to rip somethin' to pieces . . ."

"What do ya mean?" the boy asked.

"Ya think this is the first *unusual* thing I've heard about yer quirk family? Besides bein' gallsy enough to try and leave Hop, that is."

The only other strange thing Gai knew about his family was that his father, Stav Izz, left five years ago on the only ship to leave Hop in many, many years. The ship was called the *Lady Merry*. And she hadn't returned. But that was a completely different kind of disappearance; Pa left with Uncle Baald and a whole crew on a real ship. Lynd was there one second, gone the next. Surely, Tanning didn't think those were the same? And what about the destruction of Boulie? Gai couldn't have made that up. It was there. The mayor released him for the day with a glare that said, "Oh, yeah, investigations *will* be ongoing."

The boy laid awake that night again, piecing together every moment of the encounter with the spryt like a puzzle. He tossed from side to side, glancing at the rope blanket he made his sister, which she had torn to shreds and used to escape out the window. As wild as it was, the destruction of Boulie seemed like just an extreme example of what already happened when Lynd got upset. Instead of snapping a piece of wood, Boulie snapped. Lynd couldn't have destroyed *herself*, could she?

By the second day, an unforgiving crowd had gathered outside 76 demanding answers, tossing stones and painting all sorts of stinky words on the Board planks in front. "Ya heard about that Izz family? Mhm. I heard that mamma's been drivin' 'em right off Boulie one-after-one!" Three days of no new evidence passed, so the girl was declared "dead to us, at least" by Tanning. He planned a small funeral where he'd rename the tattered, splintering end of Boulie Board to "Lynd's Pier" for — how did the mayor put it? — "Any soggs who actually bought their story."

That evening, Mape held back her tears as she went up to Gai and Lynd's room. She palmed open the door and found their schooling books stacked in front as a doorstop. Education, like anything one built or made, wasn't highly regarded in Hop anymore. It could just be unmade, couldn't it? Kids forget their lessons all the time. Still, Mape had been trying to teach them their letters, just in case Stav's trip succeeded and they got off that ugly wooden prison. Lynd hadn't quite gotten the hang of reading yet. Mape imagined now she never would. She again swallowed her welling emotions as she addressed her son, who was sitting quietly on his floor-bed with their pet turtle, Emilie, cupped in his hands. "How ya bein', she asks?"

The boy didn't look up.

Mape, for one, believed her son's story. If her children ran out in the middle of the night and one of them vanished after an encounter with a strange red light, then that was just life giving her a good kick in the guts again. And life was wearing some spiky boots that day. After all the kicks Hop had given her, she learned how to hide their impact. She believed wearing her sadness just smeared the misery to those around her. A lump grew in her throat. "H-had a chance to gather Lynd's things?" She plodded into the room. "It's only right to give those lost at sea their things back, she says."

Don't be alarmed by the way Mape talks. She had an odd habit of narrating her own sentences, seemingly unconsciously and rather randomly. Rumor had it she lost a few marbles after Stav left.

Gai's eyes rolled up, his head motionless. No words came out. Emilie, the turtle, crawled from his left hand to the right.

Mamma Mape approached him carefully. "It's one of the few Hopper traditions I actually buy into." She bent down and put her hands under his. "I don't say it much, but I know how hard it is to—"

"Lynd is *not* dead." He stood abruptly and paced toward the door with the tiny turtle still in hand. "But I'm gonna give Emilie back at the funeral for show. I don't want them thinkin' . . . whatever they think."

"That turtle is yers both?" Mape stared at Lynd's pulled-apart blanket. "Yer not supposed to throw back yer own things."

Monotonous and detached, the boy replied, "Lynd found her." He ran his thumb gently over Emilie's scaly nose. "She saved her from an old crab cage on Bleek Board. Em still has the scar she got from bein' trapped." Gai paused, staring at his mother for some hint of emotion from her. "Ya think she's really gone, don't ya?"

But Mape was bent on keeping it all in.

Gai felt himself simmering. "'Nothin' last but salt in yer . . . ya-know-where . . . Pa was right, all we do here is stare around at the pieces when things break, pointin' fingers. Maybe if we weren't such soggs, somethin' might actually last! I wish we left on that ship right with him!"

Mape let out a breathy sigh, listening to Gai stomp down the stairs on his way to Lynd's funeral. She reached up to her chest where her necklace *used* to be. The necklace had a small ship's wheel charm, believed to be a symbol of Zeea — a mythical figure who many believed granted luck and clarity. Zeea was something of a patroness of Hop, though few still bothered bargaining with gods anymore. Still, that necklace made Mape feel guided during rough emotional currents. She had forgotten she bet that trinket three nights ago at Tanning's Vice House. It was no longer there. She never got Lynd a present. "I can't help but stare. The pieces is all I got, she says."

Gai opened the front door to jeers and boos from the eleven angry Hoppers that had gathered outside. They demanded justice for Lynd. Apparently, they believed the rumors that Mape had something to do with her disappearance. The boy pretended they were just the regular hoots and hollers he overheard from his intolerant neighbors.

Mrs. Shakk was there in front, hay-haired and bucket-shoed, with her usual sickly-yellow hue, just blowing her yelling horn at him like always — *Whaaah!* She wore an old roof tile around her neck and used it write people messages, usually rude ones. Why she wouldn't actually *talk* to anyone at all was really the least interesting thing about her. She even claimed to know what spryts were. She was the one who lobbied Tanning to hang spryt warning signs all around Hop.

The boy ignored them all, hobbling into some thick, sticky fog that had settled over Hop's area of the Domus Gulf. Mape came out after, rushing past the crowd with her head down and her own offerings to Lynd draped over her arm.

Gai marched forward to the fateful pier, reliving every step anew from that night along the way. He could practically hear Lynd's fiddle plucks coming from the white fog all around. He remembered Lynd's last moment still on the Board. How she was there with the spryt playing the fiddle and how suddenly everything around her tore apart in a flash of crimson light. "It was my fault she was even outside . . ."

Mother and son joined the mayor, who was tapping his foot at the end of the about-to-be-named "Lynd's Pier." He wore a black tarp with a hole cut out for his sun-battered head, just for this special occasion, which was honestly more than either Izz expected. The crowd of justice-seeking Hoppers didn't follow them to the funeral, thank Zeea, though a few of their nasty chants could still be heard. A random scooper was there as well, but it was unclear if he actually meant to attend or just happened to be scooping there. It was kind of him to take his cardboard hat off, though.

"As mayor," boomed Tanning, his long arms swinging way over their heads. "It's my obligation to officiate yer loss, Mrs. Izz. But per Hopper Law, the family must first agree to *accept* the loss by offering their loved one's personal belongings to the sea. How do ya feel about these terms, Mrs. Izz?"

". . . Like a ship crashed into me," she said.

The mayor continued, unmoved by Mape's obvious distress. "Very well. I understand ya have *two* losses ya'd like to accept?"

Two? Gai thought, shooting his eyes at her. By Zeea, did her skin look pale. He noticed both Lynd's *and* his father's patchy raincoats draped over her arm. Light-headed and heavyhearted, he wondered if she was really going to do this? Were they done waiting for Pa to come home? Was five years long enough?

Mape sniffled back a tear. "Yeah." But her eyes soon filled with them. "Today, I accept bo—" She couldn't finish.

"Ma," said the boy, his voice trembling. "Lemme go first."

Tanning moved from the edge of the destroyed pier, "Very well, young Izz. Please hurry this up. It's almost sunset, and the water levels predict another spryt swarm tonight. I trust ya understand the dangers of that, *now?* Won't be ignorin' any more of Tanning's signs, will ya?"

"No." The boy stepped to the splintering end of Lynd's Pier with Emilie in his hands, her tiny turtle feet dangling over the rushing water.

Mraaw, she cried quietly.

As the boy looked down at the drop, he saw the real impact of

Lynd's destruction to the Board. It wasn't like the planks were simply snapped and cracked. They were warped at the ends like they were torn then twisted and smooth almost like melted wax. It was truly a bizarre sight. "Lynd . . . I offer ya back our best friend. I know Em remembers how nice ya were to her. Goodbye, my sister." He then whispered to the turtle, very softly so no one would hear but her. "If ya bring Lynd and Pa home, I'll scoop ya every crabby in the Under Board."

Had the mayor heard, he would've canceled the ceremony right there. Gai and his mother were supposed to be *accepting* death, not asking for help from turtles. The boy let Emilie fall straight down into the currents, where she vanished in the white, rushing water.

"Mrs. Izz," Tanning said, "if ya could please make yer gesture of acceptance. So I can leave."

Mape crept to the end near her son. She couldn't look at him. How could she? She was about to officially accept the death of his father after hardly speaking about him for years. With the loss of Lynd, too, all her hope had dried up like a jellyfish on the beach. She dangled the coats over the pier. "I . . ."

Whaaah! Whaaah!

The ugly sound of that damned yelling horn came from back down Boulie. Though, no one could see that far down the Board through the fog.

"It's just that Mrs. Shakk," said Tanning. "Continue, Mrs. Izz."

Whaaah! Whaaah!

. . . Whaaah!

Mrs. Shakk wouldn't stop furiously blowing in that irritating horn.

Baaanng! A bell then rang so loudly that it shook all the Boards of Hop. Tanning almost fell into the water, shouting, "What in Esa's goin' on down there?"

It was the bell atop Garris Hall in the center of Hop. Its powerful ring was meant to shake anyone from their sleep in case of an imminent disaster, like an invasion of Electrians or a particularly nasty swell. *Bannng!*

"Wh-what is *that?*" yelled Gai, pointing out at sea. A giant shadow was quickly growing in the milky fog over the water. Something truly gigantic was barreling right at Lynd's Pier. "It's bigger than our house!"

All four of them, Tanning, Gai, Mape, and that random scooper, stared at it in silence as it got bigger and more threatening every moment. Every heart rate quickened. More bells started ringing all over the port town. Mrs. Shakk kept blowing that horn.

Tanning shouted, "Every mayor for himself!" He scurried down Boulie toward the center. The scooper shot up and followed, his soggy hat rolling behind.

Mape caught a body chill and accidentally dropped both coats into the water. She bent down tried to catch them, but Gai yanked his grieving mother from the edge before the giant shadow, whatever it was, crashed into Lynd's Pier.

Everyone on Boulie ran toward Hop's center as fast as they could. The Board jolted hard as the object finally collided. Planks rippled under Gai and Mape's feet, nearly tripping them. The boy peered back — the pointed bow of a *ship* was chewing through the Board and Under Board like a hungry whale.

Tanning tripped.

"Ma!" said Gai, pointing to the mayor ahead, the planks popping like puny twigs behind. The boy picked him up, and they all ran together. The mighty currents of the Domus Gulf hurled that ship forward so fast, with jagged wood chunks flying through the air like arrows. The ship was so close to them it was pushing the stumbling mayor's bottom forward.

They were about to be ship food. But the bow veered suddenly off Boulie and *Booom!* It dashed cleanly through Bleek Board.

Boom! Tanning's Vice House lost one of its corners. Then *Booom!* It finally came to a rigged rest in Hop's center, crumbling everything behind it.

The bells still belled all around. The mayor looked down the path of destruction and saw where the ship came to rest. "My home! My home! *My* beautiful home!" he yelled, running past the protesters outside 76.

Mape and Gai looked down the path of destruction, then immediately at each other. "I don't believe it," said Mape.

They knew this ship. It was Uncle Baald's ship, the *Lady Merry*. It was the same one Stav Izz left on five years ago. They'd done it; they actually survived leaving Hop. Pa was home.

Stunned and elated, they raced to the impact zone. Even the

angry crowd outside the Izz home went too, yelling at every house they passed, "A ship crashed! A ship has *crashed*!"

Flocks of Hoppers were already scouring Tanning's bulbous home through the rubble when they arrived. They were trying to find a way up to the shipwreck from his house. A few called up to the ship's deck, "'Ey! 'Ey! If yer still alive, say it!" With every Hopper gathered in one place for once — that's at least two hundred people — Mape and her son couldn't get close enough to get a good look.

"I knew they'd make it back," said Gai. "Unc's the best sailor! Even with the rough landin'."

"Gulf currents are unforgivin'." Mape wouldn't take her eyes off the ship, trying to get a peek through the spaces between all the heads, hungry to see if her husband and cousin would climb down. Or if she was about to add a third family member to the funeral ceremony. Yet another kick.

Gai pointed. "What's that they're passin' around?"

"Hurry! Here it comes. Grab it, she says!"

The boy snatched the piece of paper and quickly brought it to his mother to read it together.

"It's the passenger list," Mape said. She searched with her finger through the names of all the people aboard from the last port, Electri City. Halfway down the page was the name STAV IZZ.

"By Zeea," she shouted, barely staying on her feet. She locked eyes with her son, "Gaiel, Pa *is* back! They made it all the way to Electri City and back! I hope he's . . ."

"Ya hope he's what, Ma?"

Her eye twitched. "Nothin'." She pulled him in for a hug, "Yer father's home. Maybe yer right about Lynd, too. Maybe some things do last." Tears filled up their eyes as they held each other.

The anticipation of good news and hope was driving them mad. They both stood on the very tip of their tippy-toes to see how the passengers were faring. Gai looked over every corner of the *Merry's* deck, trying to see someone. Anyone. "Why's no one comin' off yet?"

CHAPTER 4
THE VOICE BOX

When waiting for something life-changing, minds tend to imagine every possible possibility of what might happen when that wait is finally over. That's why moments spent waiting are so much longer than the ones spent having fun. People aren't in one space, as they are when playing. But living in two, four, fifty scenarios at once, each taking its tug on the nerves. Gai and Mape had imagined many scenarios while waiting for Pappa Stav to walk off that ship. And their nerves were getting rather gnarly.

"What is this crap? We been soggin' out here for an hour, she says!"

"'Ey," Gai pointed at someone poking over the rails of the deck. It was the first person they'd seen on the ship.

Mape sighed. "Oh, that's just Tanning's bald head."

The mayor waved down to the Hoppers from the top deck of the *Lady Merry*. He'd been able to find a way into the ship through the wreckage of his home. Everyone, including the hopeful Izz family, yelled up for news. Tanning shrugged his shoulders and shook his head. He yelled something like, "*Esa hostess!*"

"What's he goin' on about?" said Mape.

No one in the crowd seemed to know what he was saying either.

He called down as loud as he could into his coned hands, "It's a ghost ship!"

All of Hop gasped at once.

"*Ghost* ship?" Gai dropped his jaw.

Where was the crew? The captain, Baald Penn? Stav? The Hoppers all whispered their own wild theories. Some said they must've run out of food and jumped overboard. Or ran out of rum and jumped overboard. Maybe the crash knocked them off? "Quick, check the water!" The crowd grew more and more anxious, ready to burst onto the *Merry* and have a look for themselves. Someone had to be responsible for wrecking their ugly town.

Mape reached her hand to where her necklace used to be. Shaking, her empty fingers came back down to her sides. "Don't tell me . . ."

Gai started to think out loud. "They're gone . . . like Lynd?"

"Speak up, she says."

"Ma, what do ya think spryts are, again?"

Mape stared blankly.

The Hoppers near him heard Gai say the word spryts and immediately got panicky. "Spryts? Where? Who saw 'em?" Then the people around them spread the word in a wave of whispering fears. "Spryts are comin', I heard! The red tide!" The people parted around him and his mother like they were two misplaced drops of oil in water. Gai shrank, having so many eyes on him.

The mayor saw the budding chaos below, saw that it involved the Izz family — *per course*, it involved the Izz family — and sent word for them to get up on the *Merry's* deck with him. When the order reached Mape, she swallowed another heavy lump and gripped her son's arm. "Spryts might be the best we can pray fer."

"Why?" he said. "Do ya know what's goin' on?"

"Tanning's starin' at us. That's what's goin' on." She pulled him forward. "Stay close."

They entered the mayor's front door and into his living room. The salty hull of the *Lady Merry* was smack in the middle of the room, cutting it in half like a poorly thought-out decoration. A coffin-sized gash in the *Merry* led right into her cargo hold from the living room. As they squeezed their way through the rough opening, the line of people who had already entered the ship all gawked at them eerily. Eyeball after stinky eyeball rolled across the other

Hopper's faces as the mother and son climbed up to the creaky stairs to the top deck.

Out in fresh air again, they saw Tanning standing with three other men in a circle toward the bow. Each were staring down at the deck boards. As Mape and Gai approached, the mayor turned to them with a dazed leer.

Mape exhaled like she'd been holding her breath for the entire walk up. "Mayor Tanning, we don't—" But Mamma Mape was stunned when she caught a look at the *Lady Merry's* front deck.

A whole side of it looked like it had been blown to bits. It was as if an explosion went off, searing deep into the wood from the planks to the mast. And the damage was too far inward to be caused by the collision with Hop.

"They're gone, Mape," Tanning said in an uncharacteristically quiet tone. He seemed like he wanted to be angry, but he wasn't quite sure what to be angry about yet. "Against all guesses, yer cousin Baald's ship came back. Too bad no one else did."

"What're ya sayin' about?" she said.

"It's completely abandoned," he stressed. "Not a damn scrap of one of 'em. No lifeboat's missin'."

Around the edges of the wrecked deck, the boards were curled up, twisted and gnarled bizarrely, not just snapped. "By Zeea," Gai said under his breath. "It's the same destruction as Lynd's Pier . . ."

The mayor locked his wrinkled lids on the boy. "Not the first *unusual* thing I've heard about yer quirk family."

Waaahhhhh!

Mape tightened her grip on Gai's arm even more. Every sight and sound seemed to make her jittery, as if danger could strike from anywhere at any time.

A Hopper yelled from down in the cargo hold, "Mrs. Shakk's comin' up, sir!"

"This should be interestin'." Tanning sighed. "Send her up!"

Gai said, "What *else* have ya heard about my family?"

Clunk. Scrape. Clank. Mrs. Shakk walked her bucket shoes onto the deck, her ear-busting horn in hand. Dangling from her neck was a fresh piece of chalk and a small roof tile, ready for fighting words. She stepped right in front of Tanning and took in a whiff of air. She then began scribbling on the tile.

Mape let go of her son and backed away a bit.

As soon as Mrs. Shakk put the final hard stroke on her roof piece, she turned it around for all to see — STAV IZZ DID THIS!

Gasps. Gasps. Gasps all around. It was like a contest to see who could suck the most air off the *Merry* deck. But Tanning didn't appear shocked at all. Instead, he nodded along as if Mrs. Shakk were confirming some deeply held belief of his. "Mrs. Shakk, I know ya have . . . a *history*, shall we say, with Mr. Izz. But that's a whale of an accusation. Don't get me wrong, I'd believe it. But do ya have any proof?"

Entirely unconsciously, Mape had been slowly turning her body away from the situation as they talked. By now, she was almost facing the stairs down.

Mrs. Shakk walked right up to Gai and opened her mouth wide for him to see inside. Off-putting as that was, down her throat was a horrifying, black scar. It had the same jagged tears as the *Merry's* deck and Lynd's Pier. She began furiously dashing that chalk hard on the tile. She turned it around — HE DESTROYED MY VOICE!

Mape pulled Gai to the stairs. "That's all, she says!"

Gai gave the destroyed deck one last glance on the way out and saw a piece of curved wood. It was a nice piece of wood. It didn't quite belong on a ship from Hop. He gave it a double-take. "Is that?" he said aloud. As Mape pulled him down the stairs, he looked a third time and swore he saw some twisted fishing wire shredding off it. "Ma, wait. I think I made that—"

"We need to get out before the whole place turns on us," she said. But it was too late. The line of Hoppers down the stairs had been passing along all the details to the crowd below. They all heard the latest: The Izz family has a history of this destruction crap. As Mape and Gai climbed out of the ship, every one of those stinky eyeballs leered at the boy like he was the spawn of a sea monster. But they saved their worst looks for Mamma Mape, the rumored sea monster herself. "The whole family is cursed!" If the crowd was on edge before, they were falling off their seats now. They chanted, "Justice!" One riled Hopper even spat in Mape's eye.

Gai grabbed her and used his body to push through them like a ship cutting through the gulf. Mother and son plowed through the crowd and hurried back to Boulie. They were chased by the same Hopper neighbors that protested outside their home already, plus a few new anti-Izzers. Mape huffed and puffed down the planks until she finally collapsed on their graffitied door. Her fingers shook so much that she dropped her keys. Gai had to finish the unlocking. Once inside, Mape slammed the door, shot their fourteen locks in place, and fell into her favorite rocking chair. It collapsed to pieces. The angry cluster gathered right outside and started bang-bang-banging.

"Ma!" Gai said, helping her back up. "It's a'kay, I'll fix it."

Bang! Bang! Bang!

"Ma, why did Pa leave Hop?"

Mape stared upward at the ceiling until her eyes teared up.

Come on out and face justice, ya bunch of quirks!

"Tell me!"

"Sorry at ya, Gaiel . . ."

The boy backed away from her. "It's true. Isn't it? What Pa did to her voice?" With the door of their home rattling from banging fists, Mape locked eyes with her son. Her lips shook like she wanted to say something but couldn't.

"For Zeea's sake, say somethin', Ma!"

"Oh, say somethin'? Easy for ya to say. What if I say the wrong thing? It's all on *my* shoulders!" Mape stared at her hands, rubbing her ring finger mindlessly, tear droplets raining down. "Yer Pa was sick, she says. I don't know what happened to him, but he was sick . . . Once ya can destroy a voice, is a ship really all that far?"

Justice! Justice! Justice! The crowd yelled and pounded on their door.

"So . . . Mrs. Shakk?" Gai touched his throat. "Pa really *destroyed* her voice that night?" Like putting the pieces of a fiddle together, Gai stitched together a frightening idea. Destruction, strangely enough, bonded everything. He remembered all the times Lynd would get angry. Her need to break things. Or things would break around her. "Sick . . . *with destruction*? If Pa was sick, I think Lynd caught it!" Gai looked up at his mother, trembling. He wasn't sure if he should tell her the fiddle he made Lynd might have been on that ship. But what would that even mean? It was too bizarre. It was all too bizarre. His head pulsed with a wave of tension. "But where did all this destroyin' stuff come from? Why do the spryts make it worse? What are they?"

"It was an awful sickness, Gaiel." She tapped her palm on her heart. "That's why Pa left with Baald to get help. That's the only reason he risked leavin'. He couldn't stay here and hurt . . . anyone else."

We're not lettin' ya out of this, Izz!

"I remember the night he left. Lynd says she doesn't remember, but she was outside with him. When she came back in, she wasn't the same! Ya remember, right? Ya ran out after Pa?" His face went red for a moment, but then water flooded his eyes, too. The memory of little Lynd bursting through the door and crying; she was so afraid. But the boy didn't know why. "I tried to fix her . . ." Gai remembered frantically searching for something, anything that could help his distressed little sister. The only thing he found that night was a rolled up pile of anchor rope. Somehow, he made it into a blanket to wrap her up in and held her until she cried herself to sleep. "I-I just couldn't fix her . . . Sogg."

Mape traced the veins on her shaking hand with her other finger. "When I got outside, a darkness overtook his whole body like his blood was black as ink! Baald thought maybe the Electrians and their big brains could cure him. They had to leave Hop that night." Mape never spoke about Stav. She would tell herself to wait just one more day, and maybe he'd be back, and she'd never have to speak of it. That's when her strange self-narrating began. "Every answer was supposed to come back on that damned ship, she says!"

Baang! All fourteen locks finally snapped off the frame, and the door to the Izz home burst off its hinges, crashing to the floor. A wall of clench-fisted Hoppers poured in. "Citizens' arrest! We charge ya with witchery and the murder of Lyn—"

"Don't ya dare say it!" Gai roared, turning to them. He held up his hand for them to stop. But they kept coming toward him and his mother. He felt a strange buzz quickly building up in his belly. The buzzing traveled up his chest and down the stiff arm he held out at the invaders. The angry Hoppers came closer. His hand grew hot. Very hot. He yelled, "Don't ya touch her!"

Mape stood up and put all her weight on his arm to bring it down. And that was almost not enough. "Been enough things destroyed today," she said, straining. "Let's not smear the sickness around."

He shook his head as if momentarily out of his body. "What just happened?"

Mamma Mape stepped between her son and the mob, offering her wrists up, "Ya think I did somethin'? I have a right to a trial, she says."

"We demand justice *now!*" shouted a neighbor.

"If Mrs. Izz wants a trial," Mayor Tanning said, stepping in the house. "She'll get one. It's either her or her husband that's to blame. Or both. I'd like to know which. Arrest her."

Per course, there was no formal police in Hop like there was in Electri. Anyone could arrest anyone else if they had enough suspicions and rope. Mape's own Boulie neighbors held the rope and tied her hands behind her back. Mrs. Shakk nudged someone out of the way so she could personally tie the final knot.

Mape stood, undaunted. "A moment with my son, she says."

Tanning nodded with an air of disgust.

"I never knew what to say," she said to him. "Maybe rather than just not sayin' the truth, I could've helped ya be strong enough to hear it."

"Ma, don't—"

"But here's what I'll say, now," Mape said as the neighbors carried her out the door to her trial. She stopped at the threshold and turned back with the slightest smile, "Give our door a fix, yeah?"

Tanning gave the boy one last dirty look before walking out with his mother. They all left the boy alone in a doorless house, motherless, fatherless, and sisterless, too. And the sun set on another Hop day.

CHAPTER 5

WICKED BLANK

The boy sat crossed-legged, gazing out the broken door frame at the words JUST JUMP ALREADY QUIRKS painted with Hopper White on the planks outside. They didn't even have the decency to put the comma. It seemed the neighbors would like them to kindly hurl themselves into the Domus Gulf. How unforgiving. They painted it right on the edge where the boy used to sit with Pa, listening to his stories about the lands beyond their crappy town, that this place wasn't how life was meant to be; there was more. All they had to do was fight for it, he'd say. "After ya left, Pa," Gai said in the broken home, his eyes glistened with tears. "All I wanted to do was fix us."

That battered door on the floor and its shattered frame seemed like the most broken thing the boy had ever seen. Its splinters even had splinters. Maybe it was his imagination, just the culmination of all the destruction around him that painted it extra rough. "A lot's broken since then," he said, looking around the small first floor of 76 and all its patchwork character. The staircase rail that broke when eight-year-old Lynd got angry one morning because Ma wouldn't let her play out on the Board. Gai replaced the rail with an old scooper handle and invented an indoor game where she had to find which hand the dust bunny was under. There was also the giant crack in the small kitchen table top from the time nine-year-old Lynd refused to eat watermoss balls for the fifth time in a week. Ma was particularly hurt about that one. Luckily Hopper White paint was so thick and sticky that when Gai painted over it, the paint filled the crack so that Ma could barely see it.

"But a lot's been fixed, too," Gai said, closing his eyes and letting the memories glide passed his mind's eye. "Better than doin' nothin'. I just try to fix it." A buzzing grew in his belly again. It was a warm feeling. "But where do I even start, now? *Everything's* in pieces. Not just the house . . . Ma, Pa, Lynd . . ."

His mother's voice came to him, clear as a yelling horn. "Give our door a fix, yeah?"

Gai opened his eyes, got to his feet, and marched to the broken Izz door with its hinges strewn around it. He picked up their graffitied door and walked it back into the frame. As he set it in place, a smile came over him. The warmth in his belly grew. "Gotta have a fixed house for everyone to come back to."

As he pressed the door firmly back to where it belonged, Gai felt a jolt cross between his palms and the wood. A brilliant blue spark lit up the edges of the frame like someone was outside, shining a light toward the door. He backed away, his nerves tingling, "S-Someone there?" he called. He bent down to peer through a keyhole. No one was there. He put his ear to the wood. No footsteps were running away. "Maybe storm lightnin'?"

The buzzing in his belly seemed even stronger. Assuming it was just because he was startled, he picked up the hinges to continue his work. He tried wiggling the bottom hinge back into place, but the frame was too torn up. "Balls at ya." His brow sweating, the boy played with different angles, to no avail. "A'way! If I can't fix a door, what chance to have of fixin' my fami—*Ah!*" Another jolt erupted from his hands, with a lovely blue glow still surrounding his fingers. He let go of the hinge and scooted back, shaking his hands like the glowy light was Hopper White paint he wanted off as soon as possible.

The glowing ceased quickly. Strange as that was, Gai's attention laid on the hinge he'd just let go. It didn't fall. It was stuck in the frame as if it was never broken.

"What in Esa?" He felt the frame, expecting a good splinter prick in the pinky. But no. Smooth as it was before. Maybe even smoother. "By Zeea." Gai's mouth hung. "Was that *me?*"

The room was getting pretty dark, but it looked to him like the splintered wood had somehow reformed around the hinge. The boy was still in shock. He knew about Lynd's destruction, but maybe there was another side to that power? Gai shot to his feet, ready to yell in celebration. But — *gurgle grr* — his stomach suddenly roared with an immense hunger. He bent over from the cramping and waddled into the kitchen. "Oh, please at ya, hope ya made some watermoss balls, Ma," he said, frenziedly feeling the nearly bare cabinet shelves. He felt a group of the squishy morsels, "Thanks at ya!" and shoveled three of them in his mouth. "I've never been so hungry in all my life!" Then he swallowed three more.

The boy looked back at their graffitied but almost fixed Izz door. He looked at his hand, where that blue glow had emerged. "Fixin'," he said, as more memories flashed in. Images of Lynd breaking pieces of wood in her hand and tearing up Boulie Board came. "Breakin'." He paused to chew over his own words as he picked some watermoss from his teeth. "Lynd and Pa had breakin' tricks . . . I just did a fixin' one." Gai looked at his hand. "Can I use it to fix *us?*"

He walked back to the door, picking up the last hinge on the way. He ran two of his fingers over the fixed frame and slid the hinge easily into place. Two thin pins fastened it all together. As the Izz family's fixed front door opened without a single creak, he said, "Not bad, for a sogg."

Gai stepped out onto Boulie in the cooling night air. He looked down at the carnage left by the *Lady Merry*. Walking to the Board edge, he said, "A'kay, Ma. First, I'll find out what happened on that ship and get ya free. Then, I'm gonna put us all back together." *Gurgle grr.* "After I eat!" He immediately turned back inside to grab three more watermoss balls. "*So* hungry! Guess that blue fixin' trick has a price. I don't remember Lynd gettin' this hungry with *her* tricks . . ."

Once his appetite was fixed, he went back outside and lowered his body back into the wooden matrix of the Under Board. Gai once again made his way toward the center under his neighbors' homes with the rushing gulf water just a short fall beneath. Step. Pivot. Round to the next. By the time he was under Tanning's Vice House, his mother was already inside with a packed crowd yelling and deciding how the trial should go down. *I say drop her in the gulf, already!*

"Hang in there, Ma. I'll figure this out." He trailed the destructive path caused by the unhelmed *Lady Merry* all the way to its resting spot in the mayor's home. Of course, Tanning was out conducting a sham trial, but Gai politely knocked on a collapsed ceiling beam as he climbed in just in case. "Hello? Anyone here tonight?"

Silence. Just a big, open room with a ship stuck in it. There wasn't even an attempt to lock the scene up. Perhaps Tanning thought he had nothing of value anymore and just left it all out for some scoopers to take. In fact, the boy suddenly wondered how in Esa the place wasn't already crawling with scoopers? This was their favorite kind of salvage — free. Even though everything in there was wrecked, that wasn't a bad deal. Gai put his hand over his stomach, thinking about how much his belly would growl if he tried to use that blue trick to fix everything in this place. And just what *was* that blue trick, anyway? He tiptoed through the crumbled mess inside, accidentally stepping his foot right on some of Tanning's pointiest knickknacks. *Yoow!*

Gai then seamlessly limped from Tanning's living room into the ship's hull. Again, politely knocking as he officially entered the *Merry*. "Hello? Anyone in *here?*"

Clunk! A barrel fell somewhere in the shadows of the hull. Its cover rolled up and hit Gai's knee before toppling over. Pins and needles rushed over his skin. He walked backward out of the ship, back into Tanning's living room. He hit a wall this time, which was oddly cushiony. And moist.

A low voice roared, "Off my gut, quirk!"

Before he could even turn, a hand came and smacked Gai to the ground. Creepy laughter and thumping boot steps poured out of the hull as some more scruffy youngsters walked out, filling up Tanning's living room. The boy pushed himself to his feet.

His attacker laughed and tapped an electri lamp, giving the room and everyone in it a yellow hue. "Funny. Ya know yer rich in Hop when ya can get Electri toys like these," the young man who hit Gai said. "But my dad told me they used to get 'em shipped by the hundreds back in Wiket."

As the small, yellow light flickered, Gai counted at least fifteen other Wikets emerging from all over the wreckage. All of them had something in their hands they were rummaging through; a stack of crumbled paper, a drawer, and one was even inside a barrel.

"Juuse," said the boy, pointing to the lamp. "Guess we'd all be happier if ya just left for Wiket. Thought it was just me."

Juuse Toho was the notorious, thick-skulled, patchy-bearded leader of the Wicked Wiket scooper gang. He dressed like he only scooped rubber mats and smelled like an old fish net. His ghostly complexion meant he almost never left the Under Board, unless at night. He claimed to be sixteen, but rumor had it he was only fifteen. "Happy. That's right. And while those 'adults' rattle on about who stunk up the Board last week, we'd actually like to do somethin' about it. We want off this death heap!"

"We all do!"

"Where's that annoying sister of yers, Izz? I owe her a kick for that mouth of hers."

Gai said nothing.

Juuse laughed. "Relax, ya little sogg. We already heard ya killed her. Guess I'll be givin' that kick to ya, then?"

"I didn't kill her!" Gai said as Juuse stepped closer. "Stop!" The boy raised his hand and clenched his teeth, hoping his little blue light trick would come and save him. Somehow. Anyhow. But nothing came out.

Juuse grabbed his hand and squeezed it hard. "Or what?"

"Ack!"

The leader of the Wikets threw him on the ground again, "Ya think anyone cares about anythin' in Hop, quirk? Unforgivin' as the sea we sit on." He went to kick the boy, but stopped, seeming satisfied at making Gai flinch. "No. No. I need ya around. Yer gonna tell us how'd that daddy and sister of yers left here."

Gai inhaled a bunch of floor dust and coughed it out. Apparently, he still had a lot to learn about those fixin' tricks, — like how to use them when it mattered. Rising for the second time, he said, "Figure out the currents."

"What do ya think we're doin' here, dumperhead? We're here to figure out how they sailed outta here. There must be some trick to it!"

"I know how," Gai said, almost unconsciously. He immediately regretted saying it, but couldn't stop. Ma was counting on him. Time was ticking. "Uncle Baald and Pa thought they came up with a way.

A bunch of maps called the Current Current maps. It was just an idea . . . until they were forced to try."

"I won't stay here. I won't!" said Juuse. "Tell me where these stupid maps are or we'll tie ya to the Under Board!"

"Tie me to the Under Board, and none of ya are goin' anywhere."

"Look," Juuse relaxed his arms by his side, "we got families to look out for, too. How can ya know how to break out of a prison and not tell the rest of us?"

Gai sighed. Tick tock. "I'm in the middle of somethin'. If ya leave me alone, I promise to help ya later."

Juuse pointed to the *Merry's* exposed hull. "Ya march on in there. Fetch them Current whatevers. And bring 'em here. Once we got 'em, I could care less what ya get into."

My, that certainly was a primitive odor coming from the Wicked Wiket leader. Sweat, dirt, and intimidation. Gai looked around the room. Not a single one of them moved. How was Ma's trial going? Tick tock. "Fine," he barked, stepping back out of the ship. "But they're not inside."

It was only by chance he knew where the Current Current maps were, anyway. Five years ago, before Baald left with sick Stav, Gai happened to catch his father shoving those maps into the *Lady Merry's* figurehead. Anyone who knew Stav Izz, which was basically just his children, Mape and Uncle Baald, knew he had big dreams. No bigger dream of his was the one to get his family off Hop someday. If there was a way, he was going to find it.

Stav enlisted Baald, who was a solid sailor in his day, to examine the currents and how they changed during the year. Did they precede a storm? Did they get worse during the winter? They watched how junk passed by in the water. The result was their special Current Current maps. They figured out that once a year, a ship weighing a certain amount, and sailed just rightly around the gulf, could theoretically make it to an area close to Electri's docks safely. It was an outrageous plan. And involved shifting sets of maps to use during different phases of the journey. When Gai saw Pa stuffing them secretly into the figurehead's mouth, they weren't ready to actually try the sail yet. But when Stav became ill, they must've been forced to take the risk and go.

Gai stepped out to the hole where Tanning's living room and the *Merry* met. He squeezed himself between them, again wiggling his way outside the hull and the broken Under Board beams. As he shimmed down, the boy heard a noise in the gushing water below — *Mrraaw.*

"Was that?" In the dark, all he could see was what looked like a slightly darker circle peeking up from the surface near the lowest Under Board posts.

Mraaw!

"Em?" Gai gasped. "Emilie?" He quickly hurried down as close to the water as he could. It sounded like her, but whatever was in the water was not the little pet he held in his hand earlier that day. "It can't be! Yer big as a boat!"

Mraw. A person-sized turtle head popped up.

Gai reached to pet her and felt the telltale scar near her mouth. "Ya *are* Em . . . How'd ya grow so fast?" He tried leaning off one of the beams to touch her big round shell, but the rise and fall of the heavy waves made it too risky.

Emilie cried out again and swam around quickly in a circle, weaving between the support beams.

"Wow, yer a good swimmer!"

Emilie began chomping at some of the trash that floated passed.

He laughed, "Growin' is hungry work, yeah?"

Mraaww.

The boy paused. "Don't suppose ya found Lynd or Pa out there yet?"

Emilie turned her head out to sea and began swimming away from the Under Board.

"All's a'kay," he said, climbing back up. "I'll keep lookin', too. Come at 76, later!"

As the boy ventured back to the ship's hull, a smile grew on his face. Emilie actually came back after being lost. A bond unmade then remade. It was reassuring to see that friendships could be fixed as well as doors could. What was to stop a family from being fixed, then?

Gai climbed to the *Merry's* figurehead, a woman bursting with a wave and a mug of vice in her hand. The crash appeared to break her cheerful arm off, however. Lady lost her Merry. "Unc wouldn't like seein' her like this." The boy reached into her mouth and felt around for the maps. He didn't feel anything but an empty hole. "Balls at ya, they moved 'em? Or they fell out. How can I get the Wikets to leave without 'em?" Tick tock. The boy began wiggling his way back down to the hull's hole through Tanning's house, wondering if he could quickly draw some fake maps instead.

As soon as he stepped back inside the *Merry*, he saw the leader of the Wicked Wiket scooper gang sitting down with his head between his knees, "Juuse? Ya'kay?" The other Wikets were all still there, too. But some were touching the hull walls with a dazed look, like they were wondering if it was made of food or something. Others were walking in circles and staring at the floor. No one was talking.

"'Ey!" Gai shook Juuse's shoulder. "Zeea's name's gotten into ya?"

"Eh? Who's askin'?" he said, glancing up and rubbing his forehead. "The Wikets already claimed this ship, get out!"

Gai stood there, wondering if maybe he was the one who'd lost touch with reality. "We made a deal . . . The *quirk*. Remember?"

"Deal?" Juuse sat up slowly and blinked a few times. "I don't even know how we got here . . ."

Gai then noticed a small black booklet right by Juuse's leg. It said Log on it in big Hopper White letters. He couldn't believe his luck; that thing might have good information about where the ship had been. A perfect place to look for evidence that might convince the Hoppers to leave Ma alone.

He walked to the Wicked Wiket leader and said, "Ya wanted to get back home." While doing so, he stealthily snatched the book and held it behind his back. "Ya made me go outside and check the ship's condition. The quirk?"

"That . . . sounds like me," Juuse mumbled. "Wikets!" he yelled, gesturing for everyone to get out of the *Merry*. "Grab what ya can outta Tanning's on the way out!" Before he left through the cracked hull, Juuse turned and gave Gai another confused look.

"'Ey," the boy said to him. "Yer gonna get to yer family in Wiket someday."

He blinked a few more times and left without another word.

With the ship empty, Gai sat on an uncomfortable barrel. Whatever insanity just struck the Wicked Wikets could wait. Mamma

Mape's trial was waiting for proof that she had nothing to do with what happened on the *Lady Merry*. He immediately opened up Baald's log and flipped around. "It goes right from Day 234, when they docked in Electri, to . . . *Day 1631*? And that's the last entry . . . Where were they all that time?"

CHAPTER 6

DAY 1631

THE *LADY MERRY* SHIP LOG, DAY 1631

My beautiful Merry ain't how I left her. Decks are peeling faster than a sunburnt nether place. The salt-eaten hull needed a good splash of tar years back. Sails so full of holes they look like dirty laundry hangin' from my mamma's line. She's not even the same color she was. The Merry, not my mamma.

Ya'd think they might give my beloved ship some basic upkeep while we were prisoners. But I guess scrubbin' ain't in those dumb Offies' job description. Seems them tiny gnomes looted her ropes. I swear I counted thirty-seven when we left Hop. Maybe they let the Merry rot to prevent us from makin' our dramatic escape. But we had Stav with us, and there was no plannin' they could've made against him.

While I'd love to record all the events that occurred in the five years since I last logged, I really don't like writing that much. It cramps the hand, and mine are full, handling the aforementioned Stav Izz. We risked takin' the Merry out this far only to help him. Complete waste, I'd say.

After we made it past Electri's disastrous sea drills and the wild waves they make, we made it to port with our little patient. Dockin' went smooth as it always does, not very, but we anchored enough. I ordered all eleven Merry crewman off to help me take Stav to the hospital. His condition only got worse over the trip to Electri. He was meaner, like a once family dog all starved and fidgety. That awful *dark rash expanded over most of him. Took all of us to wrestle him down to the street.*

We were just about to board the SkyGo, when Stav breaks loose and up and steals some little gnome's fancy pocket watch clean out of his nubby hands. He then smashes it on the ground and starts combing through the pieces until he finds a tiny spryt, like all those Electri machines use. Then he ate it. No other thing to say. Stav swallowed that little ruby like it was candy. Odder still was that, for the first time since we left Hop, Stav was able to stand on his own right after he ate it. For months he hadn't been able to speak good, but he ran back to us sayin' we needed to help him get forgiveness. Had no idea what he talkin' about. I told him it was fine the way he soiled up the sheets on the Merry.

By now, there's commotion all around, and the SkyGo goes off into the sky toward the hospital without us. Stav's cryin' and rantin' like a damned loon at the station. The gnome whose watch he just broke was screamin' for the Order Force. And twenty or so locals were busy oohing and ahhing with their beany thumbs at us. Of course, wasn't but two breaths before them Offies showed up.

Never liked Offies. Never have. Never will. Clearly, the Order Force came because of Stav's nutty behavior, so I pleaded with them to pretty please let us get him to a doctor. They scribble in some notes on those electri paper (that ain't paper) and chat amongst themselves as Stav's wild mumbling and black rash down his arm continue to draw a curious crowd.

Next, they ask if the Merry was indeed my ship. I ask 'em why they're askin'. They tell me the Merry's is full of illegal white hair dye ingredients, and we're bein' arrested!

Turns out, they weren't full of shit. 'Cuz the Merry was.

Apparently, what we use to make Hopper White paint, seagull poop, they use to dye their hair. I wasn't smugglin' no hair dye! But the commotion was already started. And Stav didn't help.

Balls. They kindly "escort" me and the whole crew — that's Avey, Knee-Knocker, all of us — with weapons zappin' us in the behind all the way. They took Stav separate, though. To the hospital, I hoped. But now, we had our own problems.

So the lot of us minus my old friend are put in front of the Minister Prime for "an assessment of the debt you owe to the citizens of Electri." For white hair dye? Wipe my nethers! They told us the gnomes use hair dye to look older, like a false identification. Put a lot of focus on lookin' gentlemanly, they do.

I could curse all I wanted, but then comes them collars pinched around all our necks. We were given the option to either work off our debt in the "myracite" mines or find some other payment way. But as long as those collars were on, we weren't leavin'.

Myracite was a new word for us, but it turns out that's what they call spryts. It's what they use to make electri power. But get this: who knew underneath the Domus Gulf is a truly bogglin' reserve of this myracite? And I'll bet ya anythin' its those awful sea drills posted all around Domus that crack up the seafloor and release spryts over to Hop, where they scare the crap outta us. Ya can sure learn a lot workin' underground. They took us all down to Lower Electri each day to help weed out the normal rocks from the myracite. Easy to spot because it glows nice and red. They gave us special gloves so the myracite didn't shock us much. Stuff is wild. They even have to keep diggin' deeper for it, as it slowly eats its way down into the bedrock of Domus. I heard the gulf was once a flat, grassy place before the myracite came. Oh, I'm sure bein' around it's all fine for my health.

I don't blame no Hopper who don't know spryts are really just special crystals the gnomes dig outta the ground. How are we little Hoppers, cut off from pretty much everythin' that happened in the past fifty years, supposed to know that's how they make electri power? They do look scary floatin' around and do cause damage pretty easy. Crazy as it sounds, we also got word there's this group up north who get this myracite shipped in to use for mystical reasons. Per course, I never believed in magic anythin'. Even praisin' Zeea was a step too fancy. But after what we saw Stav do, maybe that group up north knows somethin' we don't.

Now, I can work. Done it all my life. But not knowin' what happened to Stav or even bein' able to tell cousin Mape where we were was enough to break my soul. They got kids, ya know? We were still pretty hopeful, celebratin' each of our first birthdays down in the mines. But after three and four birthdays, with no end in sight, we started wishin' those collars would just tighten up a bit and let us off the hook, so to speak.

Then one day, our fates took a corner. It felt like a quake was comin' to knock down the whole mine and squash the Merry crew for done. That's when we finally saw Stav again. At least, what he had become.

There were Offies yellin' and blastin' electri guns, yellow balls of light all over the place. And suddenly, gruesome as it sounds, the whole line of them get ripped apart to pieces like dolls a nasty toddler don't want anymore. Done in. Each and every one. Then came our old friend. In the years that had passed, I can't tell ya what they did to him, but it wasn't healin' in some hospital bed. First, his awful dark rash covered him all but one eye. His hands were clawed like a meat-shredding beast's. Just as he cut through the Offies like a hull through smooth waters, he stops in front of us. He looks like he remembers us. I see it in that good eye. He extends his shakin' claw-hand at us like a beggin' scooper. We had a pile of myracite ready to go up. I can tell he wants it. I remembered what happened at the SkyGo — Stav eats these things. Don't know why. I take a good chunk of the red crystal in my glove and toss it to him. It was the same instinct that makes ya throw a piece of bread to a bird. He looked so desperate.

As soon as my old friend touches that glowin' rock, its light starts to pour into every openin' he had — in his mouth, eyes and ears, sure, but also into the dark wounds on his body, makin' them split open even worse.

I can't explain what happened next in any normal words. I could just say it — We were there in the myracite mines, and then we were all at the docks in front of the Lady Merry. I could go deeper in detail — bright red bolts leap out of his body once he ate that glowin' rock. Then the air got really cold. Everything went black like we entered a tunnel, bodies feelin' tugged. But if ya blinked, ya'd miss it. For me, my skin felt like it dragged over tiny pebbles way too fast. Like a rip, then a burn. All I know for sure was I was lookin' at the depressing myracite mines and then suddenly transported out, lookin' at my gorgeous ship.

Per course, we run up the gangway and set sail just as those little gnomes started comin' down the dock, firin' those zappin' guns our way. As I said, the sails were shot, but Knee-Knocker and Avey pinched them together best they could, holdin' the whole sail out. They're still holdin' them as I write this.

A hundred or so Order Force Offies lined up on the dock as we pulled out. Stav gets up on the bow and starts yellin' — roarin', I'd even call it. We all saw the electri guns zap him in the chest, over and over. And we all saw that man not even flinch. Actin' cool as a holiday. And then we all saw how those Electri docks rip apart like those Offies, collapsin' stone splashin' into Domus all around. The gnomes all fell in, splashin' like some fish caught in low tide. We made our escape clean out.

I don't know if that group we heard about up north can help him. But at this point, with even the gnomes and all their fancy electri technology unable to, I can't say I really got a choice. I can't bring him back to his family like this! I ordered Avey to steer us up into the Uncharted Sea to a city called Carpè, where this group supposedly does business. But I told Avey to keep it quiet like. Stav is unpredictable. And I'm not even sure he wants to get help anymore.

CHAPTER 7

STRANGER THAN TWO STRANGERS

Gai flipped through the pages after that entry. "Aw, a'way! What happened after?" He slammed the log closed and paced with it in his hands. He walked deeper into the ship's dark cargo hold, talking to himself, "Pa was sick like Ma said. And it sounds like the spryts made his breakin' tricks even worse. Same thing happened when Lynd touched one—*What's this?*" A splash of dust fell on his head from the ceiling. He sneezed and looked up to see why it was suddenly raining dirt on him. After cleaning a layer off his shoulder, Gai then saw the rain of dust moving down the ship. Someone was quietly walking on the deck above, disturbing the ceiling soot.

"I thought all the Wikets left?" he said, following the fresh plumes of falling dust out deeper into the hull. He was not alone; that much was clear. A short staircase led to the top deck. Every step up, he felt his stomach quake with an all too familiar fear. *Bump bump.* The same fear he had the night Lynd came crying through the door the night his father left — What was going to come through this time? The next step, he wondered if he even wanted to know. He set his hands on the oval door that led to the *Lady Merry's* top deck. *Bump bump.* ". . . Pa?"

But then a woman's voice came through, quiet and flat, saying, "You took care of the thieves, then?"

Shaking, Gai put his ear to the door.

"Of course," a gruff man's voice answered. "I used the myracle you taught me — Ruin Memory."

"Good," she said. "Best if no one knows we were here."

Gai pressed his ear harder on the door.

The unknown woman continued, "You did create a memory to replace the ones you destroyed, correct? Elix Memory?"

"Ruin? Elix?" the boy whispered, pressing his ear even harder to the point of pinching. He didn't want to miss a single word. "*What* did they do to 'em?"

"Destroy this. Create that." The man huffed. "You know how rare it is that someone can direct their myra in both directions like that?"

"You're the only one I know who can," she said. "But if you create false memories in their minds, it would lower the chance they'll detect something out of place. I just thought you'd want to do this right."

"Maybe next time," he answered coldly. "I haven't eaten all day."

"Are these even *people?*" Gai broke from the door to see if there was a crack somewhere he could peak through. "Balls at ya," he whispered, unable to find one. He then recalled the Wicked Wikets seeming confused and not even remembering the deal he made with them. Could that be what these two were talking about? A *Ruin Memory?* He pressed his left ear against the door this time. The other one was throbbing.

After more shuffling footsteps, Gai heard the man ask, "You're sure the First Void was on *this* ship?"

"The very one we're looking for," the woman said. "Yes."

"Terrible parking job," said the man. "Though if there truly was a Void aboard, the crew was probably busy running for their lives."

"They may have escaped," she said. "But it's far more likely they were turned into Voids as well."

"By Zeea," Gai whispered to himself. "Maybe they're *not* people."

"More Voids are coming?" The man exhaled as he stepped. "There aren't enough Heartbrands to take on an army of Voids."

"One Void would be too much for your entire Legion," the woman chuckled. "You know the legend as well as anyone. And the First has already been alive too long. If I can't find it soon, we'll have no choice but to take Electri's red myracite . . ."

Gai's eyes widened. He switched ears again to see if he could hear better. Without warning, the door burst open. *Wacck!* Gai tumbled down the stairs, smacking right into some barrels full of soil and fish bait.

"Oh!" said the man, rushing down the stairs after him.

The woman called down to him from the deck, "Did you find something?"

"Crew's not *all* Voids!" he yelled up the stairs to her. He then knelt down near the boy and picked up Baald's log, which had landed beside him. He offered Gai the book back, stressing, "I'm *so* sorry."

Gai's head throbbed. Then he felt a worm wiggle on his dirt-covered face. "Ah!" He stood up, shaking his hair. Some of the dirt got on the stranger. "Ugh. Sorry at ya, too," said the boy, taking back the log.

"Not a drop of trouble, young man," he said, dusting off a blue cape draping off his shoulders, revealing a polished armor underneath.

Gai nearly froze in the man's presence. Even kneeling, he was almost Gai's full height. His imposing physique was hugged by the most reflective gold metal. Everything about him seemed so *clean*. It was common for Hoppers to have dirt on their cheeks or oily hair sticking to their scalps. Where did this guy come from? He had a splash of dark hair on his chin, a curly head to match, and a pair of penetrating brown eyes dotting his handsome, deep-toned face.

"You survived the crash?" the man said. "The *ship's* crash, I mean. Not the door in the face I just gave you." He smiled warmly.

"I–ugh."

The woman's dark, hooded silhouette appeared in the doorway up the stairs. She had a cape as well, flapping in the breeze. Red, flickering spryts dotted the sky behind her like stars. "General XIII?" she said, her voice cold and dry. "Do you need some assistance?"

"No, it's alright." He waved to her casually. He looked back at Gai, "You're a crew member of this ship? Or are you with that thief band? I thought I got all of them . . ."

"*Got* all of them," Gai whispered. "Ya did use some kind of breakin' trick!"

"Looks like a local," the woman said before walking out of sight.

"Deal with it and get back to searching. We don't have the luxury of time."

"You *live* in this mesh of floating wood, then?" The man brushed off more dirt from Gai's clothes for good measure. "What's your name?"

"My-my," Gai replied, unable to stop thinking about what happened to Juuse and his Wikets — *Ruin* Memory — and if he was next to have his memory Ruin-ed, whatever that meant.

"Great name. It's lovely to meet you, My-my." The man extended his big, open palm again. "You can call me XIII." And bowed his head. "That's general of the XIIIth Heartbrand Legion."

The general seemed to radiate a presence that was unlike anyone Gai had ever met in Hop, calm but absolutely sure of himself. Apparently, he could destroy people's memories, so that would make anyone feel confident. But how do you talk to someone like that?

"No, no, my name's Gaiel. Gaiel Izz," he said, staring at the worm on the floor. "Nice to meet ya, too."

"*Gaiel*, then! Strong name," the man exclaimed cheerfully. "So, were you with the crew of this ship or no?"

"No." Gai held the book behind his back. "I just came to loot."

The woman's voice traveled down from the top decks. "General?"

XIII ignored her, pursing his lips. "Another thief, then? Town's full of you guys, huh? Can't say I blame anyone. Seems like a rough place." He glared intensely into the boy's eyes. "Would that be the ship's log behind you?"

"How did ya know?" Gai finally gained the nerve to move, and it was to take a few steps *back*. "W-What did ya do to the Wikets?"

"I'm sorry, the who's-its?"

"The thieves. The one's ya did the Ruin Memory to?"

"*Ruin Mem*—" The general's casual cool finally broke. "What did you hear? How long were you listening at that door?"

"General XIII!" the woman roared, coming to the doorway up the stairs again. "If you're done making friends, can we get back to saving Esa?"

"Uh," the general gestured to the boy. "I missed one."

"Do you need me to go over how to properly destroy a memory again?" she scolded. "Finish it and get up here!"

"But he's just another kid," the man whined.

The hooded woman scoffed, "Do what you want," and stomped back across the upper deck. "I just hope you didn't say anything *revealing* in front of him."

"Nope. He, uh, doesn't know anything." The general turned to the curious boy, raising his hands like he was praying, "Please, Gaiel. Forget about the memories." He chuckled. "Ha, 'forget about the memories.' *Ahem.* I don't use Ruin myracles any more than I absolutely must. My body can't take it much anymore. So, you go ahead and forget this, and I won't have to destroy your memory of it. Deal?"

"Sure." Gai shrugged. "If ya tell me what myracles are."

"Oh, you'd like an impromptu midnight lesson on a shipwreck, would you?"

Gai paused, then nodded.

"Does this look like an Akademy classroom to you? Do you see the majestic white Archbridges of Carpè anywhere near here? No."

"Ya *are* from Carpè! Yer the group Unc was talkin' about!" Gai said, waving the log. "Myracles must be tricks, then, yeah? I think I did one to my door. Maybe an '*Elix*' one? My sister destroys stuff — that must be what Ruin is?"

"Alright, kid. I tried. I'm sorry to have to do this." The general lifted his hand. "These deeds will all be worth it someday. She tells me." All the veins in his hand darkened and pulsed. He clenched his teeth like he was in pain, and — *Tck!* — he snapped his fingers with a red spark. Gai's eyes instantly shut, and he dropped to the floor as if he'd suddenly fallen asleep. "Oh? I must've leaned a little too hard into that one," he said, shaking his hand like it had gone numb. "Apologies for it all, young man. Not that you'll remember a thing about this week."

As XIII took the first step upstairs, the boy started to groan and roll onto his belly. It was typical behavior of someone who just had their last few days erased. By the time the man was at the top of the stairs, Gai had made it back to his feet. That was not so typical.

"Pieces," Gai muttered. "Black. Veins."

The general looked down the stairs.

"They had black veins. Everything's in pieces." Gai's mind was thoroughly scrabbled. Thoughts, ideas, faces, memories all flashed in his head like pieces of a puzzle. He struggled to put them back together. "Fix . . . Unc wrote . . . Ya have 'em, too."

"XIII!" The woman cried from up on the deck. "I found something, hurry!"

He stared down the dark stairs at the boy. "So have *I* . . ."

"Quick, come have a look at this!" she yelled.

"Commandress," said the general, approaching the woman on deck. "That kid is putting his memories back together after I destroyed them. Have you ever seen that?"

She didn't look at him. Her large, assessing eyes, deep in the shadow of a hood, were fixed on the destruction of the *Merry's* deck. "There's Ruin still radiating off it," she said.

"By the Old World," XIII mumbled. He bent down and touched the dark mark, quickly withdrawing his hand as if it burned him. "There's myra radiating off it . . . The wood's still disintegrating, slowly. You think this is where it ended?"

"I think this is where it *began*," she said. "And look here." The Commandress picked up a broken piece of curved wood. A nice piece of wood, with fishing wire melted on it. "This has Ruin all over it as well."

"'Ey!" yelled Gai from the doorway to the deck. That piece of wood in the woman's hand was the fiddle he made Lynd, he was sure. "That's my sister's. Give it back!"

XIII slapped his forehead. "Oh, right. Him."

"Give it back!" Gai ran toward them faster than they expected. He snatched the broken fiddle back from her and ran near the rails.

"Excuse me," the man said. "Don't be rude." He gestured to his companion. "This is the legitimate Commandress of Carpè! Hand that over!"

"He appears to be attached to that Ruin-covered object," she said. After XIII nodded, she turned to Gai, "That *thing* is contaminated, little boy. For your safety, please hand it over."

"No!" yelled Gai, holding the scorched fiddle.

"I'm warning you." The woman seemed intrigued by why this youngster happened to be on the same ship as the First Void. "It could . . . taint you."

"I-I can't believe Lynd was here," Gai whispered to himself, looking over the wrecked fiddle. "Did she meet Pa?" He looked over at the *Lady Merry's* wrecked deck boards.

XIII leaned in again. "I created a Mind Link earlier. He's looking for his father and sister on this ship . . . And he also shrugged off my myracle like loose dirt. Do you find those two facts interesting?"

"I do." The Commandress sighed. "Did your Link come up with any family names?"

"Yes, Izz."

"It is what?" she said.

"No, it is *Izz.*"

"XIII, I don't have time for—"

"My name is Gaiel *Izz!*"

The general unrolled a sheet of paper from a pocket in his cape and wrote the name down. I-Z-Z.

"Ah," she said. "Grab a sample of that black soot, too. If we can measure the rate it's decaying, maybe we can tell how much time we have before the First Void becomes . . . too much."

"Consider it bottled." XIII bent down, took out a thin tube, and scraped some of the charred marks into it. "Ahem. He's still holding a key piece of evidence."

"He resisted Ruin Memory, did he?" The woman whipped her cape back, away from her arms. A full-length gown covered everything but her chin up.

"Correct." The general nodded. "And it wasn't particularly easy to probe his mind, either."

"And these red lights," she looked up. "That's myracite, isn't it?"

"Yeah, funny how we're practically at war over this stuff, and here it's floating around for free. The crude way Electri mines it must make for a few leaks." XIII carefully scraped some more charred wood into a bottle. "What are you proposing?"

"That the First Void is out there, growing," she said. "And if I waste another second here, planet Esa is doomed."

The general stood up. "Are you sure it's wise for you to *touch* red myracite? You know, Ruin and Ruin . . ."

"I wasn't asking," she said. Her eyes flickered ruby red.

Gai yelled, "What're ya doin'?"

"Very well . . . my Commandress." The general raised his hand and curled his finger at the spryt — or *myracite* — and it started to slowly lower from the sky. "Just don't rip a hole in time this time, thanks."

"Stop!" Gai cried. The red hues. The lowering spryt. It all reminded him so clearly of the night on Lynd's Pier.

The man winced and hid his face with his hood. "I'll have to destroy the whole town's memories after this. Sorry again, young man!"

Gai tucked into a ball with the fiddle. "No!"

As soon as the spryt landed in the Commandress' hand, the red glow engulfed her whole body like it was on fire. As he stared, wide-eyed at the mystical display on the deck of the *Lady Merry*, he knew Lynd must have done some kind of myracle, too, when she disappeared that night.

The Commandress raised her hand to Gai with such fury in her eyes, he almost wet his newspaper pants. The entire ship seemed to be trembling. Screams came from the Boards below as onlookers gathered, fearing another storm or some other disaster.

Before he could scream, a tremendous force felt like it grabbed his back. The space behind him cracked open. It pulled him so hard and fast, all his joints popped. The fiddle pieces dropped to the deck.

Gai pushed forward against the tear in space with all his might, feeling like there were hooks in his arm yanking him back. As he struggled, a faint blue glow emerged around his body. His blue fixin' trick.

At once, his own creative power started to faithfully sow that hole in space back up. It was like the antidote to the destruction that threatened to swallow him whole. *Gurgle grr.*

"Not interesting enough, I'm afraid." The Commandress sighed.

"Huh?" His whole body ripped off the *Merry* like he was blasted out of the most powerful cannon known to any pirate. He was high up in the dark sky far, far, far from Hop in the blink of an eye. He hovered there for a moment, seeing the center's few yellow electri lights in the distance, looking like a candle flame with the black sea surrounding it.

He passed out, falling headfirst into the churning Domus Gulf below.

CHAPTER 8
LEFT AND WRONG

T he first thing the girl felt was sand rolling along the inside of her mouth. Then salty water rushed up her nose and burned her sinuses. *Cough.* She slowly became aware of a painful sting on her right palm, then of her belly pressed flat on prickly pebbles. She rolled onto her back, aching. She opened her eyes to the blinding light of a dry beach sun. Her head pulsed wildly like a bell that had been ringing for hours. Questions tried to take shape in between the throbbing in her skull. *Where am I?* would have been a good first question. Or maybe how long had she been there? But instead, she wrestled with something even more fundamental — *Who am I?*

Lynd had no memory of anything. No history, no family, no life-line to pull on the question of self. This was no mere Ruin Memory effect. It went deeper. For all she knew, this strange beach was her home, or close to it. All she knew for sure was what her body cried out for — fresh, cool water. Quickly. The warm air felt like it was sucking the moisture right out of her lungs.

It was a marvel she could even stand. She fell twice trying. Her legs were so numb that she wondered a few times if they were there at all. She peered up the beach and saw the pebbles turn to deep red-orange rocks and then into large boulders up the hill ahead. She glanced behind her at the sea and winced at the bright waves reflecting the sunlight. There was nowhere to go but up.

The boulders were hot with intimidating edges. She was about midway through the climb when the sounds of children laughing came down from over the jagged hill. They didn't sound familiar. But they didn't sound strange either. Could they be her friends? Were they having fun without her?

There were at least two lively little voices. Lynd was so glad to hear another child that she rushed and slipped, cutting the bottom of her bare foot nastily. She hurried still, undaunted, in search of water and a friendly face. The girl pulled herself up over the hill and found a stretch of flat, desert-like land as far as she could see ahead. To the left was a small, boxy house with a garden in the back facing the sea. The children's laughter continued from within those white stone gates. She approached them cautiously, asking herself, *Do I belong here?* every other second or so.

Lynd hid herself behind a rock before catching a glimpse of the children. They ran passed her, a boy and girl that were slightly younger than she was, one chasing the other. Lynd first noticed their clothes; the unknown little girl wore a long, white dress with a teal belt. Her dark hair was tied up in a matching bow. The young boy's long-sleeve shirt and pants were a clean white as well. Both had brightly colored ribbons attached to their sleeves that trailed behind in the wind. Even with her memory problem, Lynd knew she didn't belong; one glance at her own tattered, gray clothes told her that.

"Cam! Lari!" a woman called warmly, practically singing from inside the house. "Come in and eat before the parade starts!"

The children ran inside. Lynd's foot wound stung from letting it rest on the dirt. It was then that she noticed a faucet attached to the house, dripping with precious water. Her wound needed a good wash, and her mouth was sticky with dust and salt. After checking and triple checking to be sure everyone was surely inside, Lynd limped into their yard and to the life-saving drip.

She drank first. A lot. She gulped so much that her face and hair got drenched, then she began washing the dirt and blood off her heel and between her toes. Then that woman turned the corner from inside the house, saw Lynd, and screamed — *Ahhhhh!*

Lynd bolted back through the yard, limping and wincing in pain.

"No, no. Wait," she said, palm over her chest. "I'm sorry for screaming. You just startled me. Are you alright?"

Lynd stopped and bent down to hold her throbbing foot. She said nothing, staring at the woman without a blink in case there was trouble. Even without her memory, the girl's wily Hopper instincts emerged.

The woman didn't have any ribbons like the children but wore a long, white dress with her wavy hair tied up beautifully. Her features were soft and sun-kissed. She stepped closer, her eyes traveling up and down Lynd's clothing. "Oh, my dear," she continued. "Let's get a bandage on that, hm?"

Lynd didn't move. The children came rushing around the nicely dressed lady from inside, saying, "Mamma, Mamma! Who's that? Can she play with us?"

"I thought she was one of your friends?" said the mother. "No?" She then spoke to Lynd, "Are you here for the parade, dear? Do you and your family live nearby?"

Lynd stared back blankly, for a moment forgetting how to put words together. Her mind was a jumble. "I . . . Family?"

The children rushed toward Lynd to start playing, but their mother held them back. "She's hurt, dears. Don't scare her."

Lari, one of the children, unwrapped her hair bow and held it out for Lynd. "You can cover it with this if you want."

The girl was not at all tempted to get up and take it.

"That's sweet," said the mother. "But our new friend needs something clean to use." The kind woman stepped inside the house and came back with proper bandages. She confidently walked up to Lynd, bent down, and began dressing her wound. Lynd allowed her, but gave her a wide-eyed gawk the whole time.

The woman wondered to herself if she had seen this girl anywhere before. Her clothes looked and smelled worse than any fisher she'd ever met. And was that half a crab shell stuck in her hair? The most likely conclusion was that she had been part of a nearby shipwreck and washed ashore. After a final tight tug and tie of the bandage, she said, "There. That should keep it clean until you get home. Where *is* home, dear?"

Lynd sincerely searched her memory. She knew what all those words meant, but no image came to mind. "My home is . . ."

"I see. Well, today is a holiday, you know? We have a nice feast prepared, and the parade will be coming down our street soon enough." The woman smiled. "Maybe all you need is a nice, full belly to jog that memory, hm?"

"A'kay," said Lynd cautiously.

"Yay!" cheered Lari.

Cam got shy and hid inside behind a hallway door. The mother led Lynd into the well-lit, airy home. The walls within were just as white as the outside, like it was made with hand-molded putty. But the most striking thing was the scent of a roast cooking over a stone hearth. Fresh garden vegetables were simmering. Lynd's mouth immediately watered at the extraordinary smells. Her own body was reacting like all of this was new for her. This couldn't be her normal life, or she wouldn't be drooling.

The mother could see this written all over her dirty face and said, "Grab a seat, dear. I'll make you a plate this instant."

The children watched Lynd pull out the closest chair, think for a moment, and awkwardly settle into the seat. They were confused at why she would be so confused. Lari pulled out a book from a nearby shelf and opened it on the table in front of her new friend. "Do you like stories? I just got this book about the Old World," she said, flipping from page to page.

"Old world?" Lynd's eyes widened at the beautiful pictures of shining buildings with intricate carvings down the walls. She noticed the people depicted wore even stranger clothes than everyone else in the room did. "Is there a New World?"

Lari chuckled. "Yeah, I guess so. Right, Mamma?"

The woman came over with a whole roast duck on a big serving plate and placed it on the table. Then, she stepped away to gather plates and forks.

The juicy, salty, savory goodness wafted off the roast and danced into Lynd's nose. It smelled more inviting than anything she'd ever experienced before. This definitely could not be her normal life. She felt like she'd only seen in black and white, and someone suddenly put the color red on a plate in front of her. She snatched the whole thing off the table and chomped into it whole.

"Mamma, she's eating the whole bird!" shouted Cam.

"It's alright," she said, hushing him. "She . . . needs it more than we do."

Bam! Their front door shot open, followed by a cheerful man's voice. "The parade's coming down the street, now! Hurry on up in there!"

"Daddy!" Lari said, running up to him. "We found a friend in the yard."

"A friend?" he said, stepping in. "Always a nice find." He nodded at his wife. "Where'd the roast go?"

Lynd burped.

"Let's not worry about that now, dear. Everyone outside, come, come. I can hear the trumpets already!" She led the three kids out the door and whispered to her husband, "I'll tell you all about it later."

Buuh-Buuh! Colorfully dressed trumpeters trumpeted past the house just as they stepped outside, startling Lynd, who was sure she'd never heard such a sound before. Her body rattled to the percussion percussing up next. Confetti twisted in the air and landed on everyone's head. All the neighbors up and down the long, dirt street were outside cheering, hugging, and wiggling their behinds to the beats. Whether she had her memory or not, it would've all been foreign to Hopper Lynd.

The first carriage came into view behind the music numbers. Lari grabbed Lynd's hand and pointed. "See them? See them? That's the Commandress coming!"

"S-she's so pretty," said Cam from behind.

Lari smiled at Lynd, "I'm going to join the Heartbrands and be just like her."

Lynd squeezed Lari's hand back. "Commandress?"

The first in a long line of beautifully embellished bronze carts rolled down the dirt road, picking up dust, inciting hoots and praise. No people or animals pulled the carriages. They ticked as they moved like they were windup toys full of gears. But people were sitting inside them, waving out the windows. "Lively one-thousand!" they yelled from the carriage.

The people on the street returned, "To one-thousand more!"

"Can you believe it," the mother said to the father in the doorway. There was a distinct twinkle in her eye, like she was holding back tears of joy. "A full millennia since the world was reset." She cupped her hands together and shouted, "To one-thousand more!"

None of this sounded familiar to Lynd, but she didn't even know her own name, so things seeming strange were all just part of the day so far. The carriages continued to kick up the fine, reddish-brown dirt as they passed. Not enough to cough, but maybe enough to tickle the nose.

Achoo! Lynd couldn't hold back an intense sneeze. She unknowingly squeezed Lari's hand too tight when she did. And that wasn't the only unintentional consequence.

Crack! One of the ornate wheels snapped apart in front of the two girls and sent the carriage tumbling into the next neighbor's wall. Lynd shot her eyes open. She had no idea how or why, but she felt some sort of destructive force ripple out of her when she sneezed. Staggering as that was, at least no one would know it was her. Then she looked at Lari, who yanked her hand away from Lynd's with a wide-eyed shout. "Y-y-you. She shocked me; I felt it! It was her!"

No one seemed to know what in Esa was going on, but little Lari did manage to make everyone look at the girl. As strange as it was for Lynd, that destruction was the first thing that seemed even a pinch bit familiar. Finally, something felt *right*. But then why was everyone looking at her like it was so wrong? The parade had come to a crashing halt. All the spectators turned their frowning chins at her. Lynd watched as two-by-two, their narrow eyes all focused on her.

Then someone shouted, "Ruin! Ruin!" The neighbors began to shuffle about, some even stepping back into their homes for safety. Two battle-suited women quickly leaped out of the wrecked carriage. When they stepped into the sunlight, their armor was so polished it made Lynd squint. The metal was silver with flashes of teal as they moved in the light. They offered their hands to someone still inside the carriage. An elegant hand clasped with theirs, and a pair of ornate sandals hit the street. The woman who emerged smiled gracefully at the crowd in a golden gown. Her hair was dark and cut to shoulder. Her ivory cheekbones floated like moons on either side of her slight amber eyes. The two guards stood beside her tightly, darting their gaze back and forth to assess the danger.

"It was her!" yelled Lari, pointing at Lynd. "Mom! It was her! She broke it!"

It was very clear whatever the girl did with that sneeze, it was not right. She watched as that nice mother who had so warmly bandaged her foot pulled her children inside their house, acting as if the girl were some kind of monster that had come out of the sea. *Was* she a monster that came out of the sea? Lynd's heart was pounding.

The two guards locked their peepers on her. Then, with a flick of the wrist, both of them drew a brilliant sword into their hands from out of nowhere. With their vibrant yet pointy weapons, they marched forward on the offending girl.

"General XI! XII!" The beautifully dressed woman halted them immediately. "When has it *ever* been part of Heartbrand training to threaten a child?"

One of the armored women said, "Did you not see, Commandress? She exhibited powers of destruction. At you, no less. How *should* we react?"

"Don't be so critical. She sneezed." The Commandress whipped out a tissue and stepped to the girl, then bent down to meet her in the eyes. "Bless you," she said, handing it to her.

Lynd sniffled. "T-thanks at ya."

"Thanks at ya," the Commandress repeated, smiling. "That's an interesting phrase. Where are you from, little flower?"

The wife who fed the girl stepped up, quickly rattling from her doorway. "She doesn't know. W-we found her in our backyard. We don't know her. How could we have known she was . . . *like that?*"

"I see," said the Commandress.

Lynd's hands started shaking.

"There's no reason to be afraid." The Commandress peered to the broken wheel. "Ruin is nothing that can't be fixed." She then began to hum a few notes and wave her hand gently to the rhythm.

At first, it worried Lynd. But it was such a relaxing melody; the crowd even began to calm down a bit. The guards stood at ease by her side and let go of their shiny swords as they disappeared to wherever they came. Then, the Commandress started to sing the notes full-throated, and the people clapped to her increasingly cheery song. Lynd shrank back to the wall, unsure of almost everything around her.

The broken shards of wheel wood developed a blue aura and began to dance to her music as well, soon lifting right off the dirt road. A few more notes and the wheel had pieced itself back together flawlessly, maybe even better than it was before. People on the street gathered to help pick up the carriage as the wondrous new wheel slid into place as if nothing had happened.

The crowd erupted into cheer. The Commandress lady smiled a sunny smile and bowed at their admiration. She then came to Lynd and gently reached for her trembling hand. "My name is Ada. And I don't think anything that's broken has to stay that way." She looked up to the family who found her. "You say you don't know her. But you're the closest I can get to asking a parent for now; would it be alright if I showed your young friend the Akademy? I think we may be able to help her."

The husband and wife looked at each other. "Sure," she said. "We wouldn't know how to help the likes of . . . S-she's in better hands with you."

Ada gave Lynd's hand a few reassuring squeezes. "The choice is yours, then. I know it's scary, but if you have some memories that are broken, I believe we can help patch them up in no time. Just like that wheel. Then, we'll get you back to your family. What do you say?"

Lynd looked at her hand being held so tenderly by Ada's. She looked up to her and did the only rational thing she could think of. She yanked her hand out, about-faced, and ran like mad through the gasping neighbors into the crack between two homes. The two generals, XI and XII, started after her. But the Commandress halted them one more time.

The girl ducked into the thin alleyways of the white stone houses in a full-body panic. Was she a monster? What all this "Ruin" talk about? Her heart wouldn't calm up. Who *was* she? Lynd burst around a corner, thirsty to catch her breath. A cornered sea monster, she was.

"We all have special talents," Ada said quietly, leaning against the opposite wall. She peeked around the corner like a child playing tag with her. Her sudden appearance should've been frightening, but there was just something so guard-shatteringly sweet about her. A sort of relentless kindness.

"Ya don't look at me like they do," said Lynd, huffing a bit still. "What do they think I am?"

"It's not you." Ada stood tall and confident, waving for her to follow her back to the street. "We just have very old fears. Come.

You'll ride in my carriage back to the Myracles Akademy. We can chat along the way."

Lynd thought for a moment. Ada gave her all the time she needed, holding out her hand for a few long beats. Maybe, just maybe, this woman was on the up and up. She certainly was charismatic. And the only other option was to run. Maybe the woman could fix Lynd like the broken wheel.

". . . A'kay."

The two walked back slowly to the parade route and got in the Commandress's carriage. The two guards watched with a slight sneer, either because they didn't like her destructive power or because they no longer got to ride in the front of the parade with Ada. The trumpets and drums resumed. But the locals didn't restart their cheering. They just watched the carriage take off in a cloud of reddish dust with that strange girl. Lari and Cam came running out of their house and ran alongside the carriage, waving goodbye, with their parents chasing after.

CHAPTER 9
SOMETHING LIKE FORGIVENESS

Gai awoke to a scorching sun on his cheeks and the *plat-plat* of lapping water all around. His body was stretched out like a starfish pressed over a rock. He rolled up and saw nothing but the straight horizon of ocean and sky on all sides. One look down and he realized he was sitting on a little island the size of a house in the middle of a water world. Nothing and no one was there with him. "Am I . . . *dead?*" He tapped on the barren rock underneath him. His private island rumbled a bit. Then it began to sink.

Water rushed up the edges. He stood up on the rickety, round rock, shouting, "Zeea, help me!" He held his breath for the dip to come. Then, just as the rising tide was about to swallow his knees, the rock suddenly stopped sinking. There he was in the middle of the ocean, up to his knees. "What in Esa?" His island then shot back up like a spring, hopping up out of the water again. Maybe it was an island that wasn't sure it wanted to be an island. Or perhaps it was alive.

There were small grooves in the rock that pressed a swirling design into his bare feet. He traced them with his finger, noting they were like fish scales the size of dinner plates. "Or turtle scales," he said aloud. "*Emilie?*"

The turtle's bulbous head burst up from the waves. Her voice was deep, matching her new, impressive size — *Mrrawww!* Her eyes were like two pinched moons. Emilie glared at the boy standing on the peak of her shell. Was she going to eat him? Did turtles have an eating face?

Gai figured she had grown larger than the entire Izz house, easily. She could swallow three of him without getting the hiccups, easily. "Are ya really . . . Em?"

Mraaw.

"Is that a 'yeah'?" said Gai. "A 'yeah, and yer my dinner'?"

Mraaww!

"Yeah, but yer lettin' me go?"

Mraw.

"Oh, thanks at ya." He scuttled down her hill of a shell to pet her head. The scar by her nose was still there. It was definitely Emilie. Just one-hundred times the size. "Look at ya," he smiled. "Yer incredible!"

As lovely as it was to be once again reminded that friends could be remade, Gai was faced with the chilling question of how exactly he ended up in the middle of the sea on Emilie's shell. His arms and legs felt weak and throbbed at the joints. His neck was strained as if he'd been holding his head upside down too long. His left hand had a little wood splinter in it, stinging.

"Lynd's fiddle," he yelled, "I had it in my hands!" He picked at his palm to wiggle the splinter out. "And that lady. She touched the red myracite like Lynd did, then I was up in the sky! What if they're still in Hop?" He looked around him frantically. "Em . . . Where *is* Hop?"

The turtle arched her head, pointing her nose to the right of the sun.

Gai climbed to the top of her shell, hoping he might get a better view. "That little crumb? We can't be that far." *Mrraw!* "Yer right, Em! We gotta get back! I need to make sure Ma's a'ka—"

Emilie took off so fast the boy nearly slid down her back-shell into the white ripply water she left in her wake.

The turtle's powerful hind fins paddled them faster than any swimmer or ship. She hustled over wave after wave of the always rough Domus Gulf, sometimes spearing through them with a great splash. Wind and salty sea spray whipped across the boy's face as he watched Hop go from a small crumb to the size of a plate, and from a plate to a gray, depressing port. Finally, the wildly shattered posts of Lynd's Pier became clear. "That's Boulie Board, Em. Take me there!"

As they got closer, the boy could see a line of people near Lynd's Pier. In fact, there were Hoppers lined up halfway down Boulie. "Why's everyone outside?" he asked, putting his hand up to block the high sun in his eyes. They were all yapping to one another — another unusual activity for Hoppers to do. They must've had a good rumor to spread. Whatever the topic was, it was far too interesting for them to even notice Gai approach on a turtle-ship just a stone's throw below them.

"Looks like they're tossin' stuff into the water?" Another strange thing for them to do. Nothing could be wasted in Hop. Throwing stuff into the water was only permitted when someone died, like when Gai and Ma dropped Lynd's belongings into the water for her so-called funeral. "What if they're outside throwin' Ma's stuff over? Please at ya, Zeea, I hope I'm not too late!"

As soon as Emilie pulled up to the Under Board, Gai leaped off her and climbed the lattice like a ladder. He passed two snoozing scoopers in the scaffolding; they scurried right away at the sight of Em the giant turtle. As soon as the boy rounded himself over the lip of Boulie, he dashed toward the line of people, heart pounding. "What kind of sogg isn't there to help his own mother?"

"'Scuse me." Gai wove his way around the Hoppers in line. In his haste, he bumped into someone holding a bucket of liquid. And did it ever splash all over everyone around. "Sorry at ya!"

"Get back here, ya quirk!"

The boy didn't stop, frantically searching for his house as he passed everyone. "68. 73. 76!" Gai burst in his door and yelled for his mother. He checked upstairs. No one was home. He ran down the rickety stairs so quickly that he slipped and bashed his forehead against the bottom. "Balls at ya!" He shot back out onto Boulie up the line toward Lynd's Pier, rubbing his head.

"What's that quirk doin'?" someone yelled as he passed.

Then the boy heard, "Gaiel?"

"Ma!" He ran up to her on the edge of Boulie like everyone else and hugged her tightly. "What's goin' on? Why're ya here outside? What's *this*?"

Mape dumped the contents of a small dirty bottle into the water, "Oh. Ain't it the craziest thing?" She looked at her son's throbbing, red forehead. "What's this? Ya get smacked around by those Wiket brats, again?"

"I'm fine, Ma. Why's everyone outside?"

"Tanning says a batch of bad vice-drink been goin' about."

"Bad vice?" said Gai. "What happened to—" Then the mayor suddenly stomped by them with a scowl, glaring. "Mayor Tanning. Is-is everythin' a'kay?"

Tanning's brow twisted with curious contempt. "Is everythin'—A ship cut through my town!" He raised an empty bucket in his hand. "And I got a bad batch of vice makin' us all nuts!" The mayor mocked him. "Is everythin' a'kay." Then he stormed down the Board.

". . . Bad vice," the boy repeated.

"Oh, Gaiel," said Mape. "We're almost out of watermoss some-how. Can ya tell Lynd to be on the lookout, too?"

Gai almost choked on air. "*Lynd?* Ya want me to . . ." The boy looked around at everyone dumping bottles and barrels. "Why does Tanning think there's a bad batch of drinks goin' around?"

"Somethin' happened, she says. We were all at the Vice House and had no idea why! I don't frequent it. But there we were suddenly starin' at each other like we had somethin' to say. Anyway, we ran outside and saw Baald's ship had crashed right into town. But he'd already fled. Poor thing must be so embarrassed, hidin' in the Under Board someplace. Tanning's lookin' into that now. Ah, nothin' lasts, do it?"

". . . How's Mrs. Shakk?"

Mape's eyebrows pinched together. "Why ya askin' about Mrs. Shakk?"

"By Zeea," Gai said under his breath. "That guy wasn't jokin'. He destroyed all their memories."

"What're ya goin' on about with yer whispers?"

"A'way, Ma. Let's go home. I need to tell ya somethin'." He grabbed her hand and pulled her to 76.

"What's all this about?"

Once inside, he pointed at her rocking chair, the one that broke after they ran home from neighbors. "Do ya remember how that happened?"

"Oh, that," she said. "Figured it was my little girl, again."

Gai remembered the general looming over him in the cargo hold and destroying his memories. The feeling of it was strange, like forgetting one's words in the middle of a sentence; you know you *were* saying something, but it just flew out. Yet, that strange night, the boy managed to piece his memory back together. Having been the victim of that "Ruin Memory," he felt almost like he understood it. He looked to his mother. The boy felt like he might, just *might* be able to fix such an attack. Maybe he could help Ma piece her memory back together. "Can ya have a seat in the kitchen?"

Mape shrugged and did as he asked, but not without a strong air of impatience.

As the boy gazed on his mother, he couldn't help but think of her innocence in that moment. She didn't know that her daughter and cousin Baald were missing and presumed dead, and that her husband might have had a hand in it. If he helped her, she would regain an immense sadness attached to the memory.

"Well, she asks? Out with it."

Gai wondered if he could just leave Hop and find Lynd, their father, and the whole *Merry* crew before Ma realized anything was out of place. Maybe he could make up another reason they weren't there. And she would be happy. And ignorant. What was the *right* thing to do? What was better, the truth or less pain?

As Gai looked down into his mother's anxious brown eyes, he realized that she must have asked herself that very same question on whether or not to tell him the truth about Stav and his illness. Compassion welled up within him for her; he understood why it was so hard for her to say anything. Which was better? Truth? Or less pain? "Ma, sit still. I wanna try somethin'."

Mamma Mape did as he asked, but not without a crinkled mouth. "Ya gonna tell Lynd about the watermoss or no?"

Shh. Gai put his warm palms over both her temples and closed his eyes. He recalled what it was like to have his memory scrambled. All those pieces fitting together like a puzzle. He imagined what her memories were like that night and for the three days after. He felt a rush of sympathy for his mother, feeling like he was walking in her shoes. A bluish light surrounded his hands.

"Gaiel! Yer hands are hot. Yer spookin' me out, now!"

The boy walked through her memory pieces one by one, the night she bet the necklace, Gai banging on the door in the middle of the night saying Lynd has disappeared, looking over at her laundry line hanging from their window. As her memories stitched together, tears pooled in her eyes. The morning of the funeral came back, as Mape was alone downstairs mulling over whether or not to accept Stav's death along with Lynd's. How terrified she was of doing the wrong thing. All the tears no one knew. Both their hearts grew heavy learning the truth. By the time he was done, both their eyes were red with sobs.

"Sorry at ya. Ya needed to know," said Gai.

Mape clenched her heart. "My baby . . . What happened to her? How did I forget such a thing? I'm a terrible mothe—"

"No!" Gai embraced her before she could finish. The two held each other for a bit in silence. He kissed her head and said, "Ya reminded me of somethin' last night."

"What?"

He gestured at their fixed door. "All that happened, but ya wouldn't know it by lookin' at the door. We don't have to be afraid of things breakin'. As long as we trust our power to fix."

She reached for her necklace that wasn't there again. "Even when there's this many pieces?"

"As long as you can find 'em all." *Gurgle grr.* Gai held his stomach.

"But how?" said Mape standing up and looking over her son. "Ya look starvin'! I may not understand much about all this magic, but I know how to fix a hungry belly, at least." She hurried into the kitchen and scraped out the bottom of a small tub. Dried dark green twig-looking things dusted out, and she palmed it into a small ball.

Gurgle grr. "I don't know much about it either," said Gai. "But I fixed yer memories the same way that door came back together. These blue light tricks."

As Mamma Mape brought the modest morsel to the boy, she glanced at the small white kitchen table. The one Gai had fixed after Lynd broke it. She handed him the food, saying, "Don't it makes sense, though? Per course ya don't have the same gifts as Lynd. Look around this place. Yer a creator, boy."

Gai gobbled the watermoss crumbs.

"By Zeea. Didn't ya already eat all the watermoss we had?"

"Last night I ate nine balls, I think."

"Nine?" she said. "Where's this appetite comin' from? Yer in a growth spurt?"

Gai licked his finger and picked up every crumb that landed on his shirt. "I dunno. Doin' these fixin' tricks makes me hungrier than I've ever been ever."

"Well, that all makes sense, too. If ya were buildin' a house, ya wouldn't do it without a lunch, would ya?"

Gai smiled. "Ya really think I'm different than . . . whatever came over Lynd and Pa?"

Mape ran back into the kitchen and pulled out a square clay dish, one of their only three plates, and held it up to him. "More evidence. Lynd took one look at my round platter, and it broke apart. But ya took up the pieces ya could find and made somethin' new outta it — a square plate. Look at my rockin' chair made outta old ship parts. And look here at the table. There was a crack in it, and ya made somethin' new. It's all got yer stink on it."

"That's probably just the Hopper White paint . . ."

"Gaiel, ya got a gift. If anyone can bring my darlin' girl back home, it's my darlin' son, she says."

The boy blushed a bit and averted his gaze. "Then why ya tearin' up?"

"I'm just so proud of ya." Mape stepped to him ad grabbed his hand. "Tell me yer plan. I see somethin' goin' on behind those eyes of yers."

After eating every last watermoss crumb, Gai walked toward the door. "Before the *Merry* crashed here, Unc's log said he was goin' to a place called Carpè. He said there's people there who understand these fixin' and breakin' tricks," he said. "I guess they call 'em *myracles*. And there's Elix ones, the kind that makes stuff, and Ruin ones that destroy. If Lynd and Pa aren't in Carpè, I'll at least find someone there who knows what's happenin' to 'em! And me."

Mape followed him. "Yer plan to get her back is to leave me, too?"

"Emilie's an awesome swimmer. I'll be there in no time!"

"For Zeea's sake. Ya can't ride a little turtle like it's the *Lady Merry!*"

Gai popped open the front door. "Oh, ya didn't get a chance to see?"

Outside, the once-dumping Hoppers were all gathered, pointing down at the largest tortoise they'd ever seen as she swam in circles easily in the rough currents.

Mape came out to the edge with him. "What in the? *That's* Emilie?"

"Anythin's possible, Ma."

Mape felt dizzy, trying to understand way too many things at once. She remembered everything she had gone through, all the kicks. But she had also witnessed her son do something incredible. Just the look on his face was enough to believe he indeed might pull this off. Something had changed in him. A focus in his eyes that hadn't been there before. "Ya better go quick. Anyone finds out ya got a way off Hop there, they'll come jumping' after ya! But can ya find me some watermoss so I can pack up some food for ya!"

"I'll just scoop what I need on the way," he said confidently. "But I'm not leavin' just yet. I need to do one last thing before I go."

"A'kay?"

"I'll meet ya back inside," the boy said. Gai then walked by the neighbors gasping at Emilie, all the way down Boulie to Mrs. Shakk's house. *Knock, knock.*

Mrs. Shakk opened the door, saw it was that Izz boy, and slammed it shut.

"Mrs. Shakk? I just wanted to say I heard what happened to ya, and I don't think it was right. But my Pa, ya see. He isn't well. That doesn't make it a'kay, but I hope ya can forgive him." No sounds came from inside. "Anyway, I'm leavin' to try and fix things. If I can, that means everythin' that happened to ya, too."

Gai listened for a few moments to see if she would open the door. She didn't. The boy backed away from her house and started walking back to 76. Then he heard something shuffling. Mrs. Shakk had slid something underneath her door onto the Board. Gai excitedly returned. It was her chalkboard. It just said THEN DO IT. Placed on the chalkboard was his mother's necklace, the one Mrs. Shakk had won from his mother that night. Not quite a ceasefire, but something like forgiveness. Gai smiled, saying, "I will."

He rushed back to 76. His mother was already waiting in the doorway with something behind her back.

"Ma," he said, handing the necklace back to her. "I'm gonna fix us."

"Thanks at ya, boy." Mape smiled and handed him three fist-sized, hard-shelled fruits. They had a hard outer coat that made them survive floating on the water after falling from their tree. But the inside was sweet as honey — a very rare delight in Hop. "I scooped these a few nights ago. I was savin' 'em for Lynd's birthday dessert. Take 'em and stay safe."

"Babanuts!" Gai said, eyes glimmering with childlike joy. "Wow, thanks at ya, Ma . . . When were ya scoopin', though? Ya don't ever leave the house?"

"My kids scoop durin' the day, and I been goin' out at night. We got better chances that way, she says."

Gai embraced his mother again. "Love at ya."

CHAPTER 10

HOW A SKIPPED STONE FEELS

Riding on epic Emilie was like having a private island that bounced with the waves. And she was quite the swimmer. She could beat a ship with a sail so wide, the boy imagined. Gai sat facing backward with his scoop over his shoulder, watching Hop disappear the same way the sun set. Even though he was leaving his home, Gai couldn't help but enjoy the sight of that gray smudge getting smaller and smaller as he bounced away to bring his family back together.

As Emilie surfed the surface, he felt like he was riding on a giant skipping stone. It brought a tear to his eye, remembering how Pa used to teach him how to flick his wrist just right to make a flat rock leap off the water. If a scoop was left in the water too long, it usually had one or two pebbles in it. They didn't have many rocks to practice with, and it was highly illegal to waste perfectly good rocks in Hop. But Pa used to say fun wasn't a waste. He loathed stuffy Hopper rules. He loathed *Hop*. Many times he'd wonder aloud what it would be like to be one of those lucky rocks that got tossed off there to the horizon. "I miss ya, Pa."

Bounce, bounce.

Once raggedy Hop was out of sight, there wasn't really much to look at. Domus Gulf to the left, Domus Gulf to the right. His mind wandered until he landed on the mystery of the myracite from Unc's log. Was it truly just a bunch of shiny crystals under the gulf? How did it get there? Why did it have the effects it did to Lynd and that Commandress lady? "Lynd already had destruction in her before touching it," he said to himself. "What about Pa? Was there a way to fix *that*?"

Those strangers on the *Lady Merry* called that destructive power Ruin. The other side, creation, they called Elix. It seemed Ruin might run in his family. But as Mape pointed out, Gai was no destroyer. Maybe a woodroach once or twice, but those were just snacks for Emilie. If anything, he was a compulsive *creator* — someone who put things together and made something new.

He remembered how good it felt when he made and remade things around the house, and Lynd's fiddle out of junk. "Then I fixed our door. Then my memories. Then Ma's." He looked to his left palm and thought about the strange blue glow that accompanied such wonders of creation. "What can this power really do? Seems like Lynd can rip anythin' apart." He took a babanut in each hand. "Does that mean I could bring anythin' together?"

Remembering the cost of such a trick, he decided to prepare some food before trying to call up that blue glow. Lest those *gurgle grr*s came rumbling. As Emilie sailed on, Gai stood up and drove his scoop into the passing water. She was swimming so fast the scoop handle bent hard. Before it broke, the boy pulled it out. The netting was full of green, goopy moss, and lumpy seaweed. "Dinner time!"

Mraaw!

"A'kay, I'll save some for ya, Em." He spilled the sea plants onto her shell and spread them out. "First, we gotta let 'em dry up, nice and crispy how I like."

Mraw. Emilie opened her mouth and caught some watermoss of her own as she swam.

"Guess yer not as picky as I am." The boy laid back and waited for the watermoss to dry up on Em's shell before eating. "What was I doin' before? Oh, right." He pulled out the two babanuts again, one in each hand, and exhaled sharply for focus. "A'kay, little trick." He closed his eyes. "I'm gonna make somethin' new with these two babanuts." He imagined what that would be. A larger babanut? "I'm gonna make somethin'." The buzzing started in his belly. "A'way." The blue glow emerged on his hands.

Slowly, the tiny hairs on each of the fruits' hardy, sea-worthy shells reached out to each other like long-lost friends shaking hands. He opened his eyes to see the little fruits surrounded in that blue aura like his hands. So he bashed the babanuts together and — *Pow!*

A new, larger fruit was made from the two smaller ones.

"I made more food!" The boy turned to his friend. "Em! Look at this! We could feed everyone in H—" *Gurgle grr.* "Oh, maybe not." In his aching hunger, he bit down on the fruit, and its shell almost broke his teeth. "Ow!" It was true babanuts had a tough coating, but not impenetrable. The boy tapped it on Em's shell. *Tap. Tap. Tap.* He tried to press his thumb into it. "It's no use. When they get this big, ya need a hammer!"

Mraw, said Emilie.

Gai let the oversized fruit roll off Em into the water. "Luck at ya to whoever finds it." He then reached for all the wet watermoss he scooped and frantically slurped it up right then and there. "At least, it worked," he said, wet seaweed stuck in his sore teeth. "I did a myracle! An Elix one." *Gurgle grr.* "Still hungry!"

Gai dipped the scoop back in the water and fished out more seaweed strands, eating them as soon as he caught them. Once his stomach was satisfied, he scooped out a bunch of extra handfuls until his arms got tired. He then laid them on Emilie's shell to dry.

Bounce, bounce.

By the time the boy looked back up, there was land on the horizon ahead. "Already, Em? Yer fast!" If there were anything more interesting to the boy than having the power to make a big babanut out of two smaller ones, it would be the sight of real, hard land. He'd never seen it, let alone set foot on it in his entire life. Solid ground was as mythical as Zeea. The boy carefully got his footing atop Em to stand tall and watch as the land got closer. His eyes darted and squinted, trying to spot . . . anything. "What sort of people ya think live there, Em?" Gai's eyes widened. "What do ya think they eat?"

It was all green coastline, with no buildings or yellow lights of Electri City just yet. The boy laid back over Em's shell to save his energy for the journey to come. "Look, Em. That cloud looks like a scoop. Ya see it?"

Bounce, bounce.

Just when he felt relaxed, a tiny red speck of light floated by. He shot up, seeing at least ten of them had come out of nowhere. "Be careful, Em. Spryts." A few more ruby beads popped out of the water and began dancing in the free air. "Em, look out!" A spryt was right by her cheek. Gai leaped up and swung his scoop at the red menace like it was a poisonous bug.

BOoM! The scoop struck the spryt in a burst of crimson zips and zaps. The netting and wood of the scoop fragmented and shattered almost instantly in his hands. And the blackened dust that remained blew off in the sea breeze. The spryt was gone as well.

"Ya'kay, Em? That was close," he said. "Maybe Tanning was right. No one should be touchin' 'em."

Mraww.

"Yeah, guess we lost our scoop. The spryt destroyed . . . By Zeea! It's the same power that Lynd has — Spryts must be made of Ruin!" Gai looked down over the edge at his reflection in the passing water. "But if spryts are myracite from underground, how did all that Ruin get down there?" He looked around at the dozen or so red dots still hovering. "And why is it all comin' up?"

Bounce, bounce.

"What's that pokin' up from the water, Em?" Gai peered a ways ahead at what seemed like a giant pole sticking right out of the water. It took almost one hundred bounces, but the tall structure became more apparent as they approached. A tower stood in the middle of a square platform, like a stick in the mud. Fifty more bounces and Gai could see the platform was big enough to hold several Hopper homes. "I bet those are the drills Unc was talkin' about in his log. He said they were in the gulf just before Electri City."

Emilie bounced closer. The tip-top of the tower suddenly lit up. It grew brighter and faded, brighter still, and vanished again.

"Someone's gotta be up there, Em. Should we ask if they could point us to Carpè?"

Mraww.

The standing tower continued to get brighter. Then wisps of yellow lightning started to sizzle out from the top. Gai wasn't sure if it was a wave of panic flushing his cheeks or if it was the heat from this light. His hair stood up from the static. That tower crackled and hummed with godly, knee-jiggling power. Finally, the light shot down the tower at a fantastic speed, passed the platform beneath it and under the water.

"Whoa! Looked like they just shot Esa!"

Bounce. Bounce.

A swelling wave rose up around the platform structure, echoing out from the blast. It quickly became like a wall of water, barreling toward them. "We're gonna be crushed!"

But Emilie charged into the epic oncoming surge. The boy started to slide back and nearly slipped off Em's shell as she surfed up the wave. She kept climbing and climbing until she was almost straight up, paddling her massive fins.

Gai held on for his life as the turtle surfed over the top of the wave. From high up there at the crest, Gai watched as the tower lit up once more, until finally it fired that powerful beam down again. He could see the yellow blast radiate out under the waves on the seafloor below. "They *are* shooting Esa!"

Emilie picked up incredible speed, sliding down the watery mountain as Gai screamed with every corner of his lungs. "Oh, Zeea, not another one!" *Ahhhhhh!*

Another colossal wave rose, and Emilie confidently swam up and around it again. Gai braced himself to have to keep doing this for the rest of his life. He locked his eyes on that tower. But it wasn't lighting up again. The water began to settle down. Emilie rode the smaller echo waves much easier until they flattened. "No wonder we got such bad currents! Why're they even doin' it?"

Mraaww.

By now, Emilie had bounced herself close enough to this planet-shooting drill for Gai to tell it wasn't made out of any material he'd ever seen. Definitely not old wood like Hop was. At the height of at least ten Hopper houses, the tower was the tallest reason to look up he'd ever encountered.

They were only about the distance of one Boulie Board away from the platform when they spotted a small figure up there, slumped down against the rails and facing away from the turtle and the boy.

"Someone *is* up there! See, Em?" Gai pointed to the corner closest to them. He yelled up to the person. But whoever they were, they didn't move. "Maybe they're . . . sleepin'? How could anyone sleep through that light show?"

Then, right beside this slouching sleeper on the drill platform, two bright blue specks popped in out of nowhere. One on either side of them. They still didn't wake up or move.

The little lights ballooned out, then faded as quickly as they had appeared. But they each left something behind. When the lights dissipated, two more bodies were standing on either side of the sleeper.

Gai immediately recognized their polished, near-illuminated armor. "They're dressed like that guy, General XIII!" Both had blue capes draped around them and appeared to be wearing matching helmets. "Hurry, Em. I got questions for these ones!"

Emilie indeed swam closer. But then a shining sword appeared into each of these armored soldiers' hands in a flash. At just a skipping stone's throw away, Gai could tell those were no ordinary weapons; they weren't metal like an anchor or wooden like Hop, but an almost clear crystalline that seemed to radiate and ripple with blue hues.

The strangers raised their sparkling swords over the sleeper, as if they were going to slice them to pieces.

Gai didn't like seeing things in pieces, especially people. He yelled up, "'Ey! Wake up!"

The sleeping person jolted. "What? Hm? *Ah!*"

One of the helmeted soldiers shouted, "Myracite belongs to us! It's *our* legacy!"

The other yelled, "You'll never understand its power!"

The now-thoroughly-awakened person screamed, rather high-pitched, at the swords about to rain down upon them.

But the two soldiers stabbed their eye-catching weapons right down into the platform floor instead. They weren't out to slice any *person*, it seemed. They then ran around the outer edge, cutting through the platform as they went. They completed the circle around astonishingly fast. In three blinks of an eye, they were done. In the next blink, another blue speck engulfed them. One more, and they vanished from the drill completely.

The structure itself began to rumble from the damage they caused. The surface of the water near the drill rippled along. The tower was vibrating and making a wild sound that got louder and louder like *BbbmmmmmmMMMM!*

"Someone's still up there, Em! We gotta help!" Gai yelled. The turtle swiftly surfed toward the destabilized drill, dodging yellow electri bolts as they randomly spit all over from the tower.

BOOMM! The entire structure exploded.

The person up there flew off into the water. Rails and chunks of the platform raining down upon them all.

The boy snatched up the remaining strands of seaweed, tight in his hands, and closed his eyes. "I need somethin' to help 'em!" His stomach buzzed. His breathing quickened. The blue radiance erupted from his hands again. "I can help. I'm no sogg!" He threw the lumpy, wet pieces into the air, and at once, they masterfully wove themselves into a long seaweed rope. *Gurgle grr.*

Emilie surfed and skirted in semi-circles, turning sharply to avoid getting pummeled by the debris. Gai whipped his new seaweed rope over to the splashing victim. They grabbed it, and Gai yanked them in as Em propelled to a safe distance away.

The boy pulled them up onto Em's shell. They were much lighter than Gai thought they'd be. In the splashing sea spray of their escape, the boy got his first look at whom he saved. He was smaller than the boy expected, but appeared pretty average beside that. Maybe he had slightly larger ears and a rounder, rosy-colored nose. He wore a tight, black jumpsuit with pockets popping out of pockets. The boy had never seen a person quite like this, but had heard about gnomes from Uncle Baald. "Ya'kay?" he asked.

The stranger immediately barked, "That wasn't my fault. They can't blame *me*! What are you waiting for? Get to the next Drillmax! We have to warn them!"

Gai was taken aback by his tone. Didn't he just survive a disaster? Didn't he realize he was yelling at the person who saved him? "*What?*"

"Hurry! That way! Tell your Plunder's Tortoise to sail us *that way!*" The gnome shot his whole arm out to the coastline. "Life. Or. *Death.* Hurry!"

Gurgle grr. "Uh. A'kay. Em, swim up that way!"

Emilie rowed her turtle arms as fast as turtle arms could row.

As they raced, the small gnome wouldn't stop nervously babbling, "I can't believe this! It's *actually* happening!"

"What's happenin'?" said Gai.

"The Second Myracite War." He shook his head. "No, no, what

am I saying? That would be the end of the world as we know it! But what else could it be?"

"Slow down. Who were the ones with the swords?"

"Oh, you saw them?" he said. "Great. You'll be my witness."

"To what?"

"That it was *not* my fault!"

Gai arched a brow. "A'kay . . ." The boy wanted to say something like, *weren't ya sleepin'?* But that seemed rude to say to someone who just exploded off a drill. Also, he was much too hungry to argue.

"I can't believe this," the newest passenger aboard Emilie said. "They've finally done it."

"Who?" said Gai. "Who's gonna start a myracite war?"

The stranger looked shocked that he wouldn't know and yelled, "Carpè!"

"Carpè?" Gai said. It actually made sense to him. He was just attacked by similar people from Carpè. And one of them destroyed all of Hop's memories. Certainly sounded like people who would also blow up drills.

Either way, Gai bit his tongue about asking for directions to Carpè. Whoever those shiny-armored people were, they clearly understood the nature of fantastic myracles, and possibly about what happened to Lynd and Pa. But the boy didn't want to get caught up in this gnome's gripes with them. "S-so where do ya need to go now?"

"The next Drillmax! I need to warn them! They could be next! It's just up ahead; you see that dot there?" He tapped a band around his wrist. "Ugh! Of all days. Why didn't I charge my com-comm?"

"Em," said Gai. "Keep forward. And fast." He turned to the stranger, "What's a com-comm?"

Booooommm! That drill up ahead lit up in a mushroom cloud of heat and metal. Small white water mountains formed as all the debris rained down, just like the first one. Gai's eyes popped open. He didn't know what to say.

The gnome sat, staring dead-eyed ahead. "It's true," he said. "The Second Myracite War." His mouth hung there. Terror came over his face. "*Kaa-Bah!* We have to get back to Electri! *None* of this was my fault."

"Go to Electri?" said Gai. "Sorry at ya, but I've got plans . . .

somewhere else." *Gurgle grr.* Still, he didn't have a scoop anymore, and wondered if he could honestly make it to Carpè without restocking his food somehow. Especially after that rope-making Elix myracle. He said, "Is there somethin' I can eat there?"

The gnome looked at him in disbelief again. "Eat? What are you —We're being *attacked*!"

"Yeah, but I . . . Never mind. I can drop ya off. Tell Emilie how to get there."

The thing about skipping stones is that there's no way to steer them once they have a direction.

CHAPTER II
THE MYRA WITHIN

C arpè's parade continued as if the Ruin run-in never happened. Lynd could feel the dried salt and sand pressing in her clenched palms in the carriage. Her entire body was in a tight knot, unmoving as the carriage rocked. Maybe it was some kind of unconscious resistance to the path she was taking. Not because the people around her were threatening. But because *she* was. The girl would shut her eyes, trying to remember anything. And they shot right back open every time the wheels bumped over a stone and made a cracking noise. She was worried she'd done it again — that Ruin thing.

Whoever Lynd was, it was someone with an extraordinary past. It was obvious to no one more than the woman sitting right across from her. Ada had tried smiling, small-talk, big-talk, medium-to-big talk. She warmly remarked on the people and places they passed. "It's a good island to live on," she said. "I've found no kinder folks anywhere." Nothing seemed to be making Lynd any more comfortable with her predicament. Who could blame her? The only real thing she knew about herself was that she was a destroyer that everyone despised. No amount of warm exchanges with the Commandress was going to change that.

Lynd felt the carriage angling up slightly as if they were traveling up a hill. She became frightened, glancing out the window to see they were very high up and over deep blue water. She slid her body closer to the center of the seat.

"These are the famous Archbridges of Carpè," said Ada. "They've stood for over one-thousand years today."

"How many is a thousand?" said Lynd.

Ada looked at her blankly for a moment before realizing she was staring. She smiled. "Why, that's ten one-hundreds, of course."

Lynd looked at her fingers. A strange feeling took over her, not quite a memory but more of an impression. She knew how to count using her fingers. Who taught her that?

"Er—flash your hands like this. All fingers out. Go ahead, do it with me."

Lynd slowly opened her palms to her riding partner, mimicking her.

"That's it. You have ten fingers, right?" Ada started flashing her hands open and closed. "If you went like this over and over, until your hands get tired . . ."

Lynd cracked a smile, repeating the ridiculous motion along with Ada as the Commandress made crinkly faces.

". . . That's about as many years these bridges have been around."

Lynd looked at her sprawled hand, adding it all up in her mind. "That's a lot of fingers."

"That's why we're celebrating! It's not every day that many fingers go by." She laughed.

Lynd slid herself back over toward the window. She wasn't ready to look out just yet, but she did finally relax her hands a bit. She felt the carriage begin to angle down, indicating they were over the hump of the bridge and heading to the other end. Where that other end would go was just as much a mystery to the girl as whether or not this place was even her home.

"We're entering the city proper, now." Ada waved to more cheering bystanders out the window. "This is all about to get much louder."

"Where are we?"

"You see, Carpè is an island surrounded by another island." Ada opened her palm and traced a circle in it with her finger. "The parade started on the outer island." Then she pointed at the center

of her palm, "We went over the Archbridges to the center island.
And there's a little water here that connects to the greater sea. Most
of the people live and work on the inner island. It's also where the
Akademy is, where you will be my guest."

Lynd finally looked out the window just soon enough to see that
dark blue water stop and the inner island begin. How anyone could
build such massive things as these bridges was mind-blowing — what
kind of *patience* that would take. She ducked back in as soon as they
past more parade-goers.

The parade traveled down cobblestone roads that were much
bumpier than the dirt roads in the smaller settlements on the
outskirts. The carriage creaked as it flexed over every stone. There
were many more things that sounded like Ruin. And the crowds got
thicker and more boisterous the deeper they went into the city.

"The Akademy is just around this corner," said Ada. "Not too
much longer."

The self-driven, golden carriage wheeled toward the entrance to
a massive white brick building. But as soon as they got into the drive-
way, a swarm of more brilliantly armored guards came running to
them. Lynd's body immediately tensed back up when she saw the two
lady guards from earlier, XI and XII, run past the window. They met
with the ones running at the carriage and spoke for a moment, their
voices frantic.

Ada began to step out. But another armored guard ran to her
carriage first. This one was a golden-clad man with a rich almond
complexion and a stiff, jet-black beard. His voice was hoarse, saying,
"Commandress, we are on the brink of war! Your diplomatic efforts
have failed in Electri—" He then looked at the girl tucking herself in
the furthest corner she could be from him. He seemed surprised Ada
was riding with someone. "The generals are assembling in the Hall
of the Arkons. Please don't delay," he said, running back to wherever
he came.

Ada appeared stunned at the news. She was uncharacteristically
quiet, and all the cheer and warmth left her face for a moment. She
inhaled softly and opened the door to the carriage, gesturing to the
girl. "You first, my dear."

"Thanks at ya." Lynd stepped her one bare foot and one
bandaged foot onto the road. Her eyes rolled up the building in front

of them. It was magnificent. Immaculate white stones and green, green vines fanning out like a thousand fingers.

Ada raised her hand. "Kora!"

It was then Lynd noticed two people were waiting almost entirely still by the large double door. One came running at Ada's order. Then the girl saw that it was no *normal* person; their skin was white as the buildings and smooth as marble. On even closer look, their features were still as stone, with eyes that were lit up blue. If the girl didn't know any better, she'd swear this person were actually made of stone. A surprisingly sweet and feminine voice came from a small slit in the mouth region. "Yes, Commandress?"

Ada appeared pressed. "My presence is needed—"

"Yes, I heard," the stone-lady said.

"And we have a young visitor," Ada continued, guiding the girl in front. "She is to be treated as my personal guest. Please show her to an open room, and help her get adjusted. I'd also like someone to come by her room and clean up a small cut on her foot as soon as possible. Do you understand?"

"Without delay, Commandress. What is your guest's name?"

"Name." Ada bent down and ran her fingers in the girl's hair. She stared into her eyes. "My dear, if you ever feel like there's nothing left, the answer is hope."

"Her name is Hope?" said Kora.

"A nickname." Ada smiled. "I'm so grateful to have met you, Hope. I have a few things to work on, but I will check in on you as soon as I can. Kora, here, is one of my best helpers. You're in good hands." The Commandress gave one last smile before breaking away to join the group of guards rushing inside. There was something so motherly about her. It made Lynd feel safe, but it also made her question where her own mother might be, if she existed at all. Either way, the girl was left with someone she wasn't even sure was a person.

"This way," said Kora, warmly.

Impeccably pearly walls, hanging gardens, golden domes. The place was more like a place of worship than of learning. But still, maybe they just worshiped learning. Kora opened the door and gracefully offered her hand to Lynd. Her skin shined in the noontime sun. The girl wondered if she had ever seen a life-form like her before. For all she knew, stone-people were everywhere. Maybe she even had a few marble friends somewhere. As she reached for the smooth hand, she asked herself if it would be cold? Did Kora have blood? What about a heart?

Perhaps it wasn't so normal for her.

Immediately inside was a long hallway of thick columns and colorful stained glass windows all the way down. As the sunlight burst through the glass, the marble walls were splashed with the one hundred shades of dazzling blues, greens, and purples over everything. Thin, geometric lines of gold decorated every angle the walls and doors made. As they stepped inside, a quick glance up was a giant dome in the center of the room. There were scenes etched in it, of people celebrating, meditating, learning. Lynd's eyes were dancing so much they started to water. Her neck began to cramp from looking up.

No, this was definitely not normal. If this were her every day, her muscles would be much more used to the workout that was being amazed. Standing there in the entrance, in her damp, salty clothes, she looked like a stain on a wedding gown.

"What are *these*?" Lynd said as she walked past three large golden frames hung along the hallway. They appeared to be more paintings, but something was remarkably lifelike about them. More like windows into another world than a painting, all were so perfectly brushed as to almost move. One was a dramatic summer field of wildflowers blooming, the next was of a quiet beach with bloated clouds passing by, the last was of a vast stretch of white mountain peaks.

"Seems like you could almost walk right into them, huh?" said Kora.

Lynd swore she could actually smell the flowers from the meadow one, and even hear the breeze. "Yeah."

"Well, you can. I mean, you could if it were allowed. These Pocket Realms were painted by an Arkon, some thousand years ago. Priceless doesn't begin to describe them."

"Ar-kon?" The girl felt like if she reached in, she'd actually touch the grass. Curiosity compelled her to try.

Kora gently guided her forward. "Ah, ah. Straight on ahead. We'll enter the dorms through the courtyard."

"This place is . . . beautiful," said Lynd.

"It should be," said Kora. "Commandress Ada has created over two hundred constructs since she took over." A small, bronze spider-like machine came around the corner, stopped, and pinched a wad of dirt off Lynd's dress with its little claw before hurrying along. "And those two hundred are just the ones designed for cleaning. We have cooks and butlers. Sowers and gardeners—"

"She make ya, too?"

"And helpful administrative assistants. Yes. Commandress Ada created two special constructs to help look after the students. I am one."

"She *made* ya?" said Lynd. "Out of stone?"

Kora cocked her head. "I never asked if I had any ingredients. I would think so."

"But yer alive?"

"As anything else."

". . . How?"

"The same way you are." Kora lifted up her brightly-colored shirt passed where a bellybutton would be. There was a compartment on her chest. She opened it, proudly revealing a small blue light pulsing like a heartbeat inside her. "Myra."

Lynd's own heart skipped again when she saw the light. Its glow seemed familiar. So far, it was the destructive sneeze and this light. Not exactly much to go on. "I think yer mistaken," she said, shrinking a bit. "I don't have that bright thing inside me."

"The myra inside me was mined from Esa, that is true. Technically, it's myra*cite*. But in essence, it is no different than the myra inside of you. Or any other living thing. Myracite is just the Arkon's myra that was left behind. It's old, *old* myra."

Lynd stared blankly. "Yer sayin' I have a light in me? What about Ada? I mean, the Commandress?"

Kora gestured her arm for the girl to step through the door to the courtyard outside. She did, prepared to be amazed again. And she was. There were gardens, with constructs shaping every hedge to perfection. Some were even playing catch with the students. "Yes, Ada has quite the light, herself," said the stone-lady.

All the countless pieces were moving in harmony like instruments at a symphony. There even *was* a symphony, played by a mix of joyous students and exquisite constructs. To the left was a professor, professing how great it was to be a professor. To the right were rows of trees with fruit so colorful it put those stained glass windows to shame. Lynd brushed her hands on a bush and a leaf came off, tumbling to the ground. It wasn't there more than a few beats before a spindly-legged construct came by to sweep it up.

Kora said proudly, "Welcome to the Myracles Akademy of Elix Artes, Alkhemy, & Maniphestation."

The Akademy grounds were heavenly. Lynd immediately got the feeling she'd fit right in if she tried. Everyone seemed so happy. So friendly.

Lynd and Kora continued straight down the middle pathway when the girl noticed that same armored man she saw earlier; the one who came to the carriage window to deliver bad news to the Commandress and gave Lynd a strange look. He wasn't hard to miss, tall with his golden armor glistening. He was also yelling at someone. A boy, maybe slightly older than Lynd, stood straight and stiff as that guard shook his rigid finger at him. The boy peered quickly at Lynd, then stared. That only got him scolded again. Everyone seemed so happy. But him.

"Here we are," Kora chirped, turning left at a fork in the path. "This is the student dormitory."

Lynd looked back at the berated boy who looked at her, wondering what *his* name was. But before too long, Kora had opened another set of gilded doors and led the way into the dormitory. After another long hallway, Kora stopped and appeared to be lost in thought or maybe powering down; Lynd wasn't sure. Suddenly, she popped back to life — "Room B76 has room!"

"A'kay. . ."

"It's just down this wing." She brought Lynd to a wall with a map on it. The map showed they were standing in a central location, with branches going around it like spokes on a ship's wheel. Lynd stared at the design. Something was familiar about that, too. Kora continued, "If you're ever lost, walk down the halls toward the center and start again."

They made their way down hallway *B*, and Lynd anxiously awaited which room would be hers and how it might look. She kept track of how many they passed using her fingers like Ada showed her, hoping 76 wasn't as big as one-thousand.

When they got to 76, Kora knocked three times. "Astel. Faan," she said, entering, "may I present your new dorm mate, Hope. I trust you will show her Akademy kindness."

"Of course!" said Astel, a curly blonde-headed girl with pink cheeks and freckles. She appeared to also be older than Lynd, but not much, and was dressed like a queen. If there were any more pouf to her shoulders, they'd be bigger than her head. She politely smiled and reached out her purple gloved hand. Before Lynd could even think, Astel grabbed her hand and shook it. "I'm Astel Osstett. Of course, my family needs no introduction. And this is Faan Mink. Her family owns the In Inn, the most luxurious little spot in town. Maybe we should take her there later tonight? What do you think, Faan?"

Faan was a bit closer to Lynd's age, a straight-haired brunette with a loose bun, deep olive cheeks, and freckles as well. But with a less polite smile. She said, "Her clothes are . . . *What are they*? Is this some kind of new performance art fashion?"

Astel gasped. "Oh, Bello. It's reminding all of us that there are less fortunate people out there. Brilliant."

"And brave," said Faan. "Good for you."

Lynd eye's glazed. "Eh?"

"Oh, but still," said Astel. "I'm afraid the In Inn isn't really the venue for performance art. What else did you bring with you? Is your bagman coming up the way?"

Lynd didn't even know where to begin. "I don't have a . . ."

Faan gasped. "Don't tell me. You have your own construct servant." She turned to Astel, "I have been trying to make one of those for *forever*."

Astel touched Faan's arm. "I told you my cousin just opened up a construct shop. You can just buy one."

"Another Osstett shop. You guys are everywhere. Potions on every corner."

Astel gasped. "Oh, remind me to show you the latest from Solution Solutions."

"Can't wait!" said Faan.

Astel turned to Lynd. "Hope, dear. *Hope* you don't mind, but until your bags get here, why don't I whip up a few outfits for you?" She put her arm around her, felt the sand, and quickly took it off. "Wow, you were really committed to the effect, huh?"

"Yeah, kudos on your commitment," said Faan. "It's *so* believable."

"I have just the look," Astel said, skipping to her desk. She picked up a large roll of paper and rolled it onto the floor, about as long as Lynd's height. The young Osstett then looked over Lynd and began to sketch the outline of a fancy new dress on the paper.

Faan stood to the side and offered suggestions. And Astel graciously brushed them off.

Lynd watched with a mix of wonder and a bit of fear. What in Esa had she gotten into?

"Done!" said Astel.

Lynd pointed at the paper. It was a nice enough drawing. Not anything she had ever imagined a person would wear. But at least the shoulders weren't as poufy as Astel's current getup. Lynd said, "Ya want me to wear the paper?"

Astel pressed her lips, looking like she was hiding her teeth.

Faan said, "Don't you know who Astel is?"

"We just met."

Astel closed her eyes. "It's alright, Faan. Everyone has a first time seeing the power of a true Fiat." She inhaled deeply, as much as her lungs could carry. Then puffed in two more times before blowing all that air out over the drawing. As the paper flapped from the passing Astel-breath, the drawing began to dance, too. It began to wiggle so much that it leaped right off the page — *pop!* — a fully-formed, real-life dress, just as she had drawn it. "On the house," Astel said, winking.

Lynd's mouth simply hung as she looked over the beautiful fabric that just came to life. Who were these people? Is this what they learned at a Myracles Akademy? Did she belong here? "T-thanks at ya."

Faan pointed her to a bathroom door where she could change, and she went. The bathroom itself and all its mysterious contraptions were another slew of questions. But she slid out of her salty clothes and put Astel's dramatic yet somewhat lovely dress on. It fit perfectly. Lynd looked at herself in a long mirror — another fascinating object. The clothes just didn't look right, something about the way they hung. Wearing *her*, as it were.

"Let's see how you look," Astel said through the door, munching on a handful of nuts. "Not that there's any guess. It'll be gorgeous."

Lynd stepped out.

"Wonderful," Astel continued. "You are a *peach*! Shall we head to the In? Oh, I almost forgot. Faan, why didn't you remind me? The latest thing from Solution Solutions I was telling you about." She went to a drawer by one of the three beds and pulled out a glass tube with a faint blue liquid inside.

"What's that?" said Lynd.

"Newest luxury potion from my parents' store, Solution Solutions. It's a breakthrough in Bio-Myra Resonance. We're sort of famous for our Alkhemy. Just like *I'm* going to be a famous Fiat."

"What does a potion do?"

"Get this. They grind up rare blue myracite crystals into a fine powder." She put a few drops on her fingertips. "Add a few herbs for stability and the effects are insane." As Astel rubbed the liquid into her cheeks, it left her skin radiant as if sunbeams were bouncing off it, even though they were indoors. She applied it all over her face and walked around looking like she was walking through some gosh-darn midday garden rays.

Faan nearly knocked Lynd over as she pounced for the bottle. "Let me try!" She rubbed it in as well and joined Astel. "Oh, Bello, I love this! When is it going to be available?"

"Not for like three years. Blue myracite is hard to get. We're going to be the *only* ones lit up like this at the In." She turned to Lynd, passing the bottle. "And of course, you, too."

"Me?" she said, taking it. Astel and Faan were beaming at her, so she smiled back. "How long does it last?"

Astel appeared puzzled. "Oh, I didn't ask. Are we making you uncomfortable, Hope?"

"No! No." She wanted to make new friends. Maybe she did fit in; maybe she was just as well-connected as these girls. Perhaps she was a Fiat, too. Whatever that was. Maybe her wonderful clothes and expensive lotions were just lost in the shipwreck. Yes, that must be it. "This is all very kind of ya. Per course, I'll try it. Just one question."

"*Of* course?" Astel squirted a few drops in Lynd's open palm.

As she rubbed the lotion on her face, she said, "What's myra?"

Astel and Faan looked at each other, each wondering if they

heard that right. This girl didn't know what myra was? How was she at the Myracles Akademy?

Both young girls realized what was going on around the same time. The terrible clothes, the uncouth manners, that sloppy *yuh* sound she was always making. She was no brave performance artist. This girl was not one of them at all. But before they could open their mouths to interrogate her, Lynd's face started doing something strange. Astel and Faan watched in horror as their new roommate's face was turning colors.

"What?" said Lynd

Ahhhhhhhhhh!

The guard in the golden armor Lynd saw earlier was still in the courtyard and heard the girls scream. He drew his luminous weapon and dashed inside the dorms in a flash.

Bursting through the door, he said, "What's going on in here?" Then he got a look at the girl. Her face appeared *purple*. The blue myracite in the potion was reacting with Lynd's red, red Ruin myra. It was causing her skin to rash severly and even cause tiny violet sparks to go off on her cheeks.

"*Who* did this?"

"W-What's happening?" said Lynd. "I just put this on!"

"General Bend, she did!" yelled Astel.

"After the lotion!" blared Faan.

The general examined the bottle on the floor. Then he ripped off a piece of his undershirt to wipe Lynd's cheek off. The girl's face calmed quickly where he cleaned it. He then looked at the blue lotion staining his rag. "Blue myracite? Where did you get this? That's pure Elix myra. Students should not be using it without supervision."

"My parents can get anything," said Astel.

"That's wonderful," said Bend sarcastically. "But, you're mixing Elix myra with Ruin myra. Creation and destruction annihilate each other, naturally. Good thing it was a fine powder, or her nose would be gone."

"Ruin?" Astel gasped. "Here? *Her?* I'm calling my mom." Astel paced back and forth like she was about to tell her the place was on fire. "Mom? There. Is. Ruin. Here." She gave Lynd a dirty look. "Yeah. In my new dorm mate." She paced to her bed and back. "Hold on, I'll ask. Is Ruin contagious?"

Bend sighed. "I don't think you're in any immediate danger."

"Mm-hm. Mm-hm. *Nope.* Mm-hm. Thanks. Bye." Astel stepped right up to the general. "My mom's suing the Akademy."

"Kora!" Bend yelled.

The stone-lady came in quickly. "Yes, General Bend?"

"Are there any other rooms available for Ms.—uh . . . This young girl?"

"Hope is staying here as Commandress Ada's guest. If you need anything to change, you'll have to take it up with her."

"Ms. Osstet," said General Bend. "Please tell your mother that you'll be under my personal guard during . . . *this.*" He then stepped out of the room, mumbling, "I'll deal with the Commandress."

Lynd picked up the empty bottle and set it on Astel's bed. "Thanks at ya for the cream."

CHAPTER 12
GURGLE GRR

Gai watched as the sun set over the Domus Gulf. Instead of the deep blue of night coming in, a yellowish color took over the horizon. Electri City and its famous lights weren't far. His companion, the gnome, seemed as bossy as anyone the boy had ever met. "Turn left," he huffed. "Who taught you to sail? Well, straight on, now!" The looming clouds became brighter and brighter gold. The air was thick with emergency. Bounce, bounce.

The first pieces of the shining city to appear were a set of massive central buildings. Slightly less massive ones filled in on either side. All of them were illuminated, flowing electri energy. The gnome kept a stern eye forward, looking like he was getting ready to leap off Emilie as soon as she swam close enough to a street. But Gai was frozen in awe; he couldn't believe something that wasn't the sun could make his eyes water in its brightness.

"Alright, turtle," said the gnome. "Keep swimming to the right. We want to dock between those two gates."

The mystique of the buildings only grew as they got closer, as did their incredible size. By the time they approached the docking area, Gai was in total shock at the scale of this place. Up until then, that drill tower was the tallest thing he'd ever seen. Nothing in his small port life suggested such grandeur could exist. He quickly guessed the buildings ahead couldn't just fit ten or eleven Hopper houses, but ten or eleven *Hops* in them. And the big one in the center must've been able to fit fifty Hops.

Rows and rows of people were looking out over the city guardrails, not to look at the boy and a gnome riding in on a giant turtle; no one noticed them. Instead, the citizens were all panicking and pointing at the drill explosions.

"Guess they saw," the gnome muttered, as if anyone could miss the trails of amber smoke. "I bet the Minister Prime is already declaring war. He's going to want a report of what happened. I just know it. Why me?"

Emilie slid comfortably into a roofed wharf littered with small, docked boats. Whether it was the dark and shiny materials that made up the structure or the bizarrely shaped vessels, everything Gai laid his eyes on was absolutely alien. Electri City had sprung up rapidly as the world's capitol of technological innovation, thanks almost entirely to their total control of the red myracite beneath the gulf. They learned to harness its power to run "electri" generators, which in turn ran all sorts of wondrous machines. Most of these extraordinary sights had popped up in the fifty years after Hop was abandoned. Not in even his wildest dream had the boy imagined such possibilities.

The gnome stood up, "Right. Spot Z24, right here, that's mine. There we go." And he leaped off Em's shell onto a sleek, polished black street.

"A'kay. Well, good luck." *Gurgle grr.*

"What do you mean good luck? You're coming with me!"

"For what? No! I need to go to . . . I need to *go.*"

"And *I* need a witness! This. Was. Not. My. Fault." He slapped his hands together at each word. "No one's going to believe me without a witness."

Gurgle grr. The boy was famished. Could he really sail all the way to Carpè with no supplies? "A'kay. But what about Em?"

Mraaww.

The gnome waved over a second gnome standing by the entrance. "Official business with Minister Prime," he said to him. "This Plunder's Tortoise is with me. Feed her. Clean her up. The works." He turned to Gai. "Happy? Let's. Go!"

Gai's faced crunched. ". . . Can we eat first?"

"What is with—" The gnome paused and exhaled forcefully to calm himself. "Fine. A quick stop. On the way. But if anything else gets blown up, it's on you! You'll be my witness to that, too!"

Gai hopped off her shell onto the hard dock platform. He walked over to her cute-yet-large turtle face. "Ya'kay with this, Em? I won't be long."

The dock worker stepped over with his small arms full of crisp, leafy greens. Emilie sniffed it once, then chomped it all down like she'd never eaten something so good before. *Mraaw!*

"She's fine," said the bossy gnome. "Come. We don't have time!"

"A'kay, Em," said Gai. "I'll get some food, and we'll be back on our way to Car—carryin' ourselves along." He smiled at his gnome companion as he took his first steps on real land. "I don't even know yer name."

"Kabbage Blip."

"I'm Gaiel Izz. But I like Gai better."

"Gaiel. Got it."

Gai's knees jiggled as he walked. It was the first time he had ever stepped on anything other than floating wood, and it felt really hard. Like, *how* was it so hard? Nothing about this place was like Hop. Everything was much bigger than it should be. As soon as they walked out of the wharf and onto the city's famously bustling streets, he saw people of all shapes, sizes, shades, and dress. A lot of them were gnomes, like Kabbage, but there were more than a few Gai-sized citizens in the crowd as well. Electri City might have been *tightly controlled* by the gnomes, but anyone was free to live there, so long as they followed their strict social structure. Most people, whatever their stature, were still running to the water's edge, watching the smoke plumes from the exploded drills. Many shouted ideas about what could've happened.

"This way," said Kabbage, taking a right down the most lit up street yet. Then he took a quick veer into the quickly moving masses.

Gai panicked. Didn't this gnome know he wasn't from here? The boy's heart raced as his eyes searched for Kabbage's outfit amongst the crowd, but many of them had the same one. *Wham!* A tall man bashed Gai's shoulder as he walked by and knocked the boy to the ground. "'Ey!" he yelled, looking back. But the man just kept right on walking. The collision hurt. A lot.

"Hey!" Kabbage waved from a ways ahead. "Why are you lying down?"

Gai swore there was something off about the man who just hit him. Something about his face? Or maybe it was just the blur of getting bashed in the chin? Either way, people in this city were rude. He stood up, "Comin'!"

Electri's skyscrapers were even more massive and intimidating when walking right next to them. They were on either side, like a row of rectangle giants all standing shoulder to shoulder. Lights and pictures danced across all their surfaces. There were people talking on some, and others played music. All were loud. Gai slowly turned in a circle to see them. His jaw was practically hanging down to his chest. Who should he be paying attention to? How did anyone know? It was sensory overload. But all the Electrians, big and small, seemed to be ignoring them.

As they continued down the street, all the screens suddenly went completely white. All of them. A row of white giants. A gentle tone played, and *now* everyone looked to the closest screen. Something important was happening. Even Kabbage stopped in his hasty stride. He whispered, "Here it comes."

The same face popped up on all the screens. "My fellow Electrians," this white-haired gnome gentleman called out. His voice was so booming that even the people inside the buildings must've heard it. "This is Minister Prime Wynk, addressing you all from the Capitol Sector. Earlier this evening, we were attacked by the Heartbrands of Carpè."

The crowd booed and hissed.

"We are still assessing the situation," he continued. "But the culprits have been arrested and will be interrogated immediately."

The crowd cheered.

Kabbage exhaled a sigh of relief. "Oh. Good."

"We believe the threat to be contained, but anyone with information is hereby ordered to report to the nearest Order Force office. Immediately."

Kabbage scoffed.

"This is a tragic event," the Minister Prime continued, "and my thoughts are with the families of those lost. I want to promise you all — Carpè *will* pay for these crimes against us. We have been patient.

We have been fair. And they came to terrorize our great city. We've been here before! It's no secret what they're after — control of our birthright. Myracite. We will back down from these monsters no longer!" The screen changed to show a group of massive, black and angular ships setting sail from the golden city. His voice continued over the scene of soldiers pressing buttons on giant, fearsome cannons. "And if Carpè doesn't respect our claim. If they think we are the same Electri City we were during the First Myracite War, the Wonder Weapon is ready to *destroy* every one of them!"

Gai was getting a bit sick of the sound of such loud clapping.

Next came an image of the whole city, with more of those ships tightening in a circle all around it. "For your safety during these difficult times, we have initiated a lockdown of our city. We do have the culprits, but our intel suggests one Heartbrand may have escaped our grasp. No one will be allowed in or out for the next twenty-four hours."

"Lockdown?" Gai pulled Kabbage's shoulder. "Like a door? I need to get outta here!"

Kabbage brushed him off. "Will you quiet down? It's nightfall anyway. You planning on sleeping on the turtle?"

"But I . . . I don't." *Gurgle grr.* "How long is twenty-four hours?"

The Minister Prime gestured warmly to the audience. "It is no coincidence that this attack occurred right before our Electrian Pride Day tomorrow. All they want is to break our spirit!"

A passerby screamed affirmatively right in the boy's ear.

Wynk said, "We will work doubly to ensure that none of tomorrow's fabulous events will be affected by Carpè's actions. Not the Tinker's Parade. Not the Thinker's Brunch. And definitely not Uncon Con!"

Hoots and hollers all around.

"When such terrible things happen," his big head said on the screen, "it's important to remember who we are. That's why this year, we will have a special surprise. I have just sent the order for the Founder's Stone — the largest single piece of rare blue myracite in Esa — to be taken out of hiding and displayed during tomorrow's Uncon Con!"

The screens all flashed over to a scene of workers carefully wheeling out an enormous piece of blue crystal out in the center of an epic stadium floor. While they kept showing the Founder's Stone getting set up, Wynk continued speaking, "Yes, during times like these, it's important to remember who we are, and what the Founder's Stone represents — that *all* Myracite belongs to *Electri*! *Joppa joppa!*"

Everyone on the street yelled "*Joppa joppa!*" back at the screen with their fist up.

The screen went blank white followed by a gentle chime again. And then the many screens on all the many surfaces of the buildings went chaotic once more.

"That was interestin'," said Gai. "Guess there's *blue* myracite, too."

"Hm," Kabbage said. "Seems like they've got it under control. Alright, I guess we're done here. You are free to go . . . wherever, now."

"Wait," said the boy. "Yer not gonna tell 'em what happened?"

The gnome stared at him blankly. "They found the criminals. They can ask *them*." He turned around. "It's not my problem anymore."

Gai ran to him. "Can ya at least show me where to get somethin' to eat?"

Kabbage didn't want to turn around. Was any of this his fault? Absolutely not. So why was it his responsibility to get this kid food? Everything in him told him to keep walking. But he stopped and looked back at that sad boy wearing newspaper pants. "Ugh." He waved for Gai to follow him.

"Thanks at ya!"

This place was certainly not like Hop. In front of him, a seemingly endless street of busy heads bopping all the way to a giant central spire.

Gai held his stomach. "Can't we stop here?"

Kabbage turned, "No."

"Well, what about this one? This smells good. Please at ya?"

Kabbage stopped suddenly and huffed. "Nothing on this street is for us. This is a Thinker neighborhood. You can tell because there's no garbage stuck to your—Have you not been wearing shoes this whole time?"

Gai shrugged.

Kabbage rolled his eyes. "Down here. This is Kobz Street. Not quite Tinker territory yet, but there are a few options for those of us who work in this area." He stopped in a long line in front of a building. At least twenty Electrians were waiting ahead of them.

Gurgle grr. "I feel like I'm gonna pass out."

The gnome directly in front of them turned around and gave him a dirty look.

"Are you always this chatty?" said Kabbage. "It's not my fault you're hungry."

"Actually," the boy said, recalling how he used the last of his strength to create that seaweed rope to save his life. Of course, he wasn't going to push the issue. ". . . A'kay."

The line moved up by one person. Gai groaned again.

Kabbage huffed and tapped the person in front of him. "Excuse me. My friend is dying. Would you mind if we skipped ahead of you?"

This other gnome Kabbage tapped looked shocked he'd dare ask. "I'm sorry, how is that *my* problem?"

"Can't argue with that," said Kabbage.

"So, ugh." Gai shifted his weight. "How do ya feel about all this Carpè stuff?"

"Despicable," he said. "I always said it was a matter of time."

"A matter of time," repeated the gnome in front of them, nodding along.

The boy said, "So there's really bad people there?"

"*People?*" said Kabbage. "No, no. Those are monsters. Evil. Monsters."

"I see. And ya fight over myracite?"

"Evidently so."

The line moved two more people. All the boy could think about was eating. But there was also a creeping worry that he still needed to find a way past those ships and out of the city. "Why can't we eat at the other place? Without the line?"

"Must you press on that button? I've had a long day."

"Sorry at ya . . ."

The line moved another two people.

Kabbage exhaled. "You see how everyone in this line has red hair?"

"Really more of a dark red." He peeked down at Kabbage's head. "I thought it was brown like mine."

He ran his fingers through it, insisting, "It's reddish in the sunlight. Anyway. *Darker* hair is for Tinkers — working class. That restaurant is for *Thinkers* — the bosses."

"What's hair got to do with it?" said gurgling Gai.

"When a gnome 'becomes an adult,'" he said, mockingly with air quotes, "we get white hair. It's a gnome thing. It's a status thing. It's an annoying thing."

Gai remembered Baald's log again. "So *that's* why ya use white hair dye?"

"Shhh!" Kabbage waved his arms frantically.

The gnome in front of them turned around again. "Did he just say white hair dye?"

"No, no," said Kabbage. He said, 'might wear pie.' Kid's awful hungry."

That gnome in front came close to whisper, "Because if you have some, I know a few guys that would lov—"

"Nope," Kabbage interjected. "No one has any. *Ha, ha!*" He turned to Gai, whispering, "You have about as much brains as you do shoes, my friend."

Gai said. "I don't have any shoes . . ."

"Fancy that."

The line moved four more people.

"Alright, we're getting close." Kabbage jingled some coins in his pocket. "Do you know what you want?"

"Do they have watermoss?"

"Do they have watermoss? Where. Are. You. *From?*"

The boy didn't want to spill too much information. He still felt weird about being in the city while wanting to meet their enemies in Carpè. "East," he said.

"East of . . ."

"East of . . . here."

Kabbage sighed, holding his forehead. "Well. They don't have watermoss. We don't get many *whales* coming here for dinner. What else do you eat?"

"Ya don't have to get snippy. How would I know what kind of moss ya have?"

Kabbage pulled out his coins and counted five. "Just look at the menu. Please."

They were next in line.

Gai said, "I'll get whatever ya eat."

"Oh? Booger Soup, then."

"Yuck, no!"

"Relax, I'm kidding. Booger Soup is only a holiday thing." Kabbage actually chucked for the first time. "No, no. Alright. Their babanut salads are pretty good."

"Babanuts!"

Kabbage pressed the button and a nice voice came out — *What is your order, please?* "We'll take the babanut salad." *That will be three binnx.* He counted out the coins he had, "One. Two. Three." *Bing.* Out came a bowl with green leaves and fleshy fruit chunks in it. "Thank you."

"I thought ya didn't have watermoss."

"This isn't watermoss, kid. Lettuce. Grows from the ground."

"Oh. And what's this?" Gai picked up a morsel of food beside the bowl. He sniffed it. His eyes lit up, and he munched the whole thing down in three satisfying bites. "What *was* that?"

". . . Bread."

"Are there more breads?"

Kabbage pressed the button again. "Can I get another loaf, please? Yeah, mine fell on the ground. Yeah." *Bing.*

Gai scarfed the second one down just as quickly. "Oh, Zeea! This is the most incredible thing I've ever eaten!"

"Relax, kid. It's just bread. You have the whole salad."

"Yeah, yeah," he said, shoveling handfuls in his mouth. The people waiting in line were watching with disgust.

"Yeah. Who needs a utensil?" said Kabbage. "Get those dirty hands all over it."

"Can we get more bread, now?"

"Kid." Kabbage pulled out his remaining two coins and jingled them. "I'm not made of binnx here."

"Ya trade these things for food?" Gai opened his palm for Kabbage to give 'em to him. The gnome obliged, so the boy looked over the coins.

"Yeah, I guess you could say that."

"I can help! Watch this." Gai closed his eyes and brought the two coins together. As soon as his belly started buzzing, he brought the two binnx together, and *Pow!* A blue burst of light shot out, and only one oversized binnx remained. "Can ya trade a big coin for a big bread?" *Gurgle grr.*

The people waiting in line gasped.

"Oh, my—" Kabbage grabbed the boy's hand and pulled him into the crowd. "Nope! No brains! You can't just—*Ugh!*"

"Where are we goin'?"

Kabbage ducked behind an alleyway, pulling Gai. "You're one of *them?*" he yelled. "Are you the one they're looking for? I could get arrested!"

"If ya mean the Carpè people, no. I know nothin' about 'em, actually."

"Ugh, I knew none of this was my problem. Why did I . . . Wait. You really know *nothing* about them?"

"No."

"Watermoss. Bread-awe. Open-toe footwear. Somehow, I buy that you know nothing." Kabbage sighed. "But how do you explain the . . . Was that a myracle?"

"I think so."

"So you can just . . . make things out of nowhere? Like a *real* myracle?"

Gai shrugged.

"Like, you could make *money* out of nowhere?" said Kabbage.

"I don't think it's out of nowhere. It makes me real hungry. Could we go back to the bread—"

"My friend, I have plenty of bread at my place."

"Yer place?"

"Of course. You're going to need a place to sleep, aren't you? Friend?"

"No," said Gai. "I'm thinkin' me and Em can probably sneak past those ships. She's pretty fast."

"What a cruel thing, indeed."

"What is?"

Kabbage folded his small arms. "Dear Emery needs to sleep, too, you know?"

"It's Emilie. But maybe yer right. I am thinkin' a lot about what *I* need." Gai yawned. One side of his brain said he had a mission to do. The other said he didn't know how far Carpè was, and even if he did, was it really right to make Emilie keep swimming so hard? Past all those powerful looking ships? What was a Wonder Weapon, exactly? "I can stay with ya 'till early mornin'?"

"What are friends for?"

"Thanks at ya! Let's go tell her were settlin' in for the night."

"Mm. Whatever, kid."

CHAPTER 13

MAKING TIME

L ynd's night in the pristine, lush and beautifully smelling dorm room was absolutely intolerable. Somewhere around midnight, Faan had built a dividing wall between her bed and the new girl's out of big suitcases and frilly pillows. Around half an hour later, Astel got up and locked herself in the bathroom and never came back out.

Lynd pretended to be asleep. She didn't want to give either of her dorm mates the satisfaction of knowing they were getting to her. In truth, she only got about one and one quarter hours sleep when Kora — *Bang-bang-bang!* — knocked on the door, saying, "Time for breakfast! A day of Elix myracles requires a full stomach."

Faan's head popped up from her barricade, which had grown to encircle her bed completely. She yawned, "What did the chefs make, Kora?"

"Nut butter waffle sandwiches topped with Amplified funberries and purpleberries. And a side of home fries with fresh herbs."

Astel groaned behind the bathroom door.

"Ugh, again," said Faan, plopping back down on her plush bed. "Just leave it outside."

Kora knocked again, saying, "I'm afraid I must come in. There's been a change in your schedules today. One you've been on a long waiting list for."

Astel poked her head out of the bathroom. "Don't tell me?" She then ran to the dorm door and yanked it open excitedly.

"Excuse me." Kora stepped in with a tray of three magnificent breakfast mountains and a pot of sweet-scented tea.

Faan came out of her protective suitcase barrier and stood right beside Astel, and grinned. "Come on, tell us!"

Kora rested the tray on a small table by the window. "I am here to inform you that space has opened up in the Intro to Time Elix class with Professor Hosp."

The two girls dropped their jaws and hugged each other, squealing, "Finally!"

"Oh, Bello, this is incredible," said Astel. "I was worried I'd never get in before Hosp went back to his own universe."

Faan screeched, "This is so unreal."

"I'm glad you're excited," said Kora. She tilted her marble head to Lynd, who was still in bed with the blankets over her face. "Hope, you should eat soon. You've been scheduled for this class as well."

"What?" barked Faan, eyebrows curling.

"Are you serious?" Astel whined. "That girl tormented us all night! Ruin in *our* room! It was like having a sleepover with a murderer! But she gets to attend a prestigious class with the most sought-after professor at the Akademy?

"She doesn't even know what *myra* is!" said Faan.

"Commandress Ada agrees with you," said Kora on her way out the door. "That's why she's been scheduled into all of your regular classes as well today."

"*What?*" Astel and Faan collectively decried.

"The Commandress sends her sincerest thanks for your considerate patience," Kora said. "Now, we expect full attention, so get your stomachs nice and full. I will see you all at the cafeteria for lunch."

Astel grabbed a waffle sandwich and marched to the bathroom. She stopped, took a bite, and gawked at Lynd. "I'm *not* making you any more clothes." Then she slammed the door shut.

Faan took her sandwich back behind friendly lines, crumbing up her bed with waffle flakes as she pouted. "This is so unfair."

Lynd threw the covers off and walked over to the table. She'd slept in the dress Astel made for her. Not because she liked it; it was actually quite crinkly and stiff. She wore it because she didn't have any other options. One of the clean-up constructs came into the room the night before and swept her hole-y clothes right up along with any garbage.

Lynd took one look at the enormous "Amplified" berries and dug right in. They exploded with gooey juices. The dark, sweet berry guts dipped down her mouth, so she wiped it with her sleeve. Some drops got on her belly as well. Before long, the dress Astel made her had gained a few new color splashes. She sat and enjoyed the incredible breakfast by herself. Chewing it over, she thought it wasn't *so* bad being alone or disliked. At least the breakfast still tasted good.

When the girl finished, she quietly waited by the dorm room door, ready to see what was so interesting about this Time Elix class. About an hour of fussing over outfits later, Astel and Faan were ready to set out for their school day, begrudgingly allowing Lynd to walk "twelve, no, *thirteen* steps behind us, please."

Lynd attended a class on the Underlying Principles of Alkhemy, another on Quintessence Theory, then another called Enhancing Elix Myra Through Dance. Neither Astel nor Faan were any help as the girl tried to understand the subject matter. Lynd's dorm mates had been trading between bored daydreaming, to whispering and giggling with other students at her, and back to daydreaming all day. But as time drew closer to that Time Elix class, they grew noticeable more awake. They practically sprinted to the courtyard, where it was to be held. But maybe that was just them trying to lose their special shadow.

Under the rows of colorfully fruited courtyard trees, five students sat crossed-legged by a man whose back was turned to Lynd and the girls as they approached. This man wore a staggeringly ornate robe with drooping sleeves that could hide a full-grown gnome. At first, he appeared very pale, but once he turned to greet them, it became clear his complexion actually had a slightly blue tint to it. He was a redhead but much closer to orange when the sun hit it right. He looked almost normal; he could pass in a large crowd for sure. But upon closer inspection, there was just something a bit off with him everywhere the girl's eyes landed.

"Welcome to Introduction to Time Elix," he said warmly, waving them over. "Have a seat anywhere near. No formalities, just sit and listen. Very good. My name is Professor Hosp. I'm a visiting professor at this Myracles Akademy. As the name implies, this will be a beginning course on time creation. No previous experience with time myracles is necessary."

Astel shot her hand up, and Hosp pointed to her. "My parents put me on the waiting list for this class because they heard you were from another universe." She leaned forward. "Is that true?"

"Your parents heard correctly. You might say I'm a *really* visiting professor." He chuckled.

All eight students, including Lynd, leaned in wide-eyed.

"That's not the subject of today's lesson," he said. "But I suppose you'll focus better once that curiosity is cured. Yes, I am from another universe, separate but not *un*connected from yours. My home-world was called Oof. And the official story is that I came to Esa to collect data on the rate at which Elix myra maniphests new matter here. Commandress Ada liked my work on time myracles and asked that I give the Heartbrands a few lessons. That was years ago now, and I've begun teaching Time Elix to younger and younger students." He smiled wide and opened his arms in the sun rays. "I started to love teaching. So I decided that's what I'll be — an Inter-Universe Professor. It didn't matter that that wasn't a thing yet. Because that's what Elix myra is all about, isn't it? Taking your will, your life-force, and making something new from it. Leave your mark!"

Faan spoke up, "What's it like where you're from?"

"That's not the subject of today's lesson." Hosp smirked. "But if you ever *master* today's lesson, you might have the ability to visit other worlds whenever you wanted."

"Wow!" said Astel.

"I want to go!" said Faan.

"How can that be," Lynd asked from the back row. All the students leered at her. "How can there be another space? I don't get it."

"Universes are ultimately geometric in nature," said Hosp. "But what is geometry but the connection of points? And what are points but imaginary dots in space? Make sense?"

"No," Lynd said.

"Of course it doesn't," the professor said, gesturing grandly.

"Those are advanced topics. And you asked advanced questions. But we can't get to advanced ideas without learning the basics, hm?"

Lynd nodded.

Hosp continued, "If any of you are planning on joining the ranks of the Heartbrands someday, creating time, or Time Elix, is now standard arsenal. They create time in a field around their enemies in battle, effectively slowing them down. It's a formidable skill. *If* you don't drain your myra too quickly."

All eight students shifted excitedly on their bottoms. This was going to be an interesting class.

"I was informed you all have basic geometric creation skills." Hosp waded between the sitting students. "I know you're not all *Fiats*, so I don't expect you to be able to maniphest items from nothing, from your myra alone. If you're at the Alkhemist level, you may use All Powder as a starter ingredient if need be. And so, however you're able, form a small white sphere on the grass in front of you, please."

"I am a Fiat," said Astel. She closed her eyes and inhaled. Then — *pop!* A small white ball appeared out of nowhere, right in front of her. "I can maniphest from nothing but my imagination."

"That's nice," said Hosp, unimpressed.

"My imagination's not that good. I'm still trying to get the hang of Alkhemy." Faan pulled out a small sack of white powder and poured some in her hands. "I still need something to start with." She tossed the fine powder into the air and then willed all the particulate pieces into a ball shape — *pop!*

Pop! Pop! One by one, each student created their white ball.

Lynd sat there, looking at her empty hands. They began to shake. She felt sick to her stomach. *Pop!* But a white ball formed in front of her on the grass. "Where did—" She felt someone staring at her from the left, so she glanced over. A boy was looking at her; it was the same boy she saw the day before being yelled at by that golden-armored general. He must've snuck into class late.

He smiled shyly and Lynd got nervous. She looked down at the white ball. Did he make it for her? Why would he help her? Didn't he know by now about the Ruin girl on campus? She peeked back once more at him. He smiled again. Lynd turned away.

Hosp clasped his hands, "Excellent, excellent. Now, I want you to focus on the ball. Feel its Quintessences sliding from one moment to the next. It's rolling, alright. Just not down a hill, but through time. Stay with this for a moment. Imagine you want to slow this ball from rolling down the hill of time." A pocket watch popped into his hand in a blue flash. "Here's how we'll test. Everyone hold out your ball and let it fall naturally at the count of three. No myracles. One. Two. Three." Everyone dropped their ball, and he stopped the timer once they hit the ground. "Alright, it took just over half a second for them to fall. Each of you will come up here, drop the ball, and employ Time Elix to create extra moments as the ball falls, and increase the time it takes to hit the ground. Are we ready?"

Hosp made the rounds calling each student up. "Astel. Zero point nine seconds. Well done! Almost twice as slow."

Lynd was busy in her head, asking herself what in Esa she would do when he called her? The only myracles she's ever been able to do seemed to make people rather upset and not want to be her friend. And she sort of wanted that nice boy who helped her to be her friend.

"Faan. Zero point seven seconds," said Hosp. "Very nice for your first try."

Lynd couldn't even make the ball, for Zeea's sake. How was she supposed to slow it down? What was myra again?

Then Hosp called the boy who made the ball for Lynd. "Kal, your turn."

The girl watched him get up in front of the class. He was perhaps older than her but younger than Astel. He was kinder than Astel, she knew that. Lynd wasn't sure why, but she couldn't take her eyes off him. Maybe it was how well the blue Akademy uniform looked with the brown tones of his skin. But there were four other students in class with the same uniform and features, and she wasn't ogling *them*. She couldn't like him, could she?

Kal dropped his ball.

"One and a half seconds," said Hosp. "Wow! Someone is definitely Heartbrand material. Exactly what I'd expect from your family. Excellent work, Kal."

The students clapped for him, and he bowed quickly, smiling awkwardly all the way back to his seat on the grass.

"Let's see who's next? Hope. Please make your way to the front, here."

Lynd was busy watching Kal take his seat. She liked the way only one side of his mouth curled up when he smiled. He was apparently very good at Elix myracles. But he wasn't at all pompous about it.

"Hope?" Hosp called as the students started laughing. "Hope!"

"Hm? Oh! A'kay." Lynd stepped to the front of the class. There wasn't a chance for Kal to help her again with all the attention on her. She held out the ball.

"Relax," Hosp said, taking note of how tense her shoulders looked. "When we stress, we can cut ourselves off from our own myra. This isn't a graded test; it's a learning exercise. Failure isn't possible. Ready when you are."

She could feel the cold stares of her dorm mates on her. She exhaled deeply. The worst thing that could happen was *nothing*. Right? "Think of it rolling down a hill?"

"That's a way to visualize, sure," said the professor. "Or whatever works for you."

She dropped the ball. It crashed to the ground in a flash.

"Oh!" Hosp exalted. "It fell so fast I didn't even have a chance to start the timer." The visiting professor picked her ball up from the ground. It was hard as a rock.

"She has Ruin," said Astel. "She destroyed time instead!"

"Settle down," Hosp said. "Settle down, class. Now, it is true that the reverse of creation is destruction. In the context of time, that means it sort of *skips* a second. The ball rolls faster down the hill." He turned the ball in his hand, looking over what it had become — ashy and stone like. "But this is . . ." He looked at the girl. "Huh. You're something special, aren't you?"

"Wait," said Astel. "Why is *she* special?"

Hosp blinked a few times, searching for the right words. "There are people like you, Astel. The Fiats, who can create instantly from imagination and myra alone. In the case of Ruin . . . I suppose there are the equivalent of Fiats, who can destroy something instantly and fully." He held up the stone ball. "You didn't just skip a few seconds, Hope. You removed all time from the object, rendering it essentially fossilized, almost like stone."

The students were dead silent and still, judgmental eyes on the strange girl from who-knows-where.

"See?" Faan chimed in, "We told you guys, she's evil!"

Hosp clapped his hands. "Need I remind you that an equal number of *evil* things can be done with creation myracles, and *good* with destruction? Good and evil imply intent, which nature itself doesn't have." He looked back to Lynd. "Oh! Where did she go?"

"She ran off," said Faan. "That way."

"Professor Hosp." Kal rose to his feet. "I'll go get her."

"Very well, Kal. Take her to the Commandress, will you?" A piece of paper appeared in Hosp's hand with another blue sparkle. "Take this note explaining the incident. Ada . . . will want to know about this."

"You can count on me," Kal said, taking the paper. He then ran in her direction of the dormitories.

"Puh," Astel huffed. "A Ruin Fiat? There's no such thing."

Kal ran into the dormitory halls with only the faint sound of Lynd's running footsteps to follow. He heard her bare feet flapping down hallway *B* and took the corner. He saw her way down the end. "Wait. Wait!" Kal snapped his fingers, and a small light fixture on the wall right beside the girl burst into pieces.

He destroyed it. The first Ruin she'd seen in someone other than herself.

"I'm like you," he said.

CHAPTER 14

THE MYRA IN MYRACITE

Gai and Kabbage walked together on the busy streets of the epic city. The boy knew it had to be nighttime by all the yawning he was doing, but the extensive city lights were making it bright as day. There were also people of all sizes still scurrying around as if they were late for lunch.

Kabbage tapped him on the arm. "See. I told you she'd like your salad."

"Wasn't it cute? She was like *maoo*." Gai laughed. "Well, I can't do it like she does."

"Few non-turtles can," Kabbage joked, tapping the boy to take a turn down yet another well-lit street. "So this . . . putting-things-together thing you do. How does it work?"

The boy exhaled. "Ahh, no idea. But the type of myracles yer talkin' about are called Elix. There's another kind that breaks stuff apart called Ruin."

"Elix and Ruin. Who named these?" Kabbage sighed. "Thirty years old and still learning new things . . ."

Gai tripped over his own foot. "Yer *thirty*?"

"Thirty-three, actually. *Why?*"

"Nothin'," said the boy, looking over his small stature. "I just . . . Ya look even younger than my little sister?"

"That's called size-bias. Common issue with you commonilk." Kabbage mumbled.

"Commonmilk?"

"Not common*milk*. Commonilk," he stressed. "Non-gnomes."

"Non . . . gnomes? Ya mean people like me?"

"Yes, and stay on track," said Kabbage. "You said there's an energy type that brings things together and another that does the opposite. Sounds simple enough."

"Yeah, and I think that's why Carpè wants yer myracite. I think the red myracite is basically bottled up Ruin. Maybe it's the same with the blue myracite for Elix? I didn't even know there was a blue kind until that Wynk guy showed it off."

"Red myracite is wild stuff," he said, gesturing up at the blinding city lights. "The vacuum effect it has turns electri generators, giving us all this power. But it couldn't be the same thing as this Elix or Ruin businesses. That would mean you could make blue myracite, wouldn't it? *Can you?*"

Gai shrugged.

"I didn't think so. What a wild idea." Kabbage stopped at a gnome-sized black box against one of the buildings. "Speaking of myracite." He pressed some buttons on the box and it lit up, playing an adorable little tune. Then a small, black square about the size of a binnx coin slid out at the bottom. He pulled it out and plugged the little box into the band around his wrist.

"What's that?"

"Myracite, of course," said Kabbage. "My com-comm died."

"I thought myracite glows, no?"

"Sure does. It's just inside this cell. You can't touch red myracite directly; it'll shock you."

"I heard that." Gai thought about when Lynd touched it. It was definitely a shocking experience.

"Why are you looking at me like that?" said Kabbage. "You really think this is the same as that breaking-apart energy?"

He didn't think. He knew. He'd seen Ruin come from a person. He'd also seen the same destructive effects happen when he bashed his scoop into a piece of red myracite. There was no doubt in his mind myracite and myra were related somehow. But where did it all come from?

Kabbage waved him to start walking again. "Either way, it would be great if we didn't have to carry around something so hazardous."

If red myracite were indeed Ruin, that would explain the epic reaction when Lynd touched it. Ruin plus Ruin must equal *bigger Ruin*. Still, the boy was mesmerized at how these Electrian folk seemed to harness the power of spryts. They managed to make it do work for them. What a clever use of something so dangerous. "I bet," he said. "Yet yer all walkin' around with touchy little Ruin rocks."

"Ruin or not, it's all business." Kabbage took a deep breath in. "What we need is someone really smart to invent an electri broadcaster. Wireless, free energy for the whole city. We could keep the myracite far away from citizens that way." *Beep.* Then his wrist band lit up.

Gai pointed to it. "And what does a com-comm even do?"

"Compact communicator," he said, putting his wrist to his ear. "Hold on. I'm going to check my messages." Kabbage then winced like whatever he was hearing was too loud. The boy thought he heard a person screaming but couldn't quite make it out due to all the city noises around. After a few long exhales, Kabbage put his wrist down.

"Ya'kay?"

Kabbage appeared concerned, but after one more exhale, he relaxed. "It was the Minister Prime's office."

"Ya still need a witness?"

"I'm not going."

"Why?"

All Kabbage said was, "Thing's have changed." It then started to rain. He pulled out a silver cylinder from his pocket, jiggled it, and soon a beam of yellow electri shot out. The electri opened up into a dome shape over his head. "Umbrella," he sighed. Kabbage offered it to Gai, who was taller, to hold it so they could both walk under it.

"Thanks at ya." Gai took the astonishing piece of technology with somewhat trembling hands. For some reason, fixin' tricks that make doors come back together in a flash, or make babanuts bigger, was easy to swallow. But electri technology seemed cold and soulless to him, like it shouldn't be trusted. Dozens of golden umbrella domes turned on all over the wet street. Rain was the first familiar thing the boy had seen in the city yet.

"Come," said Kabbage, pointing to a staircase leading up to a platform above them. "We'll take the SkyGo to my place. Time for some sleep."

"A'kay."

They approached a two-story station with large tracks coming out of either end that extended high up, nearly as tall as the buildings. The boy watched as shining spheres glided along the tracks. They were small, fitting maybe three Gai-sized people, or five or six Kabbage-sized. But they appeared to be just lights. "Definitely not like Hop," he muttered, staring up. *Bonk!* He walked into a sign. He read it, rubbing his bashed nose. "SKYGO CO. SEATS UP. 'Ey, I read about this thing in Unc's log. What's it do?"

"Saves walking time so we can work longer," he said sarcastically. "Where did you say you were from again?"

Gai looked worried. "Uh . . ."

"Alright, geez. I'll stop asking all these hard questions."

"No, no," said Gai. He whispered, "Where can I, ya know? Pee?"

"Okay, are you *from* the turtle? You can tell me. Have you been living on that thing? Because—"

"Please at ya!"

"See that little sign that looks like a guy sitting on a chair with the happy face? That's the bathroom."

"Got it." Gai scurried in, expecting to see maybe a rushing river or a pool to relieve himself in, but did not see anything so familiar. He darted around nervously, ready to burst. Then he finally heard the familiar sound of rushing water. A gnome came out of a nearby stall, and the boy went in after him. Once he started to relieve himself, he began to giggle at the toilet.

Kabbage stepped into the bathroom. "You know, while we're here, I might as well—What are you laughing at in there?"

"It's just . . . It's like my own little gulf to go in. It's even got currents!"

"You truly are a strange young man." Kabbage finished and stepped out. "Hey! You don't leave without washing your hands. Soap, yes, all of that."

Gai smiled, wiping his hands. He looked up at the mirror and was startled by his reflection. "That's what I look like?"

"I've been trying to tell you, kid. You need some *clothes*. I'm not sure whether to talk to you or crumple you up into a trash can." Kabbage hadn't cared enough to actually read the newspapers that this boy was wearing, until that moment. "What is this?" He read the headline of the paper covering the boy's arm. "ELECTRI FLEET DESTROYED BY LONE GIRL. Wow, this is from the First Myracite War. This paper must be ten years old by now. Gross."

"Oh, there's a bread crumb," Gai said, smiling again.

"Yes, well. Let's hop aboard the SkyGo, shall we?" Kabbage walked out and toward another booth with buttons, similar to where he got the myracite for his com-comm. "One seat, please." *Beep.* He nodded for Gai to get his, but the boy looked like he'd just been asked to spell transmogrification. "Ugh. *Two*, please. Thank you." *Beep.*

Gai chuckled.

"What?"

"Nothin'," said the boy. "Just realized ya say 'thanks at ya' weird."

Kabbage folded his arms. "Okay."

Gai chuckled again.

"What *this* time?"

"Nothin'."

They took their tickets to the platform, which had two exposed rails on top and nothing below but a long drop down to the busy streets. Kabbage stepped right off the platform, and Gai frantically pulled him back. "'Ey, ya almost fell!"

"Don't be ridiculous," he said, casually stepping off the platform again. But he didn't fall. A floor made of golden electri revealed itself every step he took, like ripples on a pond.

Gai stepped on in absolute wonder. It seemed electri was flexible and could be manipulated to do all sorts of things and make many different shapes — first a domed umbrella, now a floor. At once, their cabin, boat, SkyGo, whatever it was called, shot out of the station and way up into the sky. The boy felt his bodyweight vanish. "We're flyin'!" he shouted gleefully as they quickly wove their way around the epic buildings of Electri City.

Kabbage leaned back and watched the boy look out at the city with such excitement and curiosity. The Tinker gnome saw these things every day. There wasn't usually any excitement at all in his

SkyGo cart on his way to work. It was oddly pleasant to see it through the boy's eyes. "Hey, kid. What's your story?"

"Mine?" He wondered if it would be alright to tell him. "I'm on my way to find some family. My Pa was in Electri not that long ago, actually, at the hospital—"

"The hospital?" Kabbage donned the first actual look of sympathy. "Ah, I'm sorry . . ."

"For why?"

On the lefthand side of the SkyGo, a whole new area of Electri was visible. Kabbage pointed to a high building in the distance. "See there," he said. There was an expansive building with a large hole blown out on one side. "It wasn't that long ago," Kabbage continued. "The official story is that it was another Carpèan attack. But word on the street is some Thinkers were doing wild experiments on that floor. Some kind of secret weapon to use against Carpè."

Per course, the boy knew from Baald's log that the giant hole was likely caused by his father when he escaped before running into Unc in the myracite mines. Gai looked at some workers on scaffolding still trying to repair the wrecked facade. The scaffolding reminded him of the Under Board a little. Soon, he was daydreaming about the time Pa taught him how to scoop. There was a particular way of using the currents to your advantage to snap the catch in just right. When little Gai finally nailed it, Pa had the brightest proud smile. Could he really be the same person who destroyed all of this? Gai started to feel the emotions swell up. How could he possibly fix all this?

"Hey." Kabbage pointed to Gai's hand. It was beginning to glow. "What's with the blue?"

"Oh! I didn't even mean to start that . . . Happens when I think about helpin' my family get back together." Gai couldn't stop staring at the shattered building. "I'm so sorry at ya guys," he muttered without thinking.

"Why would you be sorry?" asked Kabbage.

". . . Seems like somethin' that didn't need to happen."

Kabbage sighed. "Alright, then. Get ready because my stop's coming up."

"A'kay."

The SkyGo dipped down near the streets. Gai immediately

noticed how different this neighborhood was. It was darker, and no one was walking around. They pulled into the station. Kabbage hurried a few steps ahead right after stepping out.

Gai felt a chill. He got the strangest feeling someone was watching him. There were plenty of other people waiting to get on, but through the crowd, he met a pair of fiendish eyes across the platform. A tall man, dressed in black rags from head to toe, was sitting on a bench giving him an awful look. It only lasted a moment, as SkyGoers filled in between them. "Kabbage," Gai said, "that's the guy who knocked me over earlier!"

"Who? Where?"

When the bench became clear again, there was no one sitting on it.

"Maybe we both need some sleep, hm?" Kabbage led the way down the stairs.

Once on the street level, the boy confirmed that the buildings were closer to the size he was used to seeing in Hop. Some of them didn't even have an upstairs. Kabbage took a quick right down Tinker Way. "Hurry up!" Then a left on Cogg Corner, and then three more turns down roads that were apparently too small and unimportant to have names. Not only were the buildings becoming less grand, but they were starting to be made of wood, something the boy had yet to see anywhere in Electri City. Also, along with the wooden homes came more and more shadowy areas with fewer and smaller electri lamps. "Some people call this Outer Electri," Kabbage said. "I call it home."

The few electri street lights that were there flickered and got dim. The gnome huffed, "Not again." After a moment, they came back on full strength. "Ugh. Been havin' power issues lately."

A few more steps down the way and he stopped at one of those woodsy homes, one that didn't have an upstairs, and shoved a key into a square door. Without a creak, it opened, and they entered out of the drizzle. There was a slight humming noise that came about after Kabbage hit a switch on the floor. A modest yellow light turned on that almost lit up the entire room.

Bathed in a bit of light, Gai saw just how different these homes were from the fabulous architecture of the *other* Electri City. The entire house was one room, complete with a bed that seemed like it was too short for even Kabbage to sleep on, one rubber ball near a table to sit on, and the rest of the space littered with junk that the boy could only assume would take years and years of collecting to collect. There were half-built contraptions and gizmos all around.

"This is yer place?" Gai felt connected to Kabbage for once. "Ya *make* things?"

"Welcome to Tinker life. What I wouldn't give for that extra *h*."

"Extra *h*?"

"*Th*inker," he stressed. "Add an *h* to Tinker you get—do you know how to spell?"

"It's nice here, I like it," said the boy.

"That's disturbing."

"What's that?" Gai pointed to one of Kabbage's scrapheaps in another corner. This one looked like a metallic bowl barely attached to a pole with wires tangled around it.

"Oh. *That*." Kabbage said, wandering over to a stove. "It's nothing. Just my idea for that wireless electri power. The broadcasting thing?"

"What's broadcasting mean, again?"

"Like spreading electri out, so it's available to use all over the city. Like a big umbrella." Kabbage fanned his little fingers out. "Wouldn't that be something?" He fired up a pot of water on the stove. "Can I offer you some bing brew?"

"Bread, if ya have it," said Gai. The boy noticed another black square sitting on the table, like the one that Kabbage bought earlier. He picked it up and felt along a crack where the two halves of the shell met, whispering, "Is there really myracite in here?" He broke it open with his thumb, and a red light leaked out. He took the whole shell off, exposing the tiny piece of red myracite cradled inside. It looked just like a small spryt from Hop. What a haunting vibrancy it had up close. "No wonder Lynd couldn't help wantin' to touch it," he said. "It's so pretty."

"Yeah, well, myracite is highly unstable, so never touch—" Kabbage turned around, saw him, and shouted, "No, don't—"

But Gai touched it and *Boom!* The whole thing exploded violently. Gai shot up and danced around, blowing on his hurt finger and waving it around like it was on fire. "It burns!"

Kabbage grabbed his hand and ran it under some cold water in the sink. "You heard me say '*never* touch' right?"

"I wanted to see what would happen." Gai winced in pain.

"Oh, you are just not worth it. Didn't I tell you it shocks people?" Kabbage took a good look at his throbbing finger. "Although I don't think I've ever seen it *this* bad." The gnome perked up. "Not ever this bad." He looked at Gai. "Blue."

"My pointer hurts!"

"Pull yourself together," said Kabbage, letting him hold his own finger under the water. He had the wide, shifting eyes of someone with a fresh idea. ". . . This could be huge!"

"Ow! Oow!"

"It's a known fact that red myracite can't come into contact blue myracite," he said, rummaging through a drawer for a bandage. "Unless you want to loose your money."

Gai's face pinched with pain. "*What?*"

"If equal parts of red and blue touch, they cancel each other out, and you end up with nothing." Kabbage snapped his fingers as an idea struck him. "It's like having just enough thread to fix a tear in your shirt . . . Putting together, ripping apart."

Gai held his poor, throbbing finger. "I told ya myra and myracite were the same."

"Yes." Kabbage picked up a strange doodad, jiggled it and tossed it aside. "Yes, I have discovered something, haven't I? Myracite must be crystalized myra, either blue or red."

"That's what I said."

The gnome grabbed his chin and started pacing. "Hold on, I'm thinking. What did you call the breaking apart force, again?"

"Ruin," said Gai, still blowing on his finger. "But if I have a lot of blue myra, wouldn't that mean I'd *disappear* if I touched enough red myracite?"

"I think anyone would if there was enough." Kabbage finally remembered he used a small bandage to wrap some wires on his broadcaster. He went and unwrapped it from his nonworking invention and wrapped it around the boy's finger instead. "Think of it in colors. You clearly have a lot of *blue*. So a small amount of red isn't going to be enough to cancel you out. But it will hurt."

"Ya can say that again," Gai said, watching the gnome take care of him. "So what would happen if I touched some blue myracite?"

". . . *More blue*, I suppose?" Kabbage shrugged. "But we can't get ahold of any of that. A grain of blue myracite is worth more than every house on this street. Now, if you could be a doll and make some of *that*, we'd be billion-binnxers."

The boy paused. "What about when Ruin touches Ruin? I-I mean when red myracite touches red?"

"Oh, that I do know. If red and blue cancel each other, red and red reinforce each other's negative energy. It's even more dangerous. I mean, I'm sure some Thinkers do it somewhere — experiments in some highly controlled setting. But it's not at all something to play with."

"What happens?" Gai said, thinking of Lynd.

"You called the red one Ruin, right? Well, Ruin and Ruin colliding is like that ripping-apart force ripping itself apart. It breaks down reality as we know it. Space and time start looping, with unpredictable effects."

"Lynd . . ."

"Just like you and that small piece of red myracite, the *size* of the two sources of Ruin would matter, though. I imagine a big source of Ruin would chew through a smaller one. But still not without wild consequences." Kabbage paused, then blurted, "Gaiel, I want to enter the Uncon Con. I think what we're learning here could lead to something truly great!"

"What's an Uncon Con?"

"Unconventional Convention. It's where the latest in myracite technologies are unveiled. You know, electri concentrators, electri suppressors, multi-directional electri splitters. Anyway, the Uncon Con is being held tomorrow. And I finally think I can enter."

Gai pointed to the strange contraption he had in the corner. "Yer gonna finish the broadcastin' thing?"

"Free electri power for everyone? No, no. That was too hard. But you, *you* are my ticket in, kid . . ."

The boy's eyes went wide as two babanuts. "Me?"

"You're even better than a broadcaster!" He wrapped his arm around the boy. "If we can prove people can generate a power source, it will change . . . *everything!* I'll be famous. No. Better. I'll be a Thinker."

"I really can't sta—" Before he could finish, the small light in Kabbage's home flickered and then went completely dark. Gai froze, eye's darting.

"Don't panic," said Kabbage. "Electri flow's been weak—Hey!" The boy yanked Kabbage's head down out of the window.

"Did ya see that?" he whispered.

Kabbage muttered, "This better be good."

"I saw someone's shadow in front of yer house. Someone was watchin' us."

"Stop freaking me out, kid."

Per course, this brought Gai right back to the time he was ten, and waiting behind the Izz family door only to see little Lynd come rushing through, never the same. Everything changed for the worse that night. He summoned every pinch of bravery he could find, whispering, "How can I fix the lights?"

"There's a generator box at the end of the street. Someone usually goes down and smacks it around until the electri flows again."

"A'kay. Ya wait here." Gai slowly peered out the window and saw no sign of the shadow from earlier. He sighed with relief. "Maybe I do just need a nap." The boy stepped out the door.

"Hey!" Kabbage whispered. "Someone else can do it!"

The boy saw the far-off lights of Electri's large buildings in the distance, but it was so dark on the street itself. Everyone there lost their lights.

There was a corner up ahead with a large metal square that kept humming, with tiny yellow electri sparks shooting out every once in a while, so he reasoned it must be the generator. As Gai approached it, he kept hearing crunching, like someone stepping on a can. Finally, the box jiggled violently and ripped open at the top.

Gai stopped in his tracks.

First, long claw-like fingers came out over the side. Next, a shadowy, humanoid creature emerged. Beaming in its sharp claws was a hunk of red myracite. The red glow seeped into the monster's skin. It had the shape of an average person, but with black veins overrunning all its features. The dark, blistering rash spread wider and deeper the longer it absorbed the red myracite. Even though this horrid condition appeared to be getting worse, the creature was clearly grinning. It seemed to *like* eating all that Ruin. The monster peered right at the boy with a staggering, intense gaze — a lion caught with its prey. Then the creature, whatever it was, catapulted out of the generator box and sprinted away to the bright city.

"Black veins . . . *Pa*? Wait up!"

CHAPTER 15

AN UNCONVENTIONAL UNCON CON

Gai's heart pounded as he raced down Kabbage's dim street after the bizarre creature. It was pumping so hard he thought a rib might crack at any moment. His lungs burned. Could that monster truly be who he thought it was?

As the boy's bear feet slapped the hard ground, Unc's frightening words from the *Lady Merry* log came to him: "As soon as my old friend touches that glowin' rock, its light starts to pour into every openin' he had — in his mouth, eyes and ears, sure, but also into the dark wounds on his body, makin' them split open even worse."

The fiend dashed around a corner with incredible speed. Following it was like trying to eye a firefly flashing in the dark — first, it was there, then another spot down the way, then somewhere else unexpected. The boy's feet scraped up as he charged on.

Kabbage yelled from behind, "Wait! Wait! I called the Order Force! Our lighting issue is not your problem!"

"I'm not gonna let him get away again!" Gai turned the corner to the street where the SkyGo station was. To his horror, the boy saw the shadowy beast pushing people out of the way to get aboard. A lone Order Force officer stood in its fearsome path to stop it from getting on the public transport. The boy heard the officer scream for the creature to halt. And shockingly, the monster did.

Kabbage caught up to Gai, and then both watched the event unfold. "What is that thing?"

"Oh, Zeea! It's attackin' that Order Force guy!"

A red zap shot out from the fiend's shadowed body and struck the gnome officer. He fell to the ground, and the man-creature hopped into the SkyGo, speeding off into the skyline.

Gai ran to the station and Kabbage followed. They pushed their way through a screaming crowd running away from the station in terror. The platform was vacated by the time they arrived, except for the officer writhing in pain near the platform edge. The boy bent down to help, but a scarlet-colored discharge leaped from the fallen gnome's body.

Kabbage yelled, "What did it do to him?"

Trying to get himself up, the officer reached out to a nearby bench. But another red bolt of power came from his hand, ripping apart the seat instead.

"Ruin must spread!" said Gai, backing up. The boy recalled that Commandress lady saying that something called a Void had been on the *Merry*, and that such creatures might've turned the crew into more Voids. "I think he's turnin' into one of those things!"

"What is this? Some kind of red light virus?" Kabbage cried.

"We gotta stop that first one!" Gai pulled Kabbage onto the next SkyGo and up they went, immediately behind the monster.

"Alright, kid!" Kabbage was screaming at the top of his little lungs. "Now's the time to start opening up!"

Gai focused on the SkyGo cart just ahead, searching for anything that might reveal who that creature was. He studied how it sat and moved, and tried to get glances at its disfigured face every time it looked back. And whoever it was kept looking back a lot. It did not want to be chased.

"Gaiel!"

"Huh? Oh. Remember how I was lookin' for my Pa?"

"Vaguely?"

Gai nodded up at the yellow-lit cart in front of them.

"Oh, you've got to be kidding me? Him? I knew I should've just left you with that turtle!"

"I'm not sure it's him," said the boy. "But they both like red myracite. Maybe it's like bread to 'em?" The two SkyGos were flying high above the city streets on the same rail, one after the other. The Void's cart was just close enough to Kabbage and Gai's that they could see the outline of its claws as it stood up and faced them.

"What's it doing?" Kabbage yelled, ducking behind Gai.

The creature's palms started to glow red. It rose them up. At once, the rail just behind him — but in front of Gai — began to splinter into chunks of searing metal.

"The rail!" Kabbage pointed ahead. "We're going to fall off!"

Gai rose his hands, too, focusing on putting that rail in front of them back together. He closed his eyes as the big metal pieces of the rail gained an aura of blue. The rail then ceased splitting and wiggled a bit. With a screech the pieces bent back together well enough for their SkyGo to slide passed with only a bump.

Gurgle grr.

"*Joppa!*" Kabbage said, "That was amazing!" But then he pointed ahead. "Wait! He's doing it again!"

For the second time, the rail shook violently and cracked apart behind the Void.

"All's a'kay." Gai huffed and puffed but managed to summon enough Elix to smooth the heavy rail hunks back down for them to pass over again. His stomach roared with hunger.

"You're incredible, kid!"

As they whooshed along some of Electri's highest buildings, Gai's vision started to double. If he were actually steering, they would've veered right into someone's twenty-story window. All the city lights blended into a bright blob in front of him. He sat down, thinking he wasn't just going to be sick; he was going to be *violently* sick.

Kabbage screamed, latching onto Gai's arm with both hands. "I think he's gearing up to do it again!"

The Void was relentless. It clasped its hands together. Even more red Ruin power leaped out and shattered the rail behind him a third time. Thick metal slabs began raining down on the streets below.

"Gai?" He shook the boy. "We're going to hit it!"

Gai couldn't stand up or even respond.

"Gaiel!"

Gai and Kabbage's SkyGo cart slid right off the broken rail, hurtling down to the city far below. As soon as it left the rail, the electri shell that enclosed the cart disappeared, and the two were free-falling through the open air with the wind whipping their cheeks.

Kabbage screamed so loud it was almost like he was trying to force enough air out of his mouth that they'd stay afloat. It wasn't working.

The boy cracked open his eyes — their splattered death flashing before him. He didn't even have the energy to yell. But he needed to survive. He needed to restore his family. Beside him was Kabbage, flailing his arms in sheer terror. He needed to save his friend. Gai's stomach buzzed like it never had before. His whole body erupted in a blue glow, speeding to the ground like a burning comet. As they struck the ground, the boy created a shield of blue myra in front of them that ate up most of the impact. But it dissipated quickly, and their bodies still smacked the street hard and tumbled like lost wheels.

The whole left side of Kabbage's face was scraped up nasty. He laid groaning for a moment. Then the fallen SkyGo pieces exploded and started a fire on the street.

The gnome got himself to his feet and went over to Gai. "H-hey," he barely managed to say, shaking Gai's motionless body. "He's still breathing."

The sounds of electri guns started to *Pff-Pff* down the street.

"That's the Order Force." Kabbage looked at Gai, "*You* are a lot of work." He then heard loud crashes, like pieces of the nearby building were falling to the ground. He feared the whole thing was collapsing. And then he spotted another one of the creatures, claw-climbing up the walls, ripping them apart as it went. "Are you *kidding* me?"

A swarm of twenty or so Order Force officers raced past next, chasing this second Void as it leaped from one side of the street to the other, from wall to wall off the tall buildings. They fired blast after blast. *Pff* after *Pff*. But the monster was just too darn fast.

Kabbage was ready to call it quits. This wasn't his problem. And he certainly didn't ask to be involved in some creepy villain chase either. No one would blame him for leaving. He turned to run in the opposite direction. He took one last look down at the half-dead boy who saved him twice now.

"Dammit!" Kabbage dragged Gai's body off the street and toward a nearby set of large doors. It wasn't easy, either; Gai must've weighed two or three times what the gnome did.

The officers kept firing at the Void as it jumped down from a building and raced up the street, right to vulnerable Kabbage and Gai. Kabbage lifted up his arms straight up and just screamed.

A lucky officer nailed an excellent shot right in the Void's back, just before it clawed down the prone boy and gnome. The creature froze. Kabbage exhaled. But the monster didn't fall. If anything, it seemed to like getting shot with electri. The Order Force gnomes closed in, all shooting furiously at the fiendish target. But the Void just looked like it was getting a nice massage and even appeared to be growing with each electri hit, absorbing their power.

"What in Esa are these things?" cried Kabbage.

As the wild event unfolded, he got his bearings. He realized what part of Electri they had crashed in — the entrance to the Stadium Gnomic, where the Uncon Con would be held in the morning, was just a short sprint further up Thinker's Way.

Another dark, bug-eyed Void dropped from a building behind the officers shooting. The other Void was still getting zapped by the Order Force, and somehow loving it.

"We gotta go!" Kabbage slapped the boy's face to wake him. "C'mon, kid!"

It was no use. Gai was unresponsive. Kabbage tried pulling him down the street again. But the new Void went running after them fiercely.

Pff. Pff. Pff.

The Order Force group split their fire on both the Voids. The creatures soaked in the electri bullets like a plant did with sun rays. And they were growing like weeds.

Kabbage dragged Gai to the stadium doors, yelling for help from anyone inside. Finally, he got to the giant metal doors and banged on them as hard as his little gnome fists could bang.

A small gnome face popped up in the window of the door. It was another officer. Kabbage waved to her frantically, but she took one look at the unfolding action on the streets and ducked back down.

"Hey!" Kabbage banged so hard on the thick glass. "You let us in! I'm a Thinker! I'm exhibiting today! I demand entrance!"

The officer poked her head back up again, looking over his obviously brown hair with a squinty eye.

"I'm undercover; just open up!" Kabbage roared.

A third Void dropped down by the entrance to the stadium from out of nowhere.

"Please!" Kabbage screeched.

Another Order Force member pushed the first one aside and helped Kabbage and Gai get in.

The group of five officers within locked the door tight as the Void smashed against it. *Bunk!* Instantly, the glass window went dark as if singed. Every surface these creatures came into contact with, including the ground, corroded at its touch. If it had the patience, it could probably just lay its claw upon the metal door and gnaw a hole right through; even their skin had the power of destruction. Still, it bashed and bashed and bashed. *Bunk!* Then it was joined by another handful of Voids, descending onto the stadium entrance.

Kabbage was shaking. "Ohh, what do I do? What do I do?" He looked around the room and noticed a concession stand with buns and cookies lined up against the wall. "Shoot those open," he demanded at the officers. They hesitated, so he yelled, "Now's not the time for rules. Get this kid some food, or we're all dead!"

Pff! Pff!

Kabbage grabbed a warm bun from the opened display and waved it under Gai's nose.

Gai's eyelids fluttered open. ". . . Bread?"

"You're alive!" Kabbage shoved the bun in his mouth. "Now save us before we die!"

Bunk! Bunk! The monsters were throwing their bodies against the thick doors, weakening them, *thinning* them with every touch.

Gai chewed the flakey baked good and his eyes lit up with joy. With his cheeks full, he said, "Where are we?"

"Stadium. We landed on the street, and I dragged you in here!"

"Ya saved me?"

"Sure, I guess." *Bunk! Bunk!* "But there's no time!"

Gai saw the doors flex and rattle. "What's out there?"

"That ugly thing you were chasing? Your mom or whatever. Now we're being hunted by all its cousins, second cousins, aunts!"

Bunk! Bunk! Bunk!

Gai shook his head. "There's more than one?"

Kabbage ran behind the officer. "Yes, now . . . Go get them."

"What do ya want me to do?" said the boy, shrugging.

"Don't you *know* them or something?"

Bisshhh! The glass window of the door finally shattered from their pounding.

Two Order Force officers stepped in front of Gai and Kabbage and opened fire. The remaining three cleared another set of doors further inside the stadium, yelling for the boy and gnome to follow. Kabbage went but Gai watched the group of Voids hungrily tearing through the stadium's front doors. "Maybe it wasn't Pa . . ."

"Let's go!" roared Kabbage as the doors finally gave way.

All fled to the doors further within that led to the lower rows of seats. They closed and barricaded them with their small bodies just as — *Bunk!* — the Voids rushed that set as well. *Bunk! Bunk!*

"What can we do?" Kabbage yelled, backing away as he watched the doors bend and whittle away under the monsters' power. A claw burst through, singeing the metal.

"Don't touch it!" an Order Force officer called out. "It's like they're made of acid!"

"They're tryin' to get in," said Gai.

Kabbage barked, "No *shit!*"

"No!" The boy pressed all his weight on the crumbling doors, "The one we were chasing could destroy whatever it wanted, remember? These ones are babies."

"So?" Kabbage pointed. "They got claws long as my—"

"Look!" Gai nodded to the middle of the vast, green stadium Gnomic field. There was a haunting blue light shining under a large tarp.

"That's the Founder's Stone," said Kabbage. "They're showing it during Uncon Con."

Two more Voids emerged over the tip-top rim of seats, crawling up from the outer walls of the stadium, and began lurking down like panthers. Another three came over behind them. Then four on the other side. Soon one after another were pouring over all the stadium's high walls from the outside.

Even if they wanted to shoot at the oncoming ones, all five officers were glued to those doors, trying to keep the first batch of monsters at bay.

Kabbage clapped his hands. "Gaiel, the Founder's Stone!"

"What?"

"It's the biggest piece of *blue* myracite in Esa," said Kabbage, holding up the door in his place. "You know what to do! Get down there!"

"A'kay." Gai went to the field railing and looked down at the field full of stands and machines set up for the convention. Then he looked up at the creepy creepers creeping down the seats all around. He leaped over the rail and raced to the center field.

The officers and Kabbage were able to buy him a few moments, but soon were pushed aside by the last *Bunk!*

"We're going to die!" Kabbage cried as the creatures broke in.

Gai made it to the Founder's Stone, a crystal twice his size. He yanked off the tarp and every corner, every seat, every stair was bathed in intense blue light. It was almost blinding being so close.

All the ravenous Voids halted in their tracks as soon as the blue light landed on their corrosive skin. They looked down at themselves, almost horrified by the feeling.

The officers and Kabbage took the moment to run to the center with Gai. "Gaiel," shouted Kabbage, pointing back at them. "Remember when you touched the red myracite. Give them an overdose of blue!"

Gai went to touch what was essentially a massive blue spryt. He hesitated, but Kabbage kept pleading and the Voids pressed toward them.

The boy touched it.

Immediately, his body became engulfed in a dazzling blue aura that was so strong it knocked the gnomes to their bottoms. Gai yelled as even his pupils crackled with power. The Voids started to turn away. But the enormous surge of pure Elix myra flowed into the boy and burst out all around him in a growing dome of dazzling brilliance. It expanded rapidly, spreading out across the grass field, encouraging all the blades to sprout taller and taller. Flowers bloomed from the ground, and vines erupted through the seats. The Voids ran for their shadowy lives.

The mighty blue aura continued growing. Gai was at the center, the conduit of this storm of creation with the help of the world's largest piece of blue myracite. It got so large it encompassed the lower seats and smashed into the first set of Voids who burst through the doors. Like zipping up a zipper, the blue myra canceled out the destructive potential of the Voids upon contact. And then they were nothing.

The Elix dome ballooned to the upper seats and struck into the fearful Voids as they scattered away through upper seats. And then they were nothing.

The clouds reflected the intense glow back down and it could be seen all over the city. And in a few more moments, the blue went out all at once.

"Kid," said Kabbage, running through the tall grass to him. "You don't look so good! Gaiel!"

The boy dropped to his knees, breathing heavily. "All's a'kay." It was all likely too much power for his body to take all at once. "What a jolt! Feels like every cell in my body is humming!"

The two took a look around the Stadium Gnomic. The field had turned into a thriving, lush jungle. If there were any cracks in the stairs, they were fixed. It was like a beautiful new stadium.

"Elix . . ." Gai looked up to Kabbage and said, "Yer a hero."

"I'm a he-he . . . what?"

"Ya saved me on the street! And it was yer idea to use the Founder's Stone. I never would've known Elix and Ruin could cancel each other out like that without ya!" The boy reached out to shake his hand. "Yer a true hero. I'm glad we're friends."

Kabbage sheepishly looked away, like the gesture was too much for him. He was even blushing a tiny bit. He grabbed the boy's hand, "Okay. Frien—"

Banng! The stadium doors burst open with a large group of Order Force members piling in with guns so big they had to lump them over their shoulders. They spread out all over the newly created forest in the field and into the vine-wrapped seats. Kabbage was still holding Gai's friendship handshake, so he pushed the boy into the overgrown grass to hide him.

"What're ya—"

"You won't understand. Stay low and get out!" Kabbage whispered to him as the wave of Order Force officers started cutting a path from the front door out to the center field where the Founder's Stone used to be. Then Minister Prime Wynk walked down it.

"This is the last time I put a Tinker in charge of something this important," said Wynk, approaching Kabbage. "You were supposed to keep an eye on that Carpè spy." He whipped a piece of tall grass out of his face. "Not let him run amok through the streets, performing all those unnatural myracles everywhere! And where is the Founder's Stone? Don't tell me he . . ."

Gai ducked down and peeked through the thick blades of grass. "Is he talkin' about me?"

Kabbage was silent.

"Kabbage Blip," the Minister Prime continued, "I was ready to honor our deal — you keep tabs on the spy, and you will receive official Thinker status. But this is unforgivable." Wynk darted his eyes around the epicenter of Gai's expansive creation. "Where is he?"

Kabbage just stared at the ground. But the tall grass beside him began to shake as someone appeared to be walking out. Wynk's Order Force aimed their weapons at the commotion.

Kabbage yelled, "No, don't—" But stopped when he saw it was the five officers who were in the stadium with them when the boy touched the blue myracite. They emerged, picking twigs and blossoms off their uniforms. They all appeared to be in a state of awe.

The Minister Prime narrowed his eyes. "Mr. Blip. I am willing to overlook that you let him grow weeds in my stadium. Tell me where he is, and I will bestow Thinkerhood upon you. Right here and now."

Kabbage wouldn't look to his Minister Prime. "He . . . saved this city." He gestured out to the five officers. "*They* saw it. I can't—"

"Order Force," said Wynk. "Sweep this field and find that myracle-working scum immediately!"

"Wait!" Kabbage said. "He's gone."

"What do you mean *gone*," the Minister Prime stressed.

"Just like the Founder's Stone," said Kabbage. "The explosion was too much for his body and . . . he's gone."

"Offer withdrawn, Blip." Wynk looked around at the officers. "What are you waiting for? Search every corner of this stadium for that boy!"

"Sir, if I may," said one of the five officers who witnessed the Voids. "We have an incredible problem on our hands. We couldn't stop those creatures. But that kid did."

"It's true, sir," said another nearby officer. "We tried shooting them, but it only made them stronger. We have no defense against them. T-they destroy with just a touch! That commonilk child isn't what we need to focus on. Electri's in danger."

A third chimed in, "We'd be dead if it weren't for him!"

The rank and file Order Force members started to loosen their stances and chit-chat. Wynk was losing their attention. As hardline anti-Carpè as he was, especially after the recent attack on the Drill-maxes, he wasn't foolish enough to risk morale before the all-important war even started. "The spy is truly dead, then?"

Kabbage nodded.

"Fine," blurted the Minister Prime. "At least he took care of a few flies for us. However, you, Mr. Blip, will not be gaining Thinker status. In fact, for your role in breaking in here and losing our Founder's Stone, the pride of Electri, you are hereby exiled from the city."

"Exiled?" Kabbage said. His eyes were wide with disbelief.

"Would you like to stay and face the hordes of citizens after they find out who used up their beloved Founder's Stone?" Wynk waved the Order Force to follow him out. "You have one hour before the news hits. Consider that delay to be your thanks."

Ex-citizen Kabbage sat on the grass as the officers left him alone to ponder his fate. Where was he supposed to go? Electri was the only home he'd ever known. The tall grass beside him shook. His stomach dropped. Gai poked his head out. "Oh, kid! Geez, I thought you left already. Get out of here. While you still can."

"'Ey, ugh. Em's shell is pretty big, yeah?" Gai said, reaching out his friendship handshake one more time. "Room for ya."

Kabbage smirked. He paused, looking at that hand for a good three sighs, then shook it.

CHAPTER 16

THREE SECRETS AND AN INNER ISLAND

L ynd hadn't met anyone who could do the type of myracles she could. She'd been made to feel like she was the only one on the whole planet with this Ruin thing. Yet standing down the dormitory hall was someone who could destroy things, just like her. But was it enough to trust him?

"It'll be our secret," Kal said, approaching her cautiously. "I-I've never shown anyone. You can trust me."

Lynd immediately darted down the hallway in the opposite direction, away from him.

Kal remained where he was, second-guessing whether or not exposing his secret was wise. "Do you need a place to hide?" he added.

Lynd stopped. Dorm room B76 was close by, where she'd spent the night. It was either head in there and be sneered at by Astel and Faan when they came back, or listen to what this fellow Ruin-person had to say.

"I know somewhere safe," Kal continued.

Lynd turned around. A place to hide away from all the awful stares of the other students sounded brilliant. Maybe she didn't have to trust him all the way, maybe just enough to sneak away for a little while. She crept toward him, cautious as ever.

He smiled and whispered, "Follow me." Kal then ran outside to the sunny courtyard and waited for her to come. When Lynd finally peeked out, he waved her over to another building, "This way." Kal turned quickly up a set of stone steps just off the emerald green grass. The girl felt herself smiling wider as she trailed him. He'd gone into the largest building on campus, where she hadn't yet been. Not that she'd been given a proper Akademy tour.

Lynd entered right after him, through the wide columns and into the high-ceilinged, echoey space inside. Almost touching the top were giant statues of people dressed in outfits so exotic they made Professor Hosp's look basic. These looming figures were lined up in a semi-circle, glaring down at her as she walked in.

"This is the Hall of the Arkons. They're our ancestors from the Old World." He pointed to the row of massive marble statues. "These are the ones we know about — Bello, Agor, Zeea — all the ones from the surviving records. But there were surely countless more Arkons in their day, one thousand years ago."

"One thousand," Lynd repeated, looking at her fingers.

"They say this is a place of many secrets." Kal walked over to the first statue and slid into a space between the wall and the statue's round base. "And I know a good one." He gestured for her to follow. The way this statue's cape draped down made it possible to climb from one loop in the stone fabric to the next, like climbing the limbs of a tree. He jumped up the first one. "Come on." Then rose to the next, "Almost there."

All this hiding and climbing made Lynd feel happy for some reason. It felt familiar. Kal reached out his hand to help her up. "This is my secret spot." From the statue's shoulders, they could carefully step over to the molding ledge at the top of the massive walls. "No one else knows how to get up here. That's the second secret I shared with you."

Lynd squatted on the ledge, her knees trembling. They were *very* high up. A fall from there would break every bone she had. But it was freeing to think she had a place to get away from the other students, should the need arise.

Kal said, "Do you trust me yet?"

"I . . . want to, but—"

Kal scooted down the rest of the ledge to the far corner. "Come. You need to see the view."

Lynd saw that if she scooted more than a couple of times, she'd no longer have the statue to climb down if she needed. She'd be up on the molding, dangling her feet with no way down. She went anyway. The adventure, the risk, the secrecy, and even the camaraderie thrilled her like nothing else at the Myracles Akademy of Elix Artes, Alkhemy, & Maniphestation thus far.

Kal opened a small decorative window just under the ceiling and slithered his body out. Lynd followed to emerge out on the Hall's sun-drenched roof, with a vista of the entire Akademy grounds and even to Carpè City beyond. She saw the sea completely cutting off the inner island. She saw the surrounding outer island in a hugging crescent, with the pearly white Archbridges reaching across to it.

"This is the best view in all of Carpè," said Kal. "How do you feel about me now?"

"Look how calm the water is," said Lynd, practically dazzled. "Why ya want me to trust ya so much?"

Kal lay back on the sky-blue roof tiles. They were a bit hot from the rays. "Honestly, it's been hard not having anyone to talk to about Ruin. It's seen as the worst thing anyone can be, but I'm not—"

"A sea monster?" Lynd smiled. "I'm not either."

"Of course not." Kal leaned over and pointed down to the sea. "You know why that outer island surrounds this one?"

"Why?"

"Carpè is a volcano." He grinned like he'd been waiting all day to tell someone. "It erupted long ago in the age of the Arkons. That outer island there is the rim of its mouth, see? During the eruption, part of it collapsed and the sea water rushed in. This inner island we're on right now was the lava, cooled into rocks by the sea."

"Wow." Lynd relaxed on the warm roof tiles with him, listening. She then noticed a pretty silver chain glistening in the sun around his right wrist. "I like yer bracelet."

"Oh, oh, thanks." Kal nervously adjusted it. "M-my father gave it to me."

"Hold on." Lynd sat back up. "Ya *made* a ball for me in that class. But ya blew up that light in the hallway, too. I can only destroy things, and the other students only seem to create. How do ya do both?"

Kal got noticeably fidgety. "T-that would be three secrets." He adjusted the bracelet again. "I'm not sure I . . . I don't know if I can trust you with another."

"A'kay," said the girl, smirking. "I'd tell ya one of my secrets, but I don't even know my *name* right now."

"I thought it was Hope?"

"That's that name Ada said I could use until we bring my memory back. I woke up on a beach somewhere on that outer island."

"That's wild!" Kal sat up. "I mean, I'm sorry to hear. But that's wild! So you have no idea where you're from? No family?"

"Yeah." She shrugged. "Does that count as a secret?"

"That's a good one," he said. "And don't worry, I won't tell anyone."

"Good. We can trust each other now."

"Um . . . Alright. You're right, by the way. Normally a person's myra leans one way or the other, blue or red, Elix or Ruin. In classes, we hear about people who switched colors after some time. But never someone who has them *both* at once. It's like being alive and dead at the same time; it's just not how life works."

"But ya have both?"

"Yeah, um." Kal's hands started to shake. He rubbed his palms on his pants like they were sweating too much.

"All's a'kay." Lynd put her hand on his. "I'm not gonna tell anyone."

Kal sighed nervously and pointed down at the water again. "You see how the seawater comes in and separates the islands?"

Lynd tried to foresee where he could be going with this. "Yeah?"

"I think I may have done the same thing to myself."

"Added water?"

"No!" Kal folded his arms and tucked into himself. "I knew you wouldn't understand."

"Oh, sorry at ya," she said. "I was just tryin' to make ya feel more comfortable. I didn't mean anythin' by it. Tell me."

"No, no, I'm sorry. It's just . . . sometimes I don't understand what happened to me."

Lynd locked eyes with him. "I get that more than anyone else here would."

"That's true. You see the outer island? If someone were sailing to

Carpè, that's all they'd see — the outer island. But there's this hidden inner island, all part of the same volcano."

"A'kay?"

"The reason I can use Elix and Ruin is because I have an inner island like that, that no one can see. The wild thing is, I don't even think I can see it yet. But it whispers to me, like it's got a secret. And I'm not ready to hear it. I'm too scared to look. But I can feel that's where my Ruin myra flows from . . ."

"So yer sorta holdin' the Ruin back?" The entire time, Lynd thought she was the most interesting person in Carpè. But had she only met Kal sooner. "What happens when yer islands are reunited? When the water dries up between 'em?"

"The Ruin would take over," he said, quietly.

"Wow." Lynd withdrew into her thoughts. What a wild place, this was. A split heart leading to split myra. If myra was the source of these creative and destruction powers, she wondered if there was a way to change her myra? But then she recalled she didn't even know what it *was*. "Kora said myra is a light inside me? Is that true?"

"There is a brightness to it, sure. Some call it spirit or life-force. But don't let anyone tell you they understand myra, because no one really does — just theories. There's *no* mention of someone creating a barrier in their minds to hide from their Ruin myra, for instance. I guess I'm a freak. But we do know myra comes from the heart. We know it can either be creative, a bonding force to make new things. Or destructive, a breaking-apart kind of thing."

As soon as he said *a breaking-apart kind of thing*, a pain shot across Lynd's chest. She quickly held her hand over it and winced. Those words kept repeating in her mind. *A ripping apart kind of thing.* She saw herself on a long wooden pier. It felt like maybe a memory. Her heart felt like it was breaking.

Kal was shaking her when she came to. "Are you alright?" he said.

". . . Yeah. I dunno what that was."

Kal picked up her hand and held it in his. "Promise we won't ever judge each other?"

"Sure." Lynd looked at his bracelet, glimmering. "It is a nice bracclet."

"Thanks," he said, as a glaze of deep thought came over his eyes. "I think my mom gave it to me?"

The girl tilted her head. "Didn't ya just say yer pa gave it—"

"Wait," Kal said abruptly. *Shh.* "Someone's coming into the Hall," he whispered. Nosey as he was, he leaned toward the window to hear. "Ugh, it's General Bend, of the XIIIth Legion . . . I don't like him. I think that other voice is General Case. She heads the XIth. She's not so bad."

Lynd leaned over as well.

"We have to do something," General Bend roared from within.

"Try whispering," said Case. "Do you realize what you're asking me to do?"

"Negotiations with Electri have failed," Bend stated. "Negotiations, by the way, that we all *knew* would fail. All of us, except Ada. And now we're completely unprepared. Half the Legions aren't even nearby, but following her orders to guard some archeological site. Meanwhile, Electri has ships coming right for us!"

Case exhaled and said, "I understand—"

"And what does she do during all this?" he continued. "Picks up a child off the streets, with *Ruin*? And! And. Where does she decide to put this child? With an Osstett girl. That family is the biggest donor we have. If they cut us off, we'll never be able to defend—"

"Keep your voice down," Case interrupted. "I will discuss the legality of what you're proposing with the other generals. But Command is given by the Legionnaires. The soldiers choose who leads us. Ada was the one to give us that freedom, remember? She could've been queen. But she chose to forge a republic instead. Even then, the Legions still wanted her to at least have Command. We cannot override all those voices with one act!"

"We chose wrong, Case," said Bend. "It should've been me to replace King Tyr all those years ago. Besides, I have evidence that Ada's interest in Ruin goes well beyond picking up some girl. If leaving us flatfooted against Electri isn't enough, then going against our founding principles should convince the Heartbrands that new leadership is needed. And I will prove it to them."

Kal and Lynd held their breath, frightened to make a sound. Case left as soon as Bend finished. But General Bend lingered. The two heard his armored boots clunking on the marble floor. He seemed to be visiting each statue, then said, "Arkons. When Ruin came knocking on your door, it was the end of the Old World. I pray . . . let this not be our story." He then left the Hall, clunking all the way.

Lynd whispered, "What was that about?"

"I think they're trying to kick out Commandress Ada."

"Because of me," said the girl. "I can't stay here."

"Please, don't leave!" He grabbed her arm. "I don't want to be alone again. Please, I'll teach you anything you want. Just don't go."

"Ya heard that mean man—"

"I'll shadow the general," said Kal. "See what he's planning. Kora will be looking for you at the dorms. Head back and meet me here tomorrow night." He reached out and hugged her.

If Lynd wasn't feeling all that close to Kal before, she definitely felt closer now. If anything could've made an outcast like her feel less strange, it was meeting someone stranger. She was thankful to have met him. ". . . A'kay. I'll meet ya here tomorrow."

CHAPTER 17

ALL AROUND THE WHIRLED

Gai and his new friend, Ex-citizen Kabbage, set off to Carpè aboard his old friend, still-turtle Emilie. The duo laid back over the tippity-top of her round shell, watching the golden aura of Electri City fade into the oncoming dawn. The boy felt like he was easily five or six years older due to his experiences in the city, even though it had been less than a weekend since he had left home.

Kabbage was still trying to wrap his head around leaving *his* home. It wasn't just that he lost everything he'd ever owned — that junk took quite a while to collect, thank you — but also the chance to ever stumble onto some great invention. He'd never be a Thinker, now.

"Can ya believe Em slept through that whole thing?" Gai yawned.

"And you were going to ride her all the way to Carpè without giving her a nap," Kabbage said. "I'm surprised she was still at the dock, to be honest."

"Why? Em would never leave me."

"I mean, I'm surprised nobody swiped her."

Gai sat up quickly. "Ya said she'd be safe there!"

"We were under attack." Kabbage sighed. "I was just trying to move things along. Truth is, Plunder's Tortoises like her go for *a lot* of binnx. Black market stuff. They're prized for being able to grow to the size of their containers, big or small."

Gai patted Em's giant shell. "Well, we're not sellin' her."

The morning sun had risen just enough to warm the skin but not so high as to be hot. Neither of them had slept all night, chasing and annihilating Voids as they were. The boy then closed his eyes and enjoyed a moment of peace and air.

"So about your father," said Kabbage, spoiling the silence. "If you don't mind me asking—"

"He wasn't always a monster," Gai blurted, opening one eye.

"Oh?"

". . . Sorry at ya. He's just sick, ya know? Anyway, I don't even think that was him we saw near yer house."

"How can you tell?" Kabbage sighed. "Are the creatures that tried to eat us in the stadium just sick, too?"

"They must be someone else's pa? Or ma? Or brother, sister? I think they're all just people. I thought my father was the only one of those things out there, but I guess not."

"Or they *were* just people." The gnome went silent for a few wave bounces, then said, "You're not going to become one of them, right? It's not how all you myracle people end up?"

The skies were a gemstone blue with puffy white clouds drifting lazily. Lying on his back, Gai raised his palm, pretending he could skim the clouds off the sky like foam off a soup. There was a group of four clouds living out their cloudy lives, floating in different directions. Gai imagined them coming together, pretending each cloud was a member of his family. And the clouds merged, forming a rough circle as Kabbage watched.

"Elix and Ruin myracles are different," said the boy. *Gurgle grr.*

"One breaks apart a SkyGo rail; the other puts it back. I get it." Kabbage reached in the sack of supplies he packed during his last hour in Electri. Knowing Gai, he knew to throw at least ten rolls of bread inside. He handed him one.

"And one makes ya hungry." Gai laughed, taking the roll. He bit down on the crispy, crusty bread. "But, I think it's makin' me less hungry than it did before," he said with a full cheek. "If Elix makes ya hungry and weak, maybe Ruin makes you feel full and strong?

Maybe that's why they just keep on destroyin' and can't stop? If those were Elix myracles, ya'd eventually just pass out!"

"So, to be clear, you're *not* going to become like them?"

Gai got quiet. He thought about Lynd and how she always felt better whenever she broke something, like she was getting a soothing hug.

Kabbage said, "The silence isn't exactly reassuring . . ."

The boy exhaled. "I think Ruin is what turns people into those Voids. I think the destruction keeps piling on until . . . My little sister has it, too."

"Oh." Kabbage looked away at the horizon as if he were contemplating whether or not he could still jump in the water and swim back to Electri. "Where might *she* be?"

"I'm lookin' for her."

"Of course you are. So we've got to find two of those creatures?"

The boy shook his head, swallowing the last of his doughy delight. "I don't think she's that far along yet. At least, I hope she isn't."

Kabbage had seen Gai eat plenty of bread rolls, and not a single time was he sullen afterward. But he was now. "Alright, if we're going to be friends, you need to start sharing things."

". . . A'kay. I just wonder sometimes if any of this could've been different? Like, could I have changed it? Ya ever feel that way?"

"I thought second-guessing was just part of life?"

"The night my father left, my sister came back inside cryin'. I didn't know what happened. Ma ran outside after Pa. She didn't know what to say. I felt like I should've been able to do somethin', ya know?" Gai's heart sank. "I tried everythin' I could to help. I made her a blanket out of rope and tried to wrap her up safe and warm. But I couldn't get her to stop cryin'. How's that for a sogg?"

"Oh, my."

"Nothin's been a'kay since then," said the boy.

"I wouldn't be so hard on yourself." Kabbage sat up and smiled. "Sometimes we just don't know what to do. On the SkyGo last night? I almost threw up eleven times. That's all I could do."

Gai managed to raise a little smile, too.

"And didn't you just say you made her a blanket? That's not noth-ing. It probably made her feel like someone was *there*, at least. I know

I like a good blanket when I'm upset." Kabbage looked back in Electri's direction longingly.

"I never thought of that," he said, appearing to slosh the idea all around his mind. "Maybe I wasn't supposed to fix it, but show her I cared? I think she knows that. Thanks, Kabbage. I feel lighter."

"It's all about how ya think about things, kid." Kabbage looked up at the clouds that Gai had just brought together. "Imagination is key. It's the same when trying to invent things. Speaking of things in our head, do you even know how to get to Carpè?"

"I heard it's north?"

"That's true," said Kabbage. "But have you given any thought to how we're going to get through the Uncharted Sea alive? What about food sources? Rest stops? Bathroom breaks . . . Bing brew in the morning with a blanket at sunrise . . . I miss Electri!"

"All's a'kay. It can't be that far."

"Are you joking? Carpè is several thousand nautical miles from Electri City!"

Gai scanned the horizon and just saw a perfect flat line in all directions. No land in sight, even behind them. "Maybe we should get some rest?"

"Yes, well, wake me if we're about to die." Kabbage rolled over and curled himself in a little nap ball.

The turtle continued her steady swim, dipping her head below the waves and casually catching some fish. Gai took another look at their watery surroundings and noticed a set of small bumps forming in the east. He wondered if it was land, and if it was, who might be living on it? Did they make bread, and what kind? The churning water passing Emilie's powerful flippers was rhythmic. The boy stared down and wondered how long it would take to get to the ocean floor. *Do sea monsters exist? Octopus-people?* Soon all that imagining lulled him into dreamland. His arm fell onto his stomach, his eyes shut, his hands relaxed. *ZzzZZZzz.*

Mmraww!

Ow! Gai felt his back fall on something hard. It certainly didn't feel like Em's shell and was certainly too dry to believe he'd fallen into the water. Before he was awake enough to see straight, he heard Kabbage yell, "Help! Monsters!"

Gai rubbed his eyes, trying to get rid of the sleepy blur. The sun was now high, with three large bodies casting black shadows. They gripped both his arms hard and dragged him away. "Get off! Who are ya? Lemme go!" He banged his bare heels and tried to wiggle out of their grasps, but they were just too strong.

He turned his head and saw the wood rails of a ship like the *Merry*. His abductors pulled him up, where he got a look at their faces. They had clear crystals over their eyes in some kind of bizarre mask. Kabbage and Gai struggled as the new enemies wrestled their hands behind their backs and clasped them in iron cuffs. Next, their captors wrapped their cuff chains around the mast a few times and threw another lock on that for good measure.

Kabbage was crying, "Monsters! Help us!"

Ten or so people were running across the deck of this ship. As far as Gai could tell, they weren't actual monsters, but those strange facial apparatuses gave them a frightening look. Most of these masked people were off to one side, bending over the railing, where a blonde woman without a mask was yelling at them, "Get her, boys!" She had a long rifle clenched in one hand, held high. She roared, "Take an axe to her shell!"

"'Ey!" Gai yelled. "They got Em!"

"They got *us*," screamed Kabbage. "If you haven't noticed!"

The masked men were yanking on a huge thick-roped net. The edge of Emilie's green flipper poked up over the railing of the ship. "Get away from her!" Gai commanded, roughing up his skin trying to wiggle out of his irons.

That woman with the rifle turned to the loud prisoner boy. Her wavy light hair, locked up in a bright red bandana, caught the breeze as she walked toward the mast. "Easy, kid," she said casually. Her angular, beige face framed two emerald eyes, narrowing on them. Her long, open coat was also green. She had yellow boots that went up past her knees. "We're just takin' part of your catch. Think of it as a tax. None one's gotta get hurt."

"She's not a catch," Gai yelled, rattling his chains. "She's my friend!"

"Friend?" she scoffed.

Emilie struggled in the net and rocked the whole ship with her weight.

The woman looked over to one other person who wasn't wearing a mask either. He was barely noticeable, leaning up against a shadowed wall in a full suit of dark armor, unmoving as a statue. "Hey, Mac!" she said. "I pay ya to watch? Get over there and help 'em secure that thing!"

This lone leaner barely looked at her. The man she called Mac wore a fancy helmet with gold trims. But like the rest of his armor, it was a bit scraped, dull, and dented in a few spots. When he turned to look at the woman yelling at him, all the boy could see were his narrow, piercing eyes through a small opening in the headgear. The battle-ready man acknowledged she was speaking. Then he looked away.

A crewman shouted, "We got her!"

"Excellent," said the bandana woman, walking to the side for a look. "No thanks to you," she said, passing the armored leaner.

Mac answered in a dry, calm voice, "You paid me to raid the archaeological ship." He then pointed to a set of ornately framed paintings strapped to the wall he was leaning against. "Not to catch food. *My* meals are on the house."

Kabbage whispered, "Now would be a good time for some of that Elix!"

"With what?" the boy whispered back. "My hands are locked up."

"Use your imagination," the gnome stressed.

The blonde captain was still arguing with the helmeted man, "Okay, we got the paintings. But follow my orders from berth to berth. *That* was the agreement. If I say clean the head, you'll use your tongue if you got to, you hear me?"

"Imagination, imagination . . ." The boy thought for a moment, listening to his chains rub against each other behind him. "What could I make with iron?"

Kabbage said, "A sword, you idiot!"

The armored man stood straight, stepped to the captain, and tapped her shoulder. He pointed to Gai and Kabbage wiggling against the mast. "I'd throw them back, if I were you."

"Stuff it," she said. "Do you know how much Plunder's Tortoises are worth?"

One of the crew members by Emilie raised an axe high in the air over the turtle.

Gai yelled, "Stop it!" His hands lit up that marvelous azure light. It spread to the thick iron cuffs around his wrists and snaked down the chains. At once, the boy swung his arms in front of him as the glowing cuffs and long iron chains whipped forward, fusing into each other, creating a massive iron sword in the boy's hands. It was so heavy that Gai dropped it immediately, and it wedged right into the deck wood. "Oop!"

Mac pointed at Gai. "I meant, throw them back because they're not your average fish. That one's got teeth."

Emilie let out a giant roar that shook the ship. *Mrawwwww!*

"Hold on, Em!" Gai struggled to pick up his new giant weapon, managing to lift it just high enough to drop back down on Kabbage's chain, freeing him. They ran over to Emilie's side of the ship.

"Stop right there," said the captain, pointing her long gun barrel right at the escaping duo.

"Captain Ballette!" one of the masked crewmen shouted down from up on the mast.

"Eh?" she said, looking up and shading her eyes from the sun with her hand.

"To port!" said the crewman. "Incoming!"

Captain Ballette and the others headed to the opposite side of the ship, away from Emilie, to find out what exactly was coming at them.

Kabbage tapped Gai. "Now's our chance."

"Right," Gai whispered as the two friends went to untie the third.

The captain, the armored man, and the masked crew were scanning the horizon on the other side as Gai and Kabbage loosened Emilie's ropes. The crew was touching their masks and adjusting those crystal eyepieces. It seemed those strange masks were tiny telescopes to help them see farther.

"What am I lookin' at?" Captain Ballette yelled to Mac. When he didn't respond immediately, she slapped him. "Hey! I order ya to——"

"More Plunder's," said Mac, flatly.

Gai looked over his shoulder and saw that those small bumps he'd seen earlier had grown much larger. They looked like a group of islands.

For an instant, Captain Ballette's face went pale, like she was going to throw up over the railing. But, quickly remembering her role as captain of the ship, she swallowed her fear, yelling, "Never fear a large plate, men! To the spear-cannons!"

All of the crew, including Mac, rushed to the side where the enormous turtle-mountains were approaching. Some grabbed hold of large iron cannons and started to aim; the others formed a chain behind them to carry ammunition from the lower decks. The spear-heads they were loading into the cannons looked like the sharpest things the boy had ever seen.

"Hey! Get away from that!" The captain roared at Gai and Kabbage while they were still bent over the rail, trying to undo the knots of Em's nets.

At last, the two friends were able to release Em into the water, rocking the ship slightly. "Too late!" Kabbage said confidently. Just as they were about to hop off the ship back onto Em's shell, they saw just what was approaching.

Captain Ballette yelled, "Fire!"

Explosion after explosion, the cannons shot the giant spearheads with ropes attached at the islands — that weren't islands at all. They were more turtles like Emilie. The spearheads arced far up in the sky toward the giant turtles. Gunpowder smoke covered the deck and made Kabbage and the boy choke. *Couuh. Couhh.*

Beyond the white haze, the boy saw great waves of water leaping into the air where the spears missed their unmissable targets. There were seven of them, a family of Plunder's Tortoises, swimming faster than anything so large should be able to move. They were like speeding ships with full sails, but each must have been the size of Hop. Finally, the massive turtles broke apart and began to crescent around the captain's ship.

"They're comin' to help Em," said Gai. "They heard her cryin'."

"Fire at starboard!" yelled Captain Ballette, shuffling her tall boots around, following the swift, circling tortoises. "Bow! Stern!"

Soon long arcs of rope were shot out in all directions like they were at the center of some kind of twine flower opening into the blue sky. "C'mon!" Gai said to Kabbage, lifting his legs over the rail to leap onto Em.

Kabbage joined him but stopped. "Uh. Gaiel? Are we moving?"

Gai watched as the ship, with its anchor and sails down, began to pull away from Emilie. White ripples of the water started flowing around the hull.

"I feel like I'm gonna throw up!" Kabbage gripped the rail. "We're spinning!"

"We got a swirl, Captain!" the crewman yelled from the mast.

Immediately, Ballette ran to the helm wheel and began to turn it around and around to stop the ship from going anywhere she didn't first order it.

Free Emilie tried her best to chase after the ship, but the entire ocean seemed to be turning and turning. Those full-grown, mountainous Plunder's were swimming faster and faster in a circle around the ship, forming an epic whirlpool. The ship was twirling like a clock hand that had gone out of control. The crewman in the mast flew right off and into the water. Before Ballette could scream after him, more crew members either leaped off the deck on purpose or slipped off. It was everyone for themselves.

The jetting sea sprayed across the deck with such force, anyone who tried to stay was peeled off. The crew was all gone. But Gai clung to the heavy iron sword in one hand and Kabbage in the other.

Mraaww! Emilie was forced to the outer edge of the whirlpool. The captain's ship seemed doomed to swirl and swirl down like a bug caught in a drain.

Captain Ballette refused to lose control of her ship, white-knuckling around the wheel. She threw her whole body weight into it, digging her heels into the deck boards and scraping the deck wood right off. The hull began to shatter against the force of the flowing water. The vessel itself tilted on its side as it pressed against the walls of the sea vortex. All still aboard fell flat against the decks hard, hands and feet pinned. Down and down, they all went to the ocean floor.

Gai turned his neck as best he could and noticed that Mac had not fallen or jumped off either. That man was crawling his way up to the captain at the helm. Boards and ropes flew into the air; the sails ripped away. Kabbage's little hand was about to slide right out of Gai's. "Hold on!"

"I'm going to die!" screeched Kabbage. "And it's not. My. *Fault!*"

Ahh! They all shouted in their own times. They were in a massive whirlpool to the bottom of the Uncharted Sea, where they would soon crash into the seabed mud, the ship would finally splinter and break apart, and all lives would be lost.

The boy saw Mac pulling the captain as hard he could over one of the ornate paintings. He then threw Ballette into the beautiful artwork, clean as if it were an open window. She fell through and disappeared. Mac glanced at Gai and waved him over before leaping into it himself. Gai then looked to Kabbage, who was still screaming that his life was ending far, far too soon. The boy used the rail to drag them both to the painting as well.

"What are you doing?" Kabbage had tears racing across his cheeks.

Whatever that painting was, it was the only way out. And Gai was not ready to give up his quest. With all his might, he pushed against the massive force pinning them to the deck. He forced Kabbage in first then leaped into the frame, into the truly unknown.

CHAPTER 18
A DEFINING MOMENT

D espite the reputation she was gaining, Lynd made a friend. A friend who understood Ruin, no less. Not that it helped her as she spent her second night at the Akademy alone in her dorm room. Her dorm mates, Astel and Faan, were sleeping over at the In Inn. They claimed it was a planned vacation, but somehow the girl didn't believe them. "All's a'kay," she said to the empty room, "I don't think I like *them*, either."

When Kora knocked the next morning, Lynd woke up from the best night's sleep she'd ever had. She forced herself up from the deep mattress imprint and opened the door.

"Good morning, Hope," said Kora. She stepped in with another astonishingly colorful breakfast tray and sat it down. "I have a special note for you from Commandress Ada."

Lynd was already picking the goo off the sticky buns and licking her fingers. She looked over the note and asked, "Could ya read it for me?"

"Of course I can. With your permission?"

The girl handed the marble lady the note. Kora cheerfully read, "Dear Hope, I've been thinking about you a lot these past days. How have you been holding up? I'm sure this has all been very frightening for you. I've asked many gifted professors here about your current difficulty. I managed to get most of them to be available this morning. If you would still like our help, we will be waiting for you in the Infirmary. With Elix, Ada."

Lynd had been treated like a six-headed, fire-breathing sea monster for as long as she could remember — a whole two days. All the questions had been boiling over, none more than *why?* When the time came to learn why, she was absolutely ready to know. Or so she assumed. "Where's the Infirmary," she exclaimed, crumbs and all.

"I'll take you after you eat your breakfast."

"Good." *Gulp.* "I'm done."

"I've been here for years, Ms. Hope," she said, waving her to the exit. "And I've never seen anyone not finish an Akademy breakfast."

Lynd shrugged. "Guess I'm just not that hungry."

The idea of getting her memory back filled her with excitement, and a bit of nervous tingling in her fingertips. It was true she would finally know where she lived and who her family was. But wasn't there also the possibility of not liking the answer to those questions? Still, there was much more reason to do it than not. Even if her parents were six-headed sea monsters, they'd probably be nicer to her than Astel and Faan.

Kora walked her through the courtyard, took a right, then straight on to another one of the Akademy's stained-glass domed buildings. This one had stripes around its door that Lynd hadn't seen anywhere else, first blue, then red, then blue again. As the place where medical help is found, it needed to stand out.

"This is the Infirmary," Kora said, holding the door open for her. "Right through here."

"Thanks at ya," Lynd said as she waved goodbye sincerely and smiled half-heartedly. As the girl stepped in, she saw seven people, including Ada, standing in a central room colorfully lit by the sunlight through the glass dome.

The Commandress sighed with relief. "Thank you for coming, Hope." She stepped closer, appearing slightly rehearsed. "I'd like to introduce you to my colleagues, who have agreed to help us this morning. From left to right, we have Professors Baayl, Colt, Arkenna, Talia, and Hosp. At the end there is General Case, or General XI as she is sometimes referred."

Hosp stepped forward in front of a silver chair at the center of the room. "I'm very sorry for what occurred in my class yesterday.

No one should ever be treated that way. The rest of these professors and General Case are here because they agree. Under my agreement with the Akademy, I'm not allowed to meddle in . . . well, *anywhere*, other than in the instruction of students. But I think the Commandress and I both feel that the safety of a student should take precedent."

"Safety?" said Lynd.

Ada said, "Hope, we have found a method of repairing even the most fractured memories. But . . ." The Commandress was not her usual, confident self. She seemed flimsy, even. "But as your mind puts the pieces back together, it will feel very much to you like it's happening again. There is a chance, as with anything, for some undesirable effects."

"What could happen?" asked Lynd, who still hadn't yet even walked fully into the room. Perhaps she wanted to preserve the option to flee, just in case.

"Ruin," said General Case in the corner, her shiny armored arms tightly folded. Her light hair was cut very short, leaving her furrowed expression quite prominent. "This technique cannot cut your mind off from your body, or else it won't work. So it will be like you're sleepwalking. You'll be acting out your memory." Case looked over Lynd like she was a known thief walking through a shop. "And if this is a traumatic memory, who knows what destruction you could cau—"

"I think," Ada interrupted. "We should focus on calm thoughts for calm results."

General Case mumbled something under her breath.

"We have a seat for you here," said Ada.

Lynd thought over her option to run the heck out of there one more time. As tempting as that was, it was probably best to know *where* to run first. And that started with sitting in a very uncomfortable-looking chair with very uncomfortable-looking people doing what was described as a very uncomfortable experience. Although, that water around the island did look calm. Was it absolutely true she couldn't just sail around that forever?

Ada sensed Lynd's hesitation and sat in the silver chair first. "You'll be here, and I'll be just behind, guiding you through the entire way." She forced a smile. "I promise."

Lynd went to the center of the room and asked, "Will it hurt?"

Case blurted, "Not you—"

"No pain," Ada said, standing up.

Lynd sat in the chair that looked like a goblet with one side cut out. She hoped this would all be worth it.

Ada adjusted the chair to Lynd's height better. "Someone get her pillows, please." She leaned to the girl. "Are you ready to get some answers?"

Lynd pushed up a smile. She was getting good at that. She sat down.

"When you're ready, Hope, I'll begin healing your memories, slowly." Ada stood behind Lynd with her hands resting on her shoulders. "We believe your condition will be helped by uncovering the memories and returning you to your family where the healing can continue. When we find out who your family is, we will begin the search."

"I wanna find 'em," said the girl. ". . . I'm ready."

The Commandress put her hands near Lynd's ears, just close enough that Lynd could feel the heat coming off them. "Breathe in. Close your eyes. Repeat after me — I am home."

The girl exhaled. ". . . I am home."

Ada held her breath for a while. "Something is out of place."

"Somethin's out of place," Lynd repeated.

"I hear someone," Ada said, crinkling her brow with concentration.

"I hear—" *Crack!* The top edge of Lynd's chair split slightly. "Someone."

Ada opened her eyes and whispered, "We found it." She returned to Lynd, "How old am I?"

"I'm seven. The night is . . . um . . . it's cold out tonight."

Ada said, "Why am I outside?"

"I hear Pa." Her breathing quickened. "He's screamin'. He's in trouble. He's . . ."

Ada put one palm down on Lynd's shaking body as if to hold her from leaping right out of her seat.

The pieces of the girl's memory came together so vividly that Lynd began to believe them, live inside them, as if they were the only here and now. She lost touch with the bright Infirmary room entirely and was outside on Boulie, staring at her father in the dark just a few Board planks ahead.

"Pa," Lynd said aloud. "Ya'kay?"

Everyone in the Infirmary could hear her, but Ada could actually see what Lynd was seeing.

The Board was as black as the surrounding sea. She could've easily stepped right off the wood. The only bearing was Stav's back, faint in the night but clearly turned away from her. That, and the garbled, yelling voices. Her father threw his hands up in the air. He appeared upset.

Ada whispered, "What am I hearing?"

"Who's there, Pa?" Lynd stepped closer to Stav. Someone else was in front of him. The girl heard a woman say, "I'll tell this whole town, Izz, I swear it!"

Pa replied, "Mrs. Shakk, don't ya dare threaten my family!"

"And ya brought new stuff back, didn't ya, Stav?" Mrs. Shakk said.

"I-I don't know what yer talkin' about," he said. "Keep yer voice down."

"Ya think I was born last moonset?" said Mrs. Shakk. "I can hear the quirk sound of that fiddle from my dumper, ya know? That kinda nice stuff don't just float by Boulie!"

Stav clenched his fists. "I'm warnin' ya."

"Yer warnin' me *what?*" she scoffed. "We're out here starvin'. If Baald and ya found a way outta Hop, we outta know about it!"

"Please quiet down, Mrs. Shakk." Pa then whispered something to her.

She shouted, "I *knew* it!"

"But keep it between us," he stressed. "It was just a test sail. We didn't get far. Please, Mrs. Shakk, if word gets out, it'll be a mad house. Lemme get my family out of this place, first. I'll come back for everyone else, I promise."

"Ya vile muck," said Mrs. Shakk. "Ya listen to me. Every door in Hop's gettin' a knock tonight. And I'm gonna tell 'em Stav Izz got a way off Hop. And he's keeping' it from ya." She turned around and started walking.

"I'm gettin' my family off first, I said!"

Mrs. Shakk kept right on walking.

"If the ship's too heavy with people, it can't sail fast enough to make it!"

She kept clunking those bucket boots from down Boulie.

"Yer gonna wreck their only way out!" Pa cried. Then a small spryt, a piece of red myracite, came up from the Under Board behind Stav. It seemed to dance around him like a bee hinting at which flower it was going to land on.

Stav was boiling. His fists clenched. The one chance to get his family off Hop was crumbing before him. Mrs. Shakk had to be stopped.

Ada whispered, "How am I feeling?"

"I'm scared." Lynd's heart was racing. Her chest was heaving. "What's happenin', Pa? Are we gonna be a'kay?"

In the Infirmary, the crack in the chair quickly spread down to back and onto the actual floor.

"Look out!" yelled Case.

Ada shushed her. "I'm barely holding on, here!"

"Pa?" Lynd cried into the Hop night. Tears glazed over her eyes.

"How dare she . . ." The red myracite was drawn to the Ruin myra building within Stav and slowly crept to him. He saw that crimson glow in the corner of his eye. He didn't know what it was. But maybe it was his chance to stop Mrs. Shakk. He could chuck that spryt right at her. Get her to turn back around. Give her a headache at worst. Was that so bad? If he did nothing, his family would be nothing, he imagined. Yelling was only going to alert more neighbors. It drove him mad. It tore his heart apart. He grasped the spyrt to throw and yelled, "Don't ya say a damned thing!"

Instead of throwing the spryt, its red, red power absorbed into his skin, adding its Ruin to his own — an extra jolt of destruction to an already lit flame. Then a red bolt of lightning lashed out from his hands toward Mrs. Shakk.

She began to choke immediately and fell to her knees, gripped her sizzling throat with both hands.

"Pa?" Lynd backed up, horrified. She bawled, shouting, "Pa!"

The Infirmary room began to shake. Hosp closed his eyes and concentrated. "I'm on standby."

The last thing out of Mrs. Shakk's mouth was a gasp. With

flashes bouncing off her teeth, like a mouth full of rubies, her neck burned with the touch of Ruin.

"Mrs. Shakk! F-forgive me . . ." Stav finally turned around; his face was covered in dark veins beyond recognition. "Lynd! I told ya to go back inside!"

Lynd took one look at her father and screamed in horror on Boulie, and her cries echoed out in the Infirmary. The crack in the floor grew as Talia and Arkenna used their myra to hold it together.

Lynd didn't recognize her father, and that frightened her more than anything imaginable. Her father, her protector, a monster striking down a neighbor in the night. It was a strain too great for her young heart to bear. And so, her heart shattered to pieces.

She couldn't understand a thing. There wasn't time to understand. Something had to be done. To protect her. Following her father's example, little Lynd let the Ruin become the way out. It welled up inside the cracks of her broken heart, a volcano ready to burst. "I don't want to see him like that!" She asked the red power building within her to destroy the memory of seeing her Pa that way. Boulie began to rumble. Board planks were ripping all around. "Take it away!" she screamed.

Ahhhhhh!

The Infirmary shook violently. Piece by piece, Lynd set about destroying the memory as she did that night when she was seven. "No! No! No!"

But the victim was the building. Equipment began to dematerialize all around — stone walls to dust. The professors struggled to move everyone out to safety. Ada stayed with Lynd. The Infirmary started to crumble like a flimsy toy in the grasp of a babe. Hosp remained, holding up the dome, and indeed the entire building up with his Elix power. But even he was straining under the girl's tremendous bursts of Ruin.

Ada yelled, "Open your eyes, Hope!"

She did, as artwork, the table, bottles, the floor, and everything kept snapping with red sparks.

Hosp strained. "I can't hold it up! Too much Ruin!"

"My name is Lynd," she said to Ada. And then her eyes shut again as she collapsed, as did the Infirmary upon them.

CHAPTER 19
A VERY THIN BRUSH

A ll Kabbage and Gai could feel was the sense of falling into some dark space below. But they had no idea how far or what awaited them at the bottom. Each was screaming at the top of their lungs. Following them down was a companion stream of freezing seawater. All at once, a rush of cold struck them as they splashed into a pool of water, diving deep underneath.

Everything was so dark that the boy didn't even know which way to swim to the surface and breathe, for Zeea's sake. He flailed his arms, reaching out to see if he could feel Kabbage swimming nearby. But there was only more frigid water flowing past his fingers. Frantic as he was, he would soon die if he didn't figure out where to swim. Gai calmed himself by listening to where the rushing water was loudest. He followed it and broke the surface, gasping.

"Kabbage!" He struggled to scream while trying to catch a breath. "Kabbage!" There was such a powerful stream of water dumping in that even if the gnome *were* above water, Gai would never hear him. A faint flicker of light struck the boy's eye from a ways away. It was electri gold in color. It was the gnome's com-comm. "Kabbage!" Gai paddled himself as quickly as he could to the tiny beacon. When he got closer, he could hear his friend panting and splashing. "Hold on!" The boy scooped him up over his shoulder so Kabbage could ride him like an Emilie. "All's a'kay."

Kabbage spat out a throat full of seawater. "W-where are we? I'm blind! Where am I?"

"Yer not blind," said Gai. "Just super dark in here."

They heard a woman shout a ways away. After a few scattered splashes, she yelled, "Get that light over here, will ya?"

"That's that captain!" Kabbage garbled in between spitting out seawater. "I don't like her."

Hungry pirates-thieves, they may have been. But Gai one-arm paddled in the direction of her voice, hoping she had found land or at least something that floated. Survival was top priority. They could yell at her for causing all this later.

"That's it, this way," Ballette said in the black, black air. "Follow my musical voice."

As Kabbage and Gai got closer, they started to see the captain in Kabbage's com-comm light. She was in Mac's arms, who was standing firmly on some actual ground. "Alright," she said, sliding off him to her own feet. "Now pick these two out. That's an order."

Mac bent down and pulled Gai out of the water by his arm, with Kabbage dangling off the boy's neck, saying, "I miss Emilie." Then the barely visible, dark-armored man dropped them both on some dark, slippery rocks.

"What the hell is this place?" said Ballette.

"The water's still pouring in," Mac mumbled. "We have to find higher ground, quickly."

"Pouring in from where?" she asked.

"I'll explain later," he said, splashing the rising water with a stomp. "Move!"

"Wait," Ballette yelled. "Shine that light up again."

Kabbage did as she demanded. He was kind of frightened of her.

"There," said the captain. "Ya see that?"

Gai pointed ahead. "Looks like shiny rocks. Maybe we can climb 'em out?"

Mac grabbed Kabbage, without asking, and put him on his tall, metal shoulders where the gnome's com-comm light shined in front of them like a miner's hat.

"This is rudeness!" Kabbage insisted.

Mac started walking to those reflective rocks. "Would you rather I just took the arm?"

Kabbage huffed, "That would be ruder," and hung his wrist up high so the light would illuminate further ahead.

Ballette followed, and Gai followed her. The unlikely group of turtle-thieves and turtle-friends had no choice but to work together or drown apart.

"It's a wall," said Mac. A bewildering, glossy rockface towered in front of them. "But these aren't normal rocks."

"They're see-through," said Gai, working his head around one. The rocks were jagged and threatening in all directions, appearing almost as if a running river had burst and froze mid-stream.

It certainly seemed cold enough to freeze water in there, but Mac went ahead and touched it, saying, "It's not cold. This is *glass*."

"By Zeea." The boy went to touch it, but Ballette quickly smacked his hand.

"Get some sense," she said. "*You* don't have armor on. And these edges look sharper than a blade."

"Glass?" said Kabbage in his new post as the light atop Mac. "What's it all doing here?" He shined his com-comm light across the material like he were an archeologist studying ancient wall paintings by candlelight. "Bend down, lamppost," he said to Mac. "Check what we're standing on."

Mac leaned down, inspecting the ground they were on. "It's clear, too. Could be a giant slab of glass."

Kabbage then shined the light as high up the pointy glass rocks as possible, revealing a ledge just a short climb up.

"Go on," said the captain. She nudged Mac in the chest plate. "Climb up and tell us what we're dealin' with. That's an order."

The rising, icy water was already up to Gai's bare ankles, reminding him of their inevitable doom if they didn't find a way to escape the cavern. "We should just all go, yeah?"

"Wait," Kabbage said, pointing down at the boy. "It's too sharp! You need some shoes, kid."

Mac looked at Gai's feet and groaned. He stood still for a moment. Perhaps he was deep in thought, but who could tell what was going on in that shadowy helmet? The man sighed. "Aren't you an Alkhemist?"

"Ya talkin' to me?" said Gai.

"Maybe not," Mac said. "But I saw you make a sword out of those chains earlier?"

"I did."

Mac scoffed, "Well? Don't tell me you can't make *shoes*."

"Ya think?" Gai splashed the water as he circled, looking for materials to use. "Out of what, though?"

"Use your imagination, Gaiel," Kabbage sang, almost mockingly. Then under his breath, he muttered, "Not that it helped us last time."

"Most Akademy recruits your age could make something out of just their myra and imagination," Mac teased. He then began to climb up the jagged glass rocks, Kabbage still atop his shoulders, saying, "Hm. Good luck."

Ballette started up right behind him. "Anyone else seeing their crappy lives flash before their eyes?"

"Hey," cried Kabbage, "We're not just going to leave him!"

"All's a'kay, Kabbage." The boy slapped his hands together and rubbed them. "I accept his challenge." Of course, he said that while thinking — *It's either that or die . . .*

He was still a bit gurgle-grr-y from his last myracle with the iron cuffs. Add the spinning near-death experience and the exhausting swim with Kabbage on his back, and the boy was undoubtedly feeling deflated. "A'kay, what do boots look like?" He scanned his memories, trying to think if he ever saw Unc wear some, or maybe even Pa. Not many good ones in Hop. Mrs. Shakk had ones made of buckets. But he couldn't get a good enough image in his mind. He chose the more recent memory of Mac aboard the ship and his dark armored boots.

"I can do this." Gai held the image of Mac's footwear in his head. His stomach buzzed a familiar buzz. His hands glowed a familiar glow. The water level continued to rise. "I can do this."

"He's doin' it," yelled Kabbage aboard Mac, now high up the glass.

The boy felt his myra bend to the image in his mind, following it like a weaver following a pattern. In and out, around and through, the Elix myra wove into his desired shape. The surrounding water lit up a lovely blue. And the scuffed boots he had imagined took on a tangible form.

Mac could see the blue light of Elix reflecting on the glass as he climbed. All he said was, "Hm." He and Kabbage rounded the ledge at the top of the glass rocks.

"I did it," said Gai, stepping into them. Unfortunately, he had imagined Mac's boots a bit too well; they were fit for a full-grown man. Still, he proudly slipped into them with plenty of wiggle room. Not bad for the first time making something out of just myra. *Gurgle GRR!* The boy keeled over in extreme hunger pains.

Mac helped Ballette up over the sharp edge. He looked down in the darkness and shouted, "Learn to deal with the hunger. I've seen plenty younger than you do it!" He then whispered to Kabbage, "Hold that light so he can see."

The boy struggled through the deep ache of hunger to start climbing up in boots that were way too big for him. The water chased him up as he slowly scaled the glass structure. His stomach felt pressed, but his heart was full. For some reason, he wanted to prove he could do this more than any challenge before. He'd just recently forgiven himself for not being able to fix little Lynd, and this was like a test against his sogg-hood. He pushed through, creeping up the jagged glass, some might say running off his myra alone.

Kabbage began cheering as Gai soundly rounded the glass cliff. The boy wobbled to his feet with an aching belly and a slight smirk. He'd done the impossible. At least what seemed like the impossible just a few moments before. He created boots, rather stylish ones at that, out of nothing but myra. He even pushed through the most gnawing stomach pains he'd ever felt.

Mac stood stoically, looking over the victorious but altogether drained young man. "A short sail from the Akademy, there is a massive tree called the Everbloom." He reached into his belt a pulled out what looked like a tiny grain. "I don't recommend eating the Sap of this tree, but Heartbrand Legionnaires have used its tiny fruits like these for generations. Here, it'll feel like you've eaten a few banquets." Mac held out the tiny seed-like morsel.

The boy hardly believed such a small speck would make him feel full at all. But being as hungry as he was, he'd gladly take anything. He swallowed it immediately. His stomach gurgled and groaned, then felt warm and happy. It began to expand and expand, indeed like he'd eaten too much. But even the tight, slightly bloated feeling was better than the hunger. "Thanks at ya!"

"Just so you know," said Mac. "Recruits are almost never able to do what you did."

"I'm a little hungry, too." Kabbage dropped his open palm by the opening in Mac's helmet.

The man promptly slapped it away. "That was my last one."

"So ya lied about the recruits?" said Gai. "They can't all do that right away? That was really hard!"

"It was a lie. But so was the one you'd already told yourself. Now you know you're capable of change," said Mac. "We create our own value in this life. Don't forget that."

"By Zeea," said Gai. "You'd make a good teacher. Why'd ya help me?"

Mac stood stoically for a moment. ". . . You remind me of some-one. Someone I miss terribly."

"Sorry at ya . . ."

Ballette unsnapped the rifle off her back, shook it, and groaned. "Bet the powder's all soaked to crap, now."

"Do we even need that with these myracle guys around?" Kabbage said with his little yellow light.

Ballette blew a raspberry. "Hard to tell when we have no idea where we are! Mac! Where are we? That's an order."

Gai had just made it over the lip of the ledge before the rising water did. It began lapping again at everyone's heels. There was no going back the way they came.

"We need to keep moving." Mac began surveying options. Behind them was another massive glass wall. As far as he could tell with Kabbage's little light, there was no ledge to climb up to, just more glass.

Gai walked over to the wall. "There's a hole in this one. Can we all squeeze through?"

Mac stepped to him, inspecting the crack in the glass. It was less a cave and more like a fissure in the glass rocks. It just appeared to lead further into the darkness, but with the water still pouring in fast, the man insisted they follow it.

"Easy for you to say," said Kabbage. "You've got all that armor. It looks like a paper shredder in there!"

"Duck down," said Mac, stepping through the narrow passage in the glass.

Gai eagerly went in next, with Ballette right behind. As they all shimmied carefully along the tight walls, the water chased closely behind. Despite the danger, or maybe because of it, the boy couldn't resist but to pick Mac's brain more. Finally, someone to talk to about blue fixin' tricks. "'Ey, what's an Alkhemist?"

Mac didn't say anything at first. He didn't really want to. But darn if there wasn't something familiar about the boy. "There are . . . *levels* to Elix myracles," said Mac. "First level is anything creative, putting words or musical notes together well. We call these *Artes*. Most people stop there. The second level is called *Alkhemy* — bringing together two objects and willing them into something completely new. Most students at the Akadmey stop there. Third level myracles are done by very special people called *Fiats*. Fiats are able to infuse their myra with their imagination to create something entirely new to the world from scratch. Using myra in this way is called *Maniphestation*."

"Did ya hear that, Kabbage? I'm a very special people."

Kabbage replied dryly, "Yeah, yeah. It all sounds wonderful, kid."

Gai couldn't help but ask, "Is there a fourth level?"

Mac stopped in his wet tracks. He looked back at the boy. "You're inside one."

All at once, everyone, including Kabbage atop Mac's shoulders, said, "What?"

As plainly as anything, Mac said, "You all saw we entered a painting, didn't you? It's a *Mythik* myracle — a level beyond anyone alive today."

"The paintin'?" said Ballette. "I was too busy screamin'."

"Yes," he replied flatly, continuing to shuffle through the crevice as the water kept rising. "If we hadn't, we'd be at the bottom of the sea. Which I suppose is where the painting is, now. Explains all this water rushing in."

"Wait a minute. Wait a minute," Ballette chimed, following. "You're tellin' me my little ransom is a magic picture?"

"They're called *Pocket Realms*," said Mac. "But yes."

A Pocket Realm? Fiats? Gai didn't know what to think or

say. "There's so much I never knew was possible," he breathed. He didn't fit the boots already. But suddenly, they felt even bigger.

Kabbage said, "How can someone paint a *place* . . . and make it real?"

"With a very thin brush," Mac said. "The tunnel's widening up here."

"Just hold on!" Ballette caught up to him once they had more room in the glass crack. She slapped his shoulder. "You're serious? We're in the paintin'?"

"Would you let it go?" said Mac. "You're the one who wanted to rob your family's archeological site for Arkon relics. Didn't you know what you were stealing?"

". . . Like an *actual* paintin'?" she replied. "I was just tryin' to stick it to my snooty sister, Astel, is all. She's headin' up that dig."

Mac continued walking straight ahead into the glass tunnel. "Someone from the Old World must've made it." He turned back to Gai. "The Arkons were people who could wield fourth level myracles, as you described it. People were a lot more powerful back then. Be on your guard. Pocket Realms have their own rules. No telling what the creator created it for."

Slowly, they made their way through the reflective glass tunnel. Gai wobbled in his new much-too-big-for-him boots, accidentally chipping a few glass shards on the floor. The group couldn't really grab the tunnel sides to support themselves, fearing a diced-up hand.

"What if these 'Old' people didn't paint a way out?" Kabbage muttered.

Gai sneakily adjusted his stride so he'd end up walking side-by-side with Mac. "Where'd ya learn all this?"

"You'll have to be more specific," he answered, monotoned.

"Makin' boots," said the boy, wide-eyed. "Fiats? Arkons? Was it at the Akademy?"

Mac led the pack further into the tunnel. ". . . No."

"Hold that," said Ballette. "Your contract said you were an Ex-Heartbrand. Did I pay for a Heartbrand for nothin'?"

"You haven't paid me at all."

"Ya were a Heartbrand?" The boy stopped. He rested his boot on a sharp chunk of glass, and it snapped and rolled past Ballette.

"Heartbrand?" Kabbage said. "You were the ones that attacked my city!" He wiggled on Mac's shoulders. "I told you we shouldn't trust them!"

"I think *ex* means he's not one anymore, yeah?" the boy said.

Mac paused. "I don't do myracles anymore." He gestured to Kabbage. "Keep that light up, little man, will you?"

"I don't like them, again, Gaiel," Kabbage grumbled.

"We don't like you, either," Ballette snapped with the tone of a schoolyard comeback.

Mac stopped ahead.

"What is it?" said the captain.

"The end." Mac pounded his boot into the glass. A few shattered chunks loosened. Mac then kicked the broken glass ahead. It took many anxious breaths before they heard it hit the ground far, far below. *Bink.*

"I was hoping to see sunshine at the end of the tunnel," huffed Kabbage. He dipped his hand down so they would be able to tell if the glass theme continued into this new area. They were at the end of the glass tunnel but high up on a glass cliff, facing another ultra-black space full of who-knew-what below. "It took a while to hear that glass hit the ground," he said. "We've got a long climb down."

"Find a way fast," said Ballette. "Water's comin' up to wash us off."

The seawater had indeed caught up to them quickly, already starting to drip off the cliff.

Mac listened as the water poured over the edge. "We can't climb down in a waterfall!"

Gai walked back to the crevice opening they just came out of, where the water was beginning to gush through. He felt the edge of the opening. "Just another crack to fix," he whispered. As he touched the glass rocks, a beautiful ray of Elix emerged, searing into them. The rocks illuminated and began to grow, the ends of the fissure stretching out at each other like long lost friends.

"Some say there's no way to tell how far one's myra can take them," Mac said softly, as if journaling what he observed. "But I found all that makes the difference is imagination and the will to use it."

With a final flash of brilliant blue, the glass was sealed. The water was stuck behind it. The boy turned around to his silent audience. "We can climb down now." He smiled.

"Good work," the captain said. "I'm not payin' ya just so we're clear."

Mac glanced at him through his helmet slits. "Those boots are fitting a little better, hm?"

CHAPTER 20

WHERE IT DOESN'T STAND

A stel Osstett's illustrious parents yanked her out of the Myracles Akademy, citing health hazards in their daughter's room. Faan Mink packed her things as well to take a "mental health break." Both stayed at the In Inn for the time being. Before the incident in the Infirmary, no one had ever heard of Lynd Izz, not even Lynd Izz. But now, they all most certainly had. If anyone at the Akademy thought Ruin just *might* be something they could tolerate on campus, they didn't think that anymore. The Infirmary's marble was still crumbing onto the surrounding walkways. It wasn't safe to even approach, let alone visit if one had a stomach ache.

Commandress Ada wrestled with calls to throw Lynd face-first onto the next ship off the island and be done with her. Threats came in, saying if Ada didn't do *something* about her, someone would be forced to do so. The Commadress, for her part, was stunned that both she and Hosp weren't able to contain Lynd's power. It would take a few weeks and several skilled Elix myracle workers to restore the Infirmary. However, for all their efforts, for all the destruction, the girl did have her memory back. They had a way to find her family, at least.

While all the professors discussed the ramifications, General Bend took to action. He ordered the Heartbrand Legion under his authority, the mighty XIIIth, to descend on Akademy grounds for added student protection. This was highly unusual, both that a general would make a move on their own, and to have more than a handful of Heartbrands in Carpè, at most. But as one could imagine, between the failed Electri negotiations and this Ruin incident within the Akademy walls, the Commandress' standing had fallen quite a bit with the people of Carpè. And General Bend could smell blood in the water.

Lynd watched the shadows of the well-armored Heartbrands walking by under her dorm room door all evening. Even if she hadn't recovered her memory, it was quite clear she certainly didn't belong anywhere near the Akademy. "Mape, Stav, Gaiel," she said to herself in the empty room, worried their faces would disappear again if she didn't repeat their names over and over.

Part of her was upset at herself for forgetting them in the first place. How could she destroy her own memories? What did that mean? She thought about how worried Ma must be. And Gai was probably on some makeshift boat he scrapped together out of loose boards trying to find her, for all she knew. The shadows kept passing. It had to be getting close to morning. It was impossible not to feel watched, threatened.

"This place is a prison," she whispered. ". . . And they can't keep me."

Knock. Knock. Knock.

"Ah, ah," said Professor Talia stepping into the room with a pitcher of water.

Talia seemed to be younger than Ada. She was one of the more relaxed people Lynd had encountered at the Akademy. Even her clothing was more simple and informal than the others, maybe even a little stained. Still, she looked at the girl with the same mix of pity and caution as everyone else.

"I figured you might still be awake." The professor sat on Faan's striped bed. "But you can rest easy, now. The Commandress and the others won't take long to find your family."

Lynd forced a smile. "A'kay." She then sat up abruptly, which made the professor flinch in a wave of fear. The girl said, "Do you remember why you came in here?"

"I do," said Talia, slightly unnerved by the strange question. "I came in to see if—"

"Well, now ya don't," Lynd said, snapping her fingers. *Tik!*

A flash of red sparked near Talia's temples. She blinked a few times and laid down on the bed, entirely dazed.

Lynd jumped out of bed and peeked carefully out the door. A Heartbrand saw the girl and — *Tik!* — she snapped her fingers again, turning him into a wandering dope who had no idea why he was there. She ran down the halls of the dormitory and out to the nighttime courtyard. Normally, it would be quiet. But Heartbrands were patrolling by the handful all around. "I can't Ruin all their memories," she whispered. "Or can I?"

Thankfully, the Heartbrands were rather easy to spot. Their majestic suits of armor were so well-polished and reflective that they practically had their own glow about them. Lynd made her way, using the hemmed shrubs and bushes of the courtyard as cover. She'd prefer not to rip apart away anyone's memory if she didn't have to. Maybe she could hide in one of those Pocket Realm paintings she saw on the way in? It wasn't as if any guard could stop her from jumping into one. As she passed the Hall of the Arkons, she heard a woman shout, "How dare you! I am *still* the Commandress of these Legions!"

"That's Ada," Lynd whispered, stopping to take a peek inside from the courtyard shrubs. Within the flame-lit space, amongst the giant Arkon statues, was indeed the Commandress. There stood one of the few people Lynd ever met, in Hop or anywhere, that saw her as a person first. In front of the Commandress stood General Bend, who only saw the color red when he looked at the girl.

General Bend roared from within, "You lost your right to that title the moment you let Ruin through that gate!"

Pst! Someone made a noise from the rooftop of the Hall.

Up against the night sky, Lynd saw Kal up there waving his arms around. He was in his hiding space with the lovely view, coaxing her to join him again.

Lynd started to move away from the Hall; she wanted to go home, back to Hop. She looked back up at the only friend she'd ever made besides her brother.

"You and that girl will be the end of us!" General Bend continued, "Are you so determined to see our sacred island burn?"

"We're on the verge of finding her family, XIII," said Ada. "End this madness. Stand down!"

"Ada's in trouble," said Lynd. "Because of me . . . Can she really find my family?" The girl cautiously waited for the right moment to sneak inside the Hall, behind the back of General Bend as he continued to deride Ada. She slid behind the first statue as Kal showed her and climbed up to the upper molding. Kal was watching the events unfold through the window, where Lynd shimmied to him.

He embraced the girl immediately and whispered, "Are you alright? I heard what happened. The whole city is talking."

Lynd just nodded affirmatively.

Kal glanced back down in disbelief at what was occurring in the Hall below. He seemed to be wholly engrossed and concerned.

"After what we've faced together," shouted Bend, pacing. "We agreed, we struggled, we funded, we *breathe* to stop that threat our ancestors faced a millennia ago! And you invited it right into our sanctuary!"

"I'll not tell you again! Stand down!"

"This is not the first time your leadership has been questioned. Letting that blue man teach our students. Fumbling negotiations with Electri, who unwittingly sit on the greatest cache of Ruin on the planet, *and* bring war to us as we speak!"

"Do not dare to lecture me," said Ada. "Professor Hosp's research is critical to understanding how Elix myra changes to Ruin, and vice versa. Do not forget what we went through less than a decade ago with our old king's brother. We will prove that this disease starts with a broken heart, and if that's true, the girl deserves our compassion. All people exhibiting Ruin do."

"A broken heart?" Bend scoffed. "That's ridiculous. Hearts break all the time, and we haven't seen breakouts of Ruin all over."

"We're not talking about everyday disappointment or sadness. It's about deep wounds that fester — when the heart breaks and the cracks never fill. It's about division. And then their myra, their inner light, changes color. Its nature changes. Ruin is a slow poison; that's why it's been hard to find the cause. And knowing this, what would you have had me do with the girl? Would it have been safer to leave her on the streets without a name? Without a family? Without a home? A *child*, Bend!"

"Then you admit you brought a beast into our city walls only to study it? Have you given one thought as to how easily this *disease*, as you call it, spreads? Have you considered the safety of our students, of our people, of us who serve under you?" Bend pointed up at the statues. "The Arkons are an example of what happens when Ruin takes root. They were powerful beyond imagination, and Ruin *still* took them down. This city put its faith in you after King Tyr fell, and you are spitting in our face!"

"Command is given by the Legionnaires," said Ada. "And I am still their choice. Whether you agree with me or not, you have no right to lead the Heartbrands into Carpè without my consent. Remove them. That is an order!"

"Command is given by the Heartbrands, isn't it?" The general closed his eyes and raised his hand. After a beat, he shut his fist, and blue waves rippled throughout the Hall. "Then we shall bring it to a vote."

One by one, thirteen Heartbrands appeared out of thin air. Kal gasped and quickly covered his mouth. Lynd couldn't believe her eyes. Were they there the entire time? What sort of powers did the general of the XIIIth Legion possess?

"XIII!" yelled Ada, stepping to him. "Elix Mirage. Against your Commandress? In the Hall of the Arkons?"

"We charge you with conspiracy and weakness in the face of duty," the general said calmly. "Assembled here are the highest-ranking Heartbrands from each Legion, some against the will of their generals. But they've all heard rumors; they want to understand your motives." He chuckled. "And I think they have their answer."

The soldiers appeared uncomfortable, like they weren't sure who to believe.

The Commandress pushed Bend aside and addressed them directly. "Protectors of Carpè," she said to them. "Bear your weapons. Show me your heartbrands."

Each of the thirteen troops held out their hands as a shimmering blade emerged from out of nowhere, one after the next. These weapons appeared to be made of swirling blue light. Each one was shaped differently, as individual as the person holding it.

"A healthy blue," said Ada. "We cannot be blind to the forces that seek to divide us. *That* is where Ruin hides, not in a child. It starts with us. And it will live in us if we let it! The choice over our myra is ours alone. But the general's words will lead to the destruction of one another. So I ask you, what color will your myra be at the end of this day? Blue or red? Would you tear apart our great order? Or stand tall and stand now for what the Heartbrands truly represent?"

The Heartbrands cheered her, raising their brilliant heartbrands, "Commandress! Commandress!"

"You are dismissed," she said to them. "You will all be restationed at your previous posts out of Carpè. Await further orders at the docks." The thirteen armored men and women let their weapons disappear and quietly stepped in a straight line out of the Hall of the Arkons.

"What were those things they were holdin'?" Lynd whispered.

"Those were their heartbrands," Kal said quietly. "A powerful weapon made of myra. It's where the soldiers get their name."

Ada glared at the general. "Any more Mirages you'd like to spring on me? Any more coups before bedtime?"

Bend just stared back at her, seething. Something about her sickened him so. He could barely stand her presence, let alone her Command.

"I didn't think so," said still-Commandress Ada. She then casually walked over to one of the Arkon statues, a young man with wavy hair. She ran her hands along the base and found a compartment, then took out what appeared to be a golden box no bigger than a fist. "I have a task for you."

Bend didn't answer. He immediately recognized the box the Commandress had just pulled out. Just one of the many wonders of Arkonic technology found at the Osstett Archaeological Site. It was a small Pocket Realm, good for use as a prison cell. "In light of all that's happened . . . You can't seriously be considering freeing *him*?"

"Lynd Izz isn't on any citizen records we could find." Ada walked to him with grace and confidence. "There's no record of even just her family name. Professor Baayl sent queries, but there's not a whisper of that *Hop* location, either." She handed him the intricate gold box. "Not even General Case's Farsight was able to locate them. If you want the girl out of Carpè so badly, then we have only one more option."

"What is this? Punishment?" Bend held the box in disgust. "Have you forgotten it was *me* who arrested the Everbloom Speaker?"

Ada said, "Sail your Legion to the Everbloom with the girl early tomorrow. You are to negotiate the release of their Speaker for their help in finding her family."

Bend clenched it in his fist like he was ready to crush it.

"The Bloomers are eager to get him back," said Ada. "They won't refuse. And if they do . . . maybe there's some *other* leverage only you can bring to bear."

"Electri ships are on their way . . ." General Bend's hand shook. He wondered if he could take on Ada directly, right then and there? Did he have the power, or the guts? He'd fought side-by-side with her during the war that brought her to power; he knew well what kind of abilities she possessed. "But you'd like me to take the XIIIth Legion on a cruise to a tree instead of protecting the city?"

"The Legions were posted exactly where they were supposed to be," said the Commandress. "I'm well aware of your history with the Everbloom, XIII. I also haven't missed how many letters you've sent there over the years. We both miss her . . ."

Bend's bravado melted. He seemed shocked she knew about his letters. He had been so careful.

"Don't worry," she said. "Unlike some of my *generals*, I don't care what relationships you deem worthy of keeping."

Near the ceiling, Kal seemed confused. "Who would General Bend be communicating with at the Everbloom?" He adjusted his bracelet around his right wrist, as if it were itching him.

Lynd whispered, "What's the Everbloom?"

"The biggest and oldest lifeform on Esa," Kal said quietly. "That's *bold*. We don't usually mess with them. The Commandress is fighting really hard to find your family."

The general was furious. "I stood right here and told you the kind of risk she was. I don't care what you *think* you can learn from Ruin. You placed a bet, where we were all at risk, without our consent! You do not deserve to lead us."

Ada stepped right up to him. "Asking me to abandon this girl goes against everything this place stands for."

". . . Well, thanks to her, the place doesn't stand anymore, does it? Thank you for your leadership, Commandress. Oh, but no worries.

What does still stand will be taken care of by Electri while I take a jaunt to the Everbloom." He turned his back on her and stormed out.

"Sounds like you're going on a trip," Kal said.

Lynd hugged Kal. She held him so tightly, so he wrapped his arms around her, too. She said, "Can't I just leave? We can. Come with me."

He waited for a few long inhales before saying, "If your family isn't in any records, where would you ask someone to sail you to?"

"I dunno," she sniffled, holding back her tears. "Why wouldn't they know where Hop is? It's gotta be real. I'm not makin' it up."

"They say the people that live in the Everbloom are connected to Esa in a way most of us aren't. They're probably the best chance to find them. Don't worry about General Bend; I'll stow away on their ship and make sure nothing happens to you."

"Ya remind me of my brother," she said, curled in his arms.

"You got your memory back, right? Tell me about him."

CHAPTER 21

A LIVING LEGEND

G ai, Kabbage, Captain Ballette, and Mac carefully made their way down the tall glass cliff. Thanks to the boy, they didn't have to do it with buckets of seawater bashing them on their heads. But before they were even half way down, the entire cliff started to rumble.

"It's comin' down!" roared Ballette.

All raced down, fearing an imminent collapse of glass. Mac was the last to make it to the bottom, but as soon as he did — *Bssh!* The crevice Gai had sealed up burst back open under tremendous pressure. The tumbling water crashed to the ground beside them, forming a little lake.

"*Kaa-Bah!* Thanks for the shower," Kabbage said, shaking his hair dry.

The boy looked up at the cascading falls in shock. "I thought I fixed it, no?"

Mac stared down at him through his helmet slits. "Heartbrands learn that time is a promise." His voice was stern but encouraging, almost paternal. "A promise that no fix is permanent." He then turned and stepped into the new darkness they'd found themselves in.

Gai suddenly missed his father deeply. Something about the dark armored Ex-Heartbrand reminded him of Pa. Maybe it was the way they both spoke as if longing for something — a certain downward glance. Pa would do that, too. Every morning, for the first three or so hours of the day, he'd have his eyes cast on the creaking floor. He was imaging ways to get off Hop, or at least that's what he told his curious family. Gai remembered waiting for him every morning to look up so the day could officially begin. "Why fix anythin', then?" the boy called out to Mac.

Mac stopped. "The hope is . . . that no break is permanent either." He pointed ahead and said to Kabbage, "Shine that light up this way," and continued into the shadows.

Kabbage walked ahead, holding his little arm up to light everyone's path. "Anyone else want to know why the artist painted all this glass? Look at this. There's even glass *grass* on the ground. And glass bushes up ahead. If a glass goblin pops out, I'm going to mess up your shoulders."

"Glass or not," said Ballette, mesmerized by all the splashing. "This place is sinkin' to the depths of the Uncharted Sea! How do we get out?"

"Find the painter," Mac said casually. "Stay close. We're dealing with power unlike anything you could dream."

Gai and Ballette followed the only light source closely behind. They all wandered through the landscape until a thick glass forest emerged to block their passage. The plants and trees that jetted out at them had otherworldly shapes, indeed. They were much larger and lusher than any in the group had ever seen. Some appeared to be oversized mushrooms with strange, pointed tips as tall as two Hopper houses. One kind had serrated leaves fanning out as wide as a person. All were clear as a tear and seemingly frozen in a breeze. There was an eerie lifelessness amidst all the lifelike scenery. Everything appeared as if it should be moving, but nothing was.

The captain said, "Any bright ideas, Heartbrand?"

"*Ex*-Heartbrand," Mac muttered, studying the flora as they walked alongside, looking for a path through. "These all look like extinct plant life." He grazed his fingers carefully on some of the exotic leaves. "Welcome to the Old World." As he walked, he managed to find a large enough opening in a group of bulky vines. He slipped between them. Everyone else followed behind into the forest.

"Just who are these Old World people, again?" said Kabbage.

"You're joking." Mac stopped. "The time before the Great Reset?"

Kabbage looked up at Gai. Both shrugged.

"Don't they teach history in Electri?" Mac said, weaving through the flora. "What do they tell you the myracite is, then?"

Kabbage puffed out his chest. "It's the remains of a comet that struck Esa approximately one thousand years ago. Material: unknown. Uses: infinite."

Mac chuckled.

"What?" said Kabbage. "What's so funny?"

"No wonder you gnomes don't know how to use it," said Mac. "Though using its properties to spin generators is no doubt a clever use for it. I'll give you all that."

"Is that so?" Kabbage held up his wrist, their only light in the darkness. "I don't see anyone from Carpè wearing a com-comm."

"So what *is* myracite?" Gai asked hungrily.

"We didn't *need* com-comms in Carpè." Mac stepped and felt a crunch under his boot. He bent down to pick it up. "Shine that light here."

Ballette peeked over a large leaf. "What is it? I can't see!"

Mac moved his foot to reveal a piece of broken glass. But this one was no woodland artifact. It was in the shape of a hand.

It was the first sign of another person. Glass or not, it was unsettling. And it was just as lifelike as the plants, complete with fingerprints. Kabbage got sick to his stomach immediately. Ballette turned away. Mac picked it up, noticing a ring on the finger.

"It's just part of the painting, right?" said Kabbage. "*Right?*"

"Relax," Ballette said, loading her musket. "Anythin' pops out here I'll—Whoa!" *Bang!* She fired the gun at some unknown target. "Got 'em! Bring the light over this way!"

Mac and Gai made their way to her around some giant trunks. Kabbage followed. "What she'd do that for?"

"By Zeea, she shot the rest of the glass guy!"

Kabbage's light revealed shards of broken glass all about.

"I swear it was movin'," she said, frantically loading her gun again as quickly as she could, but her extra powder was too wet.

As the rest examined the shattered pieces, more questions arose. There were geometric details on the clothes, and the style was so foreign it might as well have been from another planet. The glass person's knees were bent like they were running.

"Oh, yuck," said Kabbage. "Here's the face."

The person's mouth was open as if gasping for air. Their eyes were dripping with fear.

Everyone's stomachs felt uneasy.

"Look," said Mac. "They were holding something in this hand." He picked it up. It was a thin sheet of glass that looked like a note the man was carrying. The letters were a strange mix of swirls and notches. But it was barely visible. "I've seen these letters before. In old Arkon texts." He held it over Kabbage's com-comm light and scrutinized the language. "It's signed, *MIT HALLO.*"

"Is it the way out?" said Ballette.

Gai asked, "What's *Mit Hallo*, mean?"

"*My love*," answered Mac, still examining every line. "Let's see. 'I know you' . . . 'I know.'" He paused. "These letters here . . . we pronounce them exactly the same to this day."

Captain Ballette stomped her foot. "On with it if you want to keep your pay!"

He translated it aloud as best he could. "It says, 'I know the *Voids* run like a chill over the spine of the world. I know you think the only way to save us is the Last Myracle. I also know you plan to trick me into being a part of it. Let me be clear; I will not lend my myra to your dangerous gambit. Ruin cannot answer Ruin. I will be where no one can find me. A place of my creation where there are no lies, and nothing is hidden. Do not look for me. You would become uncomfortable very quickly there, my love."

"Spooky," said Kabbage. "I'm definitely ready to go home, now."

"Ya think this is real?" said Gai.

Mac grew uncharacteristically unnerved. No one could see his expression, but his posture kept shifting.

"What's it mean?" said the captain.

"They told you myracite came from a comet?" The Ex-Heartbrand looked at Kabbage. "It did. But nothing natural. That red comet was the Arkon's Last Myracle. The ultimate destruction."

Gai said, "Myracite is from the Last Myracle?"

"One thousand years ago," Mac said, deep in his dark helmet. "The mighty Arkons clashed with an impossible foe to defeat.

Their only option was to either let the world be destroyed forever, or . . ."

"Or what?" Ballette chirped.

Mac caught a chill. "The Last Myracle — a collection of so much Ruin myra that it filled the sky and came crashing down to Esa. The Great Reset."

"What was the point of *that*?" said Kabbage. "Wiped out by their own hands rather than the enemy?"

Mac seemed caught between fascination and concern, incessantly looking over the glass note. "You don't understand the foe they were fighting. They were simply called 'Voids' in the Arkon texts. Their bodies were said to collapse under the weight of their own Ruin. Ravenous monsters, and they can't be killed. They destroy everything and just absorb more Ruin into themselves without end."

"Gai!" Kabbage blurted. "Doesn't that sound like—"

Gai covered his mouth. "Tell us more, Mac."

"Voids are the end. Period. Nothing remains in their wake. They would have turned our planet into less than dust. So, hard as it was, the Arkons sacrificed themselves so that the planet could remain, and so maybe life could continue someday."

Gai cautiously said, "How would someone become a—"

Ballette jumped in. "Mac, this is a beautiful story. But can we get on with findin' this painter, already? I'd like to go home!"

"Yeah, me, too." Kabbage got in the middle between Gai and Mac. "Honestly, kid. I'm getting sick of all this — *huff* — myracle stuff. If I'd known all this would happen . . . I mean I can't even *go* back home . . . I just wish . . ."

"What?" said Gai.

"Nothing," he replied. "Just tell me everything's going to be fine."

Mac wouldn't stop staring at the note. "If this painting was made right before the Last Myracle . . . 'A place of my creation where there are no lies, and nothing is hidden.'" Mac looked around at the glass world and this glass person with the note. "Did it just get quiet?"

"The water," said Gai. "I don't hear it splashin' down anymore. Maybe we not sinkin' anymore?"

"Or we're waterlogged," Ballette quipped.

The group doubled back the way they came, holding the small com-comm light to see just a stone's throw ahead at a time. When they got back to the glass cliff, they also saw the falling seawater. But it now appeared frozen solid. Mac flicked it. "The water turned to glass." Chills ran over everyone's body. He quoted the note again, "'No lies, and nothing is hidden . . . You would become uncomfortable very quickly there.'"

Gai tapped Mac's armor. "Ya think the painter of this place wrote that note?"

"I do," he said. "Whoever made this place didn't trust the people around them. I think it may be a trap to see through them."

"Trap? Oh, this is perfect," said Kabbage marching back and forth nervously. "Just *perfect!*"

Gai tried to reach out to him. "Kabbage, I—"

"No!" Kabbage moved away. "I just — *ugh*! None of this is my fault!"

"Sorry at—"

"Stop!" Kabbage shouted, lifting his hand to the boy. But when he did, everyone couldn't help but notice four of his fingers were clear as glass. "W-what?"

"By Zeea!"

"Hold," roared Mac, holding up the note. "Everyone hold. The artist who made this place was running from people with Ruin. This place was meant to reveal it. Gnome, you best calm your heart. Your destructive thoughts are generating Ruin within you!"

"But I can't—" Kabbage touched his glass hand. "How can I calm down? I can't not be aware of *this!*"

"All's a'kay," said Gai, again trying to comfort him.

"Don't give me that stupid alls a'kay, thing, *a'kay!*" Kabbage started to sob and sat on the ground. The glass transformation spread down his arm. "I wish I never met you!"

"That's right," said Ballette. "I wish I never met him, either!"

Gai was speechless.

"You and that silly turtle," she continued. "This is all your fault! And now we're all gonna die here!"

The boy watched with horror as his friend began to cry and beg for help. He grabbed the gnome's elbow. "How can I fix this? How can I fix this?" He tried to imagine a way to his Elix abilities might help.

Mac grabbed the boy and pulled him up. "It's no use. You can't 'fix' someone else's myra. They're the ones causing it . . ."

Ballette screamed. "Look! Look! My damn leg is turning see-through! I-I'm becoming glass, too!" The captain dropped to the ground, holding her leg and rolling back and forth. She kept screaming, frightened for her life. Her body turned more and more to glass every second, creeping up her hips, then her stomach.

The same happened to the gnome. Both panicked more and more as the glass spread.

Gai gripped Mac's helmet with both hands and roared, "Yer supposed to know everythin'! What do we do?"

Then the silence came again. The Ex-Heartbrand stood tall and motionless. He glanced over at Ballette. "It's over."

Ballette lay still on the ground, her face transparent and frozen in the moment of horror. There was a red heat simmering in her chest, clearly visible. Kabbage laid as a glass statue, ruby red glow within him as well.

Mac bent down to Ballette. "They were not bad people," he said. "Everyone has small amounts of Ruin occur every day. If they're lucky, they also have some creative thoughts to balance it out." He moved to Kabbage and took off his com-comm. "But the rules are different here. This place reacts with even the slightest amount of Ruin."

"W-what now?" Gai couldn't stop staring at his poor friend's frightened face. "Kabbage?" He started to bawl.

Mac quickly said, "We need to keep moving."

"I'm not leavin' them!" Gai kept looking into Kabbage's translucent eyes. "How could I," said the boy. "How could I lose another friend?"

"We don't have time." Mac's voice was becoming strained. He pointed back to the path through the woods. "The person with the note was running through the forest. There must be someone they were running to."

The boy got to his feet, staring down at his friend, lifeless as glass. "Is there any way to fix this?"

". . . The only thing I'm aware of that can't change is a Void. Come, the sooner we find a way out, the sooner you can talk to the Akademy about these two. Or, if we're lucky, you can talk to the painter themselves." Mac started walking back to the forest in the direction that glass person was running.

"Wait," said Gai.

Mac clenched his armored fist to a metallic squeak. "I don't have time!" he roared, then continued up to the Old World forest.

The boy glanced back down at Kabbage and Ballette, the red still flickering within them. "They still have myra. They must be alive in there." He bent down to the gnome. "Kabbage, if ya can hear me, I'll be right back. I-I'm not leavin' ya." With that, he marched forward through the mysterious forest with the mysterious Mac.

The trees seemed to get larger as they went. At one point, the path through got so narrow, so choked by the surrounding spindly plants, that they had to shimmy sideways as they did through the fissure. All the while, the boy thought about his lost friend. It wasn't so much that Kabbage was angry at him when it happened, but that his heart was frozen in that sentiment. The idea of no possible forgiveness made the boy feel terribly weak.

"There," Mac said with desperation, pointing at a group of blue lights dotted in the distance. "Someone's home."

Walking through the forest, a clearing of glass buildings emerged. It was like a small town plaza frozen in time, complete with what appeared to be windowed dwellings and a well. But no one was around. Gai strolled to the wide doors of the centermost building, a tower with a few small blue lights wavering all the way to the very top.

Mac remained behind, holding his right arm. It was dangling stiff beside him — stiff, like it was made of wood, or glass. He clenched his teeth, knowing that beneath his scuffed armor his arm had begun to transform, just like Kabbage and Ballette. "Must really remind me of him . . ." He caught his breath, then caught up with the boy.

Of course, the tower was as glass as a window, so Gai had the benefit of seeing inside before entering. He didn't see anyone on the first floor, so he pulled the door open without knocking. There were big squares the size of a person leaning against the inside. But, unlike everything else, those squares were *not* transparent.

"By Zeea," Gai ran inside to the objects. They were as tall as him. "More paintin's!" There were dozens of them stacked up like they were in storage. As he gazed at the gorgeous scenes within the paintings, it was almost like the scenes so realistic as to be breathing, colors shifting. Gai looked at one with an emerald, tropical forest and swore he heard bird calls from it. He passed another that was of an icy landscape, and he could practically feel a chilly breeze blowing out of it. The next was a peaceful meadow that smelled like wildflowers. "Each one of these is *another* Pocket Realm? Ya could just walk right out of one and into another?"

Shh. Mac smacked Gai's arm and pointed to the ceiling. An elaborate spiral staircase spun to the top, where the only other floor beside the bottom seemed to be. That was where the little lights led to, like dancing candles. A small shadow glided across the clear floor up there; someone was indeed home.

"It's the painter! Let's ask 'em for help!" Gai jumped up the first two steps and kept running. He turned back to wave Mac on but noticed the man was leaning on one of the paintings. It was one with a scene of a beautiful city with lush, hanging gardens all around. Mac's gaze appeared glued to it. "'Ey, ya'kay?"

The Ex-Heartbrand shook his head as if in a trance. "Yes, sorry. I just . . ." He looked at the marvelous scene again, paused for a hard exhale, and stood up straight. He then joined Gai and the two continued up the stairs.

"What was that about?" the boy asked.

". . . Just resisting the ability to disappear forever."

"Oh?"

The walls going up the stairs were adorned with more lively paintings, each more hauntingly vivid than the last. Imagining that each one was some kind of world to explore like this glass place made the boy's head feel like it would explode. And what kind of power did it take to make even just one?

Mac looked at each one as they raced up, seemingly having the same battle with whether or not to just hop in and disappear. "None of these are glass worlds. Maybe they're not all traps like this one."

The two arrived at the last stair at the same time. The top room beyond was wide open. An exquisitely gowned woman was seated on a three-legged stool with her back turned to them. The two hung their mouths at the same time. She effortlessly ran a brush — a very thin one — in long strokes over a large canvas. The subject of this painting was two people in an embrace. As Gai and Mac stepped in, she softly uttered, *"Tehu uuna louoo?"* But she did not turn around, preferring to keep excising her artform.

Gai said, "Uh, miss? Can ya help us? Our friends are—" As soon as she heard his voice, she turned her head to them.

One glance of her beauty stopped the boy mid-sentence, fluttering his belly. Her eye color was as if someone set one thousand different gemstones inside, scattering the small candlelight in mesmerizing ways. Her skin tone was a deep and cool brown, without a hint of age. In one seamless movement, she stood, looking them over with a painfully analytical stare. Then, seeming to understand that they did not speak her language, she opened up a link to their minds, to speak without words — *"From which painting did you escape, little ones?"*

Gai was still choking on her magnificence.

"We're from Esa," said Mac, getting onto his knees and bowing.

"The real world," Gai added.

"The real world? I'm not sure there is such a thing." She glided over to them like a seed caught in the breeze. *"But if you are from Esa, you must be here to convince me to be a part of that Last Myracle. Are you friends of Kaaz?"*

"Our friends need help!" Gai blurted.

"I have already spoken on this matter. Tell Kaaz that Zeea will play no role in his plan. Please leave."

"Forgive us, Zeea," said Mac, bowing again. "But . . . the Arkons already performed the Last Myracle."

"Yer Zeea?" Gai tried to take in all her magnificent features. "Yer real?"

"Do you think I'm a fool? You wouldn't have survived the Last Myracle if it happened. It would surely destroy everything."

"We are your decedents," Mac continued, never picking up his head. "The Last Myracle was performed one thousand years ago . . . And yes, it did destroy everything."

The woman repulsed and sat, holding herself as if shot through the heart. *"They actually did it. Hyro? Don't tell me . . ."* Her striking eyes came back to them. *"The Voids?"*

"They were destroyed along with them," said Mac. "The Last

Myracle contained more Ruin than even the Voids had amassed, and Esa has prospered thanks to the sacrifice of the Arkons."

"With all the respect . . . Miss," said Gai. "Our friends need help."

"More Ruin than the Voids?" Zeea wouldn't take her eyes off Mac, who was still kneeling before her with his head down, panting like he'd just run a mile. *"If Esa has prospered like you say, then why is your body filled with Ruin?"* She flicked her wrist and Mac's dented armor transformed into a flock of colorful birds that fluttered off him.

And the boy finally saw his face, a middle-aged man with a greying beard jetting from brown cheeks. His clothes beneath were frayed, dirty, and torn. A deep scar rose from his chest to his right jaw. A black substance seemed to be spreading from the scar across his skin, like an infection. One of his arms was entirely glass, revealing red light moving around his body, as if flowing in his veins.

"Mac?" said Gai, in shock. "Yer gonna become a Void! Why didn't ya tell us?"

Mac was breathing heavily.

The boy bent down near him, pointing to his scar. "This happened to my Pa, too!"

Mac looked up at him. "What? You mean there are already Voids in Esa? Why didn't you tell me?"

"Ya scooped us up on our way to stop 'em!"

The Ex-Heartbrand hunched down, almost hitting the ground. "This all my fault," he said, tearing up.

"Please!" Gai yelled to the woman. "Ya have to help us! I think we may be facing that same enemy ya were long ago!"

"You mean my people are gone, and the Voids came back? They died . . . for nothing?"

Mac's condition worsened at the news of the Voids. Only his Heartbrand training was keeping the full transformation to glass at bay. But even on the skin that had not yet turned, the black marks spread. He lay face down, sobbing on the glass floor. "I need to get back to Carpè," he said. "I have to find my son!"

"Please!" Gai ran up to Zeea and begged.

Her eyes narrowed with fury that he would even approach her. She raised her arms, which began to crackle with raw, unfathomable myra. *"And you have brought Ruin to my Realm?"*

"Wait! You have to help our—"

A gigantic mass of light enveloped everything the boy could see. He felt his whole body pushed and pressed as if through a thin door. Once through it, he fell backward into an entirely different space. The bright light was replaced with the sun, glaring down on him. The hot sands of a beach crept under his shirt. They were in the Arkon's Pocket Realm no longer.

CHAPTER 22
THE EVERBLOOM

L ynd awoke *very* before sunrise to more knocks on the dorm door. With Astel and Faan still at the In Inn, she'd had the room to herself all night again. It was another great night's sleep. The half-asleep girl said, "Come in, Kora," and the door creaked open. But instead of the friendly marble-lady, five Heartbrands fanned into the room, securing every corner as if she were a wild boar they needed to swiftly pin down.

Yawn. "A'kay," she groaned. "I'm comin'."

They were there to take her off that stuffy island to the legendary Everbloom. A bold move, indeed. Ever since Ada came to power, the Akademy's official stance was that no one should go anywhere near that massive tree. One of its more famous controversies was that the inhabitants of the Everbloom, appropriately called Bloomers, drank the epic tree's Sap to live an unnaturally long life. Some even said *forever.* No outsider knew the real truth, of course, but the Everbloom was understood to be the single most abundant source of natural Elix myra on Esa. Anything could be possible. Though the Akademy liked to pretend it wasn't there, the Everbloom has always been an area of intense interest and speculation around many Carpèan dinner tables.

The courtyard grass was still wet with morning dew as the Legionnaires escorted Lynd out of the Akademy. She examined each of the Heartbrands' faces as they marched down the street in formation around her. For professional soldiers, each one had awfully jittery, nervous eyes. The girl, however, was atingle. Not only was she going to find her family, but being escorted made her feel like someone important. In her mind, she felt like the Commandress, herself.

Daylight had barely stained the horizon when they arrived at Carpè's sprawling docks. Among the large wooden vessels was one with the name *Carrier XIII* on the side. It awaited with its gangway down like a tongue sticking out to the boardwalk. Another Heartbrand guard met them there.

He saluted and said, "General Bend is in his quarters. His exact instructions are that we are to set sail as soon as s-she comes aboard."

Lynd stomped her foot on the gangway, glaring at him. "*She's* aboard."

The Heartbrands aboard were tense as she stepped onto the top decks, like they were afraid she might blow them to pieces as she did to the Infirmary. She could practically feel all their stares, quietly assessing her for danger. But as soon as she looked at them, they diverted their gaze in a snap. Lynd kind of liked that. Not much was in her control at the moment, but she could make these fancy-armored guards dance if she wanted.

While the rest of the XIIIth Heartbrand Legion was preparing the ship for sail, the girl was brought below deck into a guest room complete with a bed, a pitcher of water, and a nice view outside. Once she was in, they slammed the door behind her and locked it, as if trapping a beast.

Lynd scoffed. "Like a door could stop me."

Then she heard "You can say that again" come from under the bed.

Lynd readied herself for a fight, but Kal popped his head out. He was hanging from the slats. "I knew they'd put the Commandress's guest in this room. The barracks can get pretty crowded."

"Kal," she breathed. "I almost blew up the bed! Ya scared me."

"I slept in here last night," he said, sliding out from under. "It's a nice mattress, but the trip to the Everbloom is pretty quick. You won't need it."

"Ya must be pretty sneaky to get past all those Heartbrands." Lynd ventured to the breezy window. The salty air reminded her of home. The sun hadn't risen, but she could see the lights of Carpè moving in the distance. They had set sail to find her family.

"I know a few tricks." Kal sat on the bed and bounced. "Any other memories come back besides your name? I like it, by the way. *Lynd*."

"Thanks at ya. I didn't pick it." She sat with him on the bed. "And what I remembered was the day I made my memories disappear. Using Ruin."

"You remembered you could forget?"

"I remembered I could *really* forget. Like gone, gone."

"Wild," he said, wide-eyed. "Anything else?"

"I also remember what happened before I ended up on Carpè. I was chasing a spryt — that's what we called myracite back home. I touched it, and . . ." Lynd's brows pinched together. She was still be trying to make sense of it all. "I must've opened up a tear in space, or somethin' — suddenly, I was on my uncle Baald's ship. All I wanted was to see Pa. So I destroyed the space between us . . ."

Kal leaned back and thought about what it could mean. "Was it *red* myracite?"

"The spryts were definitely all red, yeah."

"You're lucky that's all that happened, then. Red myracite is a crystallized Ruin. Combined with your own myra . . . the effects could be even more destructive."

Lynd looked at her palms. "Really?"

"Well, sure." Kal paused, then snapped his fingers with a fresh idea. "Say you had a weapon, a blade. On it's own, it's a tool of destruction. But if two blades hit with equal force, they could shatter to pieces, sending sharp shards everywhere. It's more unpredictable."

"So because of my Ruin myra, when I touched the red myracite, it was like two swords clashin'?"

"Not a perfect metaphor, but kind of. Elix and Ruin cancel each other out. But Ruin and Ruin just make a terrible mess together."

"Pa . . ."

"What's wrong?"

"I saw Pa that night. He was some kind of—" She caught a chill. "*Monster*." The memory of her father on the ship burned white hot in her mind. "He attacked me. Or maybe he was just tryin' to send me back home. I dunno. But I must've tried to knock the attack away and . . . Ruin and Ruin. Then I was somehow on Carpè."

"A monster?" Kal swallowed a lump in his throat. "It couldn't be a Void. Could it? I wasn't sure if they were real or just a myth to scare us away from using Ruin."

"He wasn't a'kay. That's all I know." The girl chewed over the idea, growing more concerned. "Tell me about the Voids."

Kal cleared his throat and sat up straight. "Long ago, an army of vile creatures appeared in Esa. Their only desire was to destroy. The endless hunger of a collapsed soul. The Arkons just called them Voids."

"What happened to 'em?"

"Our ancestors, the Arkons, were powerful myracle workers. More than anyone around today. But Voids destroy everything around them, they tear apart the myra in all things, and absorb it into themselves. The Arkons couldn't defeat the Voids. You can't fight something that only gets stronger the longer it exists. But since Voids are just endless wells of Ruin myra, if the Arkons threw enough Elix at them, they could've cancelled them out."

Lynd said, "So, why didn't those powerful Ark-people just do that?"

"Haven't you noticed that the more things *you* destroy, the more powerful you feel?"

She recalled how easily she destroyed professor Talia's memories in a snap back in the dorm room. ". . . Maybe."

"Destruction is about freeing up the myra within an object. If you destroy something, its myra becomes attached to you. You can become stronger. But we're told if you do that too much, all that myra collapses and you turn into a Void."

Lynd shrugged. "If ya say so."

"But Elix, on the other hand, requires energy *be put into it* to work, usually food or some other source. So, you can imagine how quickly the Voids would gain more and more Ruin as they go about wrecking the world around them. And it would get harder and harder to acquire enough Elix to balance them out."

"But the world isn't full of Voids now," she said. "So how did it end?"

"Since the Arkons couldn't gather enough Elix, their only option was to fight fire with fire, so to speak. They amassed more Ruin myra than even the Voids had. They called it the Last Myracle. They had no idea what would happen because when Ruin meets Ruin, all the rules that govern our world break down. I guess you understand that first hand."

"They *had* to use Ruin?"

"The Arkons made a bet. If the Voids destroyed them, the monsters would continue to consume everything until there was nothing left. Not even the planet. To them, even an unknown effect was better than doing nothing."

"But we're still here. So it was good, right?"

"That's where the red myracite came from," said Kal. "The Last Myracle would only work if it had *more Ruin* than the all the Voids. The massive deposit of red myracite under Electri City is that left-over Ruin. The gnomes discovered it first and learned how to harness its power. As far as the Akademy is concerned, that pile of Ruin sitting under Electri is a cataclysm waiting to happen. But it's not under our control. Obviously."

"Ya sure know a lot."

"I eavesdrop. A lot," he huffed. "Anyway, not only did their Last Myracle leave its mark, but the devastation it brought wiped out all life on the planet. We call it the Great Reset."

"Everyone . . . *died?* No Arkons, no Voids?"

"Terrible decision to have to make," he said. "But think about it. It was either let the Voids win and end up with no planet, no future. Or call it a draw, and at least the planet survives to restart life again."

Lynd sighed so heavily that her whole body slumped. "What if the Voids come back?"

". . . Now you know why everyone is so scared of you. The best solution the Akademy could come up with was never to let Ruin accumulate inside a person again."

"I don't understand. I can destroy things. I guess that means I have Ruin. But I'm not a monster. *Yer* not a monster."

Kal rolled up the sleeve of his left arm. A few thin veins near his elbow were black as a midnight river.

Lynd gasped. "Then . . . ya?"

Suddenly, the pitcher of water wiggled on the table, startling them. It must've just been a rough wave.

"No. Not yet," said Kal. "And hopefully not ever. I just wanted to show you . . . you have to be careful using Ruin. As I said, it makes you stronger, but there are consequences."

She recoiled. "I don't have anything like that!"

"Of course you do. Right there." He took her hand. "Look at this mark right by your thumb."

There was a small black scar. Lynd found herself more embarrassed he was holding her hand.

Kal continued, "It's probably from your incident in the Infirmary."

Lynd smirked. But it faded quickly, thinking about how far along her father must've been to look as scarred as he did.

"The Last Myracle is actually why we're going to the Everbloom right now, believe it or not."

"What do ya mean? I thought they're gonna help find my family?"

"The Everbloom was the only thing to survive the Great Reset. Just a small seed beneath the soil on the exact opposite side of the planet from the impact. It grew and became the source of all life in this age. They say it's connected to everyone."

Knock. Knock. Knock. "We've reached the destination waters, miss," someone called. "We'll sail the rest of the way by rowboat. General Bend requests your presence on deck immediately."

"A'kay," she yelled to them. "I'm comin'."

Kal became a bit anxious, like there was more he was planning to say, but he was out of time. He opened Lynd's palm and placed his bracelet in it, whispering, "If you happen to meet . . . I mean, if there's a girl named Tesse at the Everbloom. C-could you . . ."

"Give this to her?" Lynd finished for him.

"Yes," he blurted. "Good luck. I hope you learn what you need." He then grew even more uncomfortable and went back underneath the bed.

Lynd suddenly realized just how little she knew about Kal. He was such a strange boy. What was his last name? Was he giving his bracelet away to some girl he liked? Lynd got the distinct impression he had strong feelings for whomever this Tesse was. "A'kay," said Lynd, clenching the bracelet. "Gai, Ma, Pa. I'm comin'."

Lynd left the room, trying to stay calm as one could be when finally learning which direction their family is in. Three small boats were loaded with a dozen Heartbrands each and ready to be lowered into the water. Golden General Bend was in one, with his back turned to her, arms folded and standing stiffly. One of the guards brought her to another boat, so they didn't have to ride together.

Once in the water, the armored men and women rowed from the open sea to a small stream coming from a thick forest. The first boat with General Bend in it was in charge of slicing through some dense vines with their brilliant heartbrand weapons. As they journeyed within, the canopy above was so lush very little sunlight could pierce through it. Just thin sunbeams poking through lit the way, dancing on the babbling river.

The calls of creatures Lynd had never heard before echoed. The bushy walls of this jungle tunnel jittered about, but she couldn't tell who or what was moving through them. Out of the corner of her eye, she swore there were two people-eyes peering at her between the leaves.

The general ahead said, "This is as far as we'll get," and then ordered the three boats to close in on the river bend and tied them to the web of tree roots dipping down in the water. Next, the Heartbrands got out and began hacking at more juicy vines to clear a path inland. It occurred to the girl that no one must've come though this way in quite some time. Who lived here, again?

The Heartbrands were efficient and orderly workers. Soon they broke through the dense forest into an expansive grass field. Lynd marched through with guards on either side of her. When she first saw the epic sight of the colossal Everbloom tree flourishing in the center of the wildflower field, the girl almost tripped over her own feet. From ground level, as they were, they couldn't even see how truly massive it was, as the top green shot right through the white clouds above all. All she could say was, "By Zeea . . ."

The general, Legion, and guest didn't continue walking along its giant root-hills long before a group of six teenagers popped out of the long grass and blocked their path. A young, tan, curly-haired girl stepped in front of the others. She approached the powerful general without a pinch of hesitation, saying, "Turn back. You are not welcome here."

These youngsters were all modestly dressed, with loose shirts and pants made of heavy natural fiber. Most had some kind of white flower decorating their hair. Some had colorful swirls tattooed on their faces and arms. Aside from this girl in front, the rest stayed very close to one another, untrusting of the outsiders.

General Bend towered over this girl. He was likely twice her age, maybe more. Bend simply held out the gold box Ada gave him. The group of teenagers looked at each other but did not speak either. After a few beats, they waved for the Heartbrand group to approach the epic tree.

Walking toward the tremendous trunk was like hiking at the foot of a mountain. More youngsters, some older than Lynd, some younger, swung down from the high tree branches on very long ropes. As they landed and gather around, Lynd realized there must be hundreds of kids living there. She looked around for an adult, but each face was much too young. Who was looking after them? She looked at the box General Bend was offering to them and wondered if the adult caretaker was in *there*. Once the Legion arrived under the shade of the Everbloom, that curly-haired girl in front said plainly, "What are your terms?"

"Tesse." The general sighed. "Not even a hello?"

Tesse, this stoic young woman, seemed both surprised to see the general and unhappy to see him. She had a gaze upon him like she found a wolf in her yard — alert and ready to rescue any innocent bystanders in case he bit. Lynd recognized the name immediately as the one Kal said he wanted to have his bracelet.

"Very well," Bend huffed. He put the box on the ground in front of the Everbloom kids. "Our Commandress would like your help locating a few people. In return—*exhale*—we offer the safe return of your little Speaker."

More youngsters seemed to be coming out of nowhere, from right out of the tall grass, peeking over the large roots of the tree. Lynd looked up at the spreading branches and saw lights and people moving around way up in the tree. It was like a city in the sky.

"That 'little Speaker' told us never to trust Tamperers," said Tesse.

"Not even to save him? Well." Bend picked the box up and put it back into his pocket. "Shame, really." He turned around and ordered the Heartbrands back to the ship. "I told the Commandress this was a waste of time."

"Are the people you're looking for like *her*," said Tesse, pointing to Lynd.

The general didn't bother about-facing. "Would that change anything?" he said over his shoulder.

"She has the marks of Ruin on her," said Tesse, with her large, dark, analytical eyes. "They are mostly still beneath the skin, but visible to us."

"Would that *change* anything?" Bend stressed, with his back still to her.

Tesse paused and said, "Whom does she seek?"

The general finally turned, saying, "Her family. Being away from them can be very hard on a child." Bend's tone was very familiar with Tesse, as if the two had met many times before. "Or don't you know that?"

"I do," she answered, sharply staring at him. "Let's see if you've got Spen. Then we'll talk."

"I do." Bend put the gold box back down in front of them. This time he tapped it gently, and a mist of multi-colored, shimmering smoke came out.

When it cleared, a young, fair-featured man was coughing and waving it away with his hands. To Lynd's surprise, he wasn't an adult either. This boy couldn't have been much older than her brother, Gai.

Tesse rushed to embrace him. "Spen!" And soon he was crowded on all sides with hugs from every kid who could reach him.

"What?" said the young man. "Oh, dear. How long was I out this time?"

"What's the last thing you remember?" Tesse said, beaming at him.

"I was—" Spen blinked his eyes many times as if adjusting to the light. He noticed the general and said, "*You!*" His brow bent with rage. "You were there!" He marched toward the general. He then broke his facade of anger and scratched his head. "What were we doing, exactly?"

"One count of sneaking onto Akademy property," said Bend. "Two counts of urinating on the Arkon statues. Four counts of—"

Spen laughed. "Okay, let's just keep that between us." He then noticed Lynd and strolled over to her, saying, "My, my. Who have you brought to this sacred place?" He picked up her chin and gazed into her eyes. "There's a shade under my tree, I see." Spen let her go and strolled back to his group of youngsters. One of them handed him a small jar. "Sad that's how all you Tamperers end up, isn't it?" He tilted the jar completely up and let a thick, golden syrup slowly drip into his mouth. *Gulp.* "Ah. How I missed that grand immortal sauce." Spen then addressed the general, "The Arkons themselves used to drink it, you know? Everblooms covered the planet back then." He offered the jar to Bend.

"No," he said flatly. "I know what that Sap does." He glanced at Tesse, who immediately looked away.

"They'd like a trade," said Tesse, staring at her feet.

"Okay." Spen dropped the jar and clapped his hands, "What for what, hm?" Everyone was silently looking at him, so he said, "Oh, *me?* Am I part of the trade? Well, that's already interesting. What do you want for . . . me?"

The general appeared to be doing his darnedest to hold back his frustration. "We need you to help us locate this girl's family. Quickly."

Spen's eyes widened. "I like that. Then I'd be free to do things, rather than just in my head in that Pocket Realm prison box of yours." He pretended to think about it. "I'll take that deal."

The Speaker waved Lynd closer to the monolithic sections of tree bark on the trunk. "After the Last Myracle," he said, "life on Esa sprang up from right here. This tree is the great, great, great, great, great, etc. grandmother to us all. Her loving roots run around the whole planet, cradling us like the babes we are. And she hears all her children." He waved Lynd closer and she approached. Then Spen put the girl's hand to the bark and asked, "What's the name, dear?"

"Gai," she said to him, trying to hold back her excitement. Maybe these people really could help her. There was a strange sensation under her palm, almost like the bark was crawling.

"Hm . . ." Spen put his palms on the trunk as well as his ear. His eyes rolled around like he was listening to a story, but no one could hear it but him. He then perked up. "She doesn't know anyone by that name."

"What?" said Lynd. Or maybe they couldn't help her.

"Ask another, ask another," he said, egging her on with his flimsy gestures. "There is no one the grandmother can't hear."

"A'kay. His full name is Gaiel Izz. Try that." Lynd spoke down at the bark, as if it were listening to her.

"Ahh," Spen said, returning to his listening position. He then switched ears and listened again. "Is he a little tyke?"

"No," said Lynd. "He's my *older* brother."

Spen sighed. "Nope, not catching any flies with that one, either, honey."

"How 'bout my pa, Stav Izz, then?" said Lynd, growing impatient.

"Mmm." The Speaker kept up the same strange behavior, mumbling back to the bark as if he were part of a real two-sided conversation. "Ah. Mm-hm."

"Well?" barked the general.

Spen perked up again. "Yeah, no one's answering to that name."

The general sighed. "Glad I left Carpè undefended for this." He waved for the Heartbrands to start marching back. "Keep your freedom, Speaker. In the world that's to come, it will be rare."

Ptoo! A blowdart whistled through the air at the general. Bend's highly attunded senses alerted him to the danger. His heartbrand formed in his hand in the blink of an eye, lighting up the surrounding grass. But, just before the dart struck him in the forehead, it fell out of the air, straight down like a rock at his feet. Upon inspection, the dart looked like it *was* a rock.

"It was her!" Tesse pointed at Lynd, who had her hand up, with red power crackling around her palm.

Bend's mouth hung open. Lynd had stopped the dart from hitting him. But she did it with Ruin Time, just like she learned in Hosp's class, just like the ball of hers that turned to fossilized stone. A deadly myracle, indeed. Bend realized just how powerful the girl was becoming. His fear of her finally matched his disdain.

All the surrounding Bloomers who witnessed the event shifted their feet uncomfortably. Bend and the Legion were just as concerned as they were. Just the other day, Lynd didn't know her name was Lynd. But there was no denying the girl was becoming something truly terrifying.

"Yes," Spen chirped. "Sorry for the dart. You can't blame us for trying to dose you with a little Sap sample; a little immortal sauce for those tight nerves." He sighed. "But it would seem *she'll* do worse to you than we ever could."

Lynd felt cheated and enraged after not getting any new information about her family. It took quite a bit of willpower to relax her clenched fist. Within it was Kal's bracelet.

She tossed it at Tesse's feet, muttering, "Thanks at ya. For nothin'." Then she marched ahead of the Legion toward the boats in the river.

Tesse picked up the bracelet with a look of absolute disbelief. She closed her hand around it and shut her eyes, appearing to be holding back her tears.

Bend peered at Tesse. "*Is that?*"

Spen walked between them, saying again, "Sad that's how all you Tamperers end up, isn't it?" He then took the bracelet from Tesse and replaced it with a jar of Sap.

The general looked away as she drank it, whispering, "You're killing me." He then angrily stormed back to the boats with his Heartbrands.

CHAPTER 23
IMMORTAL SAUCE

I n the blink of an eye, Gai and Mac were knee-deep in an unknown beach. Gai collapsed onto his hands, feeling the coarse sand pass right through his fingertips, "No!" Cold ocean waves crashed down in front of them. A low sunset splashed everything red-orange. The boy yanked his legs out and ran waist-deep into the sea. "She threw us out before we could help Kabbage and Ballette!"

He stared at the sparkling sea, hopeless. He barely had time to mourn his latest loss before he spotted a fleet of Electri warships far off on the horizon. Would anyone from Carpè even be able to help him if they're dealing with some messy war?

"I dunno if I can keep goin', Lynd." The boy's heart pounded. His head felt light, and rung with too many losses. He desired above all else that his father and sister would just magically appear right next to him, that very instant, and they could just go home.

Gai heard a splash behind him and turned to see Mac crouched down almost entirely underneath the shallow water, holding his shoulder with pained creases on his face. Another loss waiting to happen.

Gai rushed to lift him out of the water and onto the dry shore. "Mac?" he yelled, laying him down. His arm was still glass but appeared to stop transforming after being removed from Zeea's Pocket Realm. His chest-to-jaw scar, however, still seeped with a dark hue. And that darkness was still spreading onto his face and behind his head. "Can ya hear me?"

Mac was clenching his teeth so hard that he could barely speak. "Please . . . take me to Carpè."

"I'd like to, but . . ." Left and right, there was only more stretching shoreline. Inland there was a forest so dense that they'd never get through without a lot of time and a lot of hacking blades. Gai picked the man up, barely able to hold his weight, and started hauling him up the uneven dunes. It was the same direction the Electri ships were headed, which must be the way Carpè was, the boy reasoned.

That inland forest remained tightly packed and impenetrable as they made their way along the coast. The boy kept peering out at the ocean to see if there were any nearby boats, Emilies, or even land close enough to hear his desperate call. The frightening thought that they might be on some lonely island away from everything crept in. But in his frantic search for any signs of life, he finally saw a few small island bumps way out at sea. The way the long shoreline curved to the water ahead, Gai thought he actually might be able to reach those islands with just a short swim.

"A'way, Mac," he huffed, stumbling over the shifty sands with the full weight of his nearly unconscious mentor pressing down. "I can't lose another."

As the sun got lower and lower, the boy hunched further and further down with Mac's weight over his shoulder. Short-winded, he peered again at those islands he was trying to reach. But they weren't in the same place as before. By a lot.

"Not islands. It's the Plunder's," he said, with a hoarse voice, squinting just to be sure. There were seven large domed shells and a smaller one trailing behind. Gai sighed. "Em's with 'em."

His first instinct was to yell to her, but she was much too far out to ever hear him, anyway. Instead, Gai watched as she slowly drifted south with her new family, a family she was meant to be with, one who could understand what *Mraw* meant. Was it the loss of a friend? Of course. But she was home, reunited. His heart filled with a mix of things, but most of all, joy for her. The boy thanked his luck for letting him see her one last time. "I'm gonna find mine, too . . ."

But then he heard the strings of a fiddle behind him on the

beach. *Ping. Ping.* It was faint in the distance. His heart lifted at the sound of the notes. *Ping. Ping.* His ears pointed him to a large group of rocks meeting out from the coast into the water a ways down the sand. Someone had to be there. Maybe they knew the way to Carpè. Perhaps they knew how to cure Mac's festering Ruin marks. Maybe they had bread.

Ping. His strength and hopes returning, he saddled Mac over his other shoulder and followed the music as fast as he could, "'Ey!" he cried out in the direction of the melody. "Anyone there? . . . '*Ey!*"

A figure moved from atop the rocks. Gai watched the person hop off, a fall of at least the height of a house. Unexpected as that was, even more surprising was that the figure coming toward them was of a young man only about the boy's age.

This light-haired teenager caught up to them very quickly, looked them over with his leafy green eyes, and said, "What do we have here?"

"My friend's hurt!" said Gai.

"I hope it wasn't another shark bite," the young man said. Then he noticed Mac's wounds and glass arm, "Oh. Even more deadly." He looked up at Gai, shot his hand out to shake, and smiled. "My name's Spen. My family isn't far from here. And I think we've got *just* the fix for him."

"Ya do?" Gai was shocked. Either this guy didn't know the seriousness of Mac's condition, or perhaps Mac's condition wasn't as severe as the boy had heard. Could there be a cure for Ruin?

"Here." Spen bent down to Mac. "I'll help you carry him. *You* get that glass side. Looks fragile."

"Thanks at ya!"

Walking with Mac was immensely easier with another shoulder to carry him. Just one extra helper, and he was already half the weight. As Gai journeyed to the forest, he thought Mac might actually feel even less than half as heavy; Spen was over carrying the burden on purpose, without breaking a sweat. Meanwhile, the boy looked like he'd just gone swimming. Gai privately marveled at how fit this guy was. First, the beautiful music, then the sprinting speed, a cure for Ruin, and upper-body brawn to boot. What a handsome picture of health he was. This young man didn't even seem shocked by Mac's wild condition. Who *was* he, exactly?

They approached that impenetrably dense wall of weaving branches. Spen held his palm over his heart with his free hand and closed his eyes like he was praying. The wind rustled the leaves, but it was otherwise silent. Gai waited patiently at the edge of the thick woods, again asking himself who in Esa this character could be? In some ways, he didn't quite care who he was. Anything to get on with his journey to find Lynd and Pa. Soon the thick, green branches opened up, soft as a mother's arms. The forest mesh continued to open like the petal layers of a flower until a path emerged through to a distant clearing.

As casually as ever, Spen smiled, saying, "Just this way."

Who was this guy?

As Spen directed them through the curves and corners of the intricate unfolded path, Gai asked where they were.

"Where do you want to be?" Spen replied.

"We're lookin' for Carpè."

"I could've guessed that," he said, smirking. "Oh, but don't worry. You're not far from the city, now."

"Why could ya guess we're goin' to Carpè?" As Gai finished his sentence, the green wooded tunnel cleared into the vast field of tall grass and little white flowers. His mouth dropped at the towering sight of the Everbloom tree extending up beyond the clouds. Not even the buildings of Electri were that high. "What in Esa?"

"Welcome to my home," Spen said. "Hurry, Mr. Heartbrand here doesn't have much time."

"How'd ya know he was a Heartbrand?"

Spen smirked again, seemingly his favorite expression. "This one, I happen to know."

"Ya met Mac before?"

A few more teenagers around Gai's age emerged from the grass to greet them. "Sap!" Spen yelled out. "Another preventable Tamperer injury coming through!"

A dozen or so youngsters approached from all around the field. One girl was dragging an ornate jug the size of her whole leg. "Lay him flat," she said, standing up the jug and scooping a small cup down into it.

Gai let the others lay Mac down as this comely curly-haired girl brought the cup to his lips. The Ex-Heartbrand seemed barely aware of his surroundings. But he did have enough awareness to turn his head away as they tried to get this *cure* into his mouth.

The boy looked on, ultimately hopeful it would indeed help with Ruin. It would be so incredible if it did. Pa solved, Mac solved, and if Lynd happened to turn into a Void as well — solved. Who were these kids, again?

A golden syrup-like liquid came out and dripped into Mac's held jaw. He continued to struggle, but Spen chimed in, saying, "How Ruin makes them relentless." Finally, they were able to force Mac to swallow some of the syrup. In a few heartbeats, his breathing noticeable slowed. His back relaxed, and his grimace softened. To Gai's astonishment, the throbbing, black wound began to lose its grip over his skin and receded to thin streaks. The strain on Mac's face melted. Even his glass arm regained its fleshy consistency. His brow settled into a soft arch above his closing eyes, and soon he appeared to fall into the most peaceful of naps.

Gai grabbed Spen's arm in excitement. "What was that stuff?"

"Why, it's the Sap from this beautiful Everbloom, of course. She was the only living thing to survive the Last Myracle, you know? We all owe our lives to her." He pointed at Mac. "Some more than others. But to answer your question more directly — We call it the *immortal sauce*. You know, for the tourists."

". . . Is he cured?" said the boy.

"I'm not sure," Spen replied. "What do you think, Tesse? Is this man cured?"

The girl who gave him the Sap glared over Mac's sleeping form. "It's hard to say. He'll need some time to rest."

Spen sprung to his feet and clapped his hands. "Well, we are actually having a little celebration ourselves this evening." He wrapped his arm around Gai and pulled him in. "Feast as big as any you've ever seen. I would be honored to have you two as my guests."

Seeing as how this stranger just healed his friend, it seemed rude to say no. He glanced down at the contently snoring Mac. "A'kay. He can rest a bit. But can ya show us where Carpè is right after?"

"Of course, I can." Spen walked him over the city-sized trunk. "But I don't even know your name."

"Oh! It's Gaiel Izz. Most people call me—"

"Gai?" he interrupted, looking at the boy curiously. "I've heard that name before . . ."

"Ya must be mistaken. How could anyone know me out here?"

"It just sounds so familiar." His eyebrows pinched together in thought. "But where have I heard it? Was it in a song somewhere?" He scratched his thick, blonde head. "This is going to drive me off a branch." Then, little fire torches suddenly started lighting up on the many thousands of Everbloom branches high above them. "Sundown," he sang. "I wish you could've seen the sunset from the tree. It's like nothing you've ever seen in your life." He gestured grandly at the pretty lights looking like flickering stars. "Luckily, we've got *plenty* of things you've never seen in your life."

"Like fixin' Ruin," Gai said. "Could I borrow some of that Sap?"

"Bloomer use only, I'm afraid. But I'll tell you what — while you're my guests, feel free to consume as much as you desire here." Spen called Tesse over, saying, "Would you mind bringing our Heartbrand guest up to a nice quiet branch to nap on? I'm going to take Gaiel and his appetite up to the festivities in the Storyteller Playhouse."

"I'm about to carry this jar of Sap to the Playhouse," Tesse said. "Perhaps you can find a good resting place for the Heartbrand?"

". . . Very well." Spen looked her over. "I will meet you both there, then."

Tesse nodded to Gai. "Would you help me?"

"Per course." The boy grabbed the other side of the jar, and they carried it to the large base of the tree. Its roots practically formed hills alongside them. "Thanks at ya for helpin' my friend."

Tesse nodded so slightly it was almost imperceptible. She reached her hand up to Everbloom bark. Instantly, the bark of the trunk curved up like peeling paint, forming a winding walkway to the top. Gai paused to marvel at the majesty of this very-much-alive creature, the Everbloom. But Tesse practically pulled the boy along with the jar. She was in pretty good shape, too.

As physically capable as these Bloomers were, the boy reasoned it must just be due to their lifestyle. His legs were already burning halfway up the climb, and these kids seemed like they went up and down multiple times a day. Gai looked at the curving bark and recalled how Spen opened up the whole forest with nothing but a prayer. He asked, "Do yer people talk to the tree?"

"All life came from this Everbloom," she said with a pinch of pride. "We practice our connection with her. Strengthen it. In doing so, we connect better to all of life." Then, seamlessly, her voice continued in the boy's mind — *"And we learn many things."*

"'Ey! I know someone else who can do that. It's—"

"Stop. If the tree can hear you, so can our leader. There is something I must tell you privately."

"How can I answer ya if—"

"Say it in your mind, and push it into mine."

"Like this," he thought.

"Very good. Now — Run for your life."

Gai thought, *"What?"*

"Stay for the festival, so Spen does not suspect. Sneak away in the middle of the night."

"What about Mac?" Gai waited, but Tesse didn't say anything back to him in his mind. Instead, she stared dead ahead as they continued their exhausting climb. *"How are we in danger?"* he insisted in his head.

"The Speaker will not hurt you. But he will take your life. We are approaching the Playhouse. Do not drink the Sap."

As if that wasn't enough to think about, the boy looked on with wonder as they got to the top; in the dense heart of the Everbloom branches was a full-blown city. There were hundreds more Bloomers up there, all young and spry as Gai, some even younger. Splitting off from the trunk, the branches formed intricate pathways to bulbous swells of wood that they seemed to use as homes. The paths themselves were alive, connecting to new branches like neurons in a brain. They seemed to move with the intentions of the Bloomers as they moved about; if a way weren't already clear, a branch would gently move to where they needed to go. In several instances, the boy saw a whole new branch grow out to accommodate a Bloomer's need.

"Welcome to our home," Tesse said aloud. "The Storyteller Playhouse is just this way."

As they walked along the mighty main branches, youngsters were popping their heads out of carved windows to get a look at the visitor. Somehow they all knew there was a stranger in their tree, as if heard on a whisper through the leaves. Tesse stopped at an especially large swelling in the wood and nodded for them to enter.

"This place is incredible," said Gai. "How could it be bad, though?"

"*Shh,*" Tesse said in his mind. "*Be careful what you say out loud.*"

The two carried the jug into the large, well-lit room inside the wide branch. There were dozens of people already inside, and not one of them could've been older than Gai. Not a single ma or pa, unc or nosey neighbor around. All the Bloomers sat around seven big round tables with mountains of delicious-looking food and golden cups filled with that golden Sap.

Tesse pointed out Spen, who was sitting on top of one of the tables and making everyone laugh. He noticed them and waved, shouting, "Hey, Gai! Come this way. I want you to meet some friends!"

"I'll take that," said Tesse, pulling the jar away from Gai, as Spen ended up approaching them anyway.

The charismatic Speaker put his arm over the boy's shoulder again and guided him down to the banquet. "Are you ready for the best food you've ever tasted?"

But what Tesse told him was at the top of Gai's mind. He blurted, "Ya said ya knew Mac before? From where?"

"Hey!" A man came bursting behind them with a large cup in his hands. "Heard my name over here!"

Gai nearly didn't recognize him. "Mac?"

"It is I," he sang, with uncharacteristic charm.

It was indeed Mac, but his cheeks seemed fuller, his eyes brighter, even the gray in his head had darkened. "Ya look . . . good," Gai said. "Like, really good. Like *younger* good?"

"And boy, do I feel it!" Mac said, chuckling. "Tesse! Where's Tesse? I can't wait to see her, again!"

Gai raised an eyebrow. "Ya were dyin' not that long ago."

Spen laughed. "Looks like someone's been drinking undiluted Sap. Very bad boy. Well, I suppose it is a party!"

"Ah, it's so much *sweeter* undiluted." Mac took another big gulp. "I must thank you for making it so available. Where's Tesse, hm? I'd like to talk to her."

"We should all sit down," said Spen. "I think the show is about to start. You and Tesse can chat about all your silly problems later."

"Excellent!" said Mac as he grabbed Gai's arm and brought them both to Spen's table, where there were two seats just for them.

"Sit next to me," Tesse called to Gai, who was at the table already.

"A'kay."

Spen whistled for everyone to start taking their seats, then claimed his own next to Mac. The Bloomer Speaker cleared his throat, booming, "Thank you all for coming!" Everyone immediately stopped talking at the sound of his voice. "I don't need to tell you all that we have two new guests in our happy home this evening." He held up his gold cup of Sap, as did everyone else, and shouted, "A salute to new friends!" Spen toasted the room and hungrily sipped his thick, golden syrup. All followed — "*Salute!*"

Tesse kicked Gai's leg gently, signaling for him to play along. The boy nodded and faked a good long taste of the Sap. "Mmm."

"Now," Spen threw his cup behind him in a fit of glee. "On with the show!"

The room full of young Bloomers all clapped as seven other kids marched out in a line from behind a curtain. A steady drumbeat started. Each of them climbed onto one of the seven dinner tables. They were all dressed in different costumes as if it were some play. The one in the centermost table was dressed in a plain-looking garb similar to the audience. He had a fake, long beard and held a hefty-looking book.

"Ahem," he said, writing with their quill on the pages. "On this night, and indeed every other, we remember the Great Storyteller and our promise to each other."

"That Storyteller," chimed another, wearing a white robe and standing on the following table. "Who has moved all the ages. As they write out our lives on all of the pages."

The next Bloomer actor stood up, dressed in a blue robe. "Yet there are many who think, and talk in this era. That they should write what they want, with the ink of their myra."

A red hooded one rose slowly on their table. "Still darker, still deeper, another is smitten, to Ruin the plot and erase what was written."

"Their temper is to tamper. And tamper by their tempers," one wrapped entirely in black clothing said. Then another black-robed figure shouted from behind him, stomping forward. "Raise their pride, and when they fall, they doom us all!"

All seven joined in, singing a chorus together, "For us, poor Esa, which is the way? Which, if any, does the Everbloom say?"

Spen leaped upon his table and raised his cup — "Here's to the only choice you'll ever need!"

They all sang, "Make. No. Waves!"

Everyone erupted in applause and saluted while downing their cups of that sweet immortal sauce. Mac sucked all the Sap down like it was the best thing he had ever eaten. Tesse gracefully tapped Gai's thigh to pretend to sip his as well again. He was still trying to figure out what that performance was all about. The one in the blue robe must've represented Elix, while the red was Ruin. It seemed like the Bloomers didn't like people who used either. Both were "Tampering," and led only to trouble.

Gai took his fake slurp, giving it extra *sloop-sloop* noises, just to be safe. Part of him wanted to know what all the fuss about this immortal sauce was, though. Could it really be that bad if it cured Ruin? Everyone around his table was busy enjoying their Sap, sticking their fingers in and scooping out what wouldn't slide out on its own.

"*Ah!*" Mac fell back in his chair, rubbing his belly. "That. Was. Amazing. I can't believe I didn't try it sooner."

"All in the right time." Spen pinched the Ex-Heartbrand cheeks.

Tesse spoke again in the boy's mind. "*The Heartbrand has already had too much. You need to convince him to break away sooner than expected.*"

"Tell me, Mac," said Spen. "Where did you get that glass arm you had earlier? I'm thinking of getting one myself."

All the Bloomers seemed just as satisfied. There were cakes and cookies all over every table in heaving baskets, all made from the generous Everbloom.

"*How can I?*" Gai thought, pushing his mental words to Tesse.

"*He can be lured by Sap to do pretty much anything now.*"

Gai got up and smiled, putting his hands on Mac's shoulders. "Feelin' good?"

"Yeah!" He laughed boisterously, taking another Sap gulp.

Tesse excused herself and started to the entrance of the Playhouse.

"Will ya come have a toast with me outside?" the boy said to Mac. "Ya know, to the next step?"

"That sounds great!" he said. "Hey, will Tesse be there?"

As Mac got up, and the two made their way to Tesse near the door, Spen shouted her name — "Tesse!" He spoke loud enough that everyone would hear. They did and all stopped chatting to listen to what their Speaker had to say. "While you're helping them escape, why not show them all the way to Carpè?"

By now, all the Bloomers sat still, stunned at what he was suggesting. Spen continued, "After all, you're such good friends with these people. Take them all the way."

"We aren't permitted beyond the forest," she said, shocked.

"Go ahead." Spen peered right in her eyes. "Do it."

The Storyteller Playhouse was silent. Everyone looked on, shifting about nervously like they were watching a horrible accident.

"He's lettin' us go," said Gai, with a bit of relief. "See? He's not so bad."

Tesse stood still as a statue in the doorway. She did not look relieved. The warmth drained from her skin. Her lips quivered. But she bowed to the room and waved Mac and Gai to follow her out.

"He has sentenced me to death," she said in the boy's mind.

CHAPTER 24

NO TIME IN THE PRESENT

L ynd was left to enjoy the trip back to Carpè in the guest room
of *Carrier XIII* again. The window was still open. The pitcher
of water remained, untouched with a cool condensation on
the glass. "We'll come to get you once we arrive safely back in
Carpè," said the guard, again locking the door behind her.

Snap! A bedpost at the foot of the bed split open like a wooden
flower. The girl was upset. Where in Esa was her family? Were those
tree-people lying to her? She hurled herself onto the bed, forgetting
Kal was underneath. *Ow!*

"Sorry at ya."

"It's fine." Kal slid out, rubbing his nose. "I'm better off than the
bedpost."

"The tree doesn't know my family."

"That's weird," he said, climbing out and sitting with her. "When
we get back, I promise to help you find them. Any way I can."

". . . I don't wanna go back, Kal."

"I don't blame you." He looked out the window at the rising and
falling waves. *Carrier XIII* had quickly set off to Carpè. "What else
could you do, though? Steal a ship and go sailing around for them?"

"I *could* steal a ship," she said, half-joking. "I'm gettin' pretty good
at destroying memories. I also just did Ruin Time again. On a flying
dart."

"Impressive. You weren't this happy about it when it happened in class." He laughed nervously.

"I forgot who I was, and wanted the students to like me. Now, I don't care what they think." *Snap!* There went another bedpost.

"Alright, calm down, Lynd," said Kal lightheartedly.

"Why is it always *me* who always has to stop?" The girl got up from the bed. "Aren't they the ones treating me like garbage? Tell 'em to calm down."

"That's true, but—"

Snap! And a third bedpost went. "This general's been the worst of 'em," said Lynd pacing around the room. "Ya should've seen the way he looked at me in front of Astel and Faan, when they put that stupid lotion on me. He's no protector. I should've let that dart hit him. It was more like a reflex, anyway."

"I don't like General Bend much, either." Kal leaped up and held Lynd's hands. "Hey, did you happen to give that bracelet to . . . anyone?"

"Uh." The girl had to think through the cloud of anger stewing between her ears. "Actually, yeah. I gave it to that Tesse girl. Do ya like her or somethin'?"

"Tesse was really there?" Kal looked away. He started to tear up, talking to himself, "The inner island. It kept whispering her funeral was a lie, but I kept building more walls around it . . . My mother is *alive*."

The pitcher of water jiggled on the table. Both Kal and Lynd's stomach's dropped and tingled with nerves as they peered at it. The waves outside were easy and flat. What reason would that pitcher have to move?

Kal was shaking.

"Ya think that girl was yer ma? She was way too young!" Lynd could tell Kal was not taking the news well. She tried to cheer him up with a nudge to the shoulder and joked, "All's a'kay. If that island thing's still bothering ya, I'll teach ya how to *really* forget it with Ruin Memory."

Then General Bend's voice suddenly echoed throughout the room, "How dare you try to spread your filthy Ruin myracles!" The pitcher started to expand like a balloon, larger and twisting in shape and color. It then morphed into the esteemed Heartbrand General XIII, sitting with his legs crossed on the table.

"Dad!" Kal blurted.

Lynd turned to him. "Did ya just say *Dad?*"

"After what this girl has done," the general said directly to Kal. "You really think I'd let her out of my sight?" He approached and loomed over his young son. "I am so disappointed." Bend grabbed Kal's arm and exposed the dark marks on it. He grimaced, grinding his teeth at the sight of them. He had no idea his son had any Ruin. How could that be? He was one of the Akademy's brightest Elix students. "*She* has done this to you. I told Ada it would spread!"

"Kal, get outta here," yelled Lynd.

"Thanks to the Commandress," Bend leered at Kal, "I can't do anything about this *monster*. But *you* are under arrest." He pulled out the golden box that Spen was trapped in and opened it in front of his son. Before the girl could react, Kal Bend was drawn into the Pocket Realm prison, and the box snapped shut.

"No!" Lynd cried.

Then someone shouted down the stairs, "General!"

"What?" he roared back.

"The Electrian Fleet has surrounded Carpè! They're straight ahead!"

The general was so upset that he was practically crushing that box in his hand. "Every piece of this is Ada's fault," he angrily whispered under his breath. Then, he shot his cold eyes to Lynd. Holding up the golden box, he said, "If you move, he'll never get out." Bend then leaped out of the room and up the stairs, leaving the girl alone with the door open.

Kal was General Bend's son. Lynd couldn't believe it. And the general just locked him away in a box meant for criminals, all because he was her friend. She could hear the general shouting up on the deck with dozens of marching footsteps rumbling the boards above her. A calm, free breeze blew in through the window, calling her attention.

She peered out and saw the line of warships, shining in the sun ahead. "Electrian?" she whispered. "Like the lights?"

Lynd asked herself if she could use this distraction to hide, making her escape in the chaos once they docked. ". . . I can't leave

Kal with that man." There was no way she would let someone be imprisoned in a box because of her. She snuck out of the room and crept under the stairs to assess what was happening on deck.

Armored boots were pounding, completely overwhelmed with preparations for the impending Electri threat. The guards were so frazzled that she was able to slip right up to the deck and hide behind a pile of rope by the door. Lynd watched as all one-hundred elite Heartbrands of the XIIIth Legion were preparing sails, aiming cannons, and up the mast shouting the enemy ships' angles. "They've made a blockade of the outer island, sir," yelled one.

General Bend was pacing back and forth, his brow pinched with focus. He then stopped suddenly. With a calm breath, he said, "Port side — lower the sails. Starboard — Wind Elix. Push the limits *of Carrier XIII's* speed! Set the bow right on the inner island — straight ahead until I say stop, understood?"

"Yes, sir!"

War was new to Lynd. The point had completely gone over the girl's head before, but now she understood these Electrian people must be dangerous enemies of Carpè. She felt oddly warm that something was finally thought to be more dangerous than she was.

One Heartbrand Legionnaire got to the ship's wheel and pointed it right at Carpè. A group of them lowered the sails, while another group used their blue, blue myra to create gusts of wind to blow into them. The ship picked up incredible speed, quickly.

"The rest of you, line up," Bend commanded. "And don't move! Not a one of you!"

The remaining Heartbrands got into formation on either side of the deck, eyes forward and hands folded behind their backs. *Carrier XIII* barreled toward the Electrian blockade, a line of metallic vessels circling the entire island, so armed and outfitted that any one of them seemed impenetrable.

"Hold," Bend shouted.

The Heartbrands kept their Wind Elix myracles blowing. The sails creaked as they bent hard catching it. As they closed in, the general roared, "Stand down!" The wind stopped. The sails were released. The Heartbrands all lined up and stood still. The ship speared the water smoothly with momentum alone.

Soon, they passed right between two of the enemy ships, only an arm's throw from their decks on each side of *Carrier XIII*. Lynd held her breath, looking at the heavy weapons poking out from those big Electrian boats. But no one aboard them was taking any action. In fact, they weren't even acknowledging the Carpèan vessel passing them by in truest daylight. It sailed by utterly undisturbed.

Lynd looked closely at Bend's hand. There was a slight blue glow to it. "Elix Mirage," she said under her breath. "He must be making us invisible or something, like in the Hall to trick Ada." The girl watched as the small gnomes across the way paid absolutely no attention to them. "He is talented . . ."

The general touched his ear as if someone was whispering in it. But no one was near him. "As soon as we dock," he said shortly after. "You'll all rendezvous with XI and XII. I am in touch with General Case. You are to follow her lead." He then left to his quarters, muttering, "*I'll* take care of the Commandress . . ." He seemed genuinely distraught, so much so that he entirely forgot about Lynd.

As soon as *Carrier XIII* settled into the port, the entire Legion ran onto the pier and lined up with two more Legions positioning themselves around the sea-facing walls of Carpè.

The docks were a much different place than when they left. Everyone was in a raw, gasping panic. Rows and rows of strange constructs, like the cleaning ones at the Akademy but larger, were rolling out in defense of the city. In the chaos of approaching battle, Lynd dropped onto the pier and hid behind a crate. She wasn't concerned with whatever problem Electri was. She focused on the city, searching for General Bend like a hawk after a rustling mouse. Thousands of Heartbrands and citizens were preparing for battle. She couldn't see him anywhere.

"He's gonna take Command from Ada," Lynd whispered. As she watched the preparations unfold, her eyes traveled up to the white stones of the Akademy buildings towering over the city. "And she's probably up there, Commanding."

Several larger Carpèan ships, fulls of those constructs, were setting sail to meet the Electrians. It took everything loyal and good within Lynd to not wipe out some poor Heartbrand's memories and take control of one of those ships, and sail it to Hop, wherever that was. "I won't leave Kal. And I can't let anythin' happen to Ada, either."

Lynd rushed toward the Akademy, finding her way down the wooden docks and onto the cobblestone streets without much trouble. And when she did happen to come across someone with the time to ask who she was or where she was going — *Tik!*

More marching Heartbrands poured out of the Akademy gates with their namesake glowing swords held high as Lynd arrived. In their wartime stampede, they barely glanced at the girl as she ran into the courtyard. Commandress Ada was addressing the Xth Legion on the green, "This line — you'll march via the Grace Archbridge to the outer island. Make a stand there in case Electri feints and swings around to the north." Her bright blue heartbrand, a fearsome, curved saber, appeared in her raised hand. She boomed, "Everyone from this side down — with me to docks! The constructs have begun the first wave. Take to the sky only after they're through. Save your myra! They will never take our city!"

"Commandress!" the Xth Legion chanted, all creating beautiful heartbrands in their hands. Each one of them appeared to have a set of technical-looking wings on their backs. "Commandress!"

As Ada marched out with roughly fifty Heartbrands, General Bend suddenly stepped onto the path in front of her. A brilliant bulky sword of his own burst into his hand, reflecting off his golden armor.

"General XIII!" said Ada, stopping in her tracks. "Reinforce part of the Xth on the outer island. It's a weak point in the defenses!"

Bend raised his weapon, shouting, "Xth Legion! This woman is your Commandress no more."

Ada was stunned.

Lynd's fists tightened.

General XIII continued, "Report to General Case at the docks with XI and XII. *We* will actually save lives today."

To Ada's second shock, the Heartbrands obeyed Bend and marched at his word without her.

"You despicable cur," Ada yelled. "A coup *now*? While we're being attacked?"

"I told you Electri would attack!" Bend screamed at the top of his lungs. "And you did *nothing*!" He swung his dazzling blue heartbrand down upon her — *Cling!* — and she blocked it with her own. "The enemy is at our gate!" He forced her through the courtyard grass, slicing bushes and leaving branches in their wake. *Clang!* "My son is infected with Ruin!" *Cling!* "All because of you!" He took a swipe at her legs, but Ada jumped up the stairs to the Hall of the Arkons.

Lynd ran after them.

At the top of the marble stairs, the Commandress shouted, "We cannot win this divided, Bend! Stand down from here and head to the battlefield. All will be forgiven!"

Bend dashed up the stairs and forced their flashy duel into the Hall.

Lynd was in a fog shock, yet unsurprised that Bend would directly attack Ada. Again, it was for helping the girl. She couldn't bear it. Something had to be done. None of this was fair. All the abuse and frustration simmered deep within her. She rushed to the Hall to do what she had to do. As she ran up the stairs, she heard Ada cry out in pain.

Lynd ran in and saw the general pinning Ada through the shoulder against an Arkon statue with his sword. Her kind face was distorted in agony. Red blood dripped at the cut of his blue heartbrand.

Ada cried, arm stretched out to the girl, "Lynd! Help me!"

"*Yer* the monster!" Lynd summoned all her power and began a Ruin Time myracle on the general's whole body. He squirmed, resisting with all his might, edging his way to the girl. But she was too strong. His skin greyed, creases forming and deepening. His weapon disappeared into the breeze. Until finally, Bend turned entirely to ashy stone, fitting in well with the tall Arkons lording over the room.

It was done. General Bend wouldn't hurt anyone anymore.

Lynd's arms fell to her side. Panting and feeling the powerful currents of Ruin flowing through her body, she immediately questioned whether it was the right thing to do. But with Ada being attacked, how could it not be?

She ran to her, "Ada! Ya'kay?"

"Yes, child. Yes." Ada stepped away from the statue where she was just pinned.

Lynd went to embrace her and happened to notice the elaborate golden box was now hanging from her belt. "Ya have to open that. General Bend . . . Why do *ya* have—?"

The Commandress smirked and began full belly laughing, stepping to the center of the room, her voice echoing amongst the statues. Her laugh became deeper and deeper pitched, finally rolling into General Bend's voice. His face then emerged from Ada's. It was the general who was pinned and the Commandress who had the upper hand.

"I knew you wouldn't let me down." He kicked Ada's ashy form; she was stiff as a statue. "Monster."

"No!" Lynd roared, clenching her fists and jaw. She looked at the victim of her powerful Ruin Time myracle. It wasn't the general. It was indeed Ada. The general had created his most diabolical Mirage yet.

"I did what I had to, to save Carpè," said Bend. "Ada would've seen to our destruction, and maybe all of Esa's. She was a traitor to every being on this planet." He turned his heartbrand to the girl. "And *you* are our greatest threat!"

Lynd was horrified at what she had done and furious at the general for making it happen. The sight of Ada's face, frozen in betrayal, drove her mad. She felt like her mind was tearing itself apart. Enraged as never before, Lynd's skin began to radiate red, staining the marble walls and statues in her furious color.

Through her tight teeth, she said, "I'll tear ya apart . . ." Then an arc of pure Ruin myra discharged from her hand, a bolt of scarlet lightning.

Bend blocked it with his heartbrand, but the sheer force of the impact sent him backward against the statue of Bello. His Pocket Realm prison box rattled onto the floor, bursting open.

In a puff of colorful smoke, Kal materialized into the center Hall of the Arkons. He quickly darted his eyes across the scene — Lynd was practically burning with Ruin power, his father was barely able to stand against the statue base, the Commandress was turned to stone in the center. The ground shook with the start of Electri's onslaught on the island.

"Dad!" He ran to him. "What happened?"

"We have to stop her, son," he said, coughing. "She's trying to take us down while we're being attacked!"

Kal looked up to Ada. He knew exactly how she ended up that way. "Lynd? Ruin Time? On *Ada?*"

"He tricked me!" Lynd shouted, "*He* attacked the Commandress!"

"Don't listen to her, son! She will destroy us all. Can't you see; her myra is red as blood!"

Kal backed away from his father, but he did not move any closer to Lynd either. Just like whenever he'd hear the whispers coming from his inner island, he wasn't sure whom to believe.

"She attacked me," said Bend, getting to his feet. He brandished his weapon at the girl. "As Commander of the Heartbrands, in self-defense of Carpè, I will quell this Ruin here and now!" He then lunged at Lynd, his sword ready to slice her down.

Clink! Another heartbrand blocked his just before it cut Lynd's nose. The myra blade that stopped him rippled between shades of red and blue. Holding it was his son.

"Kal? A heartbrand? You haven't the skill for that. And what is all this *red* in it?"

He looked at his father in the eyes, his arm rattling as he held back the general's attack. His weapon was unstable and jittery; he hadn't actually gone through Heartbrand training, only watched from the roof and absorbed what he could. "You will not hurt her!"

Bend sneered and recoiled. Rather than take another slash at his son, he began walking in a circle around the mighty statues. "Don't forget where you stand! The Arkons faced this same abomination. And it destroyed them *all!*"

Kal positioned himself between his father and Lynd. The girl looked at her friend. She might have been caught off guard by Bend once, but she didn't need Kal to fight this battle for her. Still, she recognized there was more to their fight than her or defending Carpè. This was a long-brewing feud between father and son, truth and lies.

"The Arkons used Ruin to defeat the Voids," said Kal.

"They were forced to," the general said. "We still have a choice. But she will rip that choice right from our hands! As Ruin spreads, it gains power." He pointed his rigid finger at the girl. "And *she* is gaining power. The only answer is to squash it before it's too late! Help me, Kal. Please . . . All I've ever done, wrong or right, was to protect you."

"Protection?" Kal's heartbrand ignited with a more intense reddish tint. ". . . Is that why you lied to me about mom?"

"Your mother?" Bend stepped back. "Kal, who told you that?"

"I-I always knew to truth," he answered, trembling. Tears ran down his cheeks. His two-colored heartbrand lost more blue. "Her funeral — it was all a Mirage . . ."

"What are you saying—"

"It's true, isn't it?" Kal yelled, teardrops raining to the polished floor. "Isn't it?"

"I beg you, son. Renounce that Ruin. Renounce this girl." The general walked to him. "Whatever you created to deal with my myracle . . . It's just a sign of your Elix capabilities. Together, we can fix you—"

"It's not her fault!" Kal jumped and swung at his father — *Clink!* His heartbrand was almost entirely red. The barrier he created in his mind crumbled; his Ruin was free. "You have no idea what you've done to me!"

Clink! "Listen to me!"

"I trusted you!" *Clink!* "I believed she was gone!" *Clink!* His sword swings grew more and more overbearing, nearly knocking the great general of the XIIIth Legion to his knees. "I saw her in the coffin . . . But I knew it wasn't real. I always knew . . . But my trust in you, my father. It held the Ruin back."

"Kal!"

"You still send her letters at the Everbloom, don't you? Don't you think I deserve to speak to my own mother?"

Lynd gathered a large pool of Ruin in her left hand, ready to strike down the general at any moment. But not before Kal got the closure he needed.

The general got his balance and shifted his stance in the lull. "Damn it, boy! I was going to tell you. You were just so young. And you needed an answer why she was gone . . . And she doesn't write me back. Your mother fell ill, that much you must remember? And she is only *falsely* alive, only by the Sap of that tree! If she stepped anywhere near this city, she would be dust. She *is* dead, Kal!"

Just then, an Electri ship fired an energy cannon right at the gates of the Akademy, quaking the grounds.

"The city's in trouble," Lynd yelled.

Kal turned to his friend. "You go. I can handle him."

"Yer sure?" she said, just as another Electri bolt struck a nearby building, rattling everyone's ears.

"Go!" Kal cried.

Lynd ran through the gates of the Akademy, down the hilly streets to the docks, where the battle was in full bloom. Electri's weapons streaked across the sky like yellow shooting stars. The explosions were so jolting and loud she had to cover her ears while she ran. Heartbrands stood gallantly in defense of the approaching enemy ships. Marble constructs of all leg-counts were assembling barriers and carrying the wounded to safety. And there were a lot of wounded. The Electrian guns were simply overwhelming.

After what happened to Ada, Lynd had to do something with the well of Ruin power boiling within her, ready to erupt. But she wanted it to be a good thing. The girl peered out at the Electrian fleet. Three of their ships were closing in on one of the piers. Her eyes flickered with ruby rage. Even after all the Carpèan people had put her through, she needed to redeem herself to herself. "I am not a monster!"

Back inside the Hall of the Arkons — *Clink! Clink! Clink!* —the battle between father and son intensified. The XIIIth general started dodging the boy's swings entirely, quickly weaving from side to side. He flicked his tongue with a *tsk-tsk-tsk*. Kal slashed clean through his father's sword arm. But then Bend's image began to flicker. Right before the young man's eyes, his father's form split into two, then four, doubling and doubling around him in a circle — another Mirage.

Sixteen General Bend's surrounded him, smirking, laughing. "Maybe you should consider, son." They walked in closer, each with their own weapon pointed, tightening the circle. "That your mother left us for that damned Sap!"

At his terrible words, Kal's heart finally shattered completely. The barrier he had built, the one that kept his Ruin safety on an inner island, lost its strength. The volcano was whole again. And it was ready to erupt.

"You need to tell yourself that. Deal with it how you wish. *Rot* with it if you wish. But I've split myself in two long enough! One foot in the truth, and the other in the world you wanted me to believe. And now I see you." Ignoring all other images of his father, Kal leaped at the one directly in front of him. Perhaps Bend didn't think there was any chance his son would pick the right one; he didn't even defend himself. But Kal's red, red heartbrand cut the general right down the jaw to his chest.

The mighty General XIII immediately fell in pain, shock, and horror. Looking up in his son's watering eyes, he saw every one of his own wrongs. He thought he was doing the right thing by creating the Mirage to give his son closure he might not otherwise have. The truth — that she was bound to the Everbloom and its immortal sauce, forever without them — seemed too much to tell a child. Why torture him with a mother who was all but lost anyway? But at that moment, Bend saw that all he did was make a space where broken trust would turn to heartache and Ruin. And now it was too late. "Life is cruel, Kal. I was just trying to keep you strong."

Kal put his blade tip under his father's neck and tilted the man's head up with it. "It worked."

Lynd walked down to the end of the pier steel-eyed, ripping apart any electri blasts that came near her; she was like an impenetrable shield moving out to sea. Finally, the bow of the Electrian ship came to the edge. The gnomes lined up to the railing, reading to attack on land. The girl raised her hand and released all her wrath upon the ship's approaching bow.

At once, that riveted metallic bow peeled open like a banana, twisting open to the sea with an ear-shattering screech. The hull crunched as if struck by a whale on both sides. All aboard screamed leaped off into the sea like fleas off a dog. Another of Electri's ships encroached behind it, this one even larger. The girl raised her other hand, and its bow smashed in suddenly as if hitting an invisible wall — their firing cannons exploding one by one in an epic fireworks display in the waters of Carpè.

The Heartbrands and citizens alike watching from the coasts couldn't believe their eyes. A single girl had turned the tide. Their morale renewed at the sight of this brave girl standing alone at the edge of the pier, tearing through the enemy like nothing they'd ever seen in war or peace.

General Case ran up the pier with part of the XIth Legion. "They're fleeing," said Case. "Electri is turning back. We're saved!" She turned to her Heartbrands. "We won! *We won!*"

The Legion erupted in celebration, quickly spreading down the docks, through the streets, and up to the damaged Akademy gates.

General XI couldn't believe what she had just seen. So much destruction had rained upon them. But the power of Ruin, through this girl, had saved their lives.

Kal Bend ventured down to the docks, head down and heart heavy. As everyone celebrated, he regretfully informed them, "Commandress Ada was lost in the battle."

After such joy, a silence swept through them all, Legionnaire and citizen alike. He looked down the dock at Lynd, the brave girl who'd saved them all. Raising his fist, he called out, "Lynd Izz saved me . . . She saved us all! She led us to victory!"

Case approached the girl, who was still breathing heavily. Doubts swirled in her mind, but there was no denying who was most capable of protecting Carpè now. After the Arkons' Last Myracle, could it be possible that Ruin had saved Esa once again?

The general got to one knee and bowed her head to Lynd.

With the lights of Electri's ships fading quickly in the horizon, the Legions hailed their savior, Lynd Izz — "Commandress! Commandress!"

CHAPTER 25

MIRAGES

G ai kept listening to see if Tesse would say anything to him in his mind again, but all he heard was himself asking, *What did she mean by sentenced to death?*

Tesse stared straight ahead as they left the Everbloom trunk behind, sullen and a little shock-eyed. She spoke with neither mouth nor mind.

Mac was fidgeting nervously, trading glances over his shoulders back at the tree like a hungry pup yanked away from its bowl. Finally, he said, "You guys want to—ugh—have that toast, now?"

"It's just this way," said Tesse. "There's a small river transport ahead that has a full jar of undiluted Sap."

"Undiluted?" said Mac, practically drooling. "And *full*, you say? All for me — I mean, us?"

Tesse stopped suddenly and keeled over as if her stomach cramped into knots.

Gai went to help her up. "Ya'kay?"

"Yes." She regained her composure and continued walking. "Come. It's not long, now." Tesse guided them through a maze of branches outside the Everbloom clearing to the bank of a babbling stream. A small vinc-covered rowboat waited there. "Get in," she said, picking off the rustling greenery.

The boy and Ex-Heartbrand sat in quietly enough, but as Tesse grabbed hold of the oars and pushed off into the flow, Mac insisted,

"I don't see any cups? Don't we need cups? Are we sucking it right out of a tree limb? I'd love to try that."

"The supplies are underneath my seat," she said, rowing gently. "We'll mix the undiluted Sap with fresh water from a special spring down this river. It enhances the taste tremendously."

"Enhanced? I can't imagine it getting any better!" Mac said. Then his stomach made a sound similar to a *gurgle grr*, but even crankier. "Anyone else feel funny?"

"The Ruin is regaining hold," Tesse said in Gai's head. *"His body is craving more Sap to fill in the holes."*

"*Is he gonna be a'kay?*" the boy thought.

"This river leads to a channel near Carpè. Do not tell him, or he will swim back to the Everbloom in a panic."

Gai looked Tesse over. She didn't seem well either; there was a winded looked about her, like she was rowing ten boats and not one. He thought, *"Do ya need Sap, too?"*

Tesse just kept rowing. They soon arrived at the brackish mouth of the river. She then propelled the boat out to the open water as fast as she could.

"What kind of spring is in the ocean?" Mac looked back and started breathing heavily. "Where are you taking us?" he demanded. "I-I feel like I'm—I don't know. My joints hurt." He started rubbing his neck near his wound. It appeared to be slowly reopening.

Tesse put the oars down, breathing like she just climbed the entire Everbloom in a sprint.

"Here," said Gai. "Lemme row."

As the boy took over the oars, Tesse sat by Mac and let him lay his head back onto her lap. He was clenching his jaw like he was chewing on a rock. She held the Ex-Heartbrand's head like a sick child. The black scars up his neck and jaw seemed to budge more and more with every exhale.

"So that Sap can cure Ruin, but only if ya keep drinkin' it?" Gai said aloud. "That's no cure!"

Looking at Mac's sweaty, agonized face, the boy wondered if this was how his father looked before becoming a Void; if that was how he suffered? His heart felt sorry for them both. Under his breath, he said, "How could we live in a world where there's no cure for this?"

Mac's breathing quickened. "Tesse . . . For old time's sake." His eyes were bloodshot and teary. "Just a drop? Where's the Sap?"

The curly-haired girl's lips shook as she started to tear up. "'For old time's sake.' Don't give me that. You stopped sending me letters ten years ago."

"I never stopped loving you," he said and coughed. "I want you to know that."

Tesse looked away. "Save your strength, general."

"I'm no general anymore," said Mac.

"A'kay, sounds like ya know each other? Ya look like—"

"Husband and wife," Tesse said. "Once upon a time."

"What?" Gai almost let the oars slip right out of his hands. "But yer so young!"

Tesse cleared her throat. "I was a professor at the Myracles Akademy when I met General Bend. I'm actually a bit older than he is. The age I seem now is just the work of the Everbloom's Sap. I went to live there about twenty years ago. But the Sap heals nearly all ailments, even age. That's why Spen calls it the immortal sauce. I won't have access to it anymore. And all my years will come rushing back. As you noticed," she gestured to Mac, uncomfortably shaking in her lap. "As soon as you stop drinking the Sap, it all comes back."

Gai was open-mouthed stunned for a beat. "How long before it wears off?"

"A good gulp can keep even death at bay for a few hours," she said.

As Gai watched her speaking, a wrinkle formed around her mouth. Then he noticed a few more around her eyes. It was all happening so subtly that he wondered if they had been there the whole time.

She continued, running her hands through Mac's hair, "For General Bend, the dose will be used up more quickly. This is because the Sap was satiating his Ruin myra."

The boy gazed upon struggling Mac. "Ruin's a hungry thing, yeah?"

"Yes." Tesse sighed. "That was always the trouble with Ruin."

Gai looked at what was becoming of the man. Mac was a mentor to him; without his pushy brand of encouragement in Zeea's painting, he might never have known his full potential. It was no surprise for the boy to learn Mac was once a general of some kind; he knew how to motivate. Hard lines were slowly coming back to his face as well. The gray returned to his hair. The scar down his jaw and chest was back, with thin black veins branching off. "Is there no way to stop him from becoming a Void?"

"Becoming a Void is the ultimate destination of a person with too much Ruin myra. It's a matter of nature," she said, appearing closer and closer to the Ex-Heartbrand general's age every moment. She paused, having a bit of trouble breathing. "A person that uses Ruin myracles begins to need it more and more. It's like a weight on the heart that keeps getting heavier. So they have to keep destroying, increasing their capacity to destroy as they go, like a snowball rolling down a hill. Until eventually, their body collapses under the weight of all that Ruin. They become a vortex of emptiness . . . *This.*"

Gai kept watching the horizon ahead, hoping for the city with all the answers to come up soon. He feared for Lynd. Who knew if she kept on destroying things since he saw her last? He wondered if he was already too late. He thought about Kabbage, too. His list of people to help was getting long. His nerves were working overtime, so he took it out on the oars and pumped them faster. He changed the subject before his head exploded. "Why'd ya move to the Everbloom? Is that the reason Mac has . . ."

"No," Tesse said. "I'm not sure what caused his myra to change to red." She looked down upon him. "Like many other Bloomers, I used the Sap to cure myself of an illness when nothing else worked. It was a last resort. And also like many Bloomers . . . I didn't believe it would keep me locked to it for eternity. My husband at the time, General Mac Bend, here, begged me to wait for the Akademy to find a Elix means of healing. But I was so sick and so afraid of leaving our son behind."

"I would be, too," said Gai.

"I made a choice." She sighed, reaching under her shirt and pulling a silver bracelet tied to a thin rope around her neck. "I've had to live unnaturally long with it."

Mac twitched when he saw the bracelet dangling above him. He tried to lift his head. "K-Kal!" He just couldn't find the strength to grasp the bracelet.

"I was saving this." Tesse reached up to her hair and unpinned it, letting it fall. It was much more gray than before. She held up the pin to Mac's nose. It was a single sliver of Everbloom wood, no wider than a blade of grass. "Some things even Spen doesn't suspect. Take it."

Mac bit down on the little branch and chewed it like a stalk of wheat. He stared at the morning sky as his breathing stabilized. Then, with a small amount of vitality returning, he said, "Our son, T-Tesse. I did something . . . awful to him."

"What?" she said, concerned.

"When you left, I made him think that you passed on. I regret it every d-day."

Tesse closed her eyes. "You didn't want him longing for something he could never have."

Cough. "That's not all," he struggled to say. "I felt so badly for him. Elix Mirage — your funeral. I wanted him to be able to move on. To give him closure."

Tesse popped her eyes open, shocked. "That's . . . worse."

"It backfired, Tesse," Mac said. "It only confused him. He knew the truth in his heart, but his eyes told him something else, thanks to me."

"Don't tell me — *Ruin?*" she said.

"Yes, and in a way I've never seen before." *Cough-Cough.* "He trusted me, so his Elix myra created a barrier to push back the Ruin. It must've been a constant strain on his energy. The boy was resilient. Until . . ."

"Kal . . ." Tesse's face was so sullen. All her features looked like they were melting. A tear drop landed on Mac. "I understand why Spen calls us Tamperers. Some things are not for us to meddle in. You should've told him the truth but . . . This is all my fault."

Gai felt so awful for them both. "'Ey, maybe yer son still lives in Carpè? It's not that far, yeah?"

Ex-General Bend's body began to cramp up again. ". . . I won't make it."

Ahead at the horizon, the boy spotted a few dots. "Well, here come those Electri ships," he said, rowing. "I saw 'em before I met Spen. Any ideas how we can get through?"

"Gai." Mac sat up in the boat with Tesse's help. "The last time Electri's ships surrounded Carpè, I used a Mirage myracle — made them think we were a school of fish. We snuck past. Do you remember that day, Tesse? I came with that . . . *girl*." He grabbed his neck in pain. "Ack! That must've been ten yeas ago by now. That was the last day I saw Kal!" Tesse, with her own bones and muscles weakening by the moment, rested her hand on his shoulder to soothe him. "I deserve all the Ruin that comes to me." Ex-General Mac Bend looked right into Gai's eyes. "I need to see Kal. One last time. Please."

The behemoth Electri vessels loomed larger and larger ahead. "A'kay, we can see Kal if ya do that fish trick again."

". . . I don't do myracles anymore."

"Can ya teach me, then?"

Mac's face creased in pain. "You really do remind me of him." He looked up at Tesse. "Doesn't he remind you of Kal?"

Gai felt like crying at their story. Mac wasn't even worried about what was going to happen to him. But if the goal for all was to get to Carpè, they had to get there without being Electri Wonder Weapon target practice. "Teach me Elix Mirage, quick!"

"Let him rest." Tesse laid Mac down flat on the floor of the boat for comfort. "Mirage myracles work by having a clear image in your mind of what you want the world to see. Then push it out. Add a little Elix myra, and you can fool anyone."

"So it's like when I made these." Gai kicked out his armored boots.

"You know a lot for someone who wasn't at the Akademy," she said.

"Mac taught me a lot."

"You must truly remind him of our son. Mac always disliked teaching." Tesse gazed with her maturing eyes at the rail of the boat. "We need practice. The wood from this boat is made of a babanut tree. Imagine there's a babanut right beside me."

"I wish there was." Gai stared at the seat next to her. "A'kay. I'm imaginin' there's a babanut right there. And it's makin' my mouth water."

"Still looks empty to me," said Tesse. "When students first start with Mirage myracles, it helps to close their eyes," she said. "It's harder to project an illusion while you're staring at reality. You have to learn how to trick your own eyes for that."

The boy did as she suggested, closing his eyes and picturing a nice big babanut by her. "Ya see a babanut yet?"

"Ah! I do," said Tesse, looking about sixty years old by now. "You remind me of Kal a bit, too. He was a wonder with Elix myracles."

Mac groaned on the floor. "I'm so sorry, Kal . . ."

Ready or not, they were about to be within spotting distance from the Electri ships. "Guide me," the boy said. Gai rowed forward with his eyes closed, which wasn't easy. He imagined the oars were flippers, and the boat was a small turtle shell, innocently gliding through the water.

"Good," Tesse said, appearing exhausted. "I don't see anyone moving on their decks. Keep going. A little harder on the left."

Slowly, they crossed the blockade and continued rowing toward the inner island of Carpè.

Gurgle grr.

"*Hey!*" Someone shouted from the deck of the closest Electri ship. "What's *that?*"

"Oh, no," the boy panicked.

"Keep going," Tesse strained to say. "Level your thoughts. They're just looking at the water. Just think of yer sister and that if this fails, you won't get to her."

"That's just a baby Plunder's," another person on the Electri vessel's deck said.

"Good work," said Tesse.

"How did ya know I was lookin' for my sister?" said Gai.

"Mind Link. It's a basic Elix myracle." By now, Tesse was beginning to look quite a great deal sicklier. Her eye sockets darkened. Her face thinned. Her skin drooped.

Past the metal Electri fleet, a line of wooden ships were waiting to leave the docks of Carpè. The boy had many questions brewing for the supposed experts in myra who called this island home. He struggled to keep his concentration on the moment.

"Don't let your Mirage slip just yet. Paddle the left oar for a while. We need to round the inner island."

Gurgle grr. "But I'm gettin' so hungry!"

"Around the bend here." Tesse's voice withered and whistled like a fragile, older woman. "You can drop the Mirage now."

"Thanks at ya!" Gai's empty belly hurt so much that he had to let go of the oars and press on it. *Gurgle grr.*

Tesse looked at her heavily aged reflection in the water. "Oh, my." She then cupped some water in her hand and wet the rail of the wooden boat. "I haven't done this some time." She looked up at the morning sun, relaxing into its rays. "Mm. And it'll be the last time."

The boy was still trying to get the strength back to keep rowing, "What're ya doin'?"

Tesse inhaled deeply and put her hands over the wet rail. "This boat was made from a babanut tree, remember?" A faint blue glow erupted under her hands. A small sprig with a leaf curled out, growing from the wood. She struggled to give it enough myra to keep growing, but soon a whole, ripe fruit hung from the young branch.

Tesse picked it. "Here. I'm sorry it's not more, but I'm out of practice. We don't use myra for Elix *or* Ruin at the Everbloom."

"Thanks at ya . . ." The babanut was a small one, but he was genuinely grateful for any scape of food. Gai broke it open over the rail and munched on the sweet filling inside. He was done in less than five bites and even surgically bit the remaining flesh on the inside of the hard shell. "Feels much better." He grabbed the oars and began rowing to the inner island again.

Now even weaker from performing that small Elix myracle, Tesse could barely lift her arm to point at a fissure in the rock. "There, the In Inn was built over that. There's a path they walk down to get water to wash dishes where we can climb up."

Gai looked them over. "Ya sure ya can climb?"

With the hint of a smile, the woman said, "No."

CHAPTER 26

THE BIG REUNION

T he boy rowed them into the land-wedge, where it looked like a tiny slice of the inner island pie had been taken off the platter. There was indeed a set of haphazard stairs carved up the wet rocks to a door. As the babanut tree boat softly pulled up to the edge, Gai looked up the steep climb, then down at the two older people barely able to move. "A'way! One of ya on either side of me. Ya can find yer son. I'll find out how to help Pa and Lynd. Then, we'll have a big reunion! All of us."

Mac Bend stood, rickety as a forgotten bridge. He'd saved the last of his strength for when they arrived in Carpè. Tesse wasn't as shaky but still moved poorly. It wasn't just her age coming back; the illness she had when she started drinking Sap was coming back for her, too. The trio carefully marched each step in sync with a "one, two, three — up!" all the way to the In Inn door. Thirty-three "up's" later, they squeezed through the In's back door, making their greatest effort *not* to seem like a group of random quirks coming up from the sea crack.

Inside, the In Inn was bustling; all were too busy to even notice the quirks. Artistic prints and stylish furniture decorated every cranny of the place. When they walked in, directly on the wall next to a painting of colorful swirls was a sign telling them where to stand for war effort recruitment, depending on whether they were sailors or soldiers. A bit further in was a stiff, tidy-looking woman in her forties waving forward a line of at least forty people to her desk. "Next!" she said to an elderly man who approached. "Yes?" she barked. "What can you do to help defend the city? Quickly, now!" The elderly man replied that he had three small fishing boats and a crew of four. "Approved!" She stamped a piece of paper and handed it to him. "Take these to General Osstett at the docks. Next!"

"Excuse me?" Gai said to her.

Ah! She jumped. "By Bello! You scared the peace out of me! Line starts over—" The woman looked the boy over, then at his two barely standing companions. "We need all the help we can get. But maybe you better sit this one out."

"Uh, no," said the boy. "We're looking for the Inn In?"

"You're in the In. You're also in the way, so move out! Next!"

"A'kay." As the boy made his way to the other side of the well-decorated room, he heard a commotion down a small corridor. There was a door in the small hallway, and from the tummy-tingling smells billowing from it, Gai assumed it had to be the kitchen. A really good one.

There was a heated discussion behind that smelly door. He heard a man say, "They had me prisoner for five years!" Then, "Been a sailor my whole life. There's no way I shouldn't be out their captainin' for ya! A'way, now."

Gai stopped, Tesse dangling off his right shoulder and the ex-general completely hunched over his left. The voice seemed familiar. He whispered, "*Is that?*"

A young woman wearing a peach angular suit came through the door, continuing their discussion — "If that's true, where's your ship? How about a crew? Where's anything that would prove your sea chops? Other than that musky smell."

Right behind her, a tall man turned the corner wearing raggedy striped pants and a paper hat. A stained apron draped over the front of him, and he was using it to polish up a spoon as he walked. "Honest . . . I dunno where my crew went," he said. "O-or how I got here for that matter. But I was a captain, that's true!" It was none other than Baald Penn.

"Right," the young woman scoffed. "We get a lot of that. The answer is no. Besides, I need you to scrub my toilets." She turned, barely noticing Gai and the two sickly folks leaning on him, and huffed to the front of the In.

"Unc!"

"Gai? *Gaiel* Izz!" Baald nearly choked. "What kind of nasty wind brought ya up this way? How'd ya get off Hop—oh, never mind that, come here!" Unc's dirty spoon clinked on the ground as he came to hug the boy. But then he realized he couldn't quite get his arms around all three people. "Right—uh. Who's this? A fan club?" He gave an all-over look to weak Tesse and Ruin-riddled Mac. "By Zeea! I-I know what those marks mean! Ya better back away!"

"Unc!" Gai exclaimed. Then he whispered, "Unc, I'm happy to see ya, too. But ya know how bad this is." The boy glanced at Mac. "I need to get 'em a room and some help. Please at ya?"

"How is it I keep gettin' wrapped up with these monsters?" he said. "No offense. Anyway, they're doin' *war* recruitments here. I think the rooms are all taken." Baald locked eyes with the fancy-suited lady with whom he was just arguing and shouted, "Faan!"

Faan scurried back over through the crowded room, frantically checking off checkmarks on her clipboard. She looked at him with just a splash of contempt. "What *now*?"

"My nephew, Gai, here needs a cabin to cool his sails. Ya got any?"

"Stop talking like that," she said. "I'm not going to believe you're a captain just because you reference boat things." Faan then turned to Gai with a tiny, barely-noticeable look of indifference. "We're full up at the momen—" Then her mouth just stopped moving. She came closer and looked Mac right in his barely open eyes. "General *Bend*? We haven't seen you since . . . Not since the last attack from Electri!" She glanced at them all with a very clear expression of distaste. "You all look terrible!"

"Faan," Mac strained to say. "The In Inn kept extra rooms for Heartbrands?"

"We do," she said. "But you're not . . ." Faan Mink, whose family owned the In Inn, analyzed their condition as a wave of pity came across her eyes. "Baald, help them up the stairs." She fished in her pocket and handed him a key. "Room 76."

"A'kay, kid," said Unc. "I'll take this gent up, and ya help the lady."

"Thanks at ya." The boy and his Hopper uncle carefully went up the stairs, each with their own baggage. "When'd ya get here?" Gai asked. "What happened with the *Merry*?"

"Oh, that." Baald opened the door to Room 76 and helped Mac lay on a bed, taking keen note of the stage of those black scars on his neck. "Same thing as Stav, alright. What about her? Is she?"

"No." Gai helped Tesse get comfortable in another bed beside Mac. "She's just been drinkin' Sap to stay alive. Ever been to the Everbloom?"

"No." Baald seemed a bit shocked his little nephew had even heard of it. How exactly did he get out of Hop, again? Did he get his mother's permission? "That's the famous tree, yeah? And how might ya know about that?"

"I don't think we got time, Unc. I need to find someone to help 'em. Have ya heard anyone talkin' about a thing called myra here?"

"Oh, sure. Sure," Baald muttered. "Comes with another word near it. Elitzer?"

"Elix."

"Closer than I thought I'd be."

Tesse started to *cough, cough.*

Gai went to open the window. "A'kay, so where'd ya hear it? Where can I find people who know about it?"

"Bad memories." Baald covered Mac's face with a blanket so he wouldn't have to look at his Void-ness. "Ugh, where? Myra, myra . . . Faan talks about some school with that name all the time."

"Unc . . . *How long* ya been here?"

"Maybe a week or two. Not sure how long I was unconscious for, though."

"What happened on the *Merry*, Unc?" The boy sat down at the foot of Tesse's bed. "Ya know, it came back to Hop and crashed right into Tanning's house, yeah?"

"I'll cry privately about my *Lady*, later." Baald looked over Mac's dark veins spreading to his forehead. "But what happened was yer pa, Gai. We we're headin' here, actually. But then yer sister appears out of nowhere! Right on my deck like a catch outta Domus. Now, Stav was just about where yer friend here is, but he reached out to her, tryin' to get her to go home, I guess. But that little Lynd wouldn't have it. Next thing I know, there's these two flashes and swirls, then a wild explosion. I thought I was dead, kid. Wouldn't ya know I wake up after some sailors netted me out of the sea right outside these docks here! And not just me! The whole crew aboard got sent up this way."

"What about Pa and Lynd?"

"Haven't seen 'em yet. But here's the kicker — me and the crew got sent here? Well, not at the same time, we didn't! I got here last week. Knee-Knocker said he got here a month back. Avey's been here a whole *year*. Nothin' about what yer Pa and sister did was right. Ripped a damn hole in time and just sprinkled us about anywhere!"

"Ruin and Ruin," Gai muttered.

Click! The door to Room 76 locked.

"'Ey!" Baald ran over to the knob and turned it back and forth. "They locked us in! Faan! Let us out! Faan!"

"General Bend is a traitor," Faan said behind the door. "He killed Commandress Ada during the First Myracite War. Electri is at our door, and he just happens to show up again — looking like *that*? And you with all your obvious lying! You're clearly spies!"

"Faan, please at ya," said Unc. "We need to get these guys some help. Somethin' bad is gonna happen!"

"I called the Heartbrands as soon as you went upstairs," she said. "You can explain it all to them."

Mac groaned. "Kal . . ."

Baald banged on the door. "Faan!" He heard her footsteps run back downstairs.

"This can't get any worse." Gai held his head.

They were in there! I saw them! They heard someone yelling outside. *Right in the In Inn!*

"Oh, it can get worse." Baald ran to the window. "More bad memories. We got the guards surrounding us. Tell me the truth — Do I *look* like an outlaw or somethin'?"

The boy went to the window. A crowd had gathered quickly outside around a large fountain with a statue of a woman inside. Frightened citizens, unsure recruits, and armored Heartbrands alike were on the street in front of the In. In the center, staring right at their window, was a tall man with dark features and golden armor. "I know him," said Gai. "He came to Hop after the *Merry* crashed! General XIII!"

"Kal!" Mac shouted, sitting up.

That man outside stood calmly, arms folded.

A citizen shouted with a fist. *Go get him, General Bend!*

The Defender of Carpè! cheered another.

Mac reached out his arms like he was trying to grab onto some-one. But at once, zapping arcs of Ruin energy shot from the ex-general's palms. The bed sheets, the mattress, and the rug all tore to shreds in a flourish of destructive red light.

"A'way!" Gai knocked his Unc out of the red zap's path. The zap then struck a wall and ripped all the wood beams into sawdust. A breeze blew in through the new giant hole in the room. The people on the street looked up with oval mouths.

As the golden armored General XIII, the Defender of Carpè, watched through the shattered room from below, the black scars on Mac Bend's face deepened and spread.

"Forgive me," Mac cried as his body absorbed more Ruin myra from the destroyed items around the room. The darkness cast over his outstretched hands and morphed them into cutting, black claws.

Tesse strained to speak, gasping. "He's gone . . . He's feeding on Ruin. My love is gone!"

"Not again!" Baald scurried himself to the corner near the door.

The general below yelled to his guards, "Legion XIII! Get every citizen out of the In, now!" A stunningly bright heartbrand formed in his hand.

It was a giant sword, taller than himself. It was unlike any other heartbrand weapon the boy had seen. It was jittering back and forth between a red and blue light. Whether the inner island still existed in his mind or not, Kal was still the unique young man with both extremes of myra flowing through him. And he seemed to have mastered the balance.

"Void!" he yelled out with fury. "You have relinquished your right to exist!"

Mac roared like a beast and leaped through the freshly demol-ished wall right down to the street, scattering the crowd.

All twenty or so members of the XIIIth Legion dashed across the area, helping citizens to safety. Then they poured into the In Inn, shuttling everyone to any hiding spots they could find.

Baald and Gai watched from the blown-out wall at the father-son,

Void-Heartbrand showdown about to take place on the typically quiet streets of Carpè.

Kal glanced up and noticed the boy in the destroyed room. "You?" he said in disbelief. "From that floating woodpile? Is this *your* Void?"

"Mine?" Gai yelled back. "No! But we have to help him!"

"You brought him here!" Kal roared. "Peddling Voids into the city is so bad it's not even an actual law!" He looked to his comrades. "You two — Seize that young man!"

"Oh, shit!" Baald shot up from the corner. "Pardon my Electrian. I'll fend 'em off. Ya get outta here!"

Before the boy could even start to run, he was suddenly struck with the strangest sensation. He felt like his legs were moving through a thick syrup. It seemed to take forever just to turn his head. Any way he went to move was excessively long. Time itself had slowed down. But only for him, as two dashing Heartbrands appeared quickly on either side of him. He knew they must've performed some powerful Elix myracle. They both hooked him under either arm as time returned to normal.

Baald jumped to help his nephew, but they performed the Time Elix myracle on him as well, freezing him in the room. Finally, the Heartbrands both leaped down to the street, gripping the boy tight.

"Take him to the Commandress immediately!" General XIII then shifted his eyes back to the Void.

Ex-General Bend approached the new General Bend, arms open and claws spread. The Heartbrands took Gai up the street, kicking all the way.

"Lemme go!" yelled Gai, wiggling against their armored arms. A thin layer of blue light spread across his skin. "I said let me *go!*" Gai created his myra shield around him, thrusting the Heartbrands to the dusty ground in a bright wave.

But the guards rose to their feet nimbly. Shimmering weapons appeared in their hands with a flick of their wrists. Still, they hesitated to attack the boy, realizing they weren't dealing with some everyday criminal.

"Stop!" said Gai. "I'll go." He turned his head to Kal, then to the In room with the blown-out wall. "*If* ya leave the ones in the room alone."

The two Heartbrands looked to their general for hints of how to proceed. Kal nodded in agreement, then said, "All will be unharmed. All but the Void."

"Is there really no way to help him?" the boy yelled back. "Yer Kal, yeah? He's yer father!"

"I know who his is," shouted General XIII. "That is why I'm taking responsibility for his mess . . ."

Gai couldn't believe what he was hearing; how could he give up on his own family? The guards stepped to either side of the boy, *escorting* him rather than carrying him to the marvelous gates of the Akademy that were just up the street. He looked back once more at the creature Mac had become, wishing he could fix it. "Take me to the Commandress. She's got to know somethin'. She knew about the Voids way back in Hop."

Once inside the Akademy, Gai soaked in the stained glass beauty and awe of that place just as Lynd did when she first came. But he did not have the time to enjoy it. He had friends at the bottom of the sea in some Pocket Realm painting. He had a mother whom he promised to bring back Lynd and Pa. He had a mentor morphing into a Void and adding chaos to the already panicked streets. The guards pushed him to a spiraling staircase. As he walked up, the boy practiced how he would beg this Commandress lady to help him. She must know *something*. Maybe this was all about to finally end.

At the top of the stairs, the Heartbrands gestured to an intimidatingly large set of double doors. "Commandress Lynd is in the war room."

Bump Bump. Gai's heart skipped. Chills crept down his arms and legs. "Commandress *Lynd?*" he said, nearly tripping.

He frantically tried to remember what the Commandress looked like that night in Hop. It was dark, and she was full-barreled blasting him off the *Lady Merry*. But what was her face again? Could Lynd be a common name?

The boy could hear a woman speaking behind the doors. She said, "The Electrian fleet outnumbers us." Another asked what they were supposed to do. She replied, "They are only a risk at range. Line up the ships in a thin line, thinnest at the center. When they take the bait, the center will retreat, luring them closer to the inner island.

At that point, the flanks can close in on Electri's ships, trapping them. Board them, and it's over."

The other woman asked, "What about reports of this Wonder Weapon they've developed? Can't you just . . . do what you did last time? Countless lives could be saved!"

"I will meet General Case at the back of the island and sail directly to Electri," she said. "Remember, the battle here is only a distraction."

Knock. Knock. The guard said, "Commandress Lynd? We have a dangerous criminal from the In Inn for you."

"General XIII is stationed down there," she roared back through the door. "Have him handle it!"

"We were sent *by* General Bend, Commandress. There's been a Void incident."

"Open the doors." She sighed.

As the Heartbrands palmed the doors open, the colorful brightness of three more stained glass windows dazzled the boy's eyes. Inside, eleven luminously attired people were standing around a long table, placing little wooden boats over a map of the islands. In front of the glaring window was the silhouette of an elegantly gowned young woman, facing outward. Long, black hair ran nearly the entire length of her back. When she turned to the boy, he swore for half a moment that it was Mamma Mape.

The Commandress took one glance at the boy and said, "Generals, you all have your orders. You are dismissed. Leave the criminal with me." All of them began walking out, each face more concerned than the last. They had a war to fight. The two Heartbrands that brought Gai there shut the doors behind them. And the Commandress and boy were alone at last.

She smiled warmly, and with the clearest Hopper accent, said, "Good to see ya, brother."

CHAPTER 27
ELIX VERSES RUIN

At the In Inn, Faan, the hard-trained Heartbrands, and citizens alike recoiled in terror as the Ruin began to completely overtake Mac's body. As if the impending bombardment of electri war guns wasn't enough to make them panic, they watched as a man became a monster right in front of them. The Ex-Heartbrand started gasping, his veins bulging, trying to resist the full descent into Void-hood. He gripped one of the In Inn's window boxes full of flowers, turning them to ash in his clawed fists. Black blood gushed from his coughing throat. There was no resisting. Ruin was the only thing animating him anymore.

Kal gave the signal for his Heartbrands to clear the street. "Legion XIII! Your only goal is to keep the people of Carpè safe. Not a single one of you is to interfere in this fight. No matter what." He readied his stance as the darkness around his father's neck throbbed and grew across his jaw to distort his whole face. Then, knowing full well what it meant to take on a creature such as this, Kal said, "It has been my life's honor to serve with you all."

The Void spread its arms, arched its back, and wailed with every corner of its monstrous lungs. A long tongue licked its lips around a mouth full of jagged teeth. Down its throat, just emptiness — endless emptiness. Faan screamed and finally locked the door to the In. Hungrily, the Void that was once Mac Bend strolled toward Kal, studying him like a lion that found new prey. Every step it took left a char in the stones, as anything it came into contact with began to instantly decay. Even the air around it fizzled out of existence near its skin, giving it a reddish aura of certain doom.

Once Legion XIII cleared the street of innocent people, Kal narrowed his eyes on the shadowy beast. "I wonder, Dad, how much of this monster has always been there, deep down?"

The Void snarled and feigned attacking as if it were testing the young general's reflexes. As it gestured wildly, a thick, black ooze was dripping from it like ink, which sizzled when it touched the street. No part of this being was safe to touch.

"Not without irony," said General XIII, readying a more offensive stance. "You wanted to throw a little girl out onto the streets because of Ruin. And here you are, tearing up these same streets, looking like this." Kal then quickly leaped through the air and chopped his epic heartbrand down at the Void. But the monster vanished. Kal stood up, glancing back over his shoulder. The Void had reappeared where Kal was just standing. It was toying with him.

Up in the war room of the Akademy, Commandress Lynd slowly approached her stunned brother. "All's a'kay," she said, gesturing her palms down like he used to do to her when she was upset. "It's me, Gai. It's Lynd." She stood there, a young woman in her early twenties, tall and confident as any statue, with about the same amount of detectable emotion. "I'm sure ya have questions," she said dryly. "But ya see the warships. And bringin' a Void into my city certainly hasn't bought us any extra time."

Gai's knees felt weak. He wanted someone to hold *him* up, now. His eyes were already starting to well up. "Yer . . . not. Lynd is my *little* sister. Where'd ya hear that name?"

Lynd wandered back to the window, terribly preoccupied. She peered at the distant Electri ships around the outer island and at the eleven *Carrier* ships leaving Carpè's docks just below. She glanced down the street at the In Inn for an update on Kal's unfolding battle. When she had imagined this moment, when she would finally explain things to Gai, they had more time. Much more. She would help him understand why she had to do what she was about to do. He would hate her, but she would be there for him. Unfortunately, the reality was that she was Commandress of Carpè, and the city was under double threats. "Please, Gai—"

"Don't *Gai* me!" The boy paced back and forth, growing angrier every step. He'd come all this way for help, not games. "Don't act like ya know who I am! Ya threw me off the *Lady Merry*! My sister would never do that! Who are ya?"

"Do ya wanna hear my side, or not?" The way she raised her voice, the demanding tone, that look in her eyes like she thought he was being a perfect sogg. All of them spelled *Lynd*.

Gai banged his hand on the war table, toppling the wooden boats. "Tell me who ya are!" His head felt like it was going to explode every time he looked at her, so he kept his eyes busy by tracing the coastlines on the map instead.

"It's true," said Lynd. "A few nights ago, I went to Hop for the first time since I touched that spyrt when I was a girl. It still smelled the same. Awful." She sighed and paused, trying to remember what she planned to tell him. "I was there to find Pa, but I'd just missed him. The break down of time on the *Lady Merry* made him hard to track."

"But yer not *Lynd*," the boy stressed. "I know people who can make pretty good illusions. Tell me how ya know that name?"

Lynd bit her lip, then glanced outside. She didn't have time. She sang, "We've been here before. With yer hand in mine."

The boy turned away from her, embarrassed by his tears. "Shut yer mouth. Shut yer damned mouth!"

"I wish this wasn't our lives, brother. But the cards are dealt." An explosion on the street brought her back to the window again. Kal was fighting for his life against the Void. ". . . And I'm about to lose my most powerful ally."

Kal swung his weapon gallantly, fast as a flash each time. But he never made contact with the Void. The monster was simply too quick. Within the traditions and teachings of the Heartbrands, the theory was always that a blue heartbrand made of Elix myra might be able to "cut" a Void by neutralizing its Ruin body. But at times, the Void's form seemed like it wasn't even solid, like trying to slice a thick cloud of smoke. Kal worried that maybe it was because his heartbrand was not totally blue, but a purplish mixture of both blue *and* red.

The Void roared and ripped apart the cobblestones as it charged forward at the young general, sharp jaws first. But then — *Pow!* Kal used Time Elix to slow down its fearsome movements, like the Heart-brands who arrested Gai — rolling the ball slower down the hill, creating strategic pockets of time. *Clash! Clash! Clash!* It made the Void's movements traceable and blockable, at least. Time Elix gave Kal a fighting chance. To an onlooker, their fight was like trying to catch lightning strikes in random spots in a field. It was that fierce and daunting. But it meant General XIII was burning through his myra like a wildfire just to keep up with the monster. Meanwhile, the Void was just getting stronger.

As their epic battle raged, a woman cracked open the In Inn door and walked outside. Faan was screaming within, begging her to come back. The woman's hair was grayed, her face washed out and gaunt, with a sunken discoloring around her eyes. She was frail but deter-mined to step out onto the street.

"W-wait," she said, feebly finding her way between Kal and the monster. "Wait, my boy."

Kal was about to order her back inside. But he halted at the sight of her familiar face. ". . . Mom?"

As ill Tesse stumbled to her son, the Void took an interest in her. It licked its vile lips and lunged at the poor woman.

"No!" Kal roared, dropping his heartbrand and — *Pow!* — creating so much time around the Void that its movements nearly stilled midair. The young general strained to keep up such a powerful myracle, but waved his mother back inside. "Hurry!"

"Kal, my beautiful son," she said, embracing him for the first time since he was a young child. His mother looked him over and touched his cheek. "I'm not sure I deserved—*cough*—to live long enough to see you again."

He kissed her delicate palm. "A part of me always knew you were alive. I must've gone to the Everbloom shores a hundred times but could never bring myself to go in. I didn't want seeing the truth to destroy me entirely." Tesse grew weak and collapsed, but Kal caught her in his arms, "Mom!"

"I was going to die a natural death." *Cough. Cough.* "But I chose to Tamper with nature. I did it to keep our family together, but it only assured I'd live to see us apart. It was no life."

A single tear dropped from Kal's left eye. "But you're here, now."

She was losing strength fast but forced out the words. "Will you forgive us?"

"You, I can forgive," he said, holding her in his arms, while trying to keep his Time Elix myracle fixed on the Void to give them this small moment together. "But he lied to me. I cannot forget the pain he caused. I will not set him free of that!"

Tesse opened her shaking hand, revealing she kept his bracelet after Lynd brought it a decade ago. She rested it back in his armored hand. "Things made sense once. Remember?"

Kal's hard glare at his father softened.

"Remember who you were then," said his mother. "Before you were defined by . . . our choices."

The young general got choked up. "He's a monster, mom."

"You're not setting him free. Only he can do that. Holding onto this hurts only you, not him. If you don't forgive—*cough*—that part of you that you fear will win. You will end up like him . . ." Tesse Bend could barely recover from that last cough. She was close to the end; it was clear. "Release yourself. Forgive him."

"Mom!" Kal pulled her in tighter. "Please don't go! We have new medicines. We can find a cure for you! Please, hold on!" Her hands fell down to her sides. Her body went limp. "Mom?" Tesse had taken her last breath in her son's arms. General XIII shut her eyes and carried her to the In door. Faan was watching the whole fight from a small window. She came out and took Tesse's body from him and brought it inside. It was the least she could do for the grieving Defender of Carpè.

"I know who I was before." Kal turned to the creature, who was about to break free of his powerful myracle. "And I will never be like you. You are forgiven, Dad."

At once, Kal summoned his signature grand heartbrand. But this time, the red had disappeared, with an influx of radiant blue myra. True forgiveness allowed the cracks in his heart to heal; the island was washed into the sea. Kal was free.

The proud general smiled. "We will end this together!" The Void broke free of Kal's Time Elix, and the high-speed, high-stakes combat began again — *Clash! Clash!*

The Commandress of Carpè watched it all unfold from the colorful war room window, gripping her own folded arms. "Kal's myra has shifted." She turned to her brother and said, "It's no longer split in two. He must've found some peace."

The boy just let his dagger eyes speak for him.

Lynd looked away from him. She was already burdened enough without the extra guilt. "What can I say that will help you accept this?"

And Gai just leered back.

"I have to leave for Electri," she said. "I want ya to know how much I missed ya. How much I missed all of us. Together. It seems like so long ago. Like another time. When I left Hop after touching the spryt, I found Pa on Unc's ship . . ."

Gai loosened his fists. He began to empathize with his sister. If it *really* was her. And if that was true, she had an extra decade of weight on her heart since he'd last seen her. What had she gone through?

"I panicked when I saw him, Gai," she continued. "He looked like yer friend, Mac Bend down there. I couldn't believe it. A monster straight out of a story." She locked eyes with her brother. "But I know there was still part of him in there. I think he tried to send me back home using his power, not hurt me. But I was scared. I didn't know what I was doin'. But it didn't matter if I knew or not. Our collision of Ruin was enough to blow a hole right in time and space. I ended up on a beach here. That was ten years ago."

"Yer tellin' the truth . . ." His eyes welled up again. "But if ya are Lynd, why'd ya attack me?"

"I didn't attack ya. If I did, ya'd be dust on the deck," she said. "And who do ya think put ya on Em's shell? Kal saw how much Elix myra ya had. It was a lot, even for a student here. I just wanted to see how much." Lynd slumped a bit; the first time she seemed to let her guard down. "Since Elix and Ruin cancel each other out. I thought maybe . . . ya'd have enough Elix to help us match Pa's Ruin. And then maybe I wouldn't have to go through with my plan. But ya were pretty easy to flick off that ship . . ."

"Yer sayin' this is my fault? I'm not enough? What — too much of a sogg for the good endin'?"

"*That's* why ya were easy to flick off. Yer only a sogg if ya believe it," she said flatly. "Ya may disagree with my path, but at least I write my own limits." Lynd returned to the window. Half her attention was always out of the room. "But no, it's not your fault. It was a foolish idea. Gathering enough Elix to match hungry Voids is a losing game. Just look at what happened to the Arkons." She looked out and saw that the Legion's *Carrier* ships finally were in formation, and that Electri began maneuvering their ships for battle as well. "I have to go," she said. "The Second Myracite War is about to begin."

"Wait. I saw two Heartbrands like Kal attack Electri's drills. Blue swords and all." Gai walked to the window with her. "Lynd. If yer the Commandress, did ya order them to do that? Did ya . . . start this war?"

Lynd smiled so slightly. ". . . I'm gonna fix us."

"Lynd? What're ya plannin?' What's pickin' a fight with Electri get ya?"

"Because I don't have enough Ruin to destroy Pa on my own!" Lynd merely clenched her fist, and the whole floor of the Akademy's war room split down the middle. "I need the red myracite below Electri City. Once I absorb it, pray I have enough . . ."

"So this is about gettin' *more* Ruin than Pa?"

"With control of the red myracite, I will summon the Last Myracle just like the Arkons did, and stop our father. It's the only way to save the world from being part of his endless destruction, Gai."

Gai slammed his foot down. "So, if ya don't have enough Elix, yer gonna hit Ruin with *Ruin* instead? That's what started all this!"

"When I touched the myracite that night on Boulie, I directed myself right to Pa. Our will, our *hearts*, must still play a role, even when Ruin meets Ruin. There must be a way to control it. I was young then. And these past ten years, I've grown immeasurably."

"Those Arkon people probably thought they could control it, too! And they destroyed all life on the planet tryin' this!" The boy simply could not believe he had to convince his own sister, the little sister he played with in Hop, not to blow up the planet. Just then, he noticed how her dress covered all the way down her arms. Not even her fingertips were showing. Nothing but the top of her neck and face could be seen in that elegant outfit. He wondered how many dark scars of Ruin were hidden under that gilded gown. How was she even still here? Ten years of Ruin? How had she avoided becoming a Void? "Please at ya, Lynd. Don't let Ruin force ya . . ."

Then, a loud roar near the In Inn caught their attention.

Lynd, who had already started walking out the door, went right back to see, pressing her palms against the glass. "Kal?"

General Kal Bend of the XIIIth Heartbrand Legion was on the ground, sitting back on his heels with his eyes shut. His weapon was plunged into the Void's side, with a glowing hilt sticking out. The monster screeched as the Elix blue ate through its Ruin body like an acid. It appeared Kal had finally injured it. But then the blue sword's light snuffed out, and the Void still remained, grinning. It was not enough Elix to neutralize it.

Kal watched, unfazed. He knew it wouldn't be enough. As his chest rose and sank with deep breaths, a sapphire aura spread around his whole body. With each inhale, it grew brighter and brighter.

"What's he doin'?" Gai asked, staring down from the Akademy.

"Kal . . . I mean General XIII, is performing a technique that converts his body's living tissue into pure Elix myra."

"His body into myra? Won't that hurt?"

"It will kill him," she said.

The Void arched its back and let out a screech that shattered glass all over the neighborhood, including the Akademy window where Lynd and Gai were. Lynd pulled Gai down and protected him from the shattering glass.

Kal Bend was aglow like a bonfire, humming with his newly-found, fully-realized creative power. Short blades of grass, growing through cracks in the street, grew taller under his feet as if they had been in the summer sun for weeks. Then, as all his physical structure — every muscle fiber, tissue and bone — converted into Elix myra, Kal created one last Mind Link to speak inside Lynd's mind. He said to her, "*This is the end, my Commandress.*"

Lynd closed her eyes, still ducking on the floor away from the broken window. She thought back to him, "*I know.*"

"It feels so gratifying," Kal said aloud, opening his sparkling eyes upon the monster his father had become. "That now all of me is enough to rid the world of all you wrought." Just before his body turned into pure blue light, he sent her one final thought — "*I love you, Lynd.*"

Up in the war room, Lynd shouted, "Kal!"

The young general launched himself at the Void, barreling into its shadowed body of pure, ravenous Ruin. The two collided with a thunderclap and a bright flash of purple light. And then nothing.

Gai picked a few glass shards off his hair and looked back out of the breezy broken window. "The Void's gone! Mac! He's . . . gone. So is the general! They just annihilated each other. Opposites . . . he had enough Elix."

Neither Kal nor the Void were there any longer. Not even dust remained. Only a half-burnt, silver bracelet was left on the ground.

Lynd refused to look out the window. Her bottom lip quivered a few times. Tears were building in their ducts, but she destroyed them into little red sparks before they could run down her cheek. She kept hearing his last words to her, *I love you, Lynd.*

"Lynd! Why can't we just gather enough Elix to stop Pa like he did? Why try somethin' so dangerous?"

"I told ya, I thought of that," the Commandress roared. A blast of power sparked off her skin like static off a sheet and struck the war table to instant fragments. "If it were possible, I'd do it! But Voids only gather more Ruin the longer they exist. They get stronger." She rose up slowly. "It's not a fair match. And ya haven't seen Pa — he's not like these little Voids! He's been around for years! The only way to destroy destruction." She appeared so overcome that she couldn't destroy her tears fast enough. "The only way to stop that much Ruin is to have more of it. When a greater source of Ruin hits a smaller one, the greater remains. It's how the Arkons defeated the Voids in their time — the Last Myracle. It's my only option."

"But look at the mess their stupid Last Myracle left behind with all that red myracite! Yer just shovin' a bunch of Ruin for the next generation to deal with. Not to mention killin' off this one in the process!"

A bright yellow light shined way out at sea. It was coming from one of Electri's ship's directly ahead.

It caught the Commandress's eye, and she finally came back to the fractured window. Her mouth hung for a moment, looking into the strange, new light. "Damn it. I'm out of time."

The golden light was small, far off on the distant ship. But even as far as it was, the boy could feel its heat on his face, like a little sun. "I heard 'em say somethin' 'bout a Wonder Weapon . . ."

CHAPTER 28
WONDER WEAPONS

One yellow twinkle atop an Electrian warship was frightening enough to clear every street in Carpè. The citizens slammed every window and door shut, tucking away in their homes as if waiting out a threatening storm. The Heartbrands started building extra walls of brick and myra to bolster the city against the onslaught. Those aboard *Carrier* ships maniphested great domes of blue to absorb the coming blasts. Carpè had seen such electri-infused weapons ten years ago. They remembered how easily those zaps ripped through hard stone.

Carpè expected this kind of attack. But then another frightening light flickered on at the next Electrian ship. Then another. Then twelve. Soon each of Electri's twenty vessels was charging up some new, unknown war guns. The water vibrated as they continued to pulse with greater and brighter power. Each one sizzled with focused electri energy, hundreds of times denser than those seen on a Drillmax. But electri's color was usually gold; these blossoming beams started to shift closer toward a deep red, like tiny setting suns. This was not the same attack Carpè encountered during the First Myracite War. It was the rumored "Wonder Weapon."

There was a loud *Tick!* as one of the warships finished charging their shot. *Tink!* Then the next. In turn, they all sounded once their Wonder Weapon was fired up. To the Heartbrands stationed on the *Carrier* fleet, it was like a ticking clock counting down to their last moments on Esa. Against what were they even defending, exactly?

Every watching eye widened with wonder. No one had ever seen weapons like this before. Apparently, Electri learned from its last encounter with Carpè; they could be toppled easily by the power of one girl. And they needed bigger guns.

The hissing, reddish, crackling lights aimed for the center island of Carpè and — *BZZZZ!*

The long, sizzling Wonder Weapon beams all met at one spot in the center of the Legions' fleet — *KAHBOOM!* said the epic mushroom cloud that rose in a blink.

A hot, furious eruption ballooned out from the impact point, overwhelming all shields. A tidal wave curled over any surviving ships into a wrecking roll that crashed into Carpè's walls, letting seawater up the cobbled city streets and into homes.

A shockwave cut through the air, pushing back all surrounding clouds and pummeling eardrums across the island. Lynd stood dumbfounded as the reverberation of the most destructive blast since the Arkon's Last Myracle buzzed in the air. The Commandress's entire fleet was obliterated in one fiery sweep.

"They learned how to use red myracite's power directly." Lynd bowed her head in respect for the fallen. "That wasn't just electri. That was a blast of actual Ruin!"

The Wonder Weapon didn't zap, roast or toast its target like traditional electri guns. It disintegrated the target. The most significant remains of Carpè's *Carrier* ships were splinters in the waves. The citizens and Heartbrands stationed ashore looked at their brave defense reduced to dust on the reeling sea. The sea itself looked like a land crater for a moment, a converse dome where the water had been erased from existence. The surrounding ocean rushed back in quickly to rebalance itself, as water does, causing a rebound tsunami.

General Astel Osstett was stationed near the docks with the Vth Legion and immediately shifted to a rescue operation for anyone caught in the unexpected waves. "Ace Cohort, search alongside the coast for any survivors! The rest of you — help get these people to higher ground!" The emptiness of air created by the Wonder Weapon caused wild gusts of wind. "What have they unleashed?" she cried, glancing out at the hazy horizon. The smell of rot and dust tainted every inhale.

Using the vacuum effect of red myracite, gears could be made to turn, generating electri energy. But the Wonder Weapon was no passive use of myracite. The great Thinkers of Electri City had learned how to unleash its true potential. Perhaps they had a chance to study Ruin when Stav was a patient in the hospital.

Gai looked on in horror from the Akademy war room. There were reddish bolts still hammering in the sky above Carpè. It looked like the sky itself was broken and could fall on top of them at any moment. And then there was a deep trembling — *RUUrr*.

The tower began to rumble beneath their feet. Brother and sister both looked down to the ground. Foundations were splitting up and down the streets. It wasn't just the tower that was shaking. The whole island was.

"Look what they've done!" Lynd yelled. She closed her fist as a few crackles of red Ruin power danced within it. She shot it into the center of the war room, where it snapped open a hole in space — a portal to somewhere else entirely. "Carpè is a volcano! That attack was enough to wake it up. We have to get out of here! Now!"

Looking through the portal-crack, Gai could see the shoreline and a ship's gangway drawn. There, General Case and the Xth Legion waited with Lynd's planned getaway to Electri City.

RUuRr. The ground quaked again, this time nearly toppling the boy over. Chairs fell, books teetered off the shelves.

Lynd stepped to the portal with a hand outstretched to her brother. "I'm gonna save Esa. A'way!"

Gai looked at her hand. Taking it would mean accepting her plans to call on this Last Myracle. Staying would mean certain doom. "Lynd . . . I can't."

Fury danced across her face. "That blast was made of Ruin! Every Void in Esa would've sniffed it out like a damned dinner bell! If the volcano doesn't kill ya, *they* will! Brother . . . help me end this. I know it hurts. But I can teach ya how to use this pain to add more Ruin against Pa."

The boy's pounding heart wouldn't let him budge. Though he loved his sister, and he would do anything to fix her, even give his life, she was on a path of more destruction. He was there to fix his family, but it seemed like he'd only found more pieces.

"Gaiel!"

"There has to be another way!" he shouted against the rumbling of the waking volcano beneath.

"We all want another way," she said. "There just isn't. This is my burden. And I've made peace with it."

"Well, I haven't!"

RRuUur.

Lynd withdrew her hand, saddened and disappointed. The Commandress had been wrestling with the idea of summoning the Last Myracle for years. She couldn't expect her brother to understand in a few minutes. And maybe him standing for what he thought was right was the least sogg-like thing she'd ever seen him do. ". . . The Last Myracle will only work if it has more Ruin myra than the Void does. Pa is pickin' up more and more every moment he is allowed to exist. He is our father, Gai. This is *our* responsibility. I will do what I must to fix us." She abruptly turned and marched through the portal without looking back. As soon as she went through, it snapped shut in a spark.

"Lynd!" Gai immediately regretted not going with her. He wanted nothing to do with any more Ruin. But that didn't mean he wanted to see his sister disappear again into a scarlet crack in space.

RRUrr. The first stones fell from the ceiling. Gai knew he had to escape before the whole thing came down. Or before Electri launched another Wonder Weapon attack.

The boy glanced out the window before leaving and noticed one of Electri's ships was now on fire and smoking. He wasn't sure if somehow the Heartbrands had landed an attack, or if perhaps the Wonder Weapon had backfired. He squinted through the haze. "Looks like somethin's on the ship . . ."

As the smoke rose from one of Electri's vessels, a large dark mass appeared to be moving on the deck. It was as tall as the central masts. It loomed over the entire bow, looking like a second cloud of thick, murky smoke. Or a giant Void aboard.

"It couldn't be," said the oval-mouthed boy. "It's huge!" He turned and ran out of the Akademy war room, down the quaking stairs and through the crumbling Akademy gates. "Pa?" His mind burned to know. He had to get a closer look. The ground was practically roaring as Carpè's volcano deep beneath the sea came to life once again after thousands of years.

As Gai passed the In Inn, he saw the scorch marks, the scraps of destroyed matter from Mac the Void merely stepping on the street stones. There was a silver glimmer on the ground near the fountain, where Gai found Kal's bracelet. "A piece of him survived the clash . . . He must've had more blue than Mac had red. If it were even, nothin' would be left over." He recalled meeting Kal in Hop, when Lynd came. Based on her reaction to his death, he was obviously important to Lynd, more so than just a Command-general bond.

Gai held the bracelet hard in his hand, appreciating the immense weight that must've been on the young general to have to rid the world of his own father. As the boy looked out at sea ahead, he thought of how he might have to do the same. "Mac . . . Thanks at ya for everythin' ya tried to teach me. There was more to ya than this . . . There's more to Pa. There's more to Lynd."

BOOOM! That flaming Electrian warship with the giant, unknown black mass on it exploded and began to sink. That dark smudge then leaped off and landed on the next ship, where it proceeded to shred the hull in half.

Gai ran to the wet docks. The piers were still being pummeled by the settling waves, the water crashed against his armored boots, but he needed the closest look he could get. He watched in fearful awe at whatever was attacking those ships. There was no more questioning. It was indeed a massive Void, hungrily tearing through anything in its path, delighting at the huge storage of red myracite that Electri had aboard to power their Wonder Weapon.

"Pa . . . All ya wanted was to get us off Hop. Was this the only way?" The boy looked at his right palm, pooling some bright Elix into it. He stood there knee-deep against the waves, a small blue sparkle on the stretched pier of Carpè's inner island like a little lighthouse. "Am I enough to counteract your Ruin? Like Kal could do for his father?" He recalled the lesson Mac taught him, that we write our own limits.

As the Void set its sights on the inner island, Gai remembered little Lynd running inside the night Pa left. How he tried to fix her, but all he could do was make a blanket to make her feel safe and fall asleep. Then, like a ship crashing into him, the realization hit — "We define ourselves . . . I couldn't fix her because we each define ourselves. *Lynd* has to fix Lynd. I never had any power over that. The only thing I can do is . . . not give up on her."

The Void shot over to the next Electrian ship, mauled its hull apart, and devoured the red myracite within. It was getting larger and larger through its feast.

RURrr.

"But now I do know what I have power over." Against the rumbling land, Gai stood solid as an Everbloom. "Myself." A well of luminous Elix myra swirled around him, from his toes through the tips of his hair. The broken pieces of the pier swirled thorough the air around him and snapped back into place as he walked the planks further and further out to sea. "I will not give up, Lynd. If this is my last hour, I will make it the brightest!"

CHAPTER 29
IN THE STITCH OF TIME

T he molten rock beneath Carpè continued to boil and churn, threatening to burst through the ground at any moment. Epic splashes could be heard as the city's famous Archbridges finally faltered, crashing to the waves in massive chunks. Whomever was still on the inner island was doomed to stay there.

General Osstett and her Legionnaires scoured the outskirts of the inner island for any trapped civilians. They collected many of them, some wailing with injuries. Astel had no plan of how to evacuate a single one. Every ship was reduced to dust during Electri's attack. Every quake of the ground reminded her of the race against time. As she led the Heartbrands back around to the city gates near the dock district, the general noticed the boy surrounded by Elix myra, blazing like a beacon on the pier. Could there be hope shining in that dark hour?

RUURRr.

"Vth Legion," Astel called out as the titanic First Void ripped through another Electrian ship out at sea — *BHoom!* "I've lost communication with General XIII. But his soldiers are at the In Inn. Gather everyone up there and wait for further orders." They obeyed her order without question, carrying all those who needed it to the relative safety of higher ground within the city. The general herself ran down the pier toward the shining boy. "You there! Who are you? Do you need help?"

Glowing Gai yelled back, "If yer lookin' for Kal Bend, he's gone!"

"Gone?" Astel shouted, the whip of her general authority strong in her voice. "What happened to him? Who are you?"

All he shouted back was, "Get everyone off this island, now!" Gai kept his eyes straight ahead at the lethal creature that was once his beloved father. He was prepared to give his all to stop him, the only way he knew how. "I will deal with *that . . .*"

Ah! General Osstett suddenly screamed, bringing the boy's attention behind him. A smaller Void stretched up from the lapping water and gripped her leg. Its destructive touch was practically melting her sturdy armor.

"*Another* one?" Gai rushed down the planks to help her. "This is a nightmare!"

Astel drew her radiant heartbrand and drove it into the creature's back. The clawing beast screeched and released her, falling back beneath the depths. As it sunk, she got a look at part of the Void's face and was stunned. "Talia? Talia! How did this—?"

By the time Gai joined General V closer to shore, Voids had begun breaking through the surface all around like leaping fish, each one a new nightmare.

"That weapon," Astel breathed. "They were all exposed to that Ruin! Talia, Arkenna, every Legionnaire that was out there when the blast hit — it must've infected them all!" She covered her mouth in horror. But all the monstrous heads popping up above the waves gave her no time to mourn her friends and comrades. With an outstretched hand, she yelled to the boy, "Come into the city with us! We have to defend the people as long as we can!"

Gai glanced out at sea. The gigantic First Void had just finished with the ships and turned its insatiable appetite toward the deteriorating city of Carpè. The monumental monster was so big that it walked through the open ocean like it was wading through a gentle stream. The water disappeared around its bulky legs like steam, adding to its ample body of Ruin with every step. In the foreground, smaller but no less threatening Voids emerged from the deep like swimmers on holiday. Even if he had enough Elix myra to balance out all that Ruin coming at the island before, more and more of it kept arriving on the scene. "A'way!"

As they retreated down the pier and back onto the city streets, Astel said, "I'd know anyone from Carpè with your level of power. Who are you?"

". . . Yer Commandress's brother," he answered, huffing in the sprint.

"Lynd Izz's brother?" General Osstett's lips twitched as if she had plenty of questions. She remembered the push to find Lynd's family years ago. Why was he only showing up now? Did he have anything to do with that mammoth Void? But they arrived at the In Inn with no time for chit-chat. There, her Legion was gathered tightly on the street outside with members of the XIIIth, tending to wounded and frightened citizens around the fountain.

The new Voids — the Heartbrands who'd been turned by the excessive Ruin of the Wonder Weapon — crawled onto the wooden docks by the dozens and launched up the street to the inner city, leaving charred trails of wrecked matter in their wake.

Astel grabbed a nearby soldier with "XIII" written on her shoulder. "You! I trust General Bend drills you all in mass myracles?"

She saluted her and replied, "Yes, general!"

"Good." Astel hurried to the section of the street that led up from the dock, calculating how little time they had before they were all going to be Void food. "XIIIth! Vth!" she called, the only general between the two remaining Legions in Carpè. "Form a perimeter around the In. Every civilian behind the line! I want this whole block covered. Streets, roofs, line up where you must. But do not break the chain. I will buy you a moment. Employ a mass Time Elix myracle at my word! Move!"

The Voids came rampaging up faster than anyone expected, jagged teeth first, tearing through everything they touched, growing larger with every stone, wall, or tile destroyed. The Legionnaires all positioned themselves around the In Inn and the surrounding streets as the general ordered. Together they covered an area no bigger than half-a-Hop.

"For Carpè!" The general roared, facing the coming horde. She then drove her brilliant heartbrand into the street. The Voids charged on. Astel breathed in deeply. The Voids charged on. General V then elegantly drifted from one side of the path to the other. She was practically dancing as she dragged her sword with each movement, carving an illuminated pattern on the ground. The monsters were only a stone's throw away when the Fiat, Astel, blew over her drawing on the ground, just as she did when making a dress for Lynd all those years ago.

The cobblestones rippled and bounced until her drawing, a fearsome bull made of bright blue myra, leaped up and charged — wide horns first — at the herd of hungry monsters. The bull followed the street down and clashed with them on impact. A flurry of dazzling purple sparks lit up the whole path as it plowed through them, neutralizing one Void after the next, but getting smaller and smaller each time it did. It eliminated a few dozen of them at least, all the way to the water before exhausting all the Elix myra that composed it.

But the Voids kept coming up from the sea. If every Heartbrand on the *Carrier* ships had been turned, there were hundreds ready to swarm the foundering city. Some Voids had survived the bull by jumping to the rooftops. No citizen within the Legions' perimeter breathed any easier.

Even if her attack swallowed every monster, there was still the giant one approaching in the backdrop, in case she had a pinch of hope left. General V resisted the urge to fall on her knees right there. She'd put all she had into that myracle. Astel straightened herself up and hurried back to the fountain outside the In. With the Heartbrands all in formation, she raised her fist — "*Now!*"

At once, each Legionnaire's entire body, armor and all, illuminated. They quickly opened their arms as spheres of created time burst around every one of them. The time-bubbles popped up like soap suds in a washed hand, all over the perimeter. But then the Heartbrands tuned in to one another's myracle, centering their power around the In Inn, working together toward a common goal. The bubbles merged, one after the next. And soon the entire street was under the influence of a mass myracle of extra time.

Gai peered from within the shimmering sphere at the world outside; the clouds overhead had slowed. Most critically, so had the charging Voids. How hungry they looked, open-mouthed and snarling, yet stilled. "We're inside Time Elix. A *huge* myracle!" Safe in this time-cocoon, even the volcano's impending eruption below their feet had become slower to reach them. Extraordinary as it all was, it was not a solution. The boy could see the strain on every Heart-brand's face. They could not keep this myracle up forever. But they had time to think of a plan, at least.

"Faan!" Astel banged on the In's door. "It's Astel. It's not safe here! Get everyone out and moving to higher ground! Hurry!"

The In's door cracked open and soon dozens of people seeking shelter within came pouring out, filling up the street outside, the owner, Faan, included.

"Unc!" the boy called, searching through the frenzied people. "Uncle Baald!" He spotted him looking traumatized with the rest of the *Merry* Hoppers. They were able to jostle their way to each other in the crowd, embracing for the second time; it was just that kind of day, where every time they saw each other could've been their last. "Glad yer a'kay!"

"By Holy Zeea's fist, kid." Baald gave him an extra tight squeeze. "I found my crew, at least. Did ya see all the . . . *everythin'*? What kind of Void dumper is this place?"

"We'll be a'kay, Unc."

Astel wandered to the fountain at the center of the street and grabbed its cold, stone edge to hold herself up. She was still trying to catch her breath after her myracle.

Baald resembled every other citizen looking up at the myracle dome — oval-mouthed and hopeful. "What kinda fancy . . ."

"Ya stay here, Unc. A'kay?" The boy made his way to the deflated general. With the Commandress and General Bend gone, the pressure of protecting everyone looked so heavy upon her that it was practically crushing her shoulders. "What can I do to help?" he said to her.

She winced. "Commandress Lynd has a brother, huh?" Astel then breezed her eyes across the Legions, assessing how much time they had given her to come up with their next move. "I don't suppose she gave you any training?"

"No."

"What was that on the shore, then?" Astel stood straight. "And tell me how . . . General Bend?"

Gai pointed to the scorch-like marks on the cobblestones where the Ex-General Bend had stepped after becoming a Void. "He fought against one . . . It was a draw."

"A draw," she repeated softly. "He was a good man. He did better than we'll do if I can't figure a way out of this." She glanced up at the statue in the fountain. It was of a beautiful young woman with an eerily cutting look in her gaze. "I don't want to fail Carpè." Astel directed her words up at the statue. "You're the one who made me believe in myself. Not a soldier here doesn't owe you some of their strength. We were such children at your feet back then. What I wouldn't give to hear that guiding voice now."

"Who's Ada Moira?" Gai said, reading the inscription at the base.

"Commandress Ada," Astel said with esteem. "Your sister dedicated this statue to the one who held Command before her . . . Commadress Ada had such a light."

"She looks real enough to talk back to ya," the boy muttered. He looked at her gray, stony form. "Looks like she's crackin', too."

"Cracking?" The general peered at the cracks. "Is that . . . *blue light*?" She looked around at the brilliant dome of swirling Elix above them, wondering if the light coming from cracks in the stone image of the Commandress could just be a reflection. "By Bello . . ." An idea struck her like a charging bull. She recalled the class with Professor Hosp when she was a child; that ball falling to the ground in an instant and turning to stone by Lynd Izz, back when she was known as Hope. Astel remembered the professor talking about people with Ruin would destroy time instead of creating it. "She couldn't have. But what if—"

"General Osstett!" a Heartbrand at the front lines cried.

When General V turned, she saw the lesser Voids still approaching slowly. But behind them, bursting through the tops of buildings was a vast wave of rippling red Ruin barreling at them like a massive wave. The First Void itself had finally launched an attack at sea, and it was already crashing ashore. Even for those within the mass Time Elix myracle, that energy wave was coming fast. Astel made a snap decision and ordered the Legions — "Drop the myracle and take cover!"

But the wave of Ruin smashed into the mass myracle dome before they could react, wiping it out like a pitiful sandcastle on a beach. Every person standing, Heartbrand or not, was knocked to their backs from the impact.

With the myracle down, time normalized around the In Inn. And the army of Voids were free to storm the fallen Legions. Some soldiers didn't even have time to reform their heartbrands before the creature's oozing, dark forms were right on top of them. The ones who could stand began an all-out brawl to buy as much time as they could for the civilians. The line was hardly held strong, and some Voids breached through to the innocent people near the fountain.

With Astel still weakened from her own myracle, Gai stepped in. Face-to-face with their crunching teeth, the boy yelled, "Enough!" And he clapped his hands together with a bulging barrier of Elix pushing out to the ends of the street, burning their vicious faces as if by fire and forcing all of them back. The closest Voids were neutralized. But more arrived right behind them. The Heartbrands on the roofs fought gallantly, but one after the next fell to the fiends. Astel's heartbrand shimmered to life in her hands as she joined the fray. But it was a losing battle.

And then the First Void opened its vile mouth. It let out a deep belly roar, ear-shattering and heart-stopping across the islands. Even the new Voids all stopped in their ravenous tracks and turned around, almost as if *daddy* was calling them back home.

The giant Void in Carpè's bay then breathed in, sucking in all the lesser Voids up through the air and mashing them into its own body. As if they were just pawns sent out to gather more Ruin, the First Void grew more powerful with each lesser one it absorbed.

Gai, Astel, Unc, the Legions and citizens all watched on in terror as they were spared in one moment, only to be facing a growing and more assured death the next. The First Void was filling up the sky. This creature was like a hurricane, wrecking all around and drawing the pieces into itself, where it only became greater.

RRUUrr.

"Quick!" Astel yelled to the Legions. "As many of you as can stand, Time Elix on that statue!"

Pow! Pow! Twelve nearby Heartbrands immediately followed the order and created a bubble of time around the statue.

"Not *around* it," Astel insisted. "Focus on the stone itself."

The Heartbrands homed in on only the curves of the stone. Its petrified skin cracked more and began to flake off.

"That's it!" Astel yelled. "Keep going!"

The statue of Commandress Ada and her ashy tone began to warm. Next, her hair and clothes started to dance in the wind. And finally, her eyes blinked.

"It's true." Astel was stunned. "Commandress Ada? You were here this whole time?" She bowed her head. "I'm so sorry. We thought you had died!"

Ada looked around at the astonished and frightened people at her feet, just as confused as they were. "What's going on?" She scanned their faces, and only Astel's looked vaguely familiar. The carnage of the city behind them, unfortunately, seemed the most familiar. The Heartbrands were equipped for war, with many slain on the ground. "Electri? Are we still—*Whoa!*" She then saw the approaching monster at sea, who was quite taller than the Akademy towers at his point.

Astel helped her down off the fountain. "I am Astel Osstett, now general of the Vth Legion. You were stuck by a Ruin Time myracle some ten years ago." *RUUURr.* As the island rumbled, Ada slipped off the edge. But the general caught her. "And then there's the volcano."

"Thanks for the brief," said the Ex-Commandress, getting to her own feet. She looked at the many desperate soldiers and citizens around them. Ada took a moment to collect herself, but her instincts as Commandress of Carpè quickly arose. "Is everyone gathered here?"

"Everyone we know of," Astel answered.

"Legion XIII," Ada called. "You are to comb every corner of this city using every myracle in your control. Send all you find to the Akademy courtyard. By the strength of these quakes, we should have at least three minutes until an eruption. That . . . *Void* shouldn't make landfall until then, either. Not a drop of fear from any of you. Understood?"

"Commandress!" they cried. "For Carpè!"

Shadowed slightly by Ada's radiant leadership, Astel asked, "H-how will we get off the island?"

"Ask me again in three minutes." The reinstated Commandress began walking up the street toward the Akademy gates. "Let's *go!*"

"A'way, Unc," Gai called. "We're followin' 'em."

"My *Merry*, Vice, everythin' spiced," he repeated to himself.

"What're ya doin'?"

"Oh, just listin' the things I'll miss when I'm dead."

The boy slapped his arm. "A'way!"

CHAPTER 30
POCKET UNIVERSE

Ada and Astel led the crowd of several hundred Carpèan civilians up toward the Myracles Akademy. The scattered Legionnaires arrived with a few more survivors by the time they made it to the gates. The cries of the people she once protected made Ada's heart wrench. Even more chilling for her was the creeping thought that their only hope now might be to lure the monster further inland and hope the destruction wrought by the erupting volcano would be enough to overwhelm the epic fiend. However, the Void seemed to already possess more Ruin than even the tectonic forces of a planet. There was a good chance it would simply remain.

"I need to understand our resources," Ada said to Astel. "I see Vth and VIIIth Legionnaires. But you're the only general left?"

"General VIII, Kal Bend, has been killed," she answered.

"And the other Legions?"

General Osstett kept silent and looked at the ground.

"Damn it." Ada pressed ahead. "No professors? What of Hosp? Where are my constructs?"

"Most of the professors were with the Legions when a terrible weapon of Ruin turned them into . . ." She didn't finish. "Hosp left the Akademy years ago. The constructs ran out of blue myracite even before that. As you can see, we never did normalize relations with Electri."

"I see. We won't let the Heartbrands who perished die in vain, you hear me? For Elix wielders, it's you, me, and—" Ada glanced back at the one wearing newspaper patches and black armored boots. "What's that one's story?"

"Lynd Izz's brother," Astel answered with a hint of scorn. "I don't yet know his motives. Why show up after all these years? And if it was his sister, the old Commandress, that used Ruin Time on you—"

"Hold on. *Lynd* was Commandress?" Ada nearly tripped over her dress. She turned around to the boy, who was eavesdropping on their conversation. "That makes you *Gaiel* Izz? Her family." She then slowly peered at the Void. "And that must mean . . . That's what your father has become?"

"True, true, and true," Gai said.

"I saw him in Lynd's memories," said Ada, still staring at the beastly mass moving upon Carpè.

"Of course, her father would be a vortex of destruction," Astel muttered. "Some family."

"*I'm* a perfectly normal relative," Unc added from behind. "Just for the record."

RUURRR! The island quaked its fiercest yet, forcing everyone to grab a wall or each other to keep their footing.

After a thunderous clap — *KRKkk!* — the Akademy tower cracked right down the middle and began to collapse over the city and all the innocent people below.

"Back down the street, now!" Ada yelled.

The bricks tumbled like deadly rain. But a sapphire light suddenly wrapped around every last piece of the falling tower, stopping their inevitable path to the heads and houses below. The shocked but relieved people immediately ran out of the way. The Akademy tower then began a most unnatural thing when it reassembled, floor after floor, wall after stairs, just as it was, including the war table and figurines that Lynd destroyed earlier.

Gai looked to General Astel Osstett and Ada, who were already glaring at him. "Yer doin' that?"

Wide-eyed, Astel said, "I thought you were."

"That's Elix myra," said Gai. "Who else could—" Then the boy saw a radiant woman dressed in an ornate gown stepping through the Akademy gates toward them. "By Zeea. That's *Zeea!*"

Zeea the Arkon, straight out of myth, had come straight out of her Pocket Realm paintings that hung in the Akademy entrance. With the elegance of the ultimate artist, she wielded her Elix myra to fix all the crumbling foundations, doors and floors as she passed them on the street. Not the frightened citizens, the boy, nor the Heart-brands had ever seen anyone so effortlessly powerful.

As the volcano of Carpè shook the buildings to splinter and give, she was like an anti-earthquake, her power a soothing balm to the furious tremors. She sealed up the cracks as soon as they formed. The innocent people she saved rallied behind her. Who wouldn't? Being near the Arkon seemed like the perfect umbrella for this particular storm.

Yet when this woman, in all her ancient glory, locked her luminous eyes on the immense incoming Void, even she fell short of breath. She saw what her people fought a millennia ago and couldn't defeat — a being of pure destruction that could not be contained, stopped, or even touched. It was the very thing that brought about the end of all she knew and loved. Perhaps most frightening was that Zeea was well aware that those who lost against the Voids in her time were more powerful than even she was.

"Zeea," yelled Gai, waving her closer to the group. "Zeea, over here! Thanks at ya!"

"Is she an *Arkon?*" said General Osstett, awestruck.

"She is indeed," Ada said, barely believing her own eyes. "But how is it Gaiel knows an Arkon?"

"I was in her paintin'," said the boy.

"The Pocket Realms?" Astel gasped. "The Pocket Realm paintings we found are *hers?*"

Gai turned to Astel, curious. "Ya got more of 'em?"

As soon as Zeea came to the crowded street, she laid her hands on those that were hurt and began to seal up their wounds just as well as she fixed the buildings. When General Osstett approached, Zeea reached out and touched her forehead, saying in Astel's mind, "*Don't worry. I just need to acquaint myself with this world.*"

"W-what's she doing?" said the general as Zeea's hand glowed blue on her face.

The surrounding Heartbrands leaped to her aid, but Zeea gently let her go.

"There," the Arkon said, speaking their modern language perfectly. "Thank you for your knowledge."

Astel rubbed her forehead and gestured for the Legions to back down. "You're welcome?"

Zeea then looked at the coming colossal Void, who was just about to make landfall. "When my people fought this enemy, I ran," she said. "I thought refusing to take part in the Last Myracle was as good as doing something about it. I will not make that mistake again."

"Not that we're complainin'," Gai said, "but how'd ya know it was here?"

"I felt a shockwave of Ruin from this place," said Zeea. "I feared the Last Myracle had been performed again."

Gai asked her, "What should we do?"

"I can repair some damage," said the vibrant Arkon. "But I don't have enough myra to stop what's coming." She looked around at the people huddled together, frightened and unsure. "Not one of us does."

There they were, a general with two Legions, an Ex-Commandress and an Arkon, a boy and a few hundred citizens, all trapped on a quaking island. There was no safe place to take anyone to that wouldn't just be torn apart by the approaching atrocity.

After another massive quake, part of the inner island finally cracked deep enough that the first orange glow of molten lava emerged from below. People all around screamed, desperately asking each other how they could possibly survive.

"Zeea!" Gai said. "What about yer Pocket Realm?"

Steel-eyed, she answered, "I will die before I hide in there, again."

"Not to hide," the boy insisted. "We need to get all these people to safety!"

"That's no plan." Astel shook her head. "If Carpè is destroyed, so will any Pocket Realms on it! They're subject to the whatever happens around them."

RRRURRR!

"But," Gai said to Zeea, "I saw other Pocket Realms hangin' in yer glass one. Can we get there from one of these?"

"That's how I got here, yes." Zeea nodded. "Some of my paintings are accessible from the ones hung here. If we can get to one located off this island, it would buy us time." The Arkon gestured for everyone to go through the Akademy gates, where her paintings were hung in the entrance hallway. "Know that if we don't stop that creature, there will be no safe places."

Gai immediately turned around and addressed the people of Carpè. He had to yell with all the quaking and falling buildings around them. "We're gonna be a'kay, everyone! We're gonna go Pocket Realm hopping!" He then turned to Ada and asked, "Where are they exactly?"

"Follow me," Ada said.

"A'kay, everyone follow Commandress Ada!"

Ada looked at the Void blocking the horizon like a gigantic ship about to dock. "Do not wait. If that's your father, you will be key to ending this." She then guided the civilians and Heartbrands inside the hall where they could step into one of the paintings.

When Uncle Baald passed, he grabbed Gai's arm and looked at him dead in the eye. All he said was, "Kid?"

"All's a'kay, Unc. I'll be right there! Just go with 'em. Trust me."

RRURR.

"Yer ma'll kill me if I don't bring ya back, kid!"

"A'way!"

The streets quaked as the citizens hustled to get themselves, their friends, and families into one of the gilded-framed painting portals in the hallway.

Then the massive First Void finally touched the inner island land. Globs of buildings, roads, trees, and anything else in its path tore to shreds and swirled around it, falling into and becoming a part of the Void. Gai stared up at the monster wrecking the city. By now, it was already devouring the In Inn, towering over all with a path of oblivion behind. "Pa . . ."

Once all the Carpèans were safely inside the painting of the beautiful meadow, Gai said to Zeea, "Lead them to that glass place. It's still at the bottom of the ocean, yeah? It should be safe long enough to make a plan. Go. I gotta make sure we got everyone."

The Arkon took one last glance at the creature that laid waste to everything she knew and loved one thousand years ago. "Don't make me come back for you." And then she went in as well.

Gai watched his father-Void tear up the city streets, bashing homes and absorbing all the myra everything contained. He looked left and right down the road, but no other Heartbrands were returning with survivors. He then heard some screams from a nearby collapsed home.

He ran to help. The second floor had crumbled, blocking their door and escape. He felt a buzzing swell in his belly. He then touched the crumbled stones. His Elix light spread out over every fracture and corner. Finally, after pushing through three *Gurgle grr*s, the rocks that made up the second floor lifted and sealed back into place. The family of four rushed out.

"In there!" he cried, pointing inside the Akademy entrance. "Jump into the meadow paintin'! I'm right behind ya!"

The family eagerly ran into the front hallway of the Akademy and escaped within the Pocket Realm of a peaceful meadow, the one everyone else was already running for their lives through.

Dodging more falling bricks and debris, Gai jumped in after. As soon as he landed on the green, prickly grass inside, the whole place shook wildly. The Akademy's walls behind him collapsed. Everyone in the Pocket Realm felt weightless for a moment as the frame of the painting fell to the Akademy's polished marble floors. Then came the crash, knocking everyone to the ground.

"Keep goin'," Gai yelled, spitting very realistic feeling dirt from his teeth.

Ada, Astel, fifty or so Heartbrands, Uncle Baald, and several hundred Carpèan survivors rose up and ran through the beautiful field of long grass and blooming flowers. It all felt so real, brushing up against their skin as they dashed. The lighting was as if it were twilight, meek and moody, but golden all the same. It was a shame they didn't have more time to take in such a calming scene — this unfathomable Mythik myracle. But it was crumbling around them.

The Arkon was in front of the group like a shepherd. Extraordinary as she was, there wasn't a speck of confidence to her expression. She knew she was not guiding these people through a peaceful pasture, but a waiting room between the burning fate at their heels. She was leading them to a small cottage where she kept her paintings of other worlds. This place was once her private oasis to escape from the harder days, and now it was full of strangers escaping from the world's end.

Gai hustled to catch up with Zeea, but Baald spotted his nephew and scurried through the meadow blossoms to his side. "A'kay, kid," he huffed, running alongside him — *Huuh-Huuh.* "I'm just a baby cod outta the pond for sure now. Are we dead? Is this place death? It's nice." *Huu.*

"Relax, Unc," the boy said as they ran together. "We're not dead. Zeea up there is an Arkon. She's got so much creativity; anythin' she paints is basically real. And we're in one!"

Baald kept stealing glances at Zeea, but seemed too intimidated to actually stare. He huffed and puffed some more. "I-I don't know nothin' about all this, Gai. Don't expect any help from Uncle Baald."

Gai smiled. "Ya were a bigger help than ya know, ya know?"

"How would I know?" Baald laughed nervously — *Huuuh.*

"The *Merry's* log lemme know where to go," said the boy. "If ya hadn't bothered to take notes, I wouldn't be here!"

"Can ya believe us old rats made it off Hop? Did ya like my heroic sailin' through Domus?" *Huuu.* "I tell ya, when ya got a sick passenger like him, ya find skills ya never knew ya had."

"Kinda like runnin' for yer life, yeah?" Gai said, noticing they had finally arrived at the cottage with Zeea's other paintings, thanks at ya. "I wanna hear it all when we get back to Hop."

RURRRRR. The entire Pocket Realm trembled as Carpè outside quaked.

"How should we do this?" Astel asked, standing beside Zeea as the Arkon quickly thumbed through several golden frames. "Step in like the others? Paintings within paintings?"

"These are technically paintings *of* paintings," said Zeea. "Windows into other Pocket Realms. I spent a lot of time running between them as a child, so no one could find me."

Gai stepped up. "It's like ya got yer own universe with all these."

"A *pocket* universe, perhaps." Zeea sighed with the smallest hint of a smile. As quickly as it came, it faded. "It'll be gone if the actual universe is destroyed." She thumbed through a stack of framed artworks. "Here it is — *The Glass Heart.* This is the one you'd like to enter?"

"At least we know where that one is," said Gai. "Not sure where these others are located." He came closer and whispered to Zeea, "Should we be worried about the uh—?"

"Everyone turning to glass?" She glanced down at the line of exhausted people. "It takes time to transform. We don't have that much."

RRUURRRRR.

"Everybody in!" Gai yelled.

The civilians and Heartbrands entered *The Glass Heart* painting as if stepping through a window, followed closely by Astel, Ada, Zeea. As Gai went to step in, the beautiful, calm meadow rumbled terribly, like someone was rattling it in their hands. Then, a truly epic tear opened in the painting's twilight sky as the Myracles Akademy, where it hung, suffered its most tremendous tremor yet. Zeea reached her hand out and pulled the boy inside the glass Pocket Realm before it was too late. They all watched as the meadow ripped to pieces and faded behind them.

Zeea bowed her head. "By either the volcano or the Void, my painting was destroyed. Carpè is no more."

CHAPTER 31

WHOSE MYRA IS IT

The space they entered was the Arkon's tower where Gai and Mac first met her. The people filled up the place, holding onto one another, mourning their lost city. Their faces crinkled as they held back tears. They were thankful to be alive, yes. But they had no idea where they were or if they would be safe now from that monster.

Zeea ran her fingertips on the glass wall. "If it buys us a moment to save Esa, I will gladly give up any number of artworks."

Gai looked around at the transparent world again, the spiral staircase with flickering blue flames at the top. "This place is still underwater, yeah? How long ya think we got?"

"That Void is already the size of a city," Zeea said, a look of dread washed across her comely features. "Esa has a few hours left, at most."

Ada couldn't bear the thought of what happened to her beloved city. She kept her hands and voice busy by tending to the people around the room and reassuring them they would be alright. Astel found Faan crying in the crowd and embraced her. Everyone lost so much that day.

"Zeea," said the boy. "I came with friends when I was here. Kabbage and Ballette. They were turned to glass. Please at ya, can we help 'em?"

"*Ballette* was here?" said Astel, who picked up that name right through the commotion of the crowd. She stepped forward. "I knew I'd seen this glass landscape before. We found a painting just like it at our family's dig site. But what's this about being turned to glass? Tell me she's alright?"

"Ya know her?" Gai asked.

"She's my sister."

"If they turned to glass here, you know why," said Zeea. "The paint used to make this Pocket Realm reacts with Ruin myra. But if your friends were able to transform their Ruin, yes, they would turn back. Provided they're still alive."

"How can they transform it?" Gai blurted.

"We'll have to find out." Zeea peered through the clear walls of her tower and into the dark glass wilderness. "Show me where you last saw them." She left and waved the boy to follow her outside.

"I'm going." Astel followed to help find her sister however she could.

Ada came as well, after telling the Carpèans to stay in the tower while she assessed the world they had entered.

As the painting was still somewhere on the ocean floor, it was quite dark. In a shimmering flash, a very fine brush appeared in Zeea's hand. She glided it through the air in a circle, then colored in a bright sphere. The boy saw tiny blue sparks as she made her strokes. Her myra was the paint. Mac was right; they were *inside* a myracle. And this Arkon was effectively a goddess of the Pocket Realms she created. Once the glowing sphere was filled in with her myra-paint, she threw it high, where it lit up the whole glass valley like a full moon.

"When in a painting," Ada said to the boy. "It's nice to be around someone with a brush."

They continued into the dense forest, searching for Gai's lost friends.

"Why make a Pocket Realm like this in the first place?" Gai asked. "Why turn Ruin to glass?"

Zeea gazed forward as they journeyed deeper into the dense forest. "I must seem powerful to you. I can't help but notice that the people in this age are not very connected to their myra. But in my time, I was hardly special." She became quiet, eyes downcast as if searching her memories. And they did not appear to be happy ones.

"I knew people who could disguise their myra, and thus they're intentions. So I designed a place where I could see the truth, where their Ruin would betray them. I hid here, thinking if I removed myself, I'd be safe. And I was. But the world was not."

"Sounds like a rough time ya lived in."

"We were encountering a new threat," Zeea continued. "Esa is going through the same rough times now. But we now know for sure that using Ruin against the Voids was not the right answer. It requires an extraordinary concentration of Ruin to overwhelm them, more than even they possess. The Last Myracle was an attempt to do just that. But the Ruin left over from it was just passed to a new age. This is our mess. I am sorry for it . . ."

They shuffled through the eerily lifelike glass landscape of the Old World — giant mushroom trees and lush, exotic flora.

"There's always the chance to fix somethin'," said Gai. "Don't be sorry." Gai noticed the high ridge where the water chased them, where the water poured down and had turned to glass. "Wait. If Ruin triggers the transformation," he said, pointing to the solid waterfall, seemingly frozen in time. "Why would *water* turn?"

"Elix and Ruin are inherent in all things," said the radiant Arkon. "Problems arise when Ruin collects inside a *person* and is allowed to build. As for the water, calm water is a natural source of Elix myra. That's why it is healing. But when water moves quickly, its destructive power increases, and it gains more Ruin. That's why the waterfall turned to glass here. While its potential changes, it never stops being water. People are the same. But unlike water, they have a choice."

"We define ourselves," Gai said softly to himself.

"Of course," she said. "Whose myra is it?"

Ada listened to their conversation and added, "People in our time had such an intense fear of the Voids coming back. It seemed logical to nip out any signs of Ruin before it got to that level. But unfortunately, we pushed it so far out of our society that we lost our chance to understand it. The truth is that almost all people have a bit of Elix and Ruin in them at any time. We aren't perfect, nor do we have to be. For most of us, the forces balance out, and little changes either way. It's when either Elix or Ruin starts to drastically outweigh the other that myracles occur."

"Makes sense," Gai said. "But it's the outweighin' part I wanna understand. How do ya add more to one side?" He then noticed two tiny, flickering red lights ahead. "Kabbage!" He dashed ahead of everyone to his glass comrades. "Ballette! Yer alright!" He looked over their cold, silent, and clear forms. "Well . . . yer still *here*, at least."

Ada came up behind him. "I used to communicate with my generals across long distances by creating a Mind Link."

"A'kay," said the boy. "Set us up!"

"If you wouldn't mind creating one between Ballette and me?" said Astel, catching up.

"As you wish." With two flourishes of Ada's wrist, two sets of sparkles danced around Gai and Astel's temples.

The boy suddenly heard Kabbage's voice coming from his glass body, saying, "What are they all looking at? If I don't get out of here soon, I'll—*Ahhhh!*"

"Kabbage?" Gai called out.

"Gaiel?" said glass Kabbage. "You can hear me?"

"Yeah! How ya bein'?"

"Get me out of here!" he yelled. "I've been trapped in here. I can see and hear it all but can't *move!* I watched you and that armored guy leave. It. Is. Awful. Why is this happening to me?"

"Ballette! Ballette!" called Astel. "Are you in there?"

". . . What's *she* doin' here?" said glass Ballette.

The boy bent down near his friend. "That sounds awful, Kabbage."

"That's because it is," Kabbage whined. "Imagine being completely aware of everything around you, but you can't move or talk! Not even a fluffing eyeball or a twitchy finger."

"I can't imagine—"

"Anyway," Kabbage barked. "We've been here, staring at each other's *personal space* . . ."

"Ya mean yer myra?"

"Yes. Those things. What the hell is that supposed to be?"

Gai clasped his hands together like he was begging, "Kabbage, I need ya to listen to me. That red thing inside ya is Ruin. Ya can't turn back unless ya change its color."

"Change its—What is this? A painting class?"

Gai shrugged. "It's a class *inside* a paintin'."

"How do I change it, then? Hurry! This isn't my fault!"

"Ballette!" said General Osstett, running up to hug her transparent figure. "I'm so glad I found you!"

Ballette dismissed her. "Yeah, well."

As everyone else made their way to the entrance to the glass forest, Ex-Commandress Ada said, "We had a visiting professor from Oof. We were working on a theory that, within a *person*, at least, Ruin starts with a broken heart. It alters the texture and direction of their myra. He used to say, 'a broken heart breaks all around it. Heal you, heal the world.'"

"Nothin's broken," Ballette said flatly. "Movin' on."

"Maybe there's something to that," said Astel.

"Even though an external event can break a heart," Ada continued, "ultimately, our studies showed that myra doesn't change without our consent. But sometimes, our minds don't see it as a choice. Regardless, it's always a choice to hold onto Ruin or not."

"Interesting work you were doing," Zeea said. "Our elders always told us to make sure we forgave everything from the day before we went to sleep. We even had a nursery rhyme about it. We just did it out of habit, but perhaps they knew it would ward off collecting too much Ruin."

"A'kay," Gai said, "Yer sayin' forgiveness can change red to blue?"

"If the reason for Ruin, the heartbreak, is understood," said Ada, "we can forgive it. If we can forgive, it reminds our silly minds that it's our choice. Ruin only has the weight we assign to it."

"Oh, *forgiveness*?" Kabbage mocked. "Is that all? Well, you're forgiven, Gai. I forgive that I don't have a home. I forgive that I followed you after that stupid, myracite-guzzling monster. How am I doing? Still red?"

"Yeah."

"Stunner!" Kabbage shouted. If he'd had a moving body, he sounded like he would be storming off about now.

"Does any of that help?" Ada asked.

"He's gettin' there," said Gai. "Kabbage, remember when I was callin' myself a sogg? Ya reminded me that even though I couldn't *fix* my sister, I did help her. Well, the reason I couldn't fix her is because her myra isn't mine to fix! *She* has to do it. We all have that power. That includes ya, Kabbage Blip."

"We do have ultimate control over our myra." Ada looked over the red myra inside their clear chests. "But knowing *what* to forgive can be difficult. Finding the moment we allow ourselves to be defined isn't always obvious. Especially if it's been a while. Ruin tends to become normalized the longer it's there. Like snow falling on top of footprints, we can forget it's even there."

"I know *exactly* when it was," said Ballette. "Astel got admitted to the Akademy, and everyone loved her. We were best friends before she left. I was so excited to see her again when she came back after the first year. But she ignored me, made me feel small as a spit-out crumb! I don't know if it was because I wasn't as creative as her, or I wasn't good enough, or—"

"Balle, no," Astel said, bending down to hold her glass hand. "I'm sorry. *I* felt like the crumb. I didn't know or understand what a Fiat was or why I was different. So I made it seem like I was better than everyone because I was insecure. I changed how I felt about myself, not you. And trust me, I had my own little stint with Ruin growing up."

Ballette said, "I robbed the Osstett Archaeological Site."

"I noticed that," said Astel.

"I can make things happen, too, you know?"

"It saved our lives, Balle. All these people could escape because of this Pocket Realm and this delightful Arkon you all met. So, let me suggest something. We can either keep going on about the things that happened to us as kids. Or we can meet each other in the eye as adults and move forward."

"I want to . . . try again, with us, maybe."

"I love you, too."

"Look," said Gai. "Her myra."

Ballette Osstett's inner light shifted from red to purple. As the myra turned blue, her skin regained its usual hue, and soon no one could see her myra light any longer.

"Balle, you're back!" General Osstett said, hugging her returned sister.

"Although, sometimes the defining moment is a bit more front-of-mind," Ada said, clearing her throat. "And all we need is an opportunity to voice it."

Gai turned to his friend. "Kabbage?"

"Ugh. I was afraid of this." Kabbage paused. "I need to tell you that some certain things that happened, may, possibly, could have been—"

Ballette said, "It looks like it's getting redder."

Kabbage continued, "Yes, right. Um . . . Maybe some things were my fault. *Hoo* — that was hard."

Gai tilted his head to the side. "What was yer fault?"

"Everything," he replied. "Not for the attack on the Drillmax — that was these terrible people with the blue swords. But I was asleep on the job."

"Ya were."

Kabbage sighed. "I also kind of blamed you for everything that happened after that. I didn't even thank you for saving me! That's how caught up I was. *Ha-ha* . . . The truth is I-I don't like the life I have, Gaicl. I dream every day of being someone else, a Thinker. Having status. Respect. Eating at a nice restaurant! I have great ideas; that electri broadcaster would do some real good, I think. But I never follow through with them. I guess blaming everyone else for why I didn't have nice things was easier than admitting it all came down to me."

"Nicely said, Mr. Blip." Gai smiled.

"Thanks." Kabbage sighed heavily again. "Was that enough?"

Gai watched as his friend's myra changed color, just like Ballette's. And just like the captain, his skin returned to its natural non-see-through state, just as Kabbage-y as ever. Gai ran up and gave him a swinging hug. "Ya fixed ya!"

"Alright, alright," said the gnome. "I missed you, too. Missed the daylight a little more."

The boy then noticed a few tendrils of white hair curling out the gnome's head. "Well, either ya got into some Hopper White . . . Or yer growin' up, gnome-style."

"Stop," said Kabbage. "Could it be?" He squinted at his dim reflection in the glass. "*Joppa! Joppa!*" Kabbage hopped up and down, running his hands through his hair over and over. "You were right, lady," he said to Ada. "This *was* worth it!"

Gai couldn't stop smiling. After seeing his sister go from preteen to adult in three days, and watching his giant Void-father destroy a whole fleet of the world's most advanced ships, seeing his friends still alive felt pretty good. But they didn't have much time to celebrate. What they needed was a plan.

"Wait." Gai raised his arms at the clear Pocket Realm landscape. "Zeea, can't ya trap the Void in a paintin' like this? With paint that turns it to glass? If it's made of Ruin, yeah?"

"A Void to glass?" Zeea sounded shocked he'd ask. "You don't understand their nature. They're constantly breaking down the matter around them. They'd take one step in and the painting would be less than dust. It's like asking a flame to read the words on a page as it burns the book."

"Oh," Gai huffed.

Kabbage chimed in, "*Ooh.* What about a Pocket Realm inside another Pocket Realm?"

"I'm flattered, but my power is finite," said Zeea. "Even if I could, what happens when they break out of that one? And the next? We are still dealing with a fire set to our page. Throwing more pages on it does not extinguish the flame. It only feeds it."

Ada walked to Astel, who was still hugging Ballette. "I hate to interrupt, but I'm just trying to catch up so I can be of some use. What happened after Electri attacked us . . . before this time?"

Astel stood straight and reported. "We were told that General Bend assassinated you during the First Myracite War. It's been ten years since then."

"It wasn't Bend," said Ada. "It was Lynd."

"She did what?" said Gai.

"It *was* her!" General Osstett stomped her foot. "I can't believe we trusted her."

"No, no. She called *me* General Bend," Ada insisted. "So I'm sure there was some kind of Elix Mirage running when it happened. It may have been her power, but it was only because of Bend's lie."

"Still," spat Astel. "We never should've clamored around her the way we did."

Ada paused. "The Heartbrands accepted her as Commandress . . . even though she . . . her condition?"

"Honestly, it was tough for us to swallow at first. But the truth is we wouldn't be here without her. She won the war for us. Ruin or not, she saved countless lives. The citizens have supported her since, so we did, too."

"Hold on," Kabbage said. "Your sister, the one we were looking for, was Commandress of Carpè the whole time? How'd you not know that?"

Gai looked at him side-eyed. "Last time I saw her, she was almost thirteen."

Kabbage looked around at all the people in the Pocket Realm. "Why do I get the feeling once we step out of here, there won't be a world left?"

Gai sighed. "Lynd is goin' to Electri to use all the red myracite to call on the Last Myracle. She thinks it's the only way to destroy our father and save Esa."

"I love your family." Kabbage groaned. "Who needs counseling when you can just lob death comets at each other?"

General Osstett got on her knee in front of Ada. "Commandress, would you lead us, again? We need true leadership."

"Stand up," said Ada sharply. "I never liked blind loyalty. Generals should always have a nose for who to follow." Then, she turned to the boy, "Gaiel. This is your sister and your father. What do you think we can do?"

"Me?" Gai said, shocked.

"How long do we think we have?" said Kabbage. "Don't suppose there's enough time for some bing brew before the world ends?"

"Sooner than you'd like," Zeea answered plainly. "If your sister is going to absorb the red myracite from the Last Myracle . . . history is doomed to repeat itself."

Kabbage said, "After all that self-work, we're not going to let the world blow up before I can reap the rewards." He nudged Gai. "So what's the plan, leader?"

"The first thing we have to do is stop the Last Myracle," said Gai. "Zeea, how fast could ya make a Pocket Realm?"

CHAPTER 32
THE LAST MYRACLE

The Electrian war-machine was sinking beneath the waters of Carpè at the untouchable claws of the First Void. With the help of her own destructive powers, Lynd and the Xth Heartbrand Legion arrived ominously in a flash of red just outside the golden city. Electri was still reeling from their encounter with the Voids in the Stadium Gnomic. The sight of that Carpèan ship appearing out of nowhere in the same scarlet light as those monsters used was horrifying. Lynd wasn't sailing toward them more than a few minutes before a garrison of several thousand Order Force officers lined up at the water's edge, aiming the biggest weapons they had directly at her.

From the bow, she watched the officers roll large electri tanks down Thinker's Way directly ahead. The Electrians, left and right, had the whole open dock covered in yellow, crackling cannons. Lynd ordered the ship to sail faster. The gnomes opened fire. *Pff-Pff-PFF!* The blasts came at the ship like falling stars. But any beams that came anywhere near *Carrier X* evaporated with a *Tik!* of the Commandress's fingers.

Her ship barreled at the city completely unscathed. Once they realized *Carrier X* wasn't going to stop, the gnomes leaped off the docks. The ship smashed through Electri's piers head-on, a harbinger of the destruction to come. Lynd and the ready Heartbrands jumped off the bow on impact. The electri zaps were fierce and unrelenting, a constant barrage of golden arrows. But it mattered little against those who could manipulate time. The Heartbrands overwhelmed the city's forces quickly, creating pockets of time wherever they needed, slowing the officer's movements to a crawl and striking them down. It was the ultimate advantage.

Once on Electri's streets, Lynd raised her palm and every vehicle, gun, body, and soul disintegrated like sandcastles caught in a tsunami. The myra that composed the destroyed cycled right back to Lynd as if she were the hurricane core. She took it into her own body, feeding her power, and further darkening her veins with more and more Ruin. The only way to describe the overwhelming way Lynd took control of the streets was as a force of nature. Such was the power of the woman who approached the Capitol steps. Wynk waited for her there with a meager squad of thirty elite Order Force officers, waving bright white terms of surrender.

General Case secured the area first, and then the Heartbrands lined up a pathway for the Commandress to meet the Minister Prime. Lynd walked up the steps against the backdrop of utter devastation behind her. It was no wonder Wynk was shaking, ready to give her whatever she wished. However, it did pique her interest why her brother was standing next to him with a dazzling woman she'd never seen. "Gai? Ya actually came. How'd ya get here so fast?"

"This is Zeea," he said. "She's an Arkon and knows some stuff about space myracles."

"Does she?" said Lynd. "Not bad for someone who's supposed to be dead." Lynd took a sniff at the air. "Her Elix myra is . . . more than even the legends suggest. Still not enough to neutralize the Voids, hm?"

"I'm here to help ya, Lynd." Gai looked over his sister. He couldn't get the image of her younger, innocent face out of his mind. And yet, here she was, grown up with jet black scars deepening across her features. She was as close to Void-hood as Mac was when they were rowing to Carpè. How she had avoided becoming one was a testament to her single-minded will — to do what she must to save the world from their father, even become like him. "I told Minister Prime Wynk exactly what ya need. They'll no longer resist."

Lynd turned around at the destruction in her wake. "I didn't expect them to."

Wynk spoke up, "Commandress Lynd. We are ready to surrender our full stockpile of red myracite, as well as open up Electri waters for Carpè to retrieve all the myracite that isn't yet mined."

"Good," she said.

The Minister Prime continued, "If you would please follow me into the Capitol building, where our signatures await."

Lynd didn't answer but stepped forward with the delegation into the building. Just before stepping through the two massive Capitol doors, she stopped and took another whiff. "Good with space?" she said, looking to her brother, who was nervously waiting beside Zeea. "Eventually ya realize Elix has a sort of smell to it. It's a sweetness, hovering, like a field of wildflowers." The Commandress then shot a bolt of Ruin at the doors. A fire started all around the edges. Next, the frame of a large painting came crashing down, revealing that Lynd was about to walk into a very convincing replica of the Capitol innards. "Nice Pocket Realm," she stated dryly.

Wynk ducked for cover behind some officers inside.

Lynd's marks of Ruin were stretching up into her cheeks and temples. Stepping inside, she said, "I don't blame ya, Gai. I don't. But I'm doin' this."

The boy cried after her, "Lynd!" He looked around. "General Case? All yer Heartbrands? Yer all fine with this?"

The general appeared deep in thought but never opened her mouth.

"Fine." Gai followed his sister. "Ya win."

"Win?" Lynd smirked. "Ya thought I was playin' a game? I don't *want* to do this, Gai."

Brother and sister stepped into the actual Capitol building, where Wynk was waiting with his modest Order Force, fidgeting at a table. Wynk gave a wide-eyed look to Gai, seeming to say, "I thought you said you were going to *trap* her?" The boy looked away.

The Minister Prime presented the terms of Electri's surrender on a paper-screen. Lynd signed without fanfare or hesitation.

Gai said, "So, h-how do we start?"

"*We* don't," she said. There in the middle of the echoing in the Capitol halls, Lynd brought her hands together as if praying. She then opened her hands, and in perfect unison, the marble floor roared asunder. The whole city shook, buildings toppled, and people screamed as the very ground opened to a deep scar on Esa. A faint red light emerged from below. The full well of red myracite, the leftovers of an ancient myracle, stood exposed to the open air for the first time in one thousand years. "This will be my burden."

"Wait," said Gai. "Tell me . . . Tell me what yer gonna do."

"Stallin'?"

"I just want to understand!"

"I will absorb all this red myracite, the destruction left behind by the Arkons. With it, I should have more Ruin than the First Void. Pa. It will collide with his Ruin and be his end."

"And ours," said the boy.

"I think I can control it. But if somethin' does go wrong, Esa will remain. Life will come back, just as it did before. If the Void goes free, there will be no planet, no future. Guaranteed. This is my burden."

Gai paused. "Will it cause any pain?"

The wind picked up and the ground shook as the First Void appeared over the cityscape like a looming hurricane.

". . . Maybe." Lynd broke apart all the surrounding rock with the myracite embedded in, and the giant boulders of the red crystals floated to the surface, just like big spryts in Hop.

Lynd touched the closest piece.

Red, red Ruin swirled around her, nearly burst through her skin. She directed it high into the sky, where it collected into a mass of extraordinary light, thousands of times brighter than the hanging sun. The sea below responded with giant, crashing waves looking like mountains coming into and out of existence.

Esa, herself, rumbled from Electri to the Everbloom as the giant mass of myra that rivaled the giant Void's body plummeted from the clouds. Electri City's tallest buildings were the first to vaporize as they touched the Last Myracle. Winds picked up on the street level so fiercely that they laid waste to much of the city before the meteor-sized ball even hit the Void.

Lynd grabbed her brother's hand as the Last Myracle's impossible light drowned all. "Love at ya," she said.

CHAPTER 33

FORGIVING HOP

K nock. *Knock-knock-knock* — "Who's out there, she says?"
Mape peeked her tired eyes out the door of 76 Boulie
Board. It was bright out. She saw her son with a grown
woman passed out over his shoulder

"Hey, Ma!"

To one side was a small man; to the other side was another
woman who was so striking Mape nearly slammed the door out of
shock. Her cousin Baald was behind them with yet *another* strange
woman.

Mape threw the door open and said, "What in Esa's goin' on? Ya
leave for three days and come back with a whole fan club? Baald,
where the hell ya been, huh? Where's Stav?"

"A'way, everyone." Gai stepped in, pointing to each of his new
friends. "Ma, this is Kabbage. That's yer favorite goddess, Zeea.
Commandress Ada's the one in blue. And this is yer daughter," he
said, tapping Lynd's bottom as he walked up the stairs with her.

"This is my *what?*" Mape gestured at full-grown Lynd.

"It's Lynd, Ma." Gai carried her up the stairs like a sack of
babanuts. "Told ya I'd bring her back."

Kabbage went up right behind him. When Zeea walked in, Mape
almost choked on air looking at her. "And yer a . . . ?"

"I'm not a goddess," said Zeea, gracefully ascending the rickety
Izz staircase. "I'm just really old."

"'Ey, cousin May," said Baald, sauntering in behind.

"Don't ya 'cousin May' at me," said Mape. "Five years, Baald? Where the piss is my husband, she says?"

"We were in prison, May."

"That's no excuse!" Mape narrowed her eyes, then realized what Gai just said. She ran up after him, shouting, "What're ya sayin' that's my daughter?"

Kabbage helped the boy lay his sister down on what was left of the old anchor rope blanket. Being a full-grown woman now, Lynd's legs stuck off it. The gnome said, "Smart to make her think she caught on to the Pocket Realm scheme, only to already be inside one."

"That's Lynd?" Mape said. "Ya know I meant bring back the *right* Lynd, yeah?"

"That is indeed your daughter, Mrs. Izz," said Zeea. "Ruin can do bizarre things. Especially when it hits more Ruin. When she encountered your husband, time and space did some twisting."

"Who the crap is Ruin, she says? He hit what now? Is anybody gonna tell me what happened to my darling girl?"

"It's okay, Mrs. Izz," said Kabbage. "I don't entirely understand their little *terms* either. All you need to know is that Lynd and your husband were filled with a nasty, nasty energy, and when they touched, everything turned to . . . well, *crap*, as you'd say."

Mamma Mape bent down and brushed Lynd's hair off her face. "I suppose it does look like her." She felt her forehead for any illness. "So she was sick like Pa? Where is *he*?"

"It's a long story, Ma. But we got Zeea to help us. Can't be doin' too bad, right?"

Mape stood up and looked over the Arkon with amazement. Then, swallowing a lump in her throat, she said, "Forgive the way my house looks. We don't normally have goddesses over."

"I'm not a . . . oh, never mind," said Zeea. "Your daughter is unconscious, but alright. I created a Pocket Realm that was convincing enough that she thinks the world has ended. Her eyes told her she dead and, for now, at least, her mind believes it."

"I didn't understand a damn word of that," said Mape, looking around the room. "But I guess any size daughter is better than none. Thanks at ya. When is she gonna wake up?"

"It's hard to tell," said basically-goddess Zeea. "The mind is more than happy to play dead for a little while, but it gets bored quickly."

"Pa's gonna be comin' soon," said Gai. "If this is gonna work, I'll need all yer help. Where's Ada?"

"I think she's still outside," said Kabbage.

Gai waved them all out of the room. "A'way. I need everyone on the same page. Lynd needs to rest, anyway."

When they all stepped back out to Boulie Board, Ada was listening to a scooper complaining about how awful it was to live in Hop. "That sounds terrible," said Ada. "But may I take a look at your net?" She inspected the lazy craftsmanship of the scooper's scoop. "I see. Have you thought about fixing the hole in it? Maybe it's not so much 'life hating you,' as it is just needing to set yourself up for success."

The scooper snatched his scoop back and grumbled, sticking it back down into the rough currents without taking her advice.

"If you prefer," Ada said, shrugging. She turned to everyone coming out of 76. "Ironic to spend my last hours trying to squeeze a little Elix from a stone."

"No, Ada," said Gai. "This is exactly what I need ya to do."

"What's your plan?" she asked.

Gai exhaled, "We're gonna have enough Elix to cancel out Pa . . . I mean the First Void."

Zeea didn't scoff at the idea, but she did put her head down and step to the edge of the Board. "All I sense here is a low-level Ruin underpinning this place."

"And we can change that, right?" snapped Gai. "A'kay? We just gotta change it. It's either that or *die*."

"I'm just going to jump off right now," said Kabbage.

Ada approached the boy. "It's not that I'm unsupportive. We have an Arkon here. General Osstett and the Legionnaires are all Fiats. We could create many things." Her usually bright eyes and warm smile drooped. "But from what I heard, this Void has already gathered quite a lot of Ruin. Even all the Arkons weren't able to stop the Voids in their time—"

"I don't care what yer old books say!" Gai stepped into the center of the group and puffed out his chest. "I don't care what happened before! If we base what we can do now only on what people were able to do in the past, we'd never be nothin'! What's the alternative? Take a seat on Boulie and scoop 'til the end comes? Is *the world* not worth takin' the shot?"

Ada bowed her head slightly. "I leave Command in your hands."

"My Thinker friend," Gai said to Kabbage. "Yer gonna invent that energy broadcast thing, ya hear me? We just need it to work with Elix power instead. We're gonna need to spread it around. Like an umbrella."

"That's . . . an interesting idea," he said, holding his chin and dashing his eyes all over the wooden, ugly Board. "But what am I supposed to make it with? I'll need metals, preferably in pipe form, gears—"

"Good thing we have an Arkon here who can paint anythin'," said the boy.

"Would that work?" Kabbage said to Zeea.

A very thin brush popped into her hands. She smiled. "Show me how you think a machine like that might work."

"This is a little exciting." Kabbage smiled wide as he ever had. "I've always had to worry about building materials, binnx. But with your paintin' skills, that won't be a problem!"

"Just make sure it *works*," said Gai. "Ada, ya dealt with people who're new to myra at the Akademy, yeah?"

"At every stage of knowledge," she answered proudly.

"Good. Yer about to get a bunch of new students. A'way with me to the center," said the boy. The Carpèan citizens were all waiting near Lynd's Pier with Astel and the Legions. Gai yelled for them to join him in a parade down Boulie.

Many Boulie neighbors were already outside their homes, wondering what all the fuss was about. And just who were these nicely dressed strangers in Hop? As Gai marched past on his way, he knocked on every door and waved every Hopper to join him by the crashed *Lady Merry*. They never once thought to listen to what some quirk boy was going on about. But he said it with such confidence that it made them curious. That, and he also had so many other people following him. Just what was this quirk up to? Even Mayor Tanning wanted to know. How did all the people get there? Mrs. Shakk cracked her door open but slammed it shut the moment she saw the boy. She was the only holdout.

Gai marched up and down every Board of Hop until every single Hopper got his invitation to the center. There hadn't been so much excitement happening in Hop since a ship crashed a few days ago. They recognized Baald in the procession and bullied him about it a bit, but Gai told them to zip it. Once the center was filled to the max with heads, the boy stood on a barrel that looked like it couldn't hold the weight of a cat. "Hoppers! I'm sure ya noticed we've got some guests. That's right; there are other people in the world. And this is what they look like. Us."

"Get on with it!" shouted Mayor Tanning. "Is one of 'em payin' for my house?"

"Yer angry. Maybe it's not all yer fault, even," Gai shouted to the muttering crowd. "This place we live in was ripe for Ruin. It breaks yer heart just lookin' at yer own bathroom in Hop. But none of us were involved in what made traders stop comin' here. It's not fair. It makes ya feel like tearin' the whole place up! Neighbors included. But if I've learned anythin', it's throwin' more Ruin on Ruin won't fix a thing. I know it's hard to forgive the world when it feels like it was never that nice to ya. But that's holdin' us back! *We're* holdin' us back! We gotta forgive if we're ever gonna be more than floaters in these awful currents. Forgive bein' born where ya were. Forgive yer parents for what they couldn't teach ya. Forgive yerself for lettin' it all cut ya too deep. Just like every breath we get a chance to say somethin' new, with every thought we get to *be* someone new."

The Hoppers were utterly still and silent. Actually being responsible for their own lives was an uncomfortable idea for them. They'd been stuck for so long.

The boy deflated a bit. ". . . Ain't ya tired of nothin' lastin'?"

Boom. A low rumble shook the Board and everyone on it. *Boom.*

"What's that?" Mayor Tanning pointed behind the boy. "Looks like it's cuttin' right through the currents!"

Gai turned around. His stomach felt like it dropped to his knees. A dark smudge on the horizon was approaching Hop, slowly like a stalker in the night. But it was no smudge. *Boom.*

"What's comin' at us?" someone yelled.

A Void taller than the tallest building in Electri, wide as the Everbloom trunk, shook Esa with every destructive step it took. It might have looked small now, but like an oncoming meteor, it would soon cover the sky.

"Oh, crap," Gai whispered to himself. "He's even bigger . . . Must be suckin' up all that red myracite under the gulf, too."

The end was coming right at them. Not just their end, but the end of Esa. Scared as he ever had been, the boy still knew he needed to get the town on his side. *Boom.* "That's what I'm talkin' about. That's what happens when ya let Hop get to ya too deep. *That* is our own Ruin comin' back to tear us apart. We can build a better future. But we gotta work together!"

"What do ya want us to to do, exactly, Izz?" said Tanning, arms folded, while the rest of the town grumbled.

Juuse of the Wicked Wikets came forward. "I'm in." The whole Wicked Wiket scooper gang around him gasped.

"But, Juuse," said another. "He's a quirk. Ain't all this quirk talk?"

"Could be," he answered, spitting out a piece of watermoss. "But nothin' *we* ever did got us off this rottin' heap. Been floatin' around our whole lives and got nothin' for it but empty scoops. I'm in, Izz. Ya tell me what I need to do."

"First, we practice," said Gai, stepping off the barrel. "Get our hearts the right color."

Baald yelled, cup-handed, "I know a beautiful ship that needs some Elixin'!"

"A'kay. A'kay, yeah," said the boy. "That's a good one, Unc. We can put the *Lady Merry* back together. And when we beat back that Void, we'll ride her out of here forever! Good rally cry!"

"What about my house?" said Tanning.

"Fix that, too," the boy cried out, stepping into the crowd. "If we hold on to any destruction in our hearts, we feed that thing. Turn it around, and we'll be an unstoppable weapon against it!"

Baald called out, "'Ey, ya Hoppers! We're buildin' back the *Merry* and sailin' her outta Hop for good! Let's grab our future by the oars, folks!"

"Fix it?" The mayor folded his arms tightly, appearing to resist every word. "Out of *what?*"

"Make tools with what ya got!" Gai said, "The more creative, the better."

Some Hoppers leaned into the idea. Maybe it was all the years of nothin' lastin'. They got to work, using broken pieces of Tanning's walls to help the *Merry's* hull, and extra furniture and fixtures from the ship to patch up the mayor's house. Gai looked inside and saw someone hammering with an old chair leg, and a blue spark leaped out of their hand.

"That's it," said Gai. "That's the stuff! Keep goin'!"

Ada stood in the center of Hop for those that still needed convincing. She just pretended she was in a classroom of freshmen. "Like this, see? Feel that buzz in your bellies? Listen to it. It's yours. Now move it up through the heart." She opened her hand, where a blue light pooled. "And into your palm." Next, Ada tossed the blue light into a pile of old ropes, and — *Pop!* The ropes wove themselves into a large sturdy net. She picked it up and spread the new netting open. "You're helping the world by creating something new. Now more than ever."

"But that's too big," a Hopper man complained.

"That's true," said Ada, handing him one end of the net. Then she gave the closest Carpèan the other end. "But not too big for two."

The two men looked at each other suspiciously.

"What is your name," Ada coaxed the Hopper.

"Tuuk Azus."

"Good," said the Ex-Commandress. "And you?"

"I'm Pett."

"Tuuk, shake Pett's hand. Very good. Now you know each other and can *make* a little trust, hm? You'll catch more and work less that way . . ."

Gai helped a few more Hoppers get in touch with their inner creativity. By the time he returned to Boulie Board, Kabbage and Zeea were waiting beside a beautiful bronze contraption. It looked a bit like a flower in the middle with a ring encircling it and straight pipes jetting off all around. In a way, it sort of looked like a mini-Hop.

"We're calling it the Please-Work Myra Distribution Array," said Kabbage, leaning back with pride. "She works by using—"

"Love at ya, Kabbage. But as long as it works, ya can save it for yer Thinker acceptance speech." *Boom.* The boy looked out to sea. "It's here."

The First Void was now so large it was like watching the night creeping in across the sky.

"Everyone. Help me carry this to the center—" Gai grabbed Kabbage and Zeea's Myra Distribution Array, and it immediately drew in his blue myra through his hand. *Gurgle grr.* "Whoa, what was that?"

"Oh, I think I'll just save that for my Thinker acceptance speech." Kabbage slapped him on the arm.

"Sorry at ya."

Kabbage cleared his throat. "Carry it around the ring. These other parts are made of a material that conducts electri. So I reasoned, quite correctly, thank you, that it would conduct free myra just as well."

"Wow," said the boy. "A'kay. Ma, ya got any more watermoss balls? I think we could all use a snack."

Mape opened the door to 76, "Ya kiddin'? All I've been doin' since ya left was makin' balls." She came back out with two armfuls of green seaweed balls. "Had to keep my hands busy somehow."

"Thanks at ya, Ma!" He crunched down on three right away and only chewed to make room for the fourth.

"I think I'll pass," said Kabbage.

Zeea took one whiff of the watermoss and said, "I'm good."

"A'kay," Gai said, lifting the contraption by the outer ring. "Let's get this thing to the center!"

BOom.

Mape, Zeea, and Kabbage all picked up their ends and marched to the center of Hop. Once there, they set it down by the mayor's partially repaired home.

"Hoppers!" Gai yelled out. "This is what we're usin' to collect our creative power to counter the destruction on its way. Hold hope in yer hearts, no matter what. Nothin' defines us but us!" He whispered to Kabbage and Zeea, "How is everyone supposed to touch this thing at once?"

BOOm.

"We'll hold it up here," said Zeea. "Everyone else will hold hands all the way down the piers. The Elix myra will travel from person to person."

"Like a circuit," said Kabbage.

The boy yelled out to Hop again, "A'kay, everyone. Line up one behind the other. We're gonna hold hands. Yeah, this is a community thing. A'way!"

As all the Hoppers, Legionnaires, and Carpèans got themselves lined up down all the Boards — *BOOM*. The First Void, once father to Gai and Lynd, closed in. Without a pinch of remorse, it opened its mouth and bent down to the lonely port town.

"Grab hands!" Gai shouted, watching the descending darkness. "Now! Put yer hearts in it!"

Gai, Zeea, and Ada grabbed onto the Distribution Array with one hand and held the line of Hoppers, Carpèans, and Heartbrands with the other.

Kabbage's broadcaster emitted their combined Elix myra into a sphere around Hop. The sphere crashed into the Void as the monster tried to close its mouth around them. It tried to swallow them, but all of glowing Hop was like an impenetrable egg in its maw. As the town's collective blue myra swelled, it began to chip away at the Void.

The boy belted, "We can do this! Not a sogg in the bunch!"

Lynd's eyes shot open. Her childhood bedroom came into focus. She felt the rough rope blanket Gai had made her against her back. She thought she had somehow gone back in time again, and everything was alright. But that wasn't to be true. A glance at the clash of blue and red power illuminating the whole space woke her up out of any daydreams. "Gai!" She hustled down the stairs and out the door to see the entire sky overtaken by this epic confrontation — an insatiable devouring coming down, and the will to live pushing up.

The center of Hop was practically humming with a soothing blue aura. There, the quirky boy, Ada the Ex-Commandress, Zeea the Arkon, the Legions and general, and the average folks alike let their hearts and hopes align to the myra of creation.

"This is Hop?" said Lynd, dazed by the very idea. "So much Elix . . . *Here?*" Their collective blue bubble valiantly pressed against the encroaching mouth of the hungry Void. "Ya did it, Gai."

Lynd's giant Void of a father loomed like a storm over Hop. She couldn't see anything beyond the clashing of blues and reds.

Gurgle grr. Gai pressed on, but he was pouring all he had into the effort. Everywhere bellies roared with hunger. Everyone was giving it their all. But how long would it last?

Zeea cried out, "We're losing ground!"

"Don't give up!" Ada roared back.

Lynd backed away from the edge of Boulie as the darkness crept closer to the Boards, tearing up all the waves. They were in a complete sphere of darkness as the Void closed its mouth around Hop entirely. Arcs of Ruin shot out randomly from the event horizon as it crept in like a relentless predator. Lynd ran down Boulie, past the people holding hands in a line to the center. "Gai!"

"Lynd," Gai strained. "Help us!"

"My . . . Ruin?" She put her hand over her heart. "I don't want to add to the destruction!"

The water of the Domus Gulf and even the breeze between her fingers all slipped into the Void. The sky above was just an ebony dome about to shatter on top of them all. As the Ruin unzipped every piece of matter, their Elix fought to zip it all back up, a struggle for the world itself to keep on existing.

"Lynd! Ya gotta forgive Pa!"

"A'kay! I-I forgive ya!" she shouted into the plunging, vast Void. "Are ya happy? I forgive ya!" She ran back down Boulie toward the enclosing sphere. The black dome of oblivion came closer and closer, finally gnawing at the outer edges of all the Boards, so they all looked like shattered Lynd's Pier. "Didn't ya hear me?" she cried, staring at the nothingness down the tunnel of his monstrous throat. "I meant it! Please at ya!" She faced the oncoming destruction as it chewed through Boulie, reaching out her palms at the Void's tightening grip.

Gai cried out, "Lynd!"

She touched it.

CHAPTER 34

MYRACLES IN THE VOID

L ynd turned to the people on the Board where she grew up. Her neighbors and the Carpèans held each other's hands so tightly. Their faces were pinched as they hoped and hoped to match against the Ruin falling upon them. But nothing and no one seemed to be moving at all. She walked amongst them. Hand in hand? Community? This was not the Hop she knew. She looked to the clashing colors of Elix and Ruin, and the purple seam where those opposing forces met. Even *that* wasn't moving. Time on Boulie Board, in Hop, or maybe even the entire universe, had slowed to a crawl.

As the young woman peered at the nearly frozen scene, she noticed some areas seemed to skip ahead a few seconds, then go back half a moment, like ripples of time twisting around themselves. Hard reality itself seemed to be breaking down all around her. "That's it," she said, looking at the hand that touched the Void. "It's over."

Lynd strolled down Boulie. Even moments of Hop's *past* started to play out on the Board, like ghosts from another time bleeding into this one. She saw builders excitedly hammering away in the Under Board when the port was first being made. They seemed happy, actually. Happy Hoppers, who knew? The visage of boats of all sizes, carrying excited people and crates of goods, popped in and out within the ripples of time. The more difficult moments when Hop became a stagnant place flickered through as well, with neighbors fighting with neighbors, doors slamming and locking tight.

"We've been here before," said Stav.

In another bizarre time twist, Pa was suddenly standing right in front of her, looking straight into her dark eyes. But he was no mere moment playing out; he was *there*.

"Pa?" she said to him. Tears followed almost immediately. "Where are we?"

"Where are we. Where are we?" Stav scratched his messy brown hair, a purse in his lips. He was wearing the same outfit he was in all those years ago — a sail-poncho and makeshift pants with a few passes of fishing wire holding them up as a belt. "I guess time doesn't mean much when yer a swirlin' vortex of destruction."

"So it *is* over?"

"It could be." Pa pointed to her hand, which had unconsciously been pooling with thick Ruin. "Just throw that at me, and it'll all be over. No more pain. No more anythin'."

She thought about it. The power to take it all away resting in her tired hand. "Don't tell me what to do." Lynd then clenched her fist and snuffed the Ruin. The young woman then sat at the Board's edge as the time fluctuations continued to come into and out of being. She looked down and saw the moment the rough currents really started kicking up.

Stav sat with her. "Not to be overdone, but—"

"We've been here before," she interrupted, monotone. Then she smirked. Awful as everything seemed — the end of the world and all — it just couldn't be wrong that she was finally next to him again.

"I missed ya, too," he said, wrapping an arm around. Father and daughter looked out at the slow-moving light show of absolute destruction raining down, and the power created by the heroic hearts of Hop to counter it. "Ya know I didn't—"

"I know ya didn't mean to," she said, gazing at the end of the universe as she knew it. "At least ya got our neighbors to work together."

"I never liked Hop." Stav pushed her hair back from her face. "But I was wrong. I shouldn't have let it eat me up like that. Touchin' that red thing didn't help either."

"I hear that," Lynd said, gazing out at the barely-moving collision of myra. It was an extraordinary display of meshing color and intention. "Maybe we could just stay here? The view is nice." She leaned her shoulder into his.

Stav took a deep breath in, then pointed west. "I remember a grand sun bein' over there." He pointed up. "I remember stars lookin' down at us, winkin' like we were special."

Lynd wiped a lone tear escaping. "I'm not sayin' there aren't things I'd miss." Finally, she began to bawl and couldn't wipe it fast enough. "But dammit, I missed ya for longer!"

Stav pulled her in for a deep and long-awaited, long-deserved embrace. He let her cry awhile in his arms, the weight of her tears patting him. He sat her up, locked eyes with her again and said, "And ya'll miss everythin' else again, just like ya did me. Ya gotta keep goin', little crab."

Lynd laughed through her tears. "Ya haven't called me that in so long."

"Ya remember that?" Pa smiled. "I didn't know if ya would. Given' each other play names. I said I'd be 'crab.' Ya shot right back with 'then I'll be little crab.'"

With her head pressed to his chest, she listened to his voice vibrating low. She heard him breathing. ". . . I remember."

"It'll always be ours," he said. "All the memories will. Yer hearts a window for 'em."

She picked herself up. "Ya sound like yer gonna ask me to leave?"

"There's a moment that defined ya," said her father. "One that led to all the other choices."

"Am I supposed to forgive it?" Lynd blew a raspberry. "That's what Gai was yellin' at me to do. Here we are."

"I've absorbed a lot of smart people as a Void," said Stav. "Yer brother's not wrong."

Lynd looked down Boulie at the unfolding and refolding of moments in time. She then heard her father's voice singing and a small fiddle plucking; he sang, "We've been here before."

"Pa?" Lynd turned around and saw that sitting right next to her was her seven-year-old self. It was another ghost of time playing out in the flux. In that moment, little Lynd was sitting with her father after sunset as he played a song on his fiddle for her.

"With yer hand in mine," little Lynd began to sing along with the lyrics.

Adult Lynd's eyes rushed with tears at hearing it again. She reached out, but the scene melted into other moments on the Board — whispering neighbors, frustrated scoopers throwing back their catch.

Lynd shot to her feet, breathing heavily. The time ghost just seemed so real. It *was* real, just from another time.

"We've been here before," Stav said.

Lynd turned again, and there was another moment playing out — Mrs. Shakk stomping over to Pa, interrupting his song. They started yelling back and forth down the Board. The time ghosts passed right through Lynd, with little Lynd trailing behind her father and Mrs. Shakk. Stav then yelled, "Don't ya say a damned thing!"

Bump. Bump. "This is it," said Lynd. *Bump. Bump.* "My moment." As Pa finally turned around, his face was a hideous monster, distorted and twisted, horrid beyond words. Lynd watched her younger self recoil at his image, her heart shattering at such a frightening sight of her own father, her protector. *Bump. Bump.* And then the little girl asked the Ruin that formed in the cracks of her heart to protect her from that memory, and save herself from ever seeing it again. She destroyed it.

"This is how I saw it." Adult Lynd studied Pa's hideous appearance closer. "This is how I saw it back then. I was so afraid." But Lynd's grown-up eyes saw through her father's intense image. She could see beyond it — a monster, yes, but a man in pain as well. He wasn't someone to fear. If anything, he needed *help*.

She heard her father's voice echo, "What moment defines ya?"

Lynd bent down to the time-ghost of little Lynd, saying, "All's a'kay. That must have been so scary to see at your age." She leaned in and kissed her younger self's forehead. "I didn't understand it back then. Do ya forgive me?"

Even though she was speaking to a vision of the past, Lynd knew her younger self, the one that lived eternally within her, heard every word. She felt a warmth in her heart. It spread and grew into a flutter, then a breeze, and finally a buzzing.

Lynd stood tall on the Board amongst the rippling moments and fluxes of time. "That may have been *a* defining moment," she said, walking amongst them. "But life is full of moments." She looked for current one, where Hoppers and Carpèans held hands down Boulie, Bleek, Bussa, and the rest of the Boards just before the Void won the clash. This was not a familiar Hop, yet there it was. "Just like the Hoppers can choose a different path the very instant they realize they can. I can define me at any moment."

She walked through the line of her neighbors to the center where Gai, Ada, and Zeea were making their last stand against the endless nothing. The shattered, black sky was about to press down on their heads. Their expressions frightened, but a glint of hope was still in their eyes. Lynd kissed her brother on the cheek. "Thanks at ya for not givin' up on me."

Stav appeared again, weaving through the people who were trying to rid the world of *him*. He passed Gai and smiled, a warmth growing in his heart. He looked to his daughter. "So what moment defines ya?"

Lynd turned to him. "What moment defines me?" Her lip quivered. "What about ya?"

Pa exhaled heavily. A weight seemingly left his shoulders as he did. "I just know that no matter what I've done . . . my kids were my real myracles. The good kind, yeah? I wanna be known for that. I wanna be remembered for that." A tear rolled off his face. A small blue glow emerged from his chest and enveloped him. "I'll live on through ya. Now, tell me what moment defines ya?"

Lynd felt her whole body fill with a warm blue light of her own. She grabbed her brother's hand and added herself to the chain of linked myra. Then, with one last glance to her father, she said, "*This one.*"

Stav smiled. "Love at ya."

Time then resumed in full, crushing force. Chunks of wood, tendrils of rope, and loose junk were flying through the air and ripped to splinters. The Void was about to devour them all.

Gai noticed who was suddenly holding his hand. "Lynd?"

She smiled. With an exhale that was a long time coming, Lynd released a massive burst of newly shifted, gorgeous, blue myra from within her heart. And what a powerful arrow it was, as if all the Ruin she had gained during her harder days was the force pulling back the bowstring. Now it was released. Lynd's Elix myra rivaled the impact of the Arkon beside her. Kabbage's inspired creation launched Lynd's swell of blue up with the rest of the town's will to live on.

And the Elix rose, lifting the encroachment of Ruin, beating back the Void, nearly to the win. But it was not quite enough.

"Almost there!" Zeea cried, squeezing every speck myra from her Arkon heart.

Mrs. Shakk burst out of her house, finally. She'd been doing a lot of thinking. She stomped her bucket shoes down the stairs and looked up at the Void-neighbor whom she never quite liked that much. But if it meant the end of the world — she scribbled on her board and lifted it to make sure Stav, the Void, could see it. If he could see, that is — I FERGIV YA.

Hoppers weren't the best spellers, but if it were ever the thought that counted, it was now. Even Mrs. Shakk's little myra shifted a healthy blue and added itself to the winning mix.

The Void receded — the black dome sealed up its cracks and then — *nothing*.

The last rips of Ruin were balanced out, revealing a clear, bright sky above. Brother and sister embraced as the whole gray port, almost as rickety as ever, erupted into cheer.

There was a tiny blue sparkle, barely visible in the bright blue sky. It gently drifted downwards like a little spryt.

"'Ey, 'ey," shouted Mrs. Shakk. She actually spoke. Even she covered her mouth, surprised at what she sounded like. Still, she then pointed at that spryt and said, "That little piece of magic there, that's mine! I'd know it anywhere!"

"Hm." Zeea smiled, catching her breath. "We had extra *Elix* myra this time . . ."

The sun seemed warmer than it ever had. The fishy smell of the sea hit the nose just right. It was now the smell of freedom. Hoppers and Carpèans alike mixed and hugged, kissed and danced. They had been granted a whole new day.

Gai turned to his sister. "Ya saved us, Lynd!"

Lynd's eyes were watering. "I saw him, Gai."

He looked up at the cloudless day, his smile melting. He embraced her. "Pa."

"In my heart, there's a window."

Gai started to cry with her. ". . . And it sees through time."

"As long as we see him there, he won't be gone." Lynd held him tight.

All on Hop, Tanning, the Wicked Wikets, every poor scooper, Mamma Mape, who were all so used to mourning as just individuals, who locked themselves tight in their homes, all surrounded the two Izz children to mourn as one. They all lost a good man that day.

Gai looked up again at the empty sky. "What's that?" He tapped his sister to look as well. "*What's that?*"

There was a dark smudge high up in the air, barely a dot. But it seemed to be growing. The whole town gasped, staring up. It couldn't be the Void.

Could it?

Ada yelled, "Something's falling down."

"That's a person," the boy cried out as the smudge in the sky took shape. "It's *Pa!*"

Zeea moved directly underneath his tumbling body. She created a cushion of space directly underneath him, allowing the man to gently come to rest like a feather on the planks. The Arkon bent down and picked his head up. All closed in on the scene, with Mape, Gai, and Lynd breaking through to see him.

Gai shouted, "Is he—?"

But before any hopes rose too high, Zeea shook her head, holding Stav's cold body in her warm arms. "He's gone."

Lynd immediately buried her head in Mamma Mape's shoulder. Mape herself looked away.

"It's a myracle *any* part of him survived," said Zeea.

Gai bent down and took his body from Zeea. The sobbing crowd parted for him as the boy silently carried his father toward 76. They would deal with this privately, as a family.

"'Ey, 'ey!" Mrs. Shakk yelled again, clanking on Boulie with her bucket-shoes. "My little spryt's back!"

Indeed, that small blue spryt, the tiny extra push of Elix myra thanks to Mrs. Shakk, had returned from its victory dance around Hop. All watched as the blue spark bounced around their heads as if looking for someone special. Finally, it stopped just above Gai's head and gently drifted down like a feather over Stav in his arms. It hovered above the man's heart for a moment. Every breath in Hop was held.

Then the spryt shot into his Pa's chest. Gai felt his Pa's body jerk in his arms, so he laid his father down on the Board. With a great big gasp, air filled Stav's lungs. His brown eyes popped open as if getting a shock.

Stav's first blurry sight was of his family, gazing down on him oval-eyed like he was either a monster or a myracle; they weren't sure which. "Oh," he said, scratching his head. "Um . . . 'bout all that."

Hop rumbled with hoots, cheers, claps, and hollers as every neighbor, friend, and family celebrated the myraculous salvation of one of their own.

"Get the hell over here!" Mape fell on top of him and gripped him tight. Then she slapped his cheek. "Don't ya ever do that crap to me again!"

"A'kay, a'kay. No Void-in'. Not me. Not again." Stav laughed and stood up. He grabbed his son and pulled him in for a hug. "Gaiel. Nothin' rocked yer boat, yeah? Ya stood strong no matter what. A better man than I ever was."

Gai held him close and smiled. ". . . Ya still smell like Hop."

"Ain't it the best?" Stav then turned to his daughter. "And my little crabby. My all-grown-up little crabby. I am proud of ya. Yer the strongest person I ever heard of."

"Ya showed me how free I really was." Lynd embraced him again. "True power is knowin' ya have it. And, sometimes it takes forgiveness to get there. Sometimes, it's ourselves we gotta forgive."

Pa smiled. He saw Mrs. Shakk glaring at him in the crowd of happy faces. "Shakk!" He weaved his way to her gave her a hug as well. "That was yer little light that gave me a second wind?"

"Yeah, yeah, well," she muttered, not quite returning the hug, but tapping his back. "I guess if ya made brats like these ones . . . y'ain't so bad." She smirked a bit.

Gai found Kabbage and said, "Yer broadcaster worked! Thanks at ya!"

"*Joppa.*" The gnome appeared dazed. Happy, but dazed. His hair was distinctly more white. Unless he dunked his head in some Hopper White, he may have grown up a bit. "I crossed a finish line for once. And I didn't die!"

Ada stepped to Lynd, in as many happy tears as anyone. "I'm so proud of you, too," she said.

Lynd bowed her head. "So sorry at ya 'bout the Ruin Time. I didn't know how to fix ya—"

Ada shushed her gently. "I didn't know how to fix *ya*, either." She smiled. "And I was Commandress."

"Ya can have that title back, for sure," Lynd smirked.

Ada glanced over at Zeea, who was standing by the Board's edge, staring at the calm sea. "Oh, I think there's someone who'd be better able to restore the Myracles Akademy than either of us."

CHAPTER 35

HOPPER TRADITIONS

With the *Lady Merry* proudly shipshape, and packed with eager passengers, the Izz family gathered at Lynd's Pier for one final Hopper tradition. The four of them each stood with items to return to the sea, a gesture to mourn *Hop*. They were leaving it behind forever, after all.

Mape went first by tossing in her necklace with the ship's wheel on it, the one Mrs. Shakk returned to her. "For anyone out there that needs a good steer." Mape said to Gai, "What're ya gonna give back?"

"It's from me and Lynd," said the young man. He held up the remade fiddle he tried to make his sister for her birthday. Lynd had helped tune it, so it sounded even more like Pa's.

"Maybe someone out there needs to be inspired," said Lynd. "Maybe there's a whole other Hop we don't know about somewhere. I hope this finds 'em."

Brother and sister brought the fiddle to the edge, looked at one another, and nodded. Together they let the beautifully made instrument plop into the gentle water. The Drillmaxes of Electri were still wrecked, which calmed the Domus Gulf considerably.

"It's one of the few Hopper traditions I actually buy into," said Mape. "And what about ya, Pa? Ya got anythin' left to say to this dumper of a town?"

Stav chucked a flat rock into the water and watched it skip far into the orange horizon. "Here's to our little lily pad." He pulled his family in close. "But we're ready to hop someplace else, now."

They all turned to walk down Boulie and board the waiting ship. Everyone was ready to reconnect with the world and build a new future.

Lynd stopped. "Ya go ahead. I-I be right there." The young woman walked back to the end of Boulie, whispering, "Hopper traditions . . ."

She opened her hand and looked at Kal's bracelet, warm from being pressed in her palm the whole day. A cool breeze kissed her on the cheek. "I guess I should say goodbye to ya, too." She began to choke up. "Maybe things could've been different between us . . ."

A whisper in the sea winds nestled in her ear. It sounded like a familiar voice, carrying her name — "*Lynd.*"

Her teary eyes popped open. "Kal?"

"Lynd! A'way!" yelled Gai from down the Board. "Unc's itchin' to sail this thing again!"

"Comin'!" Lynd tightened her fist around the bracelet; she would not be offering anything of Kal's back to the sea. Her free hand rested just under her belly button. "In my heart, there's a window," she sung. She clenched the bracelet hard, looking out at Domus. "And I've seen through time before . . ."

Lynd then turned and marched off to join everyone in a bright future off Hop.

On the last plank of the beautifully restored Board tip called Lynd's Pier, the smallest crack suddenly formed in the wood.

CPSIA information can be obtained
at www.ICGtesting.com
Printed in the USA
LVHW011658190522
719222LV00011B/1020